THE WAR OF KNIVES

Also by Broos Campbell
No Quarter

THE WAR OF KNIVES

a Matty Graves novel

Broos Campbell

McBooks Press, Inc.

www.mcbooks.com

Ithaca, NY

Published by McBooks Press 2007
Copyright © 2007 Broos Campbell

Cover Painting by Daniel Dos Santos © 2007.

Dust jacket and book design by Panda Musgrove.

ISBN: 978-1-59013-104-6

            Library of Congress Cataloging-in-Publication Data
Campbell, Broos, 1957-
  The war of knives : a Matty Graves novel / by Broos Campbell.
     p. cm.
  ISBN-13: 978-1-59013-104-6 (alk. paper)
  1. Sea stories. 2. Historical fiction. I. Title.
PS3603.A464W37 2007
813'.6--dc22
                        2006031084

Additional copies of this book may be ordered from any bookstore or directly from
McBooks Press, Inc., ID Booth Building, 520 North Meadow St., Ithaca, NY 14850.
Please include $5.00 postage and handling with mail orders. New York State residents
must add sales tax to total remittance (books & shipping). All McBooks Press publica-
tions can also be ordered by calling toll-free 1-888-BOOKS11 (1-888-266-5711).

Please call to request a free catalog.

Visit the McBooks Press website at www.mcbooks.com.

Printed in the United States of America

9 8 7 6 5 4 3 2 1

To Jerry Cowan

A map of the northern part of the **WEST INDIES,**

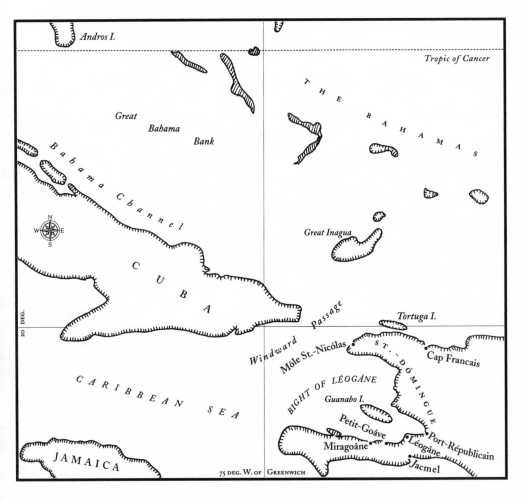

including the relative positions of
SAINT–DÓMINGUE *and the* **BAHAMA CHANNEL.**

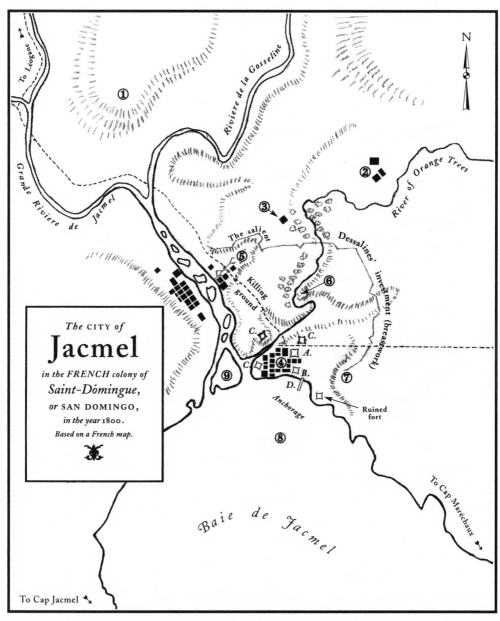

The CITY of

Jacmel

in the FRENCH colony of
Saint-Dómingue,
or SAN DOMINGO,
in the year 1800.
Based on a French map.

POINT ONE: Matty's first vantage point. POINT TWO: Toussaint's headquarters. POINT THREE: Foreign officers' billet. POINT FOUR: The citadel (A., Fort Beliotte; B., prison; C., redouts; D., jetty). POINT FIVE: The troublesome hamlet. POINT SIX: Night hunting in the ravine. POINT SEVEN: Mr. Treadwell and Sergeant Cahoon. POINT EIGHT: The *Rattle-Snake* and the *Croatan* during the night of March 11–12. POINT NINE: The triangular island.

Dramatis personae

Matty Graves, our narrator.

Cyrus Gaswell, commodore of the San Domingo squadron.

Lieutenant Peter Wickett, captain of the *Rattle-Snake*.

Toussaint L'Ouverture, governor-general of San Domingo.

Rigaud, leader of the mulatto faction in San Domingo.

Samuels, a quarter-gunner in the *Rattle-Snake*.

Brodie, a quartermaster in the *Rattle-Snake*.

P. Hoyden Blair, assistant U.S. consul at Port Républicain.

Alonzo Connor, an American adventurer.

Franklin, his secretary.

An assassin, not very good at his job.

Mr. Jeffreys, a midshipman on loan from the *Columbia*.

Mr. MacElroy, ditto.

Schmidt, master gunner in the *Rattle-Snake*.

Horne, bosun's mate in the *Rattle-Snake*.

Rogers, sailing master in the *Rattle-Snake*.

Quilty, surgeon in the *Rattle-Snake*.

Klemso, bosun in the *Rattle-Snake*.

Ambrose, wardroom steward in the *Rattle-Snake*.

A Knight of the White Hand, deceased.

Joséphine, a horse.

Grand-père Bavard, or Grandfather Chatterbox.

Juge, his keeper.

The Parson, also known as MacGuffin.

Bertrand, steward at the foreign officers' quarters.

Dessalines, commander of Toussaint's forces at Jacmel.

Major Matou, senior officer at the troublesome hamlet.

Forcené, an officer in Toussaint's army.

Cahoon, a sergeant of Marines.

Treadwell, a wandering Englishman.

Négraud, a turnkey.

Pepin, a doctor.

Pétion, commander of Rigaud's forces at Jacmel.

Cravache, his adjutant.

Christopher Block, captain of the *Croatoan*.

Williamson, his first lieutenant.

Dick Towson, his third lieutenant.

Jubal, Dick's slave.

Christophe, a colonel in Toussaint's army.

Voyou, a soldier in Toussaint's army.

Chips, ship's carpenter in the *Rattle-Snake*.

Doc, ship's cook in the *Rattle-Snake*.

THE WAR OF KNIVES

One

"My mother died before I was born, sir," I said. Through the *Columbia*'s lightsome stern window I could see the *Rattle-Snake* schooner off the starboard quarter. Peter Wickett, her captain, had edged her down from windward to wait for me; and she lay hove-to with her fore-topsail backed as she sank and rose on the Atlantic swell. Beyond her, to the south, the mountains of San Domingo loomed like jagged fangs on the horizon. "I'm told that's quite a feat."

Commodore Cyrus Gaswell crinkled up the corners of his eyes, but I'd said it solemn and he didn't laugh. He just sat there on the other side of the huge Cuban mahogany table he used as a desk, waiting for me to answer his question. He had the weather gauge on me, was the thing, and I was having to come at it in short tacks across the eye of the wind. My father had forbidden my brothers ever to speak of my mother in my presence, and to me he rarely spoke at all. Not that my old man had been there when I was born, if the way I arrived in the world can be called being born.

While I tried to figure out what to say next, I studied the commodore's elegant blue coat with its garden of gold lace and its bullion epaulets, each with a single silver star. He wasn't wearing the coat; it hung half-hidden behind a painted screen in the corner, for Gaswell was a warrior who liked his comforts. He wore a seaman's checked shirt and loose nankeen trousers in the tropic heat, and had dispensed with shoes entire; but he kept his uniform near to hand, the way some men keep a fierce and loyal dog.

And dog me if I knew how to answer him, but when a commodore sets a seventeen-year-old acting-lieutenant down on a hard wooden chair in the day cabin of his flagship and asks a question, it's best to keep right on fishing till you haul up something he wants to hear. "I don't know as I ever did get the truth of it, sir," I said. "I'm told she come from Saint-Louis in the Louisiana country. A Frenchwoman. But a portrait of her?" I shook my head as I thought of the empty walls of the house in McKeesport. "No, sir, there never was one."

"Yes, a Frenchwoman. Well," said Gaswell, shifting his bulk and coughing into his thick fist. "French is as French does, I guess. Like yourself, Mr. Graves, I never did get the pleasure of meetin' her." He hitched his reading spectacles higher up on the mottled bulb of his nose, and let them slide down again so he could see me over them. "But there *was* a portrait, a miniature in a locket. Your father carried it all during the Revolution. He showed it to me many a time at Yorktown." He rubbed one horny-nailed bare foot against the other under the table and said: "But I'm a Navy man now. Beats the hell out of the Army. There's the prize money, and no goddamn horses. You won't catch me fightin' ashore again, not if I can help it."

"Yes, sir. I don't much care for horses myself." That's the nice thing about being a commodore, I thought: you don't have to do much you don't care to do. That's what junior officers are for.

He rumpled what hair he had, as if I wasn't being as helpful as I might, which I wasn't, and said, "He spoke of her often, your old man did. Your mother was a great beauty, Mr. Graves."

"Thank'ee, sir. I didn't know that."

"Same high cheekbones as you got, and the same dark complexion. A woman like that, ye keep her near to your heart." He tapped his breast, as if reassuring himself that something was still there. He wore an old pewter chain around his massive neck, and for an odd moment I wondered if the locket he'd mentioned hung at the end of it.

I let the silence lie between us as I watched the way Peter filled the *Rattle-Snake*'s fore-and-aft mainsail from time to time to keep some way on her, lest the flagship make a sudden lurch to leeward and stove her in.

"She was a great *Creole* beauty, Mr. Graves."

My stomach flipped and sank, as if maybe the *Columbia* had indeed made a sudden lurch. Gaswell waited for his words to sink in. I waited for him to get on with it. The *Rattle-Snake* seemed suddenly far away, and the Caribbean sunshine seemed to have lost its brilliance.

"Now, ye know as well as I do that *Creole* has more than one meaning," he said. "It can mean someone that ain't all white, and it can mean a European that was born in the colonies. Besides, she weren't hardly more'n an octoroon, I'm sure," he said, dashing that hope. "So legally speaking you're probably as white as any man, have no fear o' that. Or perhaps she was part Osage or something. I'm sure *I* don't know." But it was too late for him to take back what he'd already said. He cleared his throat and drummed on his desktop with his blunt fingers.

"Now, look'ee here," he said, when I still said nothing. "You're not the first man to catch a lick o' the tarbrush. There's no shame in it, if it's far enough back. You're as good a man as any. I'll lay odds on it. I *have* laid odds on it: ain't I bucking for your promotion? Ain't I give ye your order as acting-lieutenant, free, gratis and without charge?"

I'd sunk forward till my head hung nearly between my knees. I straightened up again and said, "Yes, sir, and I'm grateful."

It weren't true he'd given it to me without obligation. I'd had to get rid of my cousin Billy for him. Billy was even then on his way home, floating in his last barrel of whiskey with a hole in his chest. But, *a lick of the tarbrush!*

"Don't think for a minute I done it just out of friendship for your old man, neither," Gaswell said. "It's because I know ye won't let me down. Ye got sand. You're copper bottomed and got saltwater in your veins, *I* allow. And never ye worry—I'll keep your secret right here." He thumped his barrel chest. "Won't breathe a word of it."

"That's white of you, sir."

"I never spoke it yet, till now."

I had to get up, commodore or no commodore. I stood behind my chair and leaned on it to keep my legs from shaking. "So why now, sir?"

"Because I need an officer to go ashore that can pass for Creole."

"If you mean mulatto, sir, I ain't aware I could pass for colored."

I was as dark as any sailor, of course, but his words cast a new light on it. I hadn't been allowed in the house much as a kid. I'd spent my days in the fields and slept in the barn. There'd been some teasing, but me and my brother Geordie had put that to rights often enough, till a Virginia dragoon shot him during the Whiskey Rebellion. It was just sunburn, anyway—I was sure of it. Pretty sure.

"Well, not exactly *colored*," Gaswell said. "I mean, what d'ye call it—mixed blood."

"*Sang-mêlée*, sir?" That was the lightest of the fifteen or twenty degrees of color recognized by French law in San Domingo.

He snapped his fingers. "*Sang-mêlée*, that's the word. Not dark enough so's a white man would notice, but a colored man, now, he might see something that a white man couldn't."

"Is that right, sir?" Which was the country way of saying *that's a damn lie*, which I guessed he knew full well—but might be he was right. A good many of the Rattle-Snakes were black, and I got on well with them. They had a way of looking at me and talking to me that was different than with the rest of the officers, although I treated them no different than I treated any of the other foremast jacks. Except the English ones—I never could cotton to an Englishman.

"And with the way ye speak French—just like an islander, don't deny it. I've heard ye." He pointed at the chair that I still leaned against. "Sit down afore ye tear that thing apart with your bare hands."

I sat. "My tutor was an émigré planter from down in the Artibonite, sir. I guess some of the accent might've rubbed off on him, but he always said it was the pure Parisian he taught me. He'd been to the Sorbonne, you know." But Gaswell wasn't listening to me, even if he knew what the Sorbonne was. He had me. He was going to offer me a job and already knew I'd take it, without waiting to hear the particulars. I needed to commit a power of mayhem to wash Billy's blood from my soul.

"Ye'll wear your best undress uniform, of course," he said, handing me a thin sheaf of papers. "It'll get sadly mauled in the woods, but Frenchmen and coloreds love an epaulet. Playing with revolution's a dangerous business, Mr. Graves, and I'm sending ye into great danger."

"'Playing with revolution,' sir?"

"Aye. Ye know there's rumors afoot that Toussaint L'Ouverture means to transplant his slave rebellion to the Southern states?"

"Yes, sir. The papers are full of it."

"I don't put much stock in 'em, myself, neither," he said, mistaking my meaning. "I think Toussaint's already bit off as much as he can chaw right here in San Domingo, what with this civil war he's got himself into with Rigaud and his mulatto renegados. His situation is precarious enough without he got to worry about planters from Georgia to Delaware getting the wild squirts that maybe a bunch of country bucks is set to come a-roaring through the countryside with blood in their eyes. He needs our trade to keep his army in corn and gunpowder. No, sir, it don't benefit Toussaint a damn. Which don't mean maybe there ain't some in his camp that'd like to see it come about."

"Yes, sir."

"Hark'ee well, now. The *Rattle-Snake* will put ye ashore at Port Républicain or Léogâne, whichever seems best." He handed me a sealed packet with the schooner's name and *P. Wickett, lt. commanding* wrote on the front. "From there ye'll make your way overland to Jacmel on the southern coast. Toussaint's General What's-his-name, Dessalines, has got one of Rigaud's armies bottled up there under a chap name of Pétion, but with as little artillery as Dessalines has got, he ain't likely to dislodge him anytime soon. I want you to keep your ears open and your mouth shut and find out which way the wind blows. That's your official orders." He fixed me with his pale blue eyes. "I dasn't write down that bit about any plot to transplant the slave rebellion, o' course. Them kinds of orders might get ye shot or worse, was anybody on either side to take it personal. But if there is such a plot, that's what

I most want to know about. Ye'll tell no one what your true mission is, except them as ye can trust with your life. And Mr. Blair down in Port Républicain, o' course. No way around that, I'm afeared."

I near about got a case of the galloping fantods at the mention of Blair's name. He'd been a friend of Billy's, if either of them could be said to have a friend.

Gaswell unlocked a cabinet beside him and rummaged around in it. "Ye'll have expenses, o' course—miscellaneous bribes and board and whatnot. To save ye the trouble of trying to get reimbursed from the Navy Department, I'm advancing ye fifty dollars out o' my own purse. You can reckon up with me personal when ye get back."

Assuming I *got* back, he meant. He slid a leather pouch across the polished tabletop and told me to count it for myself. It was in mixed coin, mostly Spanish silver but with a few French gold pieces. It seemed like a lot of money to me—more than two months' pay at my official rank of master's mate—but it didn't weigh nearly as much as my heart did at that moment.

He had me sign a receipt for it, and said, "I'd sew that purse in my boot, was I you. Harder to steal that way. Unless someone robs your boots, in which case ye'll probably be in deeper water than fifty dollars could get you out of anyway. But if all goes well, you'll go aboard of the *Croatoan* frigate off Jacmel in a few weeks—say, by the second week of March. I wrote Captain Block to fill him in on what you're up to, and ye can tell him what ye've learned when ye see him. I'm sure he'll find it useful. And if he ain't there by the time you're done, ye can report to whoever the senior officer is on the station." He looked at me in a way that was almost kindly and said, "You were pretty cocky coming in here, weren't ye?"

"Yes, *sir*," I shot back. I dropped the purse into my pocket and stood up. "I held my head high when I walked in, and I aim to walk out the same way."

"That's a lad." He held out a brawny hand and said, "Just don't get yourself kilt, that's all. And mind how you handle Mr. Blair."

Blair was the assistant U.S. consul in the nominally French colony of Saint-Dómingue; San Domingo, we called it, to differentiate it from the Spanish colony of Santo Domingo to the east. I would have to present my credentials to him before I could travel through the interior. He'd try to foul my hawse if he could. *Let him try,* I thought; I'd snap my fingers in his face. Despite what you might call *trepidations,* my state of mind was such that I actually wanted to travel through the interior. It was full of angry men with guns and knives.

Two

The Monongahela Valley in western Pennsylvania was a wild and deathsome place when I entered the world in 1782. The British had withdrawn to their forts along the Great Lakes and the Saint Lawrence, but the Shawnee were still fighting, and the tales around the watchfires at night were peppered with weird Celtic lore. You couldn't tell our Scotch-Irish neighbors nothing but that I'd sprung from the steaming blood of my mother's womb, squalling the *mallachtaí* curse of my forebears on the brave who'd tomahawked her belly open. I discount it. So far as I knew, whoever murdered her was the only eyewitness, and he never told his story to ary a white man I ever heard of. Besides which, I ain't Irish.

Howsomever it was, the circumstance of my birth was much on my mind as we rolled northwest to clear Tortuga and turned south into the Windward Passage. I watched the colored foremast jacks as they went about their business, but if they felt themselves to be any different than their white shipmates, they showed little sign of it. They were seamen first and black men a long way second.

We made our westing around Cap du Môle, the far northwestern tip of San Domingo, and John Rogers, the sailing master, turned the *Rattle-Snake* south into the Bight of Léogâne. We were coming up on the patch of sea where my cousin Billy, our former captain, had disgraced himself in January. It'd been dead calm on that day, little more than a month ago, with a sea as flat and hot as an anvil. We'd been attacked by hundreds of Rigaud's picaroons who'd mistook us for one of the merchantmen we were escorting down to Port Républicain. Billy had left the deck after we scorned his demand that we surrender to the picaroons without a fight, and it was Peter Wickett who'd saved our bacon for us in the scrap that followed. Blair, who had been on his way to take up his office in Port Républicain, had spent the battle getting drunk with Billy below stairs.

"A fair and steady breeze today," said Peter. It was a soldier's wind on our larboard beam, course southeast by east to allow for leeward drift, and we skipped along with the whitewater creaming at our bows. It was the master's watch, and Peter and I were drinking coffee on the quarterdeck. "And yet you seem indifferent to its glory."

Peter was so tall that it near about gave me the vertigo to look up at him, and he wasn't what you'd call a handsome man, anyway. He had a pink scar on his cheek that looked like something had crawled off the seafloor and rooted itself there, and a long nose and chin that seemed to reach for each other at the tips. He also had an Africa-shaped port-wine stain on his forehead. The skin around it paled when he was angry, making him look like a Cyclops. But the mark was quiescent today, the skin around it smooth and brown.

"Peter," I said. I kept my voice low, and glanced around before I spoke again. "Peter, what would you do if you woke up one morning and discovered you was a Negro?"

He blew on the coffee in the cup that he held in his bony fingers and cast an eye toward the master. Sailing Master Rogers was a brown-eyed, brown-haired, medium sort of man, with a long queue that whipped in the breeze—nothing remarkable about him, in short—and he stood next to the quartermaster and the tillerman, with a sextant in his hand as he took a bearing on a barren peak of Guanabo Island to the southeast. Satisfied that they all had their thoughts on their duty and were paying us no mind, Peter finally murmured, "What if I were to discover I were a Negro . . . Well, I shouldn't tell anyone, for starters. Why should I be an accomplice to my own ruin?"

"But what if somebody asks?"

"No one of quality would ever ask such a thing." He sipped his coffee, his long nose nearly dipping into it as he looked at me over the rim of his cup. "That sort of calumny is spread clandestinely, behind one's back where one has no chance of circumventing it. Once one becomes aware of such a thing, it is far too late. One might as well run away to sea. Speaking of which," he said as Rogers turned the glass and sent a man to the belfry to strike the bell, "the first dog-watch has begun and you have the deck."

He set his cup on the rail and strode off, twining his long fingers together behind his back and aiming his beak at this man and that, like a heron hunting for minnows.

"What do you make of her, Mr. Graves?"

"A French ship-sloop, Mr. Rogers." I handed him back his glass. The *Rattle-Snake* dipped to leeward with the roll, and I ducked down to peer out from under the topsail. "What they call a corvette."

"Could be, aye." Rogers was in the lee shrouds below me, hooked in with an elbow. He raised the glass to his eye. "Could be a frigate, too—a small one," he said, before I could argue. "A twenty-eight, maybe. Hard to tell at this distance." She lay about two leagues west of us, shaking out canvas as she emerged from the lee of Guanabo Island, the mountainous hump that divides the approaches to Port Républicain. "But the cut of her jib's got 'Johnny Crappo' wrote all over it, I give ye that."

"I don't like her, Mr. Rogers . . . She ain't trying to catch us, though."

"Maybe they ain't spotted us yet." He spat a brown arc of tobacco juice.

"Maybe they just know we can walk away from 'em to windward," I said, watching the tobacco juice to make sure it didn't land on my nice white deck.

He shifted his chaw to his other cheek. "A dog don't chase a cat that don't run."

I looked down again. "Here's the skipper."

"Where away the sail?" called Peter as he came up the after hatch.

"Starboard quarter, sir," said Rogers and I together, pointing.

Peter studied the stranger's sails from the quarterdeck rail and then looked forward toward the Princes, the islets that had given the harbor its prerevolutionary name of Port-au-Prince. He swung himself back down to the deck.

"Come alow from aloft, if you please, I need you," he called up to us. "Mr. Klemso," he said to the bosun, "I'll have chains and preventer stays. Mr. Graves," he said as I lit on the deck by way of the backstay, "clear for action and beat to quarters, please."

"Aye aye, sir." I stepped to the quarterdeck rail. "All hands," I bellowed. "All hands on deck! D'ye hear the news there? Clear for action!" That was the kind of thing I liked. Maybe I was only five-foot-three-and-a-fart, as my father used to say, but big men jumped when I raised my voice.

The watch below came pouring up on deck, and Mr. Schmidt, our German master gunner, came to me for the key to the magazine. I nodded at the Marine drummer boy, and he raised his sticks in a flourish and began beating "To Quarters."

"Mr. Jeffreys," said Peter to the signal midshipman, "hoist our private signal of the day." Jeffreys was one of our two boy midshipmen on loan from the *Columbia*.

While we waited for her reply, I said, "Think she'll catch us up, sir?"

"The question," said Wickett, "is, 'Ought I to let her?' What is she?"

"I think she's a French corvette, sir. No more'n twenty guns." I glanced at the sailing master, who'd resumed his place at the conn. "Mr. Rogers thinks she's a small frigate."

"Too far away to count her guns yet, sir," said Rogers.

"It hardly matters," said Wickett. A small frigate, a corvette—she'd have us outgunned regardless. "Was she wearing her colors, Mr. Graves?"

"No, sir." Not that you could trust anyone's colors till he fired at you. "But we're both of the mind that she's a Frenchman."

"Please, sir," said Jeffreys, "she don't answer."

"Try the British signal, then." After a few unhappy incidents, the Royal Navy had agreed to supply our Caribbean squadrons with copies of its codebooks.

She was hull-up from the deck now, wearing all plain sail and shaking out her topgallants and royals. She gave every impression of having plenty of speed in her, should she care to use it. Surely she was French-built—and French-handled, too, from the amount of time she took to set her cloth.

"If you please, sir," said Jeffreys, "she's hoisted last month's reply."

"Very well."

There was a squawking forward as Jimmy Ducks, the poultryman, snatched up the chicken coops to send them below. Some of the hands looked up and laughed.

"Silence on deck there, you chickens," I bellowed, and the men obliged me by grinning as they went about their work. The Marines were ready, assembled in full kit and with Corporal Haversham walking along their line, tugging a belt into place here and telling a man to put a new flint in his musket there. The gun captains were bent over the six-pounders, screwing the flintlocks into place that Mr. Schmidt had sent up, and the powderboys were taking seats on their wooden cartridge boxes behind the guns. Mr. Jeffreys busied himself directing the crews of the murdering-pieces, the ten swivel guns mounted on pivots along the quarterdeck rail. Mr. MacElroy, the other midshipman, stood in the waist, adjusting and readjusting his hat on his golden curls as he tried to look commanding and keep out of the way both at once.

I raised my hat in the formal salute. "Cleared for action, sir. Permission to run out the guns?"

Wickett glanced again at the fast-approaching Princes and then back at the strange ship. She was spilling her wind from time to time, seeming in no hurry to close the distance. "Not just yet, thank you. Mr. Rogers, let us stand in his road and see what he makes of it." When we'd settled on our new course, running south by southwest with the wind just abaft our larboard quarter, he turned to Jeffreys and said, "Hoist our colors where he may see them."

"Aye aye, sir!" Jeffreys was all elbows and Adam's apple, nearly as tall as Wickett and even skinnier, but a likely lad for all that. He jumped to the flag box and broke out the Stars and Stripes. As the azure and crimson and unsullied white rose snapping in the breeze, I felt that stirring in my breast that I could never quite fathom. It was just fifteen red and white stripes, and fifteen stars set in threes and twos across the blue field—just a pleasant arrangement of brightly colored silk—but I felt about it the way I suppose a parson must feel when gazing upon two pieces of wood crossed one upon the other. I saluted the colors and said, "I'll take my station, sir."

Peter nodded. The corvette—if corvette she was—kept her course. Peter would have to raise the stakes pretty soon unless he truly intended to close with her.

Young Mr. MacElroy tensed as I stepped down into the waist, where he stood by to assist me at the main battery. In spite of his boots and dirk, he looked more like a cherub than a sea officer. "All present and accounted for, sir," he squeaked, doffing his hat.

"Good afternoon," I said, touching my hat in return. "Beautiful day, don't ye think?"

He blinked up at the blue sky dotted with little white puffs of cloud. "Why, yes, sir, I suppose it is."

We all waited then in silence—not talking, I mean, for no ship at sea is ever silent—with the gun crews standing easy at their stations, and Bosun Klemso and his mates, Horne and Elwiss, aloft rigging the preventers to keep the spars from falling to the deck were the slings to be shot away.

The crews stood easy, but MacElroy looked stiffer than a parson's collar on Sunday morning. I thought he was about to piss his trousers, but with my eye on him, and maybe encouraged by my not glaring at him, he whispered, "Do you think there's going to be a fight, sir?"

"Watch and learn, Mr. MacElroy," I said, which is a handy thing to say when you don't know the answer. "Meantime, keep your mouth shut and your ears open. D'ye think you can manage that?"

"Aye aye, sir." He bit his lip. "I mean, 'Yes, sir.' Hang it, I can't never get 'em straight."

"When I give you an order, you must say, 'Aye aye, sir.' When I ask you a question, you must say, 'Yes, sir' or 'No, sir,' whichever's appropriate."

He thought about that. "But you gave me an order and asked me a question, both."

I held up a finger. "'Aye aye' means 'I hear and obey.'"

"Aye aye, sir."

"Good lad."

I looked over at the strange sail. She'd come about on a parallel course, maintaining the distance between us. I put a hand on the boy's shoulder, the way my brother Geordie used to do with me. "This is just for show, Mr. MacElroy. No need to be scared."

"Oh, no, sir," he said, looking at me in surprise and then looking away again. "I ain't scared. I'm not."

"Good. Mind your hat." I tipped it over his eyes and made him giggle.

"I'll have silence on deck, please, Mr. Graves."

"Aye aye, sir!" I winked at MacElroy.

Wickett didn't take his eye from the chase. "Come sta'board a point, Mr. Rogers, I pray you. That's well, thus. Keep her there."

"To the braces, you sail handlers," I said. "Mind her trim."

"Please, sir," said Jeffreys. "She's hoisted American colors."

"Aye, an' Oi'm a hadmiral of the facking Russian navvy," laughed the swabber at Number Three gun. He was one of four British deserters aboard that I knew about.

"Put a stopper in it, you," I said. He was right, though—she could be from any of the navies operating in the area but our own. She'd have been smarter to try her luck with the British ensign.

"Mr. Graves, I should like the guns run out. Both sides, if you please."

"Aye aye, sir. Tail on, boys."

The men jumped to the tackles, running out the six-pounders with a thrilling rumble. I looked over at the stranger. She kept her gunports shut, but her mainsail came a-shiver.

"She wavers, sir," said Rogers. "He don't know whether to shit or say howdy."

"Let us help him decide, then. Heave us to, please."

Rogers brought us up into the wind, where we balanced with the backed fore-topsail trying to push us down to leeward and the main course nudging us forward.

"Mr. Graves, there," called Wickett. "Give her a gun to windward."

"Aye aye, sir. Number One gun—fire!"

Every navy has its own way of communicating at sea, but some signals are universal. With smoke billowing across the deck from the forward gun on the starboard side, we had as much as put a chip on our shoulder and dared the other fellow to knock it off.

He came about on the starboard tack, heading away from us.

"He fills and flies, sir," said Rogers. "That dog won't fight."

"Perhaps he merely has somewhere else to go," said Wickett. "As do we. Get us underway again, if you please."

If the stranger had somewhere else to go, he wasn't in a hurry about it. We could see his topgallants peeping above the horizon as we made the outer approaches of the harbor.

Three

A toad-choker of a spring rain sluiced down the filthy streets of Port Républicain as I presented myself that evening at the walled and gated house of Mr. P. Hoyden Blair, our man of business in southern San Domingo. I'd brought only two sailors with me, having had to leave the rest of my men to guard the boat. Samuels was a tall black quarter-gunner and Brodie was a sawed-off Irish quartermaster's mate. When no one answered the jangling of the bell, I let the pair have a go at the ironbound wooden gate. They were a good way toward at least denting it aloft and alow when I heard footsteps splashing toward us from the far side of the gate.

"*Ki moun ki la-a?*" a voice demanded in Creole, and then in French: "*Qui c'est?*" And yet again, as he remembered his manners: "*Qui est la?*"

"*Je m'appel monsieur le lieutenant Graves,*" I said. "I'm here on official business. Open this gate at once!"

A Judas port opened in the gate, and a pair of black eyes in a black face peered out at us.

"What do you want?"

"I'm here to see the assistant consul." I opened my cloak and let the lantern in my hand play across my uniform. "What I want is between him and me."

"Very well, very well," he grumbled. I heard the scrape of bolts being drawn, and a moment later a black man in damp livery and a soggy white wig swung the gate open. "Your servants must wait in the yard," he said, standing aside as we came in through the gate. He slammed it shut and locked it up again. "You will follow me."

He gave me a fair dose of grumbling and dirty looks as he let me into the house. The sailors got the better part of the bargain, lounging in the fresh air under the shelter of the balcony: with the shutters closed, Blair's front parlor was as hot and damp as the inside of a barber's towel. It was near about as dark, too, as there weren't but a single candle burning.

Blair had changed in the few weeks since I'd seen him last. He had the same calculating glint in his eyes behind the square gold-rimmed spectacles, the same peevish tremolo in his voice, the same hunch to his scrawny shoulders as if he lived in dread of getting what he deserved—but something in him was different. He looked both shiftier and more arrogant; I didn't know yet where it come from, but I was pretty sure I wouldn't like it once I figured it out. Although he was old enough to know better, perhaps thirty, he neither bowed nor offered his hand as he stood looking down at me.

As he was my social superior I took my cue from him. I dropped my sodden hat and cloak on a chair, hoping to ruin the damask upholstery, but the white-wigged footman gave me a nasty look and took them away.

At last Blair stirred himself. "How is the night, Mr. Graves?"

"Coming down like a cow pissing on a flat rock, sir."

"You got good and soaked, I hope?"

"You'll be happy to know I did, Mr. Blair, but this ain't a pleasure visit. I'm here on the say-so of Commodore Gaswell." I held out my papers.

He ignored them. Instead, he clutched his dressing gown across his sunken chest and looked at the muddy bootprints I'd left on his carpet. The reflected flame of the candle writhed in his spectacles as he returned his glance to me. His eyes came to rest on my single epaulet.

"You are a lieutenant now, I see, Mr. Graves."

"Acting-lieutenant, Mr. Blair. The president has to sign my commission before it's official."

"And a long time you shall wait, too, should anyone bother to ask my expert advice." He took my orders over to the candle, where he held them too damn close to the flame for my comfort. At last he slipped his specs into a pocket of his gown and looked me over again.

"If it's only an acting appointment," he said, "how come you're wearing a sword like a gentleman?"

"Regulations, sir." The same regulations forbad my skewering him for insolence.

"Ah," he said, packing the single syllable with a bucket of resentment. "Captain Trimble approves of this, I gather?"

"I ain't the faintest, Mr. Blair."

"Captain William Trimble is your commanding officer as well as your cousin. Tell me, pray, how it is you neither know nor apparently care if he approves."

"He's dead, sir."

"Dead!" He put his fingers to his mouth. "How can this be?"

"Peter Wickett put a ball through his lungs up in Le Cap. Ain't you heard?" I wiped my curls with my kerchief and wrung it out where I stood. "No, I guess not. It ain't been but a week or so." I twisted the kerchief tighter to hide the shaking of my hands.

"Dead!" said Blair again. He groped in the air behind him. "Wickett— that terrible man! Philadelphia shall hear of this!"

I thrust a chair under his skinny legs and he collapsed into it, fanning himself with his robe and breathing whiskey fumes into my face.

"I guess the commodore's already informed the Navy Department, Mr. Blair," said I, hoping maybe he had the apoplexy. "It was an affair of honor. I calculate Secretary Stoddert will keep the president apprised." Much either one of them would care. Sea officers fought duels so often that you could read your newspaper by the light of the pistol shots. At any rate, I didn't see any need to air Navy laundry in front of Blair—nor to tell him I'd been Peter's second instead of Billy's. The memory still gave me the wicked horrors, but I'd be dogged before I'd let Blair know it.

I sloshed whiskey into a tumbler from the decanter on the sideboard. From the smell of it I guessed it was some of Billy's private store:

Monongahela rye made by my father's own hand. I thirsted for it so bad I could feel it in my bones, but I wouldn't humble myself by asking for any. I dropped the glass stopper back into the decanter and carried the tumbler at arm's length over to Blair. "As you can see, sir," I said, pointing at my orders, "I'm to make my way overland to Jacmel and deliver myself to Captain Block, who's blockading the port. I'm to see what I can see on the way. Of course that's entirely unofficial, but I'll still need a local escort—"

"Spy work is rather poaching on my territory, Mr. Graves." He narrowed his eyes as he slurped his drink.

"I ain't no spy," I said. "How you talk. The commodore just wants someone to scout out possible landing sites near the city. It might be helpful to Toussaint's efforts was we to put a contingent of Marines ashore, or maybe some large guns and the crews to work 'em. It's right there on page two, sir. All above board and plain as plain."

I also had a letter in my pocket from the rogue François Villon Deloges, a French major in Rigaud's service that Captain Oxford in the *Choptank* frigate had hanged out of hand as a pirate. It was a personal letter to Villon's wife in Jacmel. Naturally I hadn't read it, much less mentioned it to anyone.

Blair smiled, just a slight upturn of his thin lips, as he looked again at my orders. "It would not go well with you to have this in your pocket, was you to fall in with Rigaud's faction," he said, extracting the page detailing the help I was to give to Toussaint. "I think perhaps I'd best keep it in my safe—for your own protection, of course."

"Hold on there—what'll I have to show to General Dessalines, should he get suspicious of me? You know how he hates whites."

"Commodore Gaswell has a copy of it, I'm sure, and has sent another copy off to the Navy Department. He'll be able to vouch for you if need be." He held the page toward the candle. "Or perhaps I should just burn it."

"You can't do that!"

"Can't I, though? My word against yours, you know. A careless young officer loses a vital page of his orders and then blames his troubles on a poor hardworking civil servant. Now, how would that go over, I wonder."

I took a step back. "See here, Mr. Blair! A good word from Gaswell won't help me worth a damn if I already been shot."

He laughed at the thought. It sounded like a lizard choking. "Oh, you'd be safe enough, probably." He put the page back among the others. "Even Dessalines knows the value of keeping on an ally's good side, unlike yourself."

I squinted at him. "What ally? You?"

"We do in theory work for the same government, and surely you ain't as stupid as you look. But in case you are, I'll spell it out for you. Captain Block is capable of talking with the nigger generals about any assistance they might require. So, why send a jumped-up acting-lieutenant to do what Block could do better and more easily?" Behind the mask of his smile, he was pure snake. "Information is a commodity like any other, Mr. Graves. If you want my help, I suggest you start dishing some up."

"I ain't under orders to tell you. In fact, I'm under orders to keep it under my hat, which means you got to keep it quiet, too. That means no writing it down."

"The most valuable information ain't never wrote down. It's true on its face. That's what gives it currency." He sat back with his hands folded over my papers. "So, spill."

"I'm supposed to find out if it's true that Toussaint aims to transport the slave rebellion to the Southern states."

He slapped my papers down on the table. "Oh, what a lie! He wouldn't never do such a thing. Rigaud might, as a feint to draw us away and give him time to remove Toussaint, but . . . Feh." He snatched up my papers and shook them at me. "I should tear these up and have done with it."

"Do that." I looked around, wondering where that fartcatcher had gone off to with my hat and cloak. "I'll have to go back to Gaswell and tell him you thwarted him. He'll assign me some other duty and look for a way of crossing you later. Don't think he won't do it, neither."

He stroked his chin, what there was of it. "Hee hee! Maybe you know how to play this game after all. But, but—where was it?" He located a paragraph in my papers and stabbed it with his finger. "Ah yes: it says here that you are to lend me whatever assistance I might need or desire."

"That's just pro forma, Mr. Blair. The commodore don't expect me to be your errand boy while I'm doing his business."

He gave me a wicked grin. "It's all above board and plain as plain, as you so charmingly put it. However, you want a plausible excuse to be at Jacmel. I'll give you one." He returned my papers to me with two fingers and raised his voice. "Mr. Connor! Mr. Connor there! I think I have found a solution to your problem."

An elegant fellow in a blazingly white shirt and azure britches under a peacock-green silk dressing gown stuck his head out from the lamp-lit back room. In one hand he dangled a glass of ruby port and in the other he clasped a fragrant black cigar. He was about thirty, and handsome in the sort of way that makes ladies giggle with each other behind their fans.

"Mr. Connor," said Blair, "allow me to present Mr. Matthew Graves, a malapert young acting-lieutenant who needs to be delivered to Jacmel. Mr. Graves, this is Mr. Alonzo Connor. Mr. Connor is a . . . how shall I put this . . . a gentleman of color with a special commission from the War Department."

Blair pinched out the candle, and we went into the back room. It was a well-appointed parlor, with silver candle stands and silk-upholstered chairs and sofas. A black-draped portrait of Washington— rotting in his crypt these two months now—hung over the mantel, and yet another sideboard with glasses and decanters stood off to one side. "Don't bother to sit yourself, Mr. Graves," sniffed Blair, heading for the sideboard. "You won't be here long, I dare say."

Connor stood in the middle of the room with one hand on his hip and his cigar between his teeth. He studied me, tilting his head away from the smoke. "I believe I've heard of you, Mr. Graves," said he. "Ain't you the fire-eater that recaptured the *Jane* in the Bight of Léogâne five, six weeks ago?"

Blair stiffened, and I looked at Connor with sudden liking. "Well, for about an hour, sir, before I was captured myself. But it's good of you to say, Mr. Connor."

"Yet you must've escaped captivity somehow, as you stand here before us. That shows fortitude, sir. Fortitude! Your superiors must think very well of you, Mr. Graves."

We exchanged bows, and he offered his hand. It was as smooth and hard as floured marble. I had to take Blair's word for it that he was a mulatto, for his skin was lighter than my own. Now that I looked at him closer I supposed that his hair was on the crinkly side, and his nose was kind of flat and broad. But his hair had a red tinge to it, nearly blond, and his eyes were green. Despite that, he'd be considered no whiter than the blackest field hand back home, was anyone to tumble to his ancestry. Since Blair knew about it I didn't guess Connor kept it a secret. I wondered how he'd gotten an appointment from the War Department.

"Percy," he said, turning to Blair, "does the gentleman speak French?"

The assistant consul tucked his chin in and blinked at me: "A question is put to you, Mr. Graves. Do you speak French?"

"You know very well I do."

"*I* do, yes, but I ain't the one that asked. And how are you with the Creole patter?"

"I can bargain well enough in the market and whorehouses. I got a phrase or two, here and there." I knew a little more than that, but hell if I'd tell him.

The elegant mulatto chuckled, half-raising his encumbered hands in mock surrender. "Well, it's the closest I've come yet to finding a French *and* Creole speaker who's white and can be trusted."

I clasped my hands behind my back the way Peter Wickett would've done, and looked up at him. "Now that's an odd thing to say, sir." Even then, in the spring of the year zero, as the armies of Toussaint

L'Ouverture and André Rigaud rampaged across San Domingo in a savage civil war, there were still plenty of white men in the colony. Them that could afford it had sent their families off to Jamaica or to New Orleans in Spanish Louisiana, but many of the men had remained behind. "Ain't there plenty of *grand blancs* around? Surely some of them speak Creole."

Connor cocked his head. "What's a *grand blanc?*"

"The white Frenchmen that were formerly in the sugar and coffee trade."

"Oh, *them*," said he. "It ain't genteel to earn your keep, you know. They are more interested in escape than they are in throwing in with one side or the other. Some of them who ain't out-and-out Royalists have taken sides, of course. A few of Toussaint's most trusted advisers are white, as are some of Rigaud's. But that means all the good ones are taken, d'ye see."

"Then what about the *petit blancs?* The mechanics, the overseers—surely one of them would do."

He waved his cigar in a graceful semicircle. "They're all off in one army or another. Toussaint's blacks fight for freedom and Rigaud's mulattoes fight for equality. Don't know why those goals should be at odds, but they are. And so they will remain until first Consul Napoleon can gather enough ships and men to retake the colony. In the meantime, here we are, helping out the niggers. Who'd have thought it?" He sat down on a sofa, crossing his legs just so at the ankles, and sent a little half-smile toward the back of Blair's head. "The consul thinks I'm a good man for a nigger. Ain't that right, Percy?"

Blair swallowed his mouthful of whiskey a little faster than he'd intended. "Yes!" He coughed. "Yes—um, a good man, an agent of the government, come here direct from the capital in Philadelphia." He still stood by the sideboard, and poured himself another dram while he framed his words. "Best of credentials, but nary a lick of French. So happens he's headed where you are, Mr. Graves. You agree to go along as his translator, and I shall sign your passport." Under his breath he added, "Yes . . . that will do a treat, now won't it?" A bit louder, he said,

"I understand his guides don't admit to speaking English. With you along, that's one lie they won't be able to pull off—eh, Alonzo?"

"But Mr. Connor," I said, "I was just saying that I don't understand—"

"Tish tish," said he. "A soldier's job ain't to understand but to obey! Who said that? Well, never mind, I suppose I said it. How, sir, do you propose we arrive at our destination?"

Because I couldn't sit, I paced. It seemed to me that Alonzo Connor was carrying me along faster than I liked—but he seemed to be heading in a direction that was favorable to me. "First by sea, sir, to Léogâne. I calculate to strike inland from there. It should save a day at the least. Assuming tide and wind are right, which they are at the moment. We ought to be off this minute, sir, if we're to be gone by first light."

"What's first light got to do with any—" began Blair, but the handsome mulatto was already on the move.

"Good and good!" said he, springing up from the sofa. "I am to rendezvous with my guides at a certain place in the hills above Léogâne, as it happens, and I was wondering how I might safely arrive there. Percy, 'twas a pleasure." He extinguished the stub of his cigar in his port and pumped the consul's hand. "You'll sign the boy's papers and give us an indent for horses? Good and good again! I'll have Franklin pack m' kit at once." He strode off down the corridor toward the stairs, shouting, "Franklin! Rouse yourself, you black rascal, we're off to the wars at last!"

Blair hoisted himself out of his chair and perched his specs on the tip of his nose. "Wait here, Graves. I have a last word to say to Mr. Connor."

Samuels took Connor's bag as we emerged from the assistant consul's house. Brodie passed me the shuttered lantern he'd been holding. No one moved to help Franklin, Connor's bespectacled black secretary, who was encumbered by a carryall, a portable writing table, and a thick packet of papers wrapped in oilskin. He didn't seem to expect any help, anyway. Throwing our cloaks around ourselves, we splashed across the yard and through the gate. Blair's fartcatcher slammed it behind us.

"Keep a weather eye out for bravos," I said to the sailors. I glanced up and down the street. "You too, Mr. Connor, if you please."

"I doubt the gangs'll be out in this torrent," he said over the roar of the rain. "But I don't figure on being found in some filthy alley tomorrow morning with my throat and pockets cut."

I loosened my sword in its scabbard, and we set off. The seamen walked on either side with naked cutlasses in their hands. Connor took the rear, with Franklin huddling over his baggage between us.

It was a good half-mile down to the waterfront, past shattered buildings and tumbled-down walls that loomed out of the darkness, with now and then a torch sputtering in an archway or a lamp limning the bars across a window. We slipped and stumbled as we went. The cobblestones had been dug up for missiles in the late riots, and the streets were greasy with mud and turds. More than once we stopped to retrieve a shoe or boot from the sucking filth.

"Serves you right, mate," said Samuels, as Brodie groped around for one of his shore-going pumps. "Goin' around shod like a gent instead of barefoot like a sailor-man."

"Is it the naked feet I'm to be havin'," said Brodie, upending his shoe and letting the gobs dribble out of it, "like a chawbacon boobie just come in this moment from the bogs?" He swished his shoe out in a puddle and crammed his foot into it.

The rain had lessened and the gibbous moon had begun to show through rips in the clouds when we at last reached the broad marketplace. Here we walked easier. Most of the paving had been left untouched or had been replaced, and the stones were carpeted by sodden remnants of the sugar cane that blacks in San Domingo chewed constantly. The crushed cane stalks filled the air with a sweet perfume.

Soldiers wandered around in twos and threes, looking for rum or doxies and unmindful of us; but a pair left off annoying a woman and blocked our way. They both reeked of tafia, the cheap island rum. The short one shouted at me in Creole, then muttered something to the tall one out of the side of his mouth. The tall one clutched his musket, but he hadn't cocked it. He kept running his tongue over his lips and then spitting.

"What do they want?" said Connor.

"I calculate they want to rob us."

"Well, tell them something. They seem like pretty rough fellows."

I unshuttered the lantern and put the light in their eyes. *"Mwen meriken,"* I said. *"M'okipé—ralé ko-w!"* I hoped it meant, "I'm an American. I'm busy—get away!"

The shorter one set the butt of his musket on the paving stones and leaned on it. His eyes darted from me to the sailors and back again. In French he said, "We leave as soon as you pay the toll." He held out a hand. "It is two silver coins. Each!"

Samuels and Brodie edged around either side of the soldiers. I eased back my cloak to clear my sword and pistols. "We are glad to pay you in lead and steel," I said.

The soldiers both took an uncertain step back. Then the short one grinned. "But I forget," he said. "We are off duty tonight!" He gave the tall one an elbow in the ribs. They reeled away, laughing.

There was a click as Connor set his pistol back on half cock. He slipped it away inside his cloak and gave me a sad look, as if he'd caught a friend in some mild deceit. "And here you said you spoke no Creole."

"No, sir, I didn't. I said I know some useful phrases. But if the short one hadn't spoke French, might be somebody'd be dead by now."

I led the way down a maze of broken streets and narrow alleys toward the waterfront. The rain lessened and the wind turned gusty, tangling our cloaks around our legs and arms. Then we turned into a narrow passage where the wind died and the shadows crawled with rats.

"Ain't much farther now, Mr. Connor," I said. I turned to look at him, but he was hard to make out in the gloom. He drifted along like a black cloud.

"'Tis but a wee way now, sir," said Brodie. "Will you be havin' me run ahead and alert Mr. Horne, there?"

Bosun's Mate Horne was about the steadiest enlisted man I'd ever met. I'd had to leave him to see that the boat's crew didn't run off and get drunk the minute I turned my back. "Very well. No, wait—" But the little Irishman had already trotted off into the darkness. I cursed myself for a ninny. I was a sailor, not a soldier, but I knew you weren't supposed to divide your forces.

I wasn't what you'd call *scared* so much as extremely alert as we worked our way along the passage. Any number of hidey-holes lay along the way. Ali Baba and all his forty thieves could lurk in them, and we'd never know it till we woke up dead. I wished I'd brought Horne with me, and hang the boat.

I stopped to shine the light ahead. "Did you hear something?"

"No," said Connor. "Let us keep moving."

We passed a place on the left where the wall had fallen down. I shone my lantern into it, revealing a filthy room. A man lay sprawled against the far wall. A chipped enamel basin sat beside him on the muddy floor, and a foul stench hung in the air. I thought he was dead till his eyes gleamed in the lantern light. He raised his hands to show they were empty. *"Mwen malad,"* he groaned. His hands sank as if they were an unbearable weight. *"Pa anmède-m."*

Franklin poked his head in to have a look. "What does he say?"

"I think he says he's sick and not to bother him."

Connor recoiled. "Is it fever?" He whipped his kerchief out of his sleeve and held it to his nose.

That or he'd shit his pants, I thought, but I didn't say it. I lifted my head and peered down the alley. "Listen: there it is again."

"There *what* is again?"

"A shout. Samuels, did you hear it?"

"I didn't hear nothin', sir."

The close walls forced us to walk single-file. I crept along in the van, nearly on tiptoes as if that might make me invisible, with the shuttered lantern in one hand and my sword in the other. Samuels followed me, and Franklin followed him, with Connor guarding our backs.

At length the passage opened up into a small square, where water from a shattered fountain burbled across the paving stones and where the charred rafters of the surrounding houses thrust up like bones against the sky. A glow of lamps from a few streets over deepened the shadows in the square, but through an archway down at the far end I could see ships' lanterns sparkling out on the bay. Home free, I thought. Then my eyes bugged out as Samuels tripped over something in his path.

"Law!" he said. "Look-a here, sir!"

I aimed the lantern where he was pointing and saw Brodie sprawled on his back beside a broken stone bench. His arms were folded peacefully across his chest and one of his shoes was missing. I held out the lantern to Samuels and squatted down for a closer look. A welt ran across Brodie's face from his right eyebrow to the left side of his jaw— a slash, rather, beaded with blood but not too deep except across the bridge of his nose. I felt the back of his head. It was gooey from lying in the ooze, but I could feel a lump there and my hand came away bloody.

"Does he live?" said Connor.

I squinted in his direction. He stood away from the narrow beam of light, behind Franklin. In his black cloak he was no more than a shape in the gloom.

"Dunno, Mr. Connor." Brodie didn't seem to have been robbed. His pockets hadn't been turned out, his pistol was still in his belt, and his cutlass lay nearby. "Looks like we interrupted whoever—"

"Ho!" said Samuels. A shadow moved among shadows. Metal rasped on metal and a sword blade flashed. The lantern blinked out as it clattered across the square. In the sudden darkness came a thump and a gasp.

"Assassin!" cried Connor. I heard a click as he cocked his pistol.

A hooded figure loomed above me in the moonlight. I lashed out with my sword and pierced his cloak. He jabbed down at me backhanded. I threw up my arm. The dagger in his fist slashed through my sleeve and lodged in the thicker material at the cuff. He abandoned the dagger and strode past me, leveling the sword in his right hand. He lunged.

Franklin took the point of the blade—*thock!*—smack in the middle of his portable writing desk. He stumbled backward into Connor. The mulatto fired.

The would-be assassin sprawled gurgling at Connor's feet. The mulatto kicked him over onto his back. "Clumsy damned—" He stomped the man's black-masked face till the arms and legs stopped twitching. Then he stomped him again.

"Great jumping Jehoshaphat, *quit* that," I said. "I guess he ain't getting any deader."

Connor turned away.

"Well anyway, Mr. Connor," I said, looking at the corpse, "it was a pretty shot."

"Who is he? Can you tell?"

I lifted the mask from the dead man's face. Even in the moonlight it was too dark to see much, but I could see plenty that I didn't want to see. "I don't calculate I'd recognize him even if I knew him, sir. You near about turned his face to jelly."

He scraped the sole of his boot against the stone bench. "I beg pardon, Mr. Graves, for my ill temper." He snapped his fingers. "Franklin, fetch that lantern. Let us strike a light and see what the damage is."

The lantern was dented and the mica panes had splintered, but the candle was intact. In its light I could see our man was white and maybe thirty years old; but French, English, American—I couldn't tell. Connor's ball had shattered his lower jaw and blown the bones out the back of his neck, and his footwork had knocked in the man's teeth, nose, and cheekbones.

"I don't guess his own mother'd recognize him now, Mr. Connor."

"Again, Mr. Graves, I beg pardon. Sometimes it seems I have an entire army trying to do for me. Ain't that right, Franklin?"

"So it would seem, Mr. Connor." Franklin examined his oilskin packet, which he'd dropped in the excitement. Apparently satisfied that the papers had survived undamaged, he pushed his glasses up more firmly on his nose and peered at the body. If he knew him he didn't say so.

Samuels raised himself to his hands and knees with a groan. "He gimme a boot right in the cable tier," he said as Franklin helped him to his feet. "Six inches lower and the old woman wouldn't be havin' no more chil'ren."

"How's Brodie?" said I.

Samuels knelt over him, his hand outstretched. "Dead, by glory!" he said, collapsing astride the little Irishman.

"A good man ya are, Samuels," said Brodie, with a muffled air. He pushed Samuels's knee off his chest. "But have I not been trod upon enough to last me all me days?"

Four

MacElroy's treble whisper floated across the dark water. "Ahoy the boat."

"Aye aye," said Horne. He held up two fingers to indicate my rank.

"No," I said, and the big bosun's mate steered for the larboard side, where I could arrive without the bosun piping me aboard. The last thing I wanted was the attention of every vessel within earshot. I scrambled over the bulwark and nearly tripped over Mr. MacElroy.

MacElroy was all eyes under his hat as Samuels helped Brodie aboard and led him off to find Mr. Quilty, the surgeon. "Did you have a rumpus with the guard boat, sir?" He peered off into the darkness.

"How you talk," I said. "They catch so many crabs with their oars that you can hear 'em half a mile off."

"Then how'd he—" His eyes widened at the sight of Connor and Franklin. "Who's these chaps?"

"Fellows that know how to mind their own business." In the light of our battle lanterns I could make out the Marines, still turned out in full kit, and the Rattle-Snakes yarning quietly or napping around the guns. Illumined by the binnacle light, Rogers paced the old-fashioned raised quarterdeck. I doffed my hat to him and the quarterdeck, and he doffed his in return. I looked north toward the Princes. The corvette had dropped her hook there at sundown, presumably to wait till we came out again. We hadn't gone much further in ourselves, not in the dark without a pilot. "Mr. MacElroy," I said, "is that Johnny Crappo still over yonder?"

"Yes, sir." He pointed to starboard of where I'd been looking. "You can see her cabin lights over past them rocks."

"Did anyone catch her name yet?"

"Yes, sir. She's the *Rose-red Cunt.*"

That made me look at him twice. "The what now?"

As he repeated it, obviously enjoying the sound of it, I could only imagine what he'd been told about the French. He added, "She's a privateer, 'cause the officers ain't wearing uniforms. Think they'll try an' cut us out tonight, sir?"

"Not if you keep your ears open and your mouth shut, Mr. MacElroy."

"Yes, sir." He put his head down. "I mean, aye aye, sir. Oh sir, I forgot," he said, peeking out at me from under his hat brim. "Captain wants to see you immediately you come on board."

"Which you should have told me immediately I *came* on board, you wet-brained ninny," I said. "Mind your hat." He grabbed for it, but I was quicker. I set it back on his head and tamped it down over his ears. "Now, Mr. MacElroy," I continued, "put the gentleman in the purser's cabin—it's empty—and his secretary wherever he'll fit. Perhaps the gunners' mess has room for him."

"Don't wish to be any trouble, Mr. Graves," said Connor.

"No trouble, sir. And Mr. Horne," I said as I headed for the after hatch, "leave the boat in the water, and present our package to Surgeon Quilty with my compliments."

In the cuddy behind the door in the after-cabin, Peter in his shirt-sleeves was poring over the chart while his tattered tabby, Gypsy, batted at his pencil. The wooden deadlights had been shipped over the stern windows to thwart curious eyes, and the air was greasy with smoke from the lamps.

"Ah, Mr. Graves, you return to us," said Peter, without looking up. He drew a little *X* on the chart and circled it. To the southeast he had drawn another *X* within a circle. A pencil line connected the two *X*'s. He picked up a ruler and drew lines connecting the two *X*'s with one of the Princes. Then he spread a pair of compasses, measured the gap against the graph on the side of the chart, and walked off the distances between the three points of the triangle. "Light airs from the east, increasing and backing nor'easterly with the coming of the dawn. Though I wish to unmoor before then." He held the pencil out to Gypsy, who grabbed it with a crazed look and commenced to gnaw the end of it. "That Frenchman lies athwart our best passage out."

As we had engaged no pilot and hadn't asked for pratique, our certification of health, we hadn't had any official contact with the port authorities—which meant we didn't have to wait for permission to leave. Somewhere down the line it might save us a reprimand for upping anchor on the sly.

"Sir, Mr. MacElroy informs me that the Johnny Crappo is called the *Rose-red Cunt*."

"Does he now? No doubt some wag of a sea-daddy told him such. She in fact is called *L'Heureuse Rencontre*."

"The *Fortunate Meeting*, then. I think I prefer MacElroy's take on it."

His thin lips twisted in a faint smile. "Perhaps we may suggest it to her captain in the morning."

"Yes, sir," I said. "But listen, there's something I have to tell you."

"A slight north'ard current of about a quarter of a knot, and a negligible tide," he muttered, peering at the chart through a loupe. He was a tall, narrow man, and as he bent further over the chart his stern rose in the air. "I am concerned about this reef here, and those rocks under Gypsy's tail could be tricky . . . What is it you wish to tell me, Mr. Graves?"

"Blair has foisted a pair of passengers on us, sir."

"The cow. You refused, of course?"

"I couldn't, sir. He wouldn't sign my passport without I didn't, nor give me a chit for a horse. But they're going to Léogâne anyway, and they'll arrange for the horses and the guides, and pay for 'em, too."

"Very well, then. Put them wherever you wish."

"Thank'ee, sir, I've put MacElroy on it. But that ain't all."

He looked up at last. "Then pray what is all?"

"Mr. Connor's from the War Department, sir."

"And what of it?"

I told him of my meeting with Blair and what had happened in the alley off the waterfront.

The port-wine stain on his forehead stood out as the skin around it paled. "Mr. Graves," he said, "you know as well as I that the authorities will not care that he attacked you. They will assume you lie. At the very least they will raise a snit about your being ashore without their permission. I told you to take particular care in that regard."

"Yes, sir. That's why I wrapped him in his cloak and brought him with me."

"Did you now?" He grinned. "I shall have to meet this fellow as soon as we are safe at sea. Did you hoist the gig aboard?"

"No, sir. Figured it'd make too much noise."

"Excellent. The moon will not set till after daylight, but the sky is clouding up again." He tapped the compasses against the chart. "Which should provide sufficient darkness for a bit of mischief I have in mind for you."

The voices of *L'Heureuse Rencontre*'s officers drifted along the water toward us as we rowed slowly across the lie of their anchor cable. They were having themselves a time in the brightly lit after-cabin, and their singing mixed weirdly with the faint shrieking and drumming that came along the offshore breeze flowing down from the hills. The grapnel that we trailed astern was on a heavier line than might be usual, but not remarkably so. And it was a French grapnel, a souvenir from the battle with the picaroons.

"She catches, sir," said Horne.

"Belay," I whispered. The men sat their oars, letting them drift—a sudden clatter of an oar against the gunwale might bring a storm of grapeshot down on our heads. Horne tensed the line to make sure it was the cable he had caught and not some weed or rock. "Got it, sir," said he.

"Give way," I whispered. "Handsomely, now."

36

We crept toward one of the Princes islets as Horne eased out the line, keeping it taut but not hauling on it.

"Toss your oars," I whispered, and the men raised their oars out of the water as the bowman hooked onto the jumble of rocks. I went ashore, bent near double so as not to tumble on the slime and weeds that covered the verge of the islet. I looked back to see Horne easing out the line as he made his way forward. "Keep it taut," I said.

"Taut as a virgin, sir."

His wild mass of braids swung like ropes'-ends as he stepped out of the boat. We frapped the line around a pair of old barrel staves that we had fished out of the harbor earlier, and lodged them up tight and out of sight among the rocks.

The stars had faded and the morning twilight had yet to gather beyond the eastern hills. But for the lanterns of the ships in the harbor and a few lamps in the town, all was darkness. Certainly it was dark in the *Rattle-Snake,* what with all lights extinguished and the galley fire dumped over the side. Rogers had brought us round so the breeze was on our larboard quarter, letting what was left of the tide provide just enough tension to keep our single anchor in the ground. Though I couldn't see him from my perch on the bowsprit, I knew he was feeling his way with one hand resting on the tiller as he walked the schooner forward. We had muffled the capstan pawls as best we could, but still they clanked horribly as Horne and his crew took in the slack. Rogers's voice came faintly on the breeze: "She's there, sir."

"Keep her thus," said Peter.

"Heave and pawl," said Horne in an urgent whisper over by the capstan, and the clanking recommenced as the men strained against the capstan bars. "*Heave.* One more pawl—get all you can." Water hissed out of the straining cable as it rose from the sea. The boys with their nipper lines trotted back and forth in the gloom, throwing the nippers around the messenger and the cable as it came aboard, and throwing them off again as the cable slithered down into the cable tier. "Heave her 'round, boys," said Horne in a soft singsong. "Heave cheer'ly!"

I looked down. "Anchor's a-peak," I said, and the word passed along from man to man till it reached the quarterdeck. I waved my hand: "Anchor's aweigh."

"At the braces there," came Wickett's voice. "Haul taut. Brace up."

The *Rattle-Snake* swam slowly forward as her topsails filled.

"'Vast heaving," said Horne. "Rig the cat—hook the cat—walk away with her," and his crew fished the anchor as we gathered speed down the fairway.

"Heads'ls, there!" called Wickett. There was no need for quiet now that we were moving.

I jumped down to the fo'c's'le. "Man the forestays'l halyards! Clear away the downhaul and hoist away! Now haul out that jib boom!"

The breeze came astern of us and then onto the starboard quarter as we turned our nose toward the French corvette. Beyond her lay the open sea. A halo shone around her stern lantern in the morning damp, making a perfect beacon for us. We'd cross her bow within musket shot—provided she stayed where she was.

As I returned to the quarterdeck, Rogers grinned at me. "We've caught her unawares," he said. He twirled an imaginary mustache and affected a French accent. "Probablee zay all have ze snootful of claret by now and ayr snow-ring like ze saw-meels, *hein?*"

As a gentleman, Connor had been granted the privilege of the quarterdeck. Sipping his coffee—there was presence of mind for you, cadging a cup before the cook had doused the galley fire—and holding a saucer under his cup like he was at a yachting party, he looked coolly over at the corvette. "Surely if he were hostile," he said, "he'd have attacked us already."

"Not in Toussaint's harbor," I said, with more assurance than I felt. "They dassn't touch us for fear they'll be banned entire."

"Might be," put in Rogers. "And might be not. The *Constellation* gave the *La Vengeance* a first-rate thumping a couple weeks ago. It's the second time the *Connie*'s tore apart one of their heavy frigates. No, sir, my guess is they're waitin' for us to come out and play."

"It becomes clear to me, sir," said Connor. His cup rattled in his saucer. "Er . . . has either of you seen Franklin? I must find him at once." He thrust his cup and saucer at me. "You gentlemen will excuse me."

Rogers and I shared a look after he'd left. "Well, *he* left in a hurry," said Rogers.

"Yes," I said. I grinned. "For a man who was as cool as a cucumber a minute ago—"

"*Don't* say he's all of a sudden in a pickle," said Rogers. "Don't."

Peter stepped over from the windward rail. "Let us give him the benefit of the doubt," he said. "It is a passenger's right to skip below if there be a fight."

"Yes, sir," I said. "But he's a dead shot. We might need him."

"A shy man does not shoot straight," said Peter. He glanced aloft at the sails, at the dimples and eddies that marked reefs to either side, and at the ever-shortening distance between us and the corvette. "Regardless, I am sure the War Department has bigger plans for him than to get his brains dashed out in a minor action." He touched wood. "Which with luck no one will remember anyway."

We all looked up as the lookout in the maintop sang out: "Deck there! Boats in the water!"

"Where away and how many?" called Peter.

"Just for'ard o' the starboard beam, sir. Three of 'em, heading right for us."

"Anything to larboard?"

A pause. "Nay, sir."

"Run out the starboard guns," said Peter, but I was already leaping down into the waist. "Hold your fire until you are sure they mean to board," he called after me. "Or if the *Rose-red Cunt* fires upon us, of course." Peter spoke excellent French. His calculated mispronunciation of the name sent a wave of laughter through the men.

"Aye aye, sir! Cast off your guns, starboard side!"

Mr. MacElroy was waiting for me. A quick look around told me he had everything in hand for once.

"Good lad," I said, and he beamed. "Mind your hat." But he was on to me and I missed. Aft, dimly, I saw Jeffreys and his crew fitting the swivel guns into their mountings on the quarterdeck rail. That had been my job not too long ago. "Open the ports," I said. "Run out your guns."

The sky beyond the hills was turning pink. I could see a launch now, filled with men, and the shapes of perhaps a pinnace and a jolly boat behind it. The launch turned at us, crossing in front of the pinnace. There was a clatter of oars, and some choice words in French.

My gun captains held their fists in the air. "Main battery," I called, "ready for action, sir!"

"Very well," said Peter.

Pale streaks in the corvette's rigging caught my eye—her topsails tumbling home. She was getting underway.

"Why not shoot now, sir?" said MacElroy. "They're well within range."

"Hush." I raised my hand, and he grabbed his hat. "We ain't out of the harbor yet."

Port Républicain was French territory in name, but in fact it was Toussaint's. After Paris had appointed him head of all military forces in the colony, he had openly assumed control of the treasury and the civil affairs of its principal cities, while maintaining the fiction (we hoped) that he was still loyal to France. Although we fought French ships on sight on the open sea, there were some niceties about whether it would be legal to fire on them in their own waters. War had never been declared between us.

"Mr. Graves!"

"Sir!"

"Do not mind the boats for now. Aim for *L'Heureuse Rencontre*. If she fires, you may return the honor."

"Aye aye, sir."

The corvette surged forward, as if to yank her anchor from the ground on the fly. A daring move, a dangerous move, but the right one under the circumstances—except for the grapnel line that Horne and I had laid across her cable the night before. She suddenly yawed like a horse fighting the bit as she strove to break free of it. Then the grapnel line snapped and she swung the other way, only to be snubbed up short as she came to the end of her cable. Her topmasts shuddered from the shock.

The gun captains stared at her like hungry hounds as we crossed her bow. If we fired now, we'd smash her from stem to stern.

MacElroy gave me a pleading look. "We could rake her, sir!"

I clenched my hands together behind my back to calm myself. "*Could* ain't *is,* Mr. MacElroy."

"Oh, *sir!*"

The blood pounded so hard in my head that I barely heard him. I snuck a glance at the quarterdeck. *C'mon, c'mon, c'mon,* I thought.

Peter aimed his speaking trumpet toward the boats. *"Hissez pavillon!"* he shouted. "Show your colors!" He leaned forward, the cords standing out on his neck. "Stand off, or I fire!"

The men in the boats answered with a yell and a snap of musketry.

The captain of number-three gun reached for his lanyard. "Don't you dare," I growled, and he guiltily snatched his hand away.

"Corporal Haversham," Peter said. "When I give the order, have your Marines shoot the steersmen if they can." Then: "Wait for it, Mr. Jeffreys. Wait for it . . ."

The corvette had turned to starboard to lay herself alongside us. The light from her battle lanterns sparkled on the water as her larboard ports opened.

I counted the guns as they poked their snouts out: she carried sixteen guns, nine-pounders, from the look of them. We had fourteen 6-pounders. French shot weighed about ten percent more than ours, giving her a broadside weight of, say, eighty pounds of metal to our forty-two. Near enough odds, I thought: with so many of her men down in her boats, she'd have trouble maintaining a decent rate of fire. If we could get off three broadsides to her two, we'd be . . . *Shit and perdition!* We'd be thirty-four pounds short.

Her side lit up as she fired. The sea flattened between us, and the air was filled with a frightful roar. The bulwark shattered in front of me. Splinters moaned through the air. Something spun me around.

Mr. MacElroy tottered beside me, flapping his arms. Blood fountained from his neck where his head had been.

I wiped gore out of my eyes. "Fire!" Our guns boomed in a rolling volley. "Stop your vents!" Seven leather-covered thumbs came down on the touchholes. "Sponge your pieces!" I skidded in something greasy. "Get that out of the way," I snapped, and someone dragged MacElroy's body away. "Load! Double shot your guns with grape shot over all!"

The powder monkeys handed out cartridges and ran below for fresh ones. The loaders rammed the charges home. The sidemen tailed onto the tackles and ran the guns out again.

"Fire as you will!"

The guns leaped and bellowed. Powderboys came and went. The sweat gleamed on the gunners' backs as they wormed the smoldering residue out of the barrels. I forced myself to stroll down the line, thumping a shoulder here, yelling encouragement there. I found a hat and picked it up.

Here was Samuels, commanding the two forward guns. He hollered something at me and held up four fingers. I shook my head. I couldn't hear a damn thing. "Four rounds, sir!" he shouted in my ear. "Four rounds an' they ain't replied! Ain't it fine?"

Then the corvette spat flame and smoke. I braced myself for a blow, but shot howled high astern of us. And our guns no longer fired. I turned around, hot to kick someone's pants for him, but the guns were traversed as far aft as they could be, and nothing lay before them but empty sea.

"Where the hell she go, sir?" said Samuels.

There she was, off our starboard quarter and drawing astern. "Captain," I called, "the guns no longer bear."

"Very well, Mr. Graves. Helm there, one point to larboard."

That couldn't be right—we were turning away from her. I jumped up into the main shrouds, out of the smoke, and realized what Peter was about. The jagged tips of a reef burbled past our starboard side. I was startled to see it was full morning, with the risen sun sending

God-rays through the clouds. I could see *L'Heureuse Rencontre* as clear as a painting. She seemed to be glued in place on the water, canted a bit to one side.

A powder-grimed sponger peered over the rail. "She run herself on a rock, by Joe!"

The swivel guns, filled with buckshot and scrap metal, popped steadily on the quarterdeck. The Marines made good work among the boats with their rifled muskets. So did Mr. Connor, who apparently had thought better of himself than to hide in the hold. Screams rose close astern—not screams of bloodlust, but screams of failure and woe.

We cleared the Princes and made the open sea, leaving bits of men and boats bobbing in our wake. I led the men in huzzaying, till I noticed the hat I was waving was MacElroy's.

Five

Seven of us sat around the wardroom table in the heat of the afternoon watch, toying with the remains of our roasted pork, beans, and rice. We'd had plantains, too, a starchy sort of green banana that fries up gooey and sweet—better than yams, in my book. I'd taken aboard more than was good for me in the heat. So had Rogers on my left, judging by the flush in his face and the number of buttons he'd undone. A soft breeze drifted in through the hatchway and the jalousie doors of the cabins on either side, taking some of the heat with it as it exited through the open skylight. Gypsy sat on Peter's lap, sniffing at the remains of his dinner but turning away in contempt when he offered her a morsel of fatty pork. The other ship's cat, Greybar, lay under my chair with his tail wrapped around my ankle. The conversation wallowed in a dead calm, and I couldn't think of a damn thing to say.

Mr. MacElroy's empty chair was as obvious as a missing tooth. As president of the wardroom and the head of the table, I should've invited someone, perhaps the gunner or the bosun, to take his place; but I was damned if I'd dismiss his memory so easily. I had found that my job as first lieutenant was primarily to deal with an ongoing series of minor disasters, and I should've counted myself lucky that an unhappy dinner was the worst mistake I made that day, but it seemed important at the time. I had been at least thoughtless to put Mr. Jeffreys opposite the empty chair, even though that was his right and proper place. He stared guiltily into his plate—though whether that was because he missed his late shipmate or because Captain Wickett sat on his left at the foot of the table, I couldn't have said.

Between Jeffreys and Rogers, Franklin dabbed the shine off his brow with his handkerchief. I'd intended to assign him to the gunners' mess, but Connor seemed to take it for granted that his secretary would eat with us and sleep in one of the cabins, and so there he sat. His face was pinched around the temples, as if he'd put his goggles on when he was a kid and never taken them off again, forcing his forehead and jaw to bulge out around them as he grew, while his eyes stayed tiny and close-set. His forehead was as smooth as a polished plum, but his jaws and cheeks were as lumpy as a cauliflower. And he had a way of looking straight at you, as if he'd decided it didn't matter a lick that he was black but he was never going to let you forget about it, neither. He had eaten and drunk his fair share, but had contributed almost nothing to the conversation.

Not that I could think of a damn thing to say. Neither could Quilty, apparently, halfway down the table on the starboard side. Our surgeon was a man who ever had a number of things on his mind, and could talk about two things at once while juggling another half dozen in his head, but if he'd said anything more momentous during the meal than "Pray pass the salt," I disrecall it. He twiddled his knife between the tips of his index fingers, stopping now and then to contemplate it, as if the answer to a puzzle could be found there.

At last Peter broke the silence. He was a guest in the wardoom, but as captain he could talk about anything he chose. "Mr. Connor," he said. "Have you a purpose?"

Connor sat in the place of honor on my right. He leaned in front of me, the better to see past Quilty, a large man, and said, "Have I a what, sir?"

"A purpose, man. Some reason beyond the mere fact of your existence that entitles you to eat and breathe. Greybar, for instance, that beast lurking under Mr. Graves's chair, was cosseted on cream before his master died. Now he catches the flying fish that come aboard in the middle watch. I'm uncertain what purpose that serves beyond filling his belly, but I suppose it must serve some purpose or he wouldn't do it." He rubbed a finger along Gypsy's scarred muzzle. "Gypsy, here, catches rats. Catching rats is an admirable purpose. Have you a purpose as important as catching rats, sir?"

"Here now," said Connor, and laughed. "You've gone from asking if I have a purpose to asking if I have an important one. And you forget, sir, that avoiding a cat is of great importance to a rat. Let us say I do a bit of this and that in the soldierly way. But I was under the impression—" He swiveled around to look at me as it perhaps occurred to him that I was his host and shouldn't be shown the back of his head. "You'll forgive my seeming to lecture you gentlemen on a subject you know infinitely better than I, but ain't it considered not quite the *ton* to discuss professional matters at dinner?"

"Indeed, sir," said Peter. He snatched his fingers away from Gypsy's paw. "If, for instance, Mr. Graves there had bored us with a description of the best way to sweep for an anchor cable that someone had carelessly left lying about, or if Mr. Quilty here had endeavored to impress us with suggestions as to whether it is practical or even possible to take a vessel by boarding when it is underway, we should require either of them to put a stopper in it. But I was unaware that we were discussing professional matters."

"Especially was *I* to indulge in such advice," said Quilty. He was sweating profoundly in his heavy green coat with its black velvet facings, and his face was nearly the color of his scarlet vest. No one was more intimately acquainted with the squalid consequences of our chosen profession than he, yet MacElroy's death seemed to have moved him, for he had barely spoken till now. "Albeit I have spent the better part of two years at sea," he said, "I scarcely know the best bower anchor from a—well, from the regular kind. I could, however, tell you in great detail about the effects of a three-foot oaken splinter lodging in the upper thigh, say, with its jagged edges acting as perfect barbs that prevent its being drawn out by the way it went in, or why gentlemen put on silk smallclothes and stockings before a fight."

"One is reminded," said Peter, "that surgery technically falls under the ban as well. Our former captain had no qualms about what sort of conversation went on at table, and we are all filled with contrition now, I dare say."

"Silk?" said Connor. "*Silk*, for all love—"

"Now now, sir," I said. "After the cloth is cleared, we can broach any subject under the sun."

"Or the moon, as may be," said Peter, making a sort of table of his bony fingers and resting his long chin on them. His nearly colorless eyes were fixed on Connor. "In the meantime, we may have any sort of conversation at all, so long as it does not have to do with our official business. Which is why, sir, I was so bold in the meantime as to en-quire as to your purpose. You have shown me your bona fides, but you have told me almost nothing of your intentions. If I am to transport you from one foreign port to another, it could transpire that I might be held responsible in some measure for whatever it is you get up to after you leave my care."

"Ah, but there I have you," smiled Connor. "Transporting me from one place to another has everything to do with official business."

"You have me indeed, sir," said Peter, not changing his expression—or rather not allowing any expression to enter his face. "I should be embarrassed to have it thought that vulgar curiosity provoked me to speak out of turn."

"Never crossed my mind, sir."

They exchanged bows—the merest of nods—in their seats, and Peter slipped me the wink.

"Steward," I said, "clear this mess away."

Ambrose and his mate removed the dishes and cloth and laid out Madeira, a chunk of the least rancid ship's cheese, and nuts. As the decanter began to make its rounds, Connor said, "I am all a-quiver to know, gentlemen. Why *do* you wear silk in battle? Must cost a fortune keeping you in battle dress."

"Ah, but when one observes that actions at sea are few and far be-tween, the cost is seen to be quite small in the long run," said Quilty. "I'm told there are admirals in the Royal Navy who wear silk every day, though they've never seen a gun fired except in saluting other admirals and such. A matter of style for them as can afford it, I suppose. But as to silk clothing in battle—a simple answer, really. If a man be struck by a musket or pistol ball that does not kill him outright, or require the removal of a limb—which I'm very good at, by the by: should you ever require it, be sure to see me—the primary cause of death is suppuration of the wound. That is to say, the wound putrefies from the inside, even after the ball itself is removed."

"And why is that, sir?"

"Why, because of what the ball carries with it into the wound, sir. Whatever disgusting matter the ball may have come into contact with before being launched—say, the greasy film left by a Marine who has yet to learn the art of wiping his arse with oakum instead of his fingers—is quite burned away in the heat of the discharge. However, the ball generally passes through a man's clothing before entering his body. You will no doubt have observed, sir, that a ball makes a hole in a man's coat when it hits him?"

"Ah," said Connor. "And silk is less susceptible to rotting in the flesh?"

"You have hit on it precisely. The why of it I cannot say, sir, but only that repeated observation has made a commonplace of the notion."

"All of which don't matter a lick," said I, "as we didn't bother to shift our clothes before the engagement this morning, and not to mention which I ain't got any silk drawers anyway." I held up my glass. "Gentlemen, a toast."

We drank to His Rotundancy, President Adams; to free ships and free trade; and to wives and sweethearts, may they never meet. When it was Rogers's turn, he said, "Gentlemen, I give you the United States armed schooner *Rattle-Snake*. May she finally be believed!"

After drinking, Connor said, "Why ever would she not be believed?"

"It is a customary toast with us," said Peter. "Before the schooner was bought into the service, she was called *Cassandra*."

"Who was doomed always to speak the truth and never to be believed," said Franklin. "I wonder—would it be worse never to tell the truth yet always be believed?"

The party broke up soon after in response to a call from the lookout—a Connecticut privateer that forgot the private signal and had to be boarded—and we left our guests to their own devices. Connor did not take the quarterdeck after we returned but pleaded seasickness and went to his cabin. Franklin must have had a delicate stomach too, for I did not see him at all.

The sick berth was a low and cramped room in the bows, pierced in its forward part by the bowsprit and made noisy and foul by the pigsty on the other side of the bulkhead. Quilty had laid the corpse of Connor's would-be assassin out on a bit of sailcloth stretched across his operating table, the better to dissect it at this his first opportunity before the heat could dissolve it into a stinking mass of goo. The cloth was streaked with congealed blood that filled the sick berth with an iron stench.

Peter stood in the doorway, looking at the hanging cots that lined the sick berth. "Where are the wounded, Mr. Quilty?"

"Please come in, sir, and close the door behind you," said the surgeon. He removed his neck-cloth and exchanged his coat and vest for a leather apron. "Crispus Ames, who had his arm shot off this morning, expired before dinner. Otherwise I should not have come. His mates have taken him away to be sewn into his hammock. The rest of our wounded are not serious. Before we had even sank the Princes below the horizon I had given them plenty of sticking plaster and a tot of grog, which satisfied them, and sent them away." He rolled up his sleeves and hung a lantern from a hook over the table.

It was as if he was talking about bits of meat, cut to size and wrapped up in paper. The rest of us often spoke lightly about death and disfigurement to keep ourselves from getting the creepy jeebies, but I'd never known Quilty to do so. His face looked sallow and creased in the lantern light, like an old actor's will under the paint when you sit too close to the stage.

Peter closed the door with reluctance. He had to bend low under the deckbeams to enter the room, and he plucked at the handkerchief in his sleeve, as if he wanted to cover his mouth and nose with it but didn't want to seem delicate. "You said you had something of dire importance to show us."

"Indeed I do, sir." Quilty indicated the corpse. Its torso and head were covered with a sheet, with the legs and arms sticking out.

"It is a dead man," said Peter. "I have seen bodies before, Mr. Quilty."

"Yes, sir, but none like this one, I hope. Notice first the soles of the feet."

Peter and I peered at the feet as well as we could without touching them. The letter *X* was tattooed on each.

"Maybe he was a sailor," I said. "You know how Jack tattoos his feet."

"I have seen pigs and roosters used as charms against drowning," said Peter. "But never an *X*."

"Yes, sir," said Quilty. "Pray take this glass and look more closely."

Peter examined the feet through the surgeon's magnifying lens and then handed it to me. The *X* was actually a pair of crossed daggers, with the Roman numeral DXII arranged in the spaces between. I handed the glass back to Quilty and said, "five hundred and twelve?"

"If the letters are read from top to bottom and then left to right, yes," said Quilty. "But clockwise and counterclockwise both, it reads *dixi*."

"Latin for 'I have spoken,'" said I.

"Oh, thank you, Mr. Graves," said Peter, giving me a vicious look. "For we have none of us had our *amo, amas, amat* here."

"Beg pardon, sir." It'd been so long since he'd spoke sharp to me that I'd forgotten how much he could make it sting. His eyes watered, though I didn't think the body stank that much. It flavored the air, certainly, but it weren't yet what you'd call ripe.

"Observe, now, the hands." Quilty pressed them into fists, revealing the letters *DIES* on the first knuckles of the right hand and *IRAE* on the left: day of wrath—Judgment Day. He turned the hands palm up and spread them with his artful fingers. "Feel them, if you please."

"I do not please," said Peter.

"Me neither," I said. "What about 'em?"

"No callosities, and yet the body is excellently muscled in a way that suggests he was used to periodic and violent exercise, rather than steady labor."

"Perhaps he was a soldier," said Peter. "I have seen them go in for this low sort of superstition. Like sailors with *HOLD FAST* on their knuckles, to prevent their falling from aloft."

"But observe the skin," said Quilty. "Was he a soldier, one would expect him to spend his days marching about in the sun, yet his skin is as white as a fish's belly."

"Well, of course he's white—he's dead, ain't he?"

"Oh, spot on as always, Mr. Graves," said Peter. He pulled out his handkerchief and wiped his face.

"Yes," said Quilty, "but there is nary a patina of tan, not even on the backs of the hands or the nape of the neck. If he was a soldier, he fought only at night."

"But Mr. Quilty," I said, "what kind of a soldier fights only at night?"

"This kind." He twitched aside the cloth that had covered the body.

I tore my glance away from the ruined face with its eyes that stared up into nothingness, and looked at the body. It was as white as any fish belly I'd ever seen, all right, except for a lurid pink streak all along one side.

"We handled him like eggs," I said. "How did he get so bruised?"

"Death was instantaneous," said Quilty. "His heart ceased to function, so of course he did not exsanguinate—that is, he did not bleed out. The discoloration you see is where the blood settled after death." He rolled the body onto its side. "You can see the mark of perhaps a thwart here on his shoulder. And over here, this pair of marks would indicate that a seaman rested his feet on our friend here while he rowed." Giving me a sideways glance while I pretended an interest in the deckbeams overhead, he turned the body back over. "Now look you here at his breast."

"Another tattoo," said Peter. "A hand clutching a heart."

"A *white* hand clutching a *black* heart," said Quilty. "And more Latin." He pointed at the words on the scrolls above and below the hand and heart.

"*Bellum internecinum,*" read Wickett. "A war of extinction. Extinction of whom?"

"We arrive at that anon," said Quilty. "Look you at the lower scroll."

I peered around him to see. It read *Deus Vult.*

"The rallying cry of the first Crusade: 'God Wills It,'" sneered Peter. The tips of his pointed nose and chin seem to reach for each other like the horns of a crescent moon. "If God wills it, we will never see another murder in His name again."

"Exactly so, sir," said Quilty. He tapped the tattoo with a blunt forefinger. "And in the quadrants, reading from the upper left, we have the initials *A. M. D. G.,* for *Ad majorem Dei gloriam.*"

"'For the greater glory of God,'" said Peter. "So he was a papist."

"No," said Quilty. "I have seen it before, and not in a church."

"Where then?"

"In Philadelphia during the yellow jack epidemic of '93," said Quilty. "I had the honor of consulting with Dr. Benjamin Rush." He preened, a gesture he suppressed as soon as he made it. "The troubles had commenced with mumps the previous December. *Scarlatina anginosa,* or scarlet fever, also began to exhibit during that time, and continued so through the spring and into summer. By July its symptoms were of great violence, which we treated with vomits and purges—to little effect, I thought, but most of our patients survived. Toward the end of July the heat was such that the aged began to die of it. Bilious remitting fevers made their appearance at that time, as well. I remarked that it was very much like the so-called break-bone fever that struck the city in 1780."

"I make myself comfortable, Mr. Quilty," said Peter, seating himself on the edge of one of the hanging cots, "although I am pregnant with desire to know what this has to do with our friend here."

"I arrive at that anon, sir. August brought cooler temperatures.

Cholera morbus and the remitting fevers were everywhere, it seemed. Refugees from the first slave rebellion in San Domingo began to arrive at that time. They brought the influenza with them, which seized the city but caused little morbidity. A heavy rain fell on the twenty-fifth."

Peter twined his fingers around each other, a habitual gesture with him that usually portended some minor torment for whoever was annoying him at the moment.

"It was the last rain that fell for many a week," said the surgeon. "The river fell. The contents of every puddle and rain barrel grew putrid and gave rise to clouds of mosquitoes. They were a great discomfort to the well and the sick alike."

"What, Mr. Quilty," said Peter, "have mosquitoes to do with an epidemic of yellow jack?"

"Those were Dr. Rush's exact words when I suggested a connection, sir, and in just that peevish tone—he was even then the most famous physician in America, and I had yet to finish my studies. To continue: On the nineteenth of August he condescended to stop in as I was treating a woman in Water Street. She was in extremis, vomiting all the while. We gave her tonics and cordials, but she soon died. As we left that place I remarked to Dr. Rush that I had seen an unusual number of bilious fevers in the neighborhood, all accompanied by the severest malignity, and that five of my patients had died within sight of the very place on which we stood—one of them within twelve hours of the fever's onset.

"Dr. Rush investigated the matter and discovered that in each case the illness was brought on by inhaling the noxious effluvia of a great pile of coffee rotting on Ball's wharf nearby. You could hardly get away from it, the stench so pervaded the entire street. He at once pronounced the nature of our doom: the bilious remitting yellow fever."

Peter and I had bent over the corpse as Quilty talked. I near jumped out of my skin at the mention of fever, what with the way that corpse seemed to stare with its empty eyes, but Peter said merely: "Mr. Quilty, does this body exhibit any signs of yellow jack?"

"Not at all. Death, sir, was caused by that great hole in his throat."

"Then pray tell us what all this has to do with the body."

"Everything, sir, as you shall hear. I was fetched one morning in great secrecy to see a man in Arch Street. He was very far gone with the bilious remitting fever. He asked me was he to die. Naturally I laughed off the suggestion, as I find that fear of death has a way of bringing it about. However, he clutched at my coat with a strength that surprised me in one in his condition, and his eyes were as intense as a demon's. 'Do not lie,' he said. 'If my end is near, I need to be released.' Thinking he wanted a minister, I asked him what his church was. And he said, 'Hell is my church, and Lucifer is my angel.' I asked him what he meant by such a thing. And he said, 'I kill niggers.'"

"A murderer, then, confessing his sins," said Peter.

"A rectifier of divine error, in his eyes," said Quilty. "No, sir, it was no confession that he made. It was more in the line of reporting that he had done his duty."

"His duty?" said I. Maybe it was the closeness of the room, maybe it was the stench of pig shit wafting in from next door, but I suddenly had to swallow repeatedly to keep from puking.

"Yes, his duty. Naturally I feared no physical assault from one in his condition, but looking into his eyes was like looking into the depths of his very soul and finding nothing but the emptiest of voids. I have never seen such an abyss in a man's eyes . . . I confess it rattled me as no doctor should ever be. I was reminded of Milton's line about Lucifer."

"*Which way I fly is Hell; myself am Hell,*" quoted Peter. "At another time it would be instructive to ponder if Hell is an actual place of torment, or if its torment is rather the pain of exile from God's presence—but now is not such a time. Pray continue, Mr. Quilty."

"Aye aye, sir. I purged him with ten grains each of calomel and jalap, and took a few ounces of blood from him while I considered my reply. When at last I regained my composure I asked him why he would tell me such a thing. He said it was because his brother knights had fled the city and he had no one else to tell."

"Brother knights?" said I. "What was he, a Freemason?"

"Oh no, Freemasons don't go in for such wickedness, I assure you. No, he was a Knight of the White Hand."

"The White Hand?" said Peter. "It reeks of the stage."

"Nonetheless, sir, these self-styled knights take themselves very seriously. Now, during the course of my examination I had noticed an odd tattoo on his breast, the very same as this fellow has—"

"The connection at long last," said Peter, throwing up his hands.

Quilty bowed. "And he now dragged his nails across this tattoo and said—his breath came in gasps—'*Lecit,*' then '*iure divino.*' I assumed him to mean 'Divine law allows it.'"

"Allows what?"

"The murder of Negroes, sir. What, have you not been listening?"

"With every ear I possess," said Peter.

"The Knights of the White Hand, as I later discovered," said Quilty, "is a purposefully obscure brotherhood whose goal is as abominable as it is ambitious. It is to remove all the nonwhite races from America."

"And do what with 'em, send 'em back to Africa?" I laughed at the notion.

"No indeed," said Quilty, shutting me up with a frown. "It was the task of him and his fellows to hunt down runaway slaves. Philadelphia is the headquarters of many such bounty men, you know, it being the nearest city of any size above Mason and Dixon's line. Many runaways seek haven in the City of Brotherly Love. But instead of returning the poor brutes to bondage for the reward, these fiends simply murder them. They take especial delight in kidnapping free blacks to use in terrible rituals. He described these vicious rites to me in detail and with appetite, despite his rapidly fading strength and the black vomit that spewed from his throat.

"I am not a godly man, but when he had done I begged him to repent. He laughed . . . I can still hear the ghastly rattle in his chest. He was seized with rigors, and his pulse, which had been languid, became intense, as if his heart endeavored to leap from his body. He beckoned me to put an ear to his lips. '*Dixi,*' he said, and died."

"Good riddance," said Peter. "You informed the authorities, I take it?"

"I, sir, did not. Not because I was bound by the Hippocratic oath. I had not completed my studies, as I said. But in my ignorance I hoped he was simply a madman—that his Arcane Empire, as he called it, was simply the figment of a diseased mind."

"Certainly it is the product of a diseased mind," said Peter. He pulled himself out of the cot and rubbed his legs.

"Indeed, sir. But I said *figment*." Pity and disgust mixed in Quilty's face as he touched the corpse before him. "I was naïve—which is not an excuse for my failure to act, but merely an explanation. See here." He unlocked a cabinet and took from it a sword and dagger and laid them beside the corpse. Next he unwrapped the dead man's clothing and took from it a sword that seemed a twin of the first. "That sword and dagger were given me by my patient as payment for my services," he said, his lip curling. "They have given me such horrors through the years that I have never been able to part with them, for fear they should fall into evil hands." He touched the second sword with a shudder. "This one arrived with our dead friend here."

He drew the sword from its scabbard. It was a typical gentleman's small-sword on first appearance, with a black leather grip wrapped in silver wire, and a hilt and guard of steel. The steel indicated that it was a fine weapon, or at least one of a small lot made to order by a craftsman, with none of the molded brass you see on military swords turned out by the hundredweight. He pointed at the engraving on the sword's long, tapering blade. "You see here the same design and mottoes as on the body."

Peter took the sword from him. "Good Damascus steel," he said, tensing the blade, and then examining it closely. "I see no foundry mark. Which in itself is not unusual." He parried an imaginary opponent, *tierce* to *seconde, seconde* to *quinte*, bowed low though he was under the deckbeams. "The balance is excellent—murder in the hands of a good swordsman." With a lightning advance and thrust he sank the blade into the bulkhead. The pigs squealed on the other side. "I dislike the death's-head on the pommel, though," he said, leaving the sword quivering in the woodwork. "It is sufficient to know we all must die without having *memento mori* served upon us from all sides. You say the other blade is the same, Mr. Quilty?"

"Its very brother, sir."

I had been giving the dagger a going over. It, too, had a death's-head for a pommel. The grip was black leather bound with silver wire, like the sword, and the straight hilt was of steel. The blade was some nine or ten inches long and tapered to a nasty point. It bore the same Latin inscriptions as the swords and body.

"And your dagger matches this one, Mr. Quilty?"

"No, Mr. Graves, that *is* my dagger. There was nonesuch among this man's effects."

"But there was," I said. "He slashed my sleeve with it. I put it in the bundle myself."

Peter shook out the black cloak the dead man had worn, but there was no dagger in it. "Well, it is gone now," he said. "Mr. Quilty, was the body ever out of your sight?"

"Of a certainty, sir," said Quilty. "During the middle watch, when I slept. For a few minutes this morning before the engagement. When I was at dinner this afternoon with you gentlemen. And after dinner when we detained that Yankee privateer. I came on deck to watch. But while I was at my post here this morning expecting the momentary arrival of wounded men, I had a few moments to spare. I unwrapped him from his cloak and found the sword right away, of course, and having seen it, I immediately looked for a dagger. But there was no dagger even then."

"A seaman could've took it, sir," I said.

"Not likely," said Peter. "Jack's superstitious fear of the dead and his notion that theft is nearly as shameful as sodomy rules that out. Well—not entirely, I grant you, but it is most unlikely. Have Horne ask among the boat's crew anyway."

"Perhaps," said Quilty delicately, "you merely dropped it?"

"I did not, sir." I said it pretty sharp, and they looked at each other uncomfortably. "Now listen here," I said, "I told you I put it there myself."

Quilty unlocked a wooden box and took from it a pair of long knives, a saw and a pair of tongs. "Yes, yes, of course you did," he said. He picked up one of the knives and touched its tip to the body's breast. "Now, gentlemen, unless you wish to further your education . . ."

Horne wouldn't turn up anything, I was sure of it. Whatever Peter and Quilty might think, that left Franklin and Connor. They both of them had been below when the fight started.

A flock of sloops and schooners scattered like chickens before a fox as we approached Léogâne from the northeast. They were the usual riff-raff of island traders and no threat to us, but among them was a ship. We spilled our wind, waiting to see what she was up to, but she shouldered her way through the small fry and showed us her heels, rolling in the chop of the Canal du Sud and cracking on sail.

Peter handed me his spyglass. "What do you make of her?"

"A frigate, sir, a twenty-eight or a thirty-two, maybe." Her high poop, the gingerbread across her stern, and the narrow gallery below her stern windows where her captain might take a few paces in private said she was old—ancient, even. Frigates hadn't been built that way in decades. The carved figures and scrollwork that once would've been picked out in red and blue and gold were painted black like the rest of her hull. There was something pathetic but evil about her, like a poxy beggar-woman holding one hand out in supplication while the other grasped a razor beneath her rags. She heeled over and the sunlight flashed on the green stuff that grew below her waterline. "Her bottom wants breaming." I lowered the glass and squinted at her. "And she rides light, sir, like her main battery's been took out."

He took the glass back and studied her again. "Even so, she has some teeth in her. I count four guns on her fo'c's'le and perhaps half a dozen on her quarterdeck."

When we were certain she was indeed leaving, we studied the sun-washed streets and the hills roundabout the town for signs of fighting. All lay quiet and still.

Peter snapped his glass shut. "Had you not best ready yourself?"

I had been half-listening through the skylight to Connor and Franklin arguing with Ambrose about the best way to stow their gear. Ambrose, my personal servant when he wasn't the wardroom steward, tipped me the nod as I stepped below. "The gents' things is all ship-shape and Bristol fashion, Mr. Graves." He heaved the last carryall up onto the table that ran the length of the wardroom. "You want I should do yourn the same as well?"

"That's right," I said, knowing he would anyway.

Franklin stood in the doorway of his cabin. He hugged his writing desk to his chest with one hand and clutched at the doorjamb with the other against the slight motion of the schooner. Connor stood at the far end of the table, his hands on his hips. "See here, Mr. Graves," he said. "I am used to the way Franklin does my kit, and I'm not in the habit of being ordered about by a servant when it comes to my personal effects."

"Ease your mind, sir," I said. "It don't do to meddle in the little things." Franklin could always repack their stuff later; but I had to live with Ambrose, who had numerous ways of letting his displeasure be known. "The bosun is getting the pinnace in the water. Mr. Rogers will hoist your baggage aboard."

"We're off, then!" Connor bounded up the ladder.

Franklin took the steps one at a time, snatching at the siderail with his free hand as he went. His cheeks had a green tint, and from the smell wafting from his cabin I bet he'd left a full bucket under his cot.

"So, Ambrose," I said after they'd gone, and my voice rang falsely bright even in my own ears: "Was there anything unusual in their things?" I showed him a half-real.

"Oh, dear me no, sir," he said, holding his hands in fists so I couldn't sully them with silver. "The end of the month will be fine. But there's sumphin' fishy about them two." He gestured me closer and breathed tobacco and grog on me. "Everything was already bundled up into little packages, like. Couldn't tell what was what, 'ceptin' the obvious things like the brushes and razors in their housewives and such, and papers tied with red tape. Sealed with wax and wafer, too, most them was."

"But did you see anything that might've been a dagger?"

"I were on the lookout for one, sir, just like what you said. And Mr. Connor, he got a right wicked-lookin' one. Wears it around behind under his britches gusset. Odd thing for a gent to carry, but from what I hear he can't take no chances, with assassins poppin' out o' dark alleys at him."

"Well? Has it got a steel hilt and a black grip, bound in silver wire?"

"Oh, not at all sir. It's what a Guinea calls a stiletto. Plain wooden handle with a brass hilt." He held his hands eight or nine inches apart. "About yay long."

"You're sure."

"Sure I'm sure," he sniffed. "Couldn't mistake sumpthin' as plain as that, now could I, sir?" He made as if to go.

"No, no, of course not," I put out a hand to stop him. "But what about Franklin?"

"Nary a weapon nor any kind for him, sir. He's a scholar. One o' them fellas that's above such things, as long as they got someone around to protect 'em."

"Very well, then. Thank'ee."

"I'll have your things done up in a trice, sir, and lay out your duds. Traveling coat, slop trousers and sea boots?"

"I'll wear the boots, but I have to look fine. I'll wear my best undress coat and epaulet, and the blue pantaloons. Pack my white britches and a decent pair of shoes and stockings."

"Aye aye, sir." He went off grumbling about ruining good clothes in the mud and thickets.

"Oh," I called after him, "and a shoulder strap for my sword. I'll be riding."

"*Horses,* is it? A sea officer on horseback's about the pitifullest sight . . ." He disappeared into my cabin and shut the door.

The westering sunlight poured in through the stern windows of the *Rattle-Snake*'s great cabin. Peter sat on the padded locker below the windows and held up his glass. The sunlight in the Madeira bathed the whitewashed bulkheads in a golden glow. "Here is to a quick trip, Matty," he said. "May you succeed in your endeavors." We drank. "Whatever they may be."

"Thank'ee, Peter." I stretched out my legs. Peter had bought Billy's spindly gilt cabin furniture rather than ship it home to Billy's parents, but the chairs hadn't gotten any more comfortable now that they were his. "Can I tell you about 'em?"

"If you may."

"The commodore said I ain't to tell anybody but them as I trust with my life."

"And you trust me so, Matty?"

"I do."

"Then I shall strive always to live up to that," he said, as inscrutable as ever.

I told him all that Gaswell had charged me to do, even the part about the plot to raise a rebellion in the South.

"It would never work," said Peter. "It doesn't do to let a man up again after you've beat him down. Whether you should have beat him down in the first place becomes academic."

"You don't think there's a plot, then?"

"I did not say that. The heart of man is hard and strange," he said. He looked at Gypsy, crouching on his desk with her leg up as she licked herself. "The more I know about people, the less I understand them."

"You know what else is strange," said I. "Blair tried to take a page of my orders from me before he countersigned my passport. He even threatened to burn it."

"Why?"

"I don't know. Natural-born cussedness?"

"Surely he's more complex than that—here, madam, stop that." He poked Gypsy till she laid off licking herself. "Our Mr. Blair is a poltroon and a coward, yes, but not a simpleton. I do not trust him. No doubt he is still angry about the affair with the picaroons. We caught him in a lie, and I would not put it past him to harm you if he can."

"Yes, sir. And to tell the truth, I ain't too keen on Franklin, neither. There's something he ain't quite honest about, but I ain't put my finger on it yet."

He drank off his glass and set it aside. "With Connor around you should be safe enough. I shall need you back whole, and as quickly as possible. The bosun can stand your watches, but it will be hard on him. Mr. Midshipman Jeffreys hardly knows his backside from a backstay." He grunted. "I do not know yet what I shall say about Mr. MacElroy. I must write his parents, of course."

"Yes, sir. And the commodore too, of course." But that was Peter's problem, not mine, and I'd be dogged if I'd share it with him. We stepped to the chart table to examine the Bay of Jacmel once more.

"I am permitted an independent cruise of several weeks in the Jamaica Channel," said Peter. "Afterwards I am to rendezvous with the *Croatoan* off the mouth of the bay sometime in the second week of March. I shall fetch you here, at Cap Maréchaux at its eastern end—if at all possible." He tapped on the table to ward off the Fates. "If you cannot be there, leave a note nearby. I shall do the same if Rigaud or the French should have a naval presence sufficient to deny us the bay. The shoals east of the cape extend as much as five miles to seaward, but I believe we have several hands aboard capable of finding an island as large as Hispaniola." He smiled. "Even in the dark."

I didn't smile back. I kept thinking of MacElroy going over the side, sewn up in his hammock with a pair of round shot at his feet. "Aye aye, sir. Should I make a signal of some sort?"

"Yes. Say, two shots followed one minute later by two more shots, and by two more shots again, on the quarter hour. I shall fire two guns to windward in reply."

"That's kind of complex, ain't it? What if I don't have a pair of pistols?"

"Oh, for goodness sake, Matty, use your own good judgment. Set the woods on fire. Run around on the beach with your drawers on your head." Gypsy strolled over to see what we were doing, and Peter knelt down and held his hand out. She sat down with her back to him and yawned. "Paint me a picture of a rattlesnake, even." She glared sleepily as he scratched her jaw. "Anything will do, so long as it draws my attention."

Six

I gripped my reins and saddle horn together in both fists. Joséphine, the harpy our guides had foisted on me in Léogâne, laid her ears back and showed me the yellows of her eyes as we trotted along the highland track. Riding her was very much like riding a masthead in a blow, except mastheads don't bite.

Connor rode up beside me. The whites of his green eyes shone in the shade of his broad straw hat, and the ebony handles of his pocket pistols afore and the brass hilt of his stiletto astern gleamed in the purple sash around his waist. He had shucked his coat and neck-cloth and loosened his collar, which allowed his shirt to billow picturesquely. He looked so fine, so dashing, so much the romantic adventurer, that I would gladly have shot him. He smiled at me and said, "How d'ye fare, Mr. Graves?"

"I'm told—Mr. Connor," I jerked out between jounces, "that a sailor—on horseback—is a pitiful sight."

He laughed. "Oh no, not at all, sir, not at all." He clicked his tongue, and his horse danced past Franklin toward the front of the line.

Daylight flashed between Franklin and his saddle as he jolted along. His gold spectacles bounced around his sweaty face, and he was in constant torment to keep his portable desk under his arm. He had insisted on carrying it rather than let it be tied to his saddle with his carryall. "One hand for the ship and one for yourself, Mr. Franklin," I called, and he gave me such a vicious, miserable look that I almost felt sorry for him.

The older of our two Negro guides laughed. I gave him my best quarterdeck stare, but he had his back to me and missed the benefit of it. The younger one, Juge, who I guessed was only a few years older than I was, but who carried himself as if he had already crossed some imperceptible boundary into middle life, rode with a carbine across his saddle brow. We had left the Léogâne road an hour back to strike through a stretch of pine forest and thorny scrub; I didn't know much about soldiering, but it looked like a good place for an ambush. A distant thudding came intermittently on the breeze. *"Ecoutez!"* I called as I realized what it was. *"J'entend le bruit des canons!"*

Juge reined back till I caught up with him. *"Bon sang!"* he said. "Of course you hear artillery. There is a war, you know." He was a sight handsomer than the old coot, but he was an odd duck in his own right. He wore an officer's long-tailed blue *surtout* with bits of gold lace dangling from it, and didn't bother to wear a shirt under it. He flapped the coat like a rooster getting ready to crow as he spoke—the better to display his chest, I calculated. His chest was worth looking at, too; there was people back home who'd pay cash money to see it. A capital *J* had been branded on his right breast and an *E* on the left; thick scars, like the country marks you see sometimes on new-bought Guinea slaves, formed the letters *U* and *G* between them. J-U-G-E, the French word for judge. His red-and-white-striped trousers were torn off at mid-thigh, his long black cavalry boots were rolled above his knees, and a tricolor cockade and scarlet plume decorated the starboard side of his high-crowned round hat. He wore it tipped forward against the sun, but he kept his eyes moving across the trees and rocky bluffs even as we spoke. He tapped his horse's sides with his heels and cantered past the old man into the lead again.

The old man gave me an uninterested glance before returning his attention to the sides of the road. He was missing his upper teeth, and what teeth he had in his jutting lower jaw looked as weather-beaten as old wooden pilings. Juge called him Grand-père Bavard—Grandfather Chatterbox—though he didn't talk much. Like Juge he wore a blue *surtout* trimmed in red, but under it he wore a clean white shirt, a gray vest, and tight gray pantaloons tucked into Hessian boots. For headgear he wore a turban of yellow silk with a thin red stripe like a Barbary vizier, with a tricolor rosette and a tall red plume at the knot in front. He rode as if his hip joints hurt him. His horse was a fine white charger that he called Bel-Argent. I took bets with myself about how long it'd be before he got throwed; but when a flock of doves broke cover and exploded across the trail in front of him, he soothed the beast with a soft word and a single caress. The rooster claws he wore for spurs were streaked with dried blood, but it wasn't Bel-Argent's blood; he never so much as touched a heel to the horse's flanks.

The pine forest thinned out as we approached a steep ravine, where a cascade of white water rushed around a jumble of boulders. Our guides examined the trees that screened the far side while we sat our horses and waited. Finally, the old man nodded at Juge.

"Hu! Tss-tss!" Juge urged his mount forward, skittering through loose drifts of rocky debris as he scrambled down and across and up the far side of the ravine. He trotted into the shadows, leaning low in the saddle with his carbine at the ready.

"What is happening?" said Connor.

"*Chut!*" said Grandfather Chatterbox.

Connor cocked an eyebrow at me. I held a finger to my lips.

The old man looked up and down the ravine, and then back the way we had come. A thrumming of insects filled the air. The sky was dotted with high clouds, and a cool breeze with a hint of the sea in it found us. I'd had little sleep since before the *Rattle-Snake* made Port Républicain, and despite the laconic pop-popping of the field guns in the distance, I dozed.

Joséphine shook her head and snorted, and I opened my eyes with a start. Juge stood on the far side of the ravine, waving his hand. Grandfather Chatterbox still looked down the track behind us, his tongue writhing along his lips like a little pink snake.

"Monsieur," I said.

He held up his hand; I ain't much for the supernatural, but it felt as if he'd clamped it across my mouth. Then he turned Bel-Argent toward the ravine. *"Allez-y!"* he said, with a curt gesture for us to follow him. He plunged across. Our horses leaped after him, and I kept my perch by the grace of God and Connor's hand on my bridle.

Juge met us under the trees, where a squadron of dragoons knelt in skirmish order along the edge of the forest. Most of them wore shoes instead of boots, and their white pantaloons and long blue coats were patched and grimy; but their black-maned brass helmets and the silver trefoils on their shoulders shone, and their carbines looked well cared for. To the rear, a pair of troopers with freshly waxed boots sat waiting in their saddles. The old man spoke rapidly in Creole to Juge and then trotted off through the forest with the mounted dragoons on his heels.

I stared at the troopers under the trees. *"Où diable . . ."*

Juge rolled his eyes. *"Bon sang!* They have been with us all the way from Léogâne. You will never make a soldier." Then he laughed. "Get down off your horses, *mes amis,* and keep an eye open."

The horse handlers took our mounts to the rear. Franklin went with them, cradling his portable desk in his arms. Connor and I crouched down behind a fallen tree, where Juge stared across the ravine like a cat watching a rat hole. "Do not move until I say," he whispered. He put his hand on Connor's arm as the mulatto drew his pistols. "Not even a finger. *Chut*—hush now, they approach."

But then a lone white man rode quietly out of the trees. He'd been leaning over in the saddle, watching the ground, but when his horse stopped at the lip of the ravine he raised his head and stared toward us. He was dressed in a black riding cape and broadbrim hat, and wore a fringe of gray beard along his jaw, like a Quaker; but no Friend I ever met wore a sword nor carried a brace of horse pistols in his saddle holsters, nor had such a gaunt and bloodless face. Connor hissed quietly between his teeth. But we all of us kept still, the dragoons patiently waiting with their carbines trained on his breast. Though surely he couldn't see us in the shadows, the Parson—as I called him in my mind—kept his hands in sight as he craned slowly around to stare back down the trail.

"Pa tiré," Juge snapped. It was a Creole phrase I had memorized as being potentially handy: "Don't shoot." He stepped out into the sunlight, holding his carbine in one hand and raising the other. "Hssst!"

The Parson didn't move except to turn his head. Juge made an abrupt motion with his hand, as if to push him away.

With a last bleak look toward us, the Parson eased his horse around and trotted across our left along the edge of the ravine before slipping back into the trees. Juge came back and squatted beside us.

I said, "Who was that?"

"A ghost."

"He looked alive enough to me."

"He does not yet know he is dead. Do not worry about him."

A rumble that wasn't thunder or artillery rolled down the forest path toward us.

"A troop of horse?" said Connor.

"Soldats de cavalrie?" said I.

"Chasseurs à cheval," said Juge. "Mounted light infantry. They often slip through our lines at night and raise the Devil. May God punish them this day." He made the sign of the Trinity and then snapped a few orders to his dragoons. They eased back the locks on their carbines. I hauled my pistols out.

Metal glinted in the forest beyond the ravine. Over the thudding of hooves came the creak of leather and the jingle of harness. All at once a dozen riders in green and white thundered out of the woods and into the ravine. More men poured in behind them. Their muskets were strapped across their shoulders, but curved sabers flashed in their hands.

Juge sprang to his feet. *"Tiré, gason! Tiré!"* he shouted. "Fire, boys! Fire!"

The dragoons fired a volley into the chasseurs struggling up the rise toward us. Half a dozen men fell from their saddles. A horse rolled screaming back down into the gully, crushing its rider beneath it. Horses behind it bucked out of the way. The remnants of the lead riders reined up and tried to turn. The men behind crashed into them. Another horse and rider went down. An officer stood in his stirrups, waving his saber. Juge coolly put a ball through his head. Connor and I popped off our pistols. Then the chasseurs had turned and were beating hell for leather back the way they'd come.

"*Koté li cheval!*" called Juge. The horse-holders ran forward, leaning against the reins as the horses pranced and shook their heads. "*Ann alé, gason! Ataké!*" Juge swung into the saddle, and he and Connor and the dragoons charged across the ravine and down the track in pursuit.

I threw myself across Joséphine's back. "Ha! Giddap," I shouted, groping with my feet for the stirrups. We galloped in fine style into the ravine, where I promptly tumbled off and slid into the stream below.

Franklin sat with his back to a tree with his traveling desk on his knees. He finished writing something, scattered sand on it, poured the sand back into its little jar, and then blew on the paper before tucking it carefully into a sheaf of papers that he tied up with red tape. Only then did he look at me. His eyes registered neither surprise nor concern as he took in my sodden pantaloons and the ripped elbow of my coat. He wiped his pen on an ink-stained rag and locked his things up in his desk. "Did I hear you to say, 'Shit and perdition'?"

"You did. That damn bitch throwed me."

"You seem remarkably unhurt for a man who has fallen off a horse."

I slapped mud out of my coat. "I landed on one of them dead chasseurs."

"Are you sure she threw you?"

I felt a breeze and twisted around to look under my coattails. My pantaloons were ripped open across the seat, but my drawers seemed intact—uncommonly damp, but intact. "Why would I say she throwed me if she didn't throw me?"

"One might simply fall off, or even choose to fall off." He looked at Joséphine, who had followed me back and stood peeking out at us from behind a tree. "One might change one's mind about charging after who knows how many armed men." He folded his hands on top of his desk. "One might show a fitting concern for one's own safety."

"If I was concerned about my safety, why the hell would I jump off a running horse?" I gave him a sharp look. I may be slow, but I ain't that slow.

A hint of expression passed across his face. Maybe it was a smile. "I merely hoped you might have more concern for your mission," he said, "than for your own glory."

I had to sort that one out for a bit. It was too slippery to grab hold of all at once.

Joséphine scratched her rump against a tree and watched a butterfly flitting through a shaft of sunlight. I went to catch her, but as soon as I got close she scooted away. "Belay, God rot your eyes," I said. But I said it under my breath, and she waited till I was almost close enough to grab the reins before trotting off again. We made a couple of wide circuits around Franklin before I gave up.

"It would not surprise me if she were prepared to do that all afternoon," said he. "Which obviates my next question: namely, do we press on or do we wait here for our guides?"

"What's 'obviate' mean?"

"It means you are effectively without a horse. And neither of us knows the way, regardless."

The artillery still boomed away in the south. "We could double up on your horse and follow the noise of the guns."

There was a yelling way off in the woods, a clash of steel and a few shots, and then more yelling that grew rapidly distant. He said, "Hadn't you ought to recharge your pistols?"

"I guess I will, in about a minute." I eyed my saddlebags, where I'd left my powderhorn, but I misliked the way Joséphine was swishing her tail. "Why, ain't you got a pistol on you?"

He tapped his portable desk. "Properly employed, a pen is deadlier than cannons."

Maybe so, I thought, but it wanted time and distance. I tucked my pistols into my belt and went to fetch a pair of muskets off the dead chasseurs in the ravine. Joséphine clumped down after me. She nickered at a horse trying to reach its feet. Its legs were broken and it fell back again, stretching its neck out and looking at me. I checked the loads in a couple of muskets and slung them over my shoulder. Then I found another, so I shot the horse. Joséphine scrambled out of the ravine and then stood there, twitching her ears.

I tugged a cartouche belt off of one of the chasseurs and near hopped out of my boots when he spoke to me.

"*Quelle scie,*" he said. "What a nuisance. I think I have been killed." He grinned at me kind of lopsided, like he wanted me to tell him different.

Blood soaked his middle and the ground under him. I opened his coat. Blood bubbled out of a hole in his belly. "I fear you are correct, monsieur. Does it hurt a great deal?"

He shook his head. "No, I feel nothing but regret."

"Regret for what?"

"That I am not a horse, so you might shoot me too." He fumbled at his canteen.

I sat him up and dribbled some water into his mouth, but his head lolled and the water ran back out again. I laid his body down and climbed out of the ravine.

Franklin had set his writing desk aside. I held out one of the muskets, but he shook his head. I leaned them up against his tree, fished a cigar out of my pocket and stuck it between my teeth. Then I patted my pockets, looking for my flint and steel, but I'd left them in my saddlebags too. Joséphine snuffled at my cigar. I held it out to her, and while she examined it I sidled up within reach of the saddlebags. "Nice horse," I said. The skin across her shoulders quivered, but she let me unbuckle the bag and lift the flap. "*Tout doux, ma belle*—ow! Shit and perdition!" She capered away with my cigar in her teeth while I danced around flapping my hand and counting my fingers.

"Not your shooting hand, I hope," said Franklin.

I held out my hand. "That's my *left* hand," I said. "Do I look left-handed to you?"

As soon as it came out of my mouth I knew it was a foolish thing to say, but I'd meant it as a joke. I figured the least he could do was laugh; *I* was willing, but he just looked at me. That's the only way I can describe it—he didn't smile, didn't glare, didn't do a blame thing but *look* at me. It was nothing I could reasonably take offense at, but that was precisely where the offense lay, if you follow. I never met a more disagreeable man who wasn't trying to kill me at the time. I bit a chunk off a fresh cigar and chawed and spat as if I liked it. "So," I said, "what'll you do if the chasseurs come back instead of the dragoons?"

"Interesting." He put two fingers to his cheek and pretended to ponder. "I suppose I should continue to sit here quietly, to avoid alarming them, and would thus prevent my being slaughtered out of hand. They would soon discover that I speak little French beyond 'jay swee oon American,' at which point I suppose I would be taken before a magistrate of some kind, who would ask me questions in various modes—high dudgeon, low threats, appeals to reason—to which I should give him the same reply. He would then condemn me to death as a spy, detain me in some damp and unpleasant place until I had learnt my lesson, and then let me go with instructions never to return. Or perhaps I would be offered a place on Pétion's staff. One never knows."

I had swallowed some of my cigar while he was talking. When I could speak, I said: "How you talk! What kind of a dern fool plan is that?"

"An excellent one."

"Excellent, my Aunt Fanny! In what way?"

"It should serve admirably to keep me alive."

I had to look at him several times before I was sure what I was seeing. I never heard a man come so close to out-and-out saying he was a coward.

"But what about yourself?" he said. "Perhaps you ought to start walking toward the sound of the artillery. Surely it is not so very far."

I calculated he was joking, but for the life of me I couldn't tell. And he never took his eyes off me, neither. Just sat there with his legs crossed at the ankle and one hand resting on his travel desk beside him, regarding me from behind the glass mask of his spectacles. After a while I realized he was asleep with his eyes open. He didn't move even when the Parson walked his horse in a slow circle around us half an hour later, just out of musket shot and staring at us about as friendly as an empty grave before trotting off toward Jacmel.

Juge and Connor returned alone and in high spirits. Connor had blood on his right hand and sleeve, but nary a scratch on him. Juge snagged Joséphine's bridle. As I climbed aboard he said, "It was good of you to stay behind to protect the scribbler."

"That was not the way of it, monsieur." I grabbed the reins as Joséphine snorted. "I fell off."

"You look it, too, ha ha!" He ordered Franklin to his feet with a gesture. Then he grinned at me. "I have a sight for you, but we must be quick."

"What happened to your dragoons?"

"Come, come, I show you!"

The cannon fire grew louder as we rode, and the smell of spent powder drifted past on the sea breeze. In a short time we reached a high bluff that looked south over a bay and a town. "Jacmel," said Juge, with a sweep of his arm that took in the entire view. "You may dismount." Franklin scuttled off into the trees, trailed leisurely by Connor. Juge followed me to the edge of the bluff, where I compared what I saw before me against the chart in my mind's eye.

A pair of streams flowed from either side below us. The little one on the left was the Rivière de la Gosseline, the River of the Little Girl. It emptied into the big one on the right, the Grand Rivière de Jacmel, which widened as it flowed to the southeast into a swampy-looking area of low wooded islets before passing around a large triangular island and thence into the bay. A road ran along the near side of the Grand River before fording the Gosseline and then cutting across a flat field toward the town. On the left bank, hard by the bay, a group of four forts stood on a height surrounded by a long wall. The wall was little more than a heap of rubble, though whether it had been built that way a-purpose or had been knocked down and piled up again, I couldn't say. A pall of smoke and buzzards hung over all. Dismal weren't in it—the place looked like the steaming stump of a shot-off leg.

Feeling like I had a hole in my heart, I scanned the glittering emptiness of the bay and the wide sea beyond.

"One may grasp the whole situation at once from up here," said Juge. He straightened in pride as he gazed out at the battleground, but I didn't see what there was to be proud about. "Général Dessalines, who commands Father Toussaint's army of the south, has invested the citadel."

The investment—the black army's offensive line—was a long, semi-circular ditch fronted by a breastwork of logs and earth, lying more or less concentric to the defensive wall and about three-quarters of a mile from it. The ditch was full of men, and the artillery was properly dug in behind revetments, but there were far too few guns. And they were mostly three-pounders and six-pounders—field guns, not siege guns. They could bang away at the forts all year without doing much except give the defenders more places to hide. Men and horses waded along a wide, muddy path to the rear of the ditch, all busily going nowhere in particular that I could see. The scene was about as inspirational as a barnyard at hog-killing time. Even the dirt looked dirty.

Below us and off to the east huddled little gatherings of huts and tents and lean-tos. Beyond them, off to the left of the line, stood a large house surrounded by a low wall and outbuildings, with croplands around it. The croplands were a ruin of shrubs and rank weeds, as if they had lain untended for years—as no doubt they had. When the slaves had left the plantations and gathered themselves into armies some nine years before, there had been no one left to tend the fields. Toussaint's army was starving on some of the richest real estate in the world.

Juge pointed at a brushy expanse between the trench works and the citadel. "That is the killing ground, across which we make the periodic sorties to sound out the rebel defenses." At the far end of the field was a log blockhouse, in front of which a company of horse-drawn artillery had set up shop. "I see Pétion has supported his redoubt with a flying battery since I was away. If he keeps it there much longer, we will kill all his horses and then go down and steal his cannons. Perhaps even tonight. Now, see that hill over there." I followed his glance toward a rise near where the Grand River passed into the village. "Beyond it lies a little pocket of low ground that gives a great deal of trouble. We cannot cross it, and neither can he. But every night, we crawl down there and slit some throats."

A hamlet of flat-roofed houses sat in the pocket. Between the houses—with balconies running right the way round their upper stories, and well holed by cannon balls—stood heaps of broken stones, lined with sharpened stakes and strewn with swollen corpses. Puffs of smoke rose from the hamlet, provoking answering puffs from the bluffs where the trench made a sharp curve around the pocket's upper end.

"The pocket makes a salient into our lines," said Juge, "but this is to our advantage because we possess the high ground. From there we enfilade the hamlet. One knows what this 'enfilade' is?"

"Of course," I said. "You fire into the enemy from stem to stern while he can bring only a few guns to bear. It's the very acme of maneuvers at sea." A flicker of white out in the bay caught my eye, but it was just a jumble of gulls fighting over something in the water.

"Exactly," said Juge, nodding like I'd said something wise. "It is like one frigate taking advantage of another, except here the enemy cannot sail out of danger. But it is not enough." He shook his head. "He is a determined fellow, this Pétion, and his men love him."

I didn't like the ground, and I didn't like it that the *Croatoan* was nowhere in sight. "I've heard it said that the man who fights for a commander he loves," I said, intending to cut him, "cannot often be beaten."

He gave me a pitying look. "Pétion fights for the property rights of the men of color, but we fight for the liberty, the equality and the brotherhood. We carry on the revolution even as the reactionaries betray it." He thumped his bare chest with his fist. "We are true Frenchmen."

"Touché, monsieur." I doffed my hat and bowed to keep him from busting out singing "La Marseillaise."

Grinning, he pointed at a wooded watercourse to the southeast that snaked its way across the killing ground. "At the foot of the wall, that ravine becomes very deep. It prevents us from assaulting the citadel from that direction. In it is a stream called the River of Orange Trees, that flows down from our lines. Its banks are steep and covered with thick brush, which protects a man in it from the cannon fire, and it is very dark in there at night. This makes it a tempting roadway for fellows intent on the mischief. We have ambuscades set up all along in there. Every night the enemy tries to pierce our lines this way, but between our cane knives and our bayonets, we make a good harvest."

"It must be terrible," I said.

"*Bon sang!* We like this kind of fighting. It saves us the powder and ball."

I looked again at the empty bay. "Juge," I said, "have you not seen a frigate out there?"

"*Rien de rien.*" He gave me a look I couldn't read. "Just sometimes the Yankee merchantmen."

"Surely you are mistaken. We have blockaded this port at Toussaint's particular request."

He shrugged. "As long as Pétion has gold, you Americans will trade with him."

"This can't be." I wanted to tell him to shut up and be damned. "It's illegal."

He slitted his eyes. "Well." Again the shrug. "As for your navy, we have not seen it for a while. Weeks, I think."

"But I tell you the *Croatoan* is supposed to be blockading this port. American ships may only land at Le Cap and Port Républicain, and trade only with Toussaint."

His shrug grew wider. "We bought a ship to institute our own blockade, but the British stole it and imprisoned the crew. They said we meant to use this ship to invade Jamaica."

"But that makes no sense!"

"Why should it make sense?" Unable to shrug any wider, he dropped his arms to his sides. "*C'est la guerre.*"

I took another long look around the battleground. Commodore Gaswell wanted exact descriptions, positions, numbers, but—what with the way Joséphine was scratching her shoulder with a wicked-looking hind hoof—I didn't guess I could break out a sextant and a box of watercolors to make a map with right at that particular moment. However, I could make a sketch in my head and commit it to paper later. I fetched out my little pocket compass and squatted down with it on my knee.

"I bring your attention, if you please," said Juge, pointing off to the right, "to the road from Léogâne." He looked to see what I was doing, and frowned. "Why the compass?"

"Sailors don't always care where they've been or where they're going, but they do insist on knowing where they are at any given moment. It's a sort of mania with us."

He nodded knowingly. "It is the same with soldiers. I permit you to continue."

I took a few more bearings while Juge watched the road. I glanced over at it, but it was about as empty a road as I ever saw. I sighted on the main fort. "Juge," I said, "tell me about the citadel, if you please."

He reached over my shoulder and adjusted the compass so it pointed at the largest fort. "This one, he is the Fort Beliotte. The one to the right is called the Fort du Gouvernement, although Pétion governs his operations from Beliotte. That nearly untouched one on the edge of the precipice, above where the River of Orange Trees enters the bay, he is the Fort de l'Hôpital."

"It's good in you not to fire upon the hospital."

"We cannot conveniently reach it. And the edifice in the back, he is the prison. I have heard stories of that place." He recommenced his watch on the road. "And close in under the prison is the anchorage."

"How deep is the anchorage?"

"Deep."

"What about the bay?" Peter's chart had been drawn from a captured French document. There was no telling how accurate its soundings were.

He grinned. "The bay, she is deeper."

"How close can a ship come in?"

"There is a wooden pier onto which the merchantmen discharge their cargoes." He gave me a sidelong look. "Or they would discharge their cargoes there, if you did not have the bay so thoroughly bottled up."

I let that pass. Juge and I obviously would have different ideas about what a large ship was, and how deep was deep, but if a fat-bottomed merchantman could unlade directly onto a pier, I calculated it should be deep pretty close in to shore. If so, the *Croatoan* could come right up behind the forts and give 'em a good pasting. That would help shake the confidence Pétion's men had in their commander.

I stared out at the blue diamond of the bay. It was about two miles on a side, with its entrance to the sea forming the southeastern side of the diamond, and Pétion's citadel at the northern angle. Cliffs lined the bay from Cap de Jacmel on the west and Cap Maréchaux on the east, but on the northwestern shore they gave way to a long strip of black sand beach. Breakers gleamed white against the western cliffs, where the bay lay open to the current and the prevailing winds from the east. It would be a nasty place to sail in anything more than light airs. The only useful part of the bay lay directly under the walls of the citadel. If I were Pétion, I'd line the bay side of the walls with every gun I could spare. But I wasn't Pétion.

Beyond the far left of Dessalines' line rose a promontory overlooking the bay. Guns on its height would command both the citadel and the anchorage. Squinting at it against the sun, I thought I could make out a wall or two standing among the trees that crowded its summit, as if a fort had once stood there. I made a tube of my hands and peered at it. "Juge, have you a pocket telescope? I have left mine in my saddlebags."

"*Bon sang!* Yes, I have the pocket telescope. And the case clock and the four-poster bed as well! If your telescope is in your saddlebags, why do you not fetch him?"

I took a look at Joséphine. She raised her head, staring at me as she chomped a mouthful of thorns into flinders. "Perhaps later. Tell me, is there a fort on that cliff over there?"

He glanced impatiently away from the road. "There is."

"You have guns up there, of course?"

"We do not." He sneered. "The *houngan* has caused an *hounfour* to be built there."

"The what?"

"The voudou apostates have built a temple there, in which to practice their black arts at night. This is why we have no artillery in such an excellent place for artillery. It is only at night, of course, but it would not do to leave cannons around when the *loas* possess their worshippers' bodies. The *papas* and *mamans* lead them in worship of Damballah and Legba and many others." He spat in the dust. "These names disgust me. There is only one *Papa* beyond Father Toussaint, and that is our beloved Savior, Jesus Christ." He crossed himself. "You will hear their drums and screaming at night."

I stood up and shook out my legs. "Why don't you stop it if you don't like it?"

"It is too ancient to stop." He gave me an elbow in the ribs. "Besides, they are good fighters."

Connor appeared from the trees, buttoning his fly. He slapped me on the back. "Riding is like any other skill, eh? Painful until you develop the necessary calluses." His accent was from someplace along the Tidewater region—Virginia or North Carolina perhaps—but his vocabulary came from somewhere else. A northern school for free blacks and runaway slaves, I guessed.

I grinned. "Well, sir, I got plenty of calluses on my hands, but I never thought I'd need 'em on my stern." I looked back at the trees. "Where's Franklin gotten himself to?"

"Gone to dig a hole, I suppose. He ain't used to riding, and from the look on his face I didn't think it friendly to inquire." He stood with his left hand on his hip, his right foot up on a convenient rock and his right knee bent just so, with his right hand shading his eyes as he studied the arrangement of the artillery and the trenches below.

Tricolors fluttered over the black army's lines, but Tricolors dotted the mulatto's positions as well. "I expect you got a bit of experience in the soldiering trade," I said. "How do troops in the field know who to shoot at?"

"Same as at sea. If it shoots at you, shoot back."

Franklin stepped out of the woods, clutching his desk to his chest.

"Juge," I said, reaching a decision. Neither Connor nor Franklin spoke French, so I calculated I could use that language without burdening them with things that weren't their business. "I tell you in good faith what I am here to do. I am to make a survey of the terrain and your troops so I can tell my commodore what is needed. He also wants to know a good place to land a few large guns and the sailors to man them."

He smiled. "Then you must meet General Dessalines as soon as possible. But I doubt you will like him. I guarantee he will not like you." He went back to watching the road.

"Here," said Connor, snapping his fingers. "What's that he says about Dessalines?"

"He says he ain't too sociable, but I got to meet with him anyway."

"*I* have to meet with him, you mean. In the meantime I have need of you. Remember your orders from the assistant consul."

I looked at him, Connor with his wide straw hat and his gleaming white shirt with the blood turning brown on the edge of his sleeve, and wondered what I would do if he snapped his fingers at me again. "The *request* of the assistant consul," I said. "He's outside of the chain of command. I work for Commodore Gaswell, sir, not Mr. Blair."

"Mr. Blair is the sort of man who would be happy to make you unhappy, was you to cross him."

He'll be happy to do that whether I cross him or not, brother, I thought, but it wouldn't do to sound unwilling. I said, "Yes, sir."

Juge put a hand on my arm. "Now that Mr. Connor has returned to us, I wish you, please, to explain the situation to him. Down there," he said in his elegantly condescending schoolbook French, which I translated for Connor, and which Franklin dutifully transcribed in his letter book, "are ensconced the *gens du couleur*. The traitor—"

"Wait, wait," said Connor. "The John-de-who?"

79

"Sorry, sir," I said. "*Gens du couleur* means 'persons of color.' That's what they call mulattoes—the coloreds—I mean the men who ain't white nor black, if you'll forgive my saying so."

"'Persons of color' is the genteel phrase from Boston to Philadelphia," said Connor. "I would not expect a sailor to know that, but I do expect you to know I'm perfectly aware of my blood, sir, nor am I ashamed of it."

"And why, sir, should you be ashamed of it?"

"Precisely. Do not mince words on my account. I will thank you, sir, to translate everything exactly."

But I was ashamed of it, for my own sake not his, and I was ashamed of my shame. I was afraid of being found out—the way a sodomite must feel, I thought, before dismissing the comparison. A sodomite could be hanged only if he acted upon his nature, but even a hint of black blood could subject a man to humiliation and even death if he forgot for one second what he was.

"Mr. Graves," said Juge, smiling politely at Connor, "I do not trust your friend, so be careful, please, to translate exactly what I say and no more."

"*Mais oui.*"

"*Très bien.* Tell him this: Even with what the smugglers bring in, the traitor Pétion is low on food and ammunition. Yet he refuses to yield to our attacks. Unfortunately for him, Henri Christophe has marched down with two demi-brigades from the north to join forces with General Dessalines under Father Toussaint." A demi-brigade was a double regiment of foot and horse, about thirty-two hundred troops. "Together they most certainly will get results. I would suggest," he said cheerfully, "that you avoid their company beyond your necessary interviews. Chef-de-Brigade Christophe is philosophical about the necessity of including whites in our plans, but Dessalines has a thirst for white men's blood that years of the gallows and the firing squad have not slaked."

"Yes, yes, I know all that," said Connor. "You ain't leaving anything out, are you?"

"No, sir."

"As you can quite clearly see," Juge continued, "Pétion's position is strong but ultimately hopeless. Father Toussaint admires his fortitude but is saddened by the misery that must be endured down there. I show you the situation exactly, that you may truthfully explain to Pétion just how hopeless it is to resist further. The shedding of French blood by Frenchmen is a terrible thing, but when Dessalines takes the town—as he most assuredly will—all in it will be put to the sword." He stared at Connor as I translated, the round softness of his beardless face hardened by urgency. "We wish to avoid this. Pétion must be persuaded that surrender is his only option. Unless he wishes a return to the old order, he must join with us against the traitor Rigaud before France gathers an army of reconquest. He will not listen to us. We hope he will listen to you."

Connor nodded. "I will do what I can, sir."

"Listen here, Mr. Connor," I said, "you ain't planning on riding in to parley with Pétion, are you?"

"Of course I am. Why else have I come?"

"Ha ha!" said Juge, pointing down at the Léogâne road. "There! That is what I brought you to see."

Four green-coated chasseurs pounded down the road as fast as their laboring horses could carry them. They'd lost or thrown away their weapons and were making for the ford where the road crossed the Gosseline. Close on their heels rode eighteen—no, twenty—of Juge's dragoons, leaning over their horse's necks with their swords at the charge. Half a dozen riderless horses galloped alongside them, but they wore the green saddle blankets of the chasseurs.

As the chasseurs splashed across the stream, a squadron of cuirassiers in gleaming steel breastplates sallied out of the hamlet. The black dragoons broke left, placing a spur of the hills between themselves and the heavy cavalry, and hooked off toward the plantation house in the east.

A gun near the troublesome hamlet tried a ranging shot at the cuirassiers, and infantrymen appeared along the bluff. Caught between cannons and muskets, the cuirassiers gathered up the chasseurs and hightailed it back to town.

"Over there at that *habitation,* my friends," said Juge, pointing toward the plantation house, "Father Toussaint is pleased to make his *katye jeneral,* his headquarters. We ride there now." He stepped to his horse—mounting, turning and moving off in an instant. Connor leaped to his saddle and followed. Franklin grabbed at his spectacles and desk as he jounced off.

Did Joséphine wait for me to climb aboard? She did not. I hopped alongside her, one hand on the pommel and one foot in a stirrup as she shogged off down the trail. "Hi, devil! 'Vast hauling," I cried. "Whoa, dammit! Whoa!" Then I tripped over my sword and fell headlong in the dirt.

Seven

"Dern ya, belay that," I said, swatting at Joséphine with my hat. She plodded along behind me, poking me in the rear with her nose. At least she had quit trying to bite me. "Now look here, you old horse. I'm going to sit on this here stump. Go someplace where you're wanted, why don't you." I sank onto the tree stump with a wince and tugged my boots off. I was footsore and saddlesore and just plain all around sore. I hadn't been shot yet, but I guessed it was just dumb luck. Every soldier I'd asked for directions had merely glanced at my sea uniform and silently pointed me along the way.

Joséphine slopped her broad tongue across my ear. I grabbed my hat before she could run off with it again.

Across the road, two barefoot soldiers in mismatched uniforms and patched trousers stood sentry in front of a bullet-pocked farmhouse. A faded Tricolor drooped on a pole jutting out from a window on the upper floor. I had gathered that the house was where foreign officers were quartered, and I hoped to find Connor there. The long shadows of afternoon painted the whitewashed stone walls with pale gray stripes, a peacefulness that was belied by the constant background rumble of ten thousand men and horses and the popping of those damn cannons. I wouldn't have minded if they fired constantly, but they didn't. One or two would go off, and then a whole passel of them, and then they'd fall silent awhile. And just when I'd gotten used to that, up they'd start again.

Lounging in the shade across the road from the house, half a dozen dirty colonial officers of the line passed a grass-wrapped carboy around. I was sure I could smell cider. I tugged my boots back on and hobbled over to them. *"J'avoir soif, mes amis,"* I said. "I'm so dry, my friends, I could drink a bottle by putting it up my breech. May I please have a drink?"

They stared at me, some blankly, one with open hostility. The latter had a face that was all lip and nose. "You are thirsty?" he said in barely recognizable French. "So what do we care? Did you care all those years when I was thirsty?" He wrapped his lips around the neck of the jug and took a long swig. "Hah! This is good cider! And when we're done with it, you're welcome to shove it up your ass, just as you say. We wouldn't want you to think we're rude, after all, *hein?*" He looked around at his fellows, and most of them laughed.

But the oldest one looked embarrassed. *"Ase, Jean-Claude,"* he said in Creole. *"Sa pa fè anyen."*

"M bouke ak sa!" said Jean-Claude, tapping himself on the throat with the flat of his hand.

"Ça suffit," said the old one, switching back to French. "That's enough. Le'm have a drink. He's an ally, after all."

"Blòf!" said Jean-Claude. I recognized that word, anyway. It meant bullshit. "Y'old kiss-ass, he's a *gwo blan*. A Yankee Doodle, too, though you can't tell from his accent. Look at his pretty coat, so like a Frenchman's—but his ass hangs out of his pantaloons, ha ha!" He picked up a handful of dust and threw it onto my feet. "You won't be so proud when the niggers rise up on *your* plantations, hey little *gason kanson?* You'd better get away from here before I take it in mind to kill you. You're lucky I'm too drunk to chase you!"

The others muttered agreeable noises, and I retreated toward the house across the road. If Connor were inside, he'd have refreshments, surely. I was stupid not to have thought of it before. Joséphine stood quietly while I untied my carryall, but snapped at me when I tried for the saddlebags. I threw my bag over my shoulder and marched up to the house as if I knew where I was going. The sentries didn't go so far as to salute me, but they did snap to attention. A good sign, I thought; now if only they understood my French.

"Bonsoir, compagnons," I said, "I'm looking for a Mr. Connor, an

American *mulâtre*. Red hair, green eyes. Have you seen him? He has a black man with him, wears gold-rimmed spectacles. He was with an old man called Grandfather Chatterbox and an officer named Juge, don't know his last name—well, thank you." At the mention of Juge's name, one of the soldiers tilted his head to indicate that I could mount the steps and enter.

Inside, a little black man of about my size and probably three times my age, dressed in a faded but clean green suit and with a fleecy white wig on his head, introduced himself with a bow. "I, Bertrand," he said in English, "will do for you 'ere in the billet of the foreign officers. You are Monsieur Graves, I believe."

"Yes, how did you know?"

"I know many things." He was about as dignified a cuss as ever I seen. "In this case I know it because your friend 'ave arrived before you."

"Mr. Connor's here? Good."

"I regret he is not." He stood aside. "Will you make the entrance?"

"Say, you speak English." Always a firm grasp on the obvious, me. A rumpus rose behind me as the sentries tried to shoo Joséphine away from the front steps.

Bertrand shut the door. "When my charges do not 'ave the French, it is well I 'ave their language. Dutch, Spanish, I 'ave the facility with all the language."

"There's a lot of us here, I take it?"

"No, just the two of you. You may leave your bag there. Follow me, if it please you." He ushered me into one of the two downstairs rooms, bowed again, and drew the double door softly to. I heard him grunt like he was hoisting a weight—my carryall, which if I'd known it was burdensome I'd have hauled it for him—and then I heard the treads creaking in the stairwell as he tottered up to the second story.

The thick stone walls made the room almost cool. Gaps between the slats in the drawn shutters let in slender bars of light and little breaths of steamy air. Over against one wall stood a table laden with fruit. Not as good as cider, but good enough to a dusty man. I tore open an orange and squeezed its juice down my throat. As I picked up another a voice said, "I shouldn't if I were you."

Franklin sat at a table against the wall with little piles of books and papers spread out in front of him. "That fruit, Mr. Graves," he continued, "is kept for the convenience of General L'Ouverture. Not that he would begrudge you any—he lives in constant dread of poisoning. Although an orange is probably safe enough."

I threw it on the floor. "Tarnation! I wish you'd spoke up sooner."

"I wanted to see if it's true." He picked up the orange as it rolled under his chair. "How do you feel?"

I stood awhile and then said, "I'm well, I guess. No thanks to you." I sat down in the nearest chair. It was chipped and splintery and had a seat of woven cane, but at that moment it seemed the most wonderful chair ever. "Where's Mr. Connor? And why'd you ride off and leave me like that?"

"Juge was amused by your predicament and would not let us go back for you. But he has gone off on some errand of his own, now, and Connor has ridden out to look for you." He sliced the orange rind into a long spiral with his little silver penknife.

"I might've broke my neck. Damn near did, too."

"You are sure you feel entirely well?" His eyes were hidden behind the reflection on his glasses. "No nausea? No uncertainty in the bowels? No sudden rush of saliva?"

I shook my head.

"Good," he said. "I shall have to take your word for that, of course. However, I trust you. You are too innocent to lie."

"I ain't innocent!"

He chuckled—more of a grunt, really, as if his bowels griped him. "I do not think I have ever heard a man say that before. Usually a man swears he is as innocent as the newborn babe." He set the spiral of rind on the table. "But perhaps I should have said naïve. Do you know anything of the situation here?"

"Some. D'ye think there's any drink around?"

"I do not know. There might be some coffee left in that pot." He held a segment of orange up to the light that slipped in through the shutters. He looked at me. "No tremors? No headache? No blurring of the vision?" He smiled as I frowned. "I am joking, Mr. Graves."

"I don't think it's very funny." The expressionless Franklin was annoying, but ignorable. This smiling and laughing Franklin made me nervous.

He popped the orange segment into his mouth. "Do you desire to retain your ignorance?"

My head hurt, and my feet hurt, and I was sleepy. I wished Franklin would shut up. I tipped my hat over my eyes and slouched down in my chair. "I've agreed to give Mr. Connor some help as an interpreter when I can spare the time," I said. "I didn't want the job. I don't even seem to be qualified for it. Just about everybody around here who knows French talks like they got a mouthful of rocks. When Mr. Connor asks me what they're saying, I'll have to make half of it up."

"Really? You would fabricate?"

I peeked out from under my hat. He had raised an eyebrow. "No. I'll tell him whatever I can make out." I thought about the dirty officers outside. "Some of 'em speak French pretty good. And sometimes I can tell what's being said in Creole, even though I can't speak it." It seemed important to emphasize that last point.

"I understand the languages are similar."

"They're as different as a Highland burr and a Kentucky twang— the same language generally, but kind of hard to follow."

"But you're in the Navy. You've spent time in these islands. Have you acquired nothing at all of the language?"

"I told you already," I snapped. "I can say, 'Bring me some rum' and 'Which way to the whorehouse'—and not much more, see? I calculate Mr. Connor will find *that* kind of thing pretty helpful around here." My sarcasm was lost on him. "Listen, I'm just supposed to make a survey for the commodore and report aboard of the nearest American man-o'-war. And I ain't saying any more'n that to nobody."

"Not even to Connor?"

"Well, of course to Connor! I guess I can trust *him,* anyway. And don't say I can't. *Don't.*"

He wiped his knife and fingers with his handkerchief while he thought about that. He folded up his handkerchief and stuffed it into his pocket. Then he folded up his knife and stuck that in his pocket, too. I thought about three or four things in the amount of time he took to think about just that one thing. I thought about the missing *Croatoan,* for instance, and how I was going to fix my pantaloons without I had a sewing kit, and how I should've gotten my saddlebags off of Joséphine before she wandered away. I hadn't gotten very far with any one of them thoughts, though, by the time he spoke again.

"The situation here is extremely intricate." He touched two fingers to his cheek. "An enemy one day is a friend the next. And the day after that, an enemy again. Take Pétion. He admires Toussaint and used to follow him, yet now he has become a symbol of mulatto resistance to Negro rule. Rigaud would be lost without him." He wound the orange rind up into a little coil. He let go and it sprang open again. "Knowing which man to trust isn't the trick. The trick is knowing how long to trust him."

Now, I knew as well as anybody that the best way to keep a man from getting your goat is to not let him know where you keep it tied. A mild answer turneth away wrath, I thought, but what came out was, "Now what in tarnal damnation does that mean?"

He flicked bits of rind off of his fingers. "Set a thief to catch a thief."

I looked down my nose. "Thieves is worser than buggers, in the Navy."

He rubbed his temples. "You miss my point. Listen. A man is a tool like any other. A knife, say, can be used to kill a man or cut his bonds, but the knife itself is neither good nor evil."

"A man ain't a knife. A knife ain't got free will."

"Does a man have free will when he does God's work?"

I thought of Surgeon Quilty, opening up the assassin on his operating table. "Why, have you stole a knife?"

"Feh." He began gathering his books and papers together. "I might have saved my breath."

"And I mine, sir." I got up, feeling like I had a stick up my ass. "I need some air. The stuff in here stinks." I stomped off through the front room.

"Speaking of stinks, we're to share a bed," he called after me. "You're not prone to nocturnal eructations, I hope."

"If you mean do I fart in bed, don't you worry about it. I'll just kind of waft 'em over the loo'ard side." I paused with my hand on the latch. "Get you some *eau de toilette* for your handkerchee, if you're delicate." It was childish, and I regretted it as soon as I said it. But dog me if that man didn't rankle.

The officers' jug lay broken in the dirt. Joséphine stood over the shards, twitching her tail and blinking at me. The last rays of sunset shone through a gap in the clouds to the west, and then the sun dropped behind the hills. The eastern horizon showed a pale glow where the moon was rising. The evening rain began to fall. A sergeant came with the change of watch and hung a lantern on a hook by the door. The relieved sentries marched off with him, replaced by a pair that looked somewhat more promising. They wore shoes, for one thing, with white duck gaiters, leather shakos with a brass plate in front, and high-waisted coatees in the new English style. They clomped up the steps and stood beside me out of the wet. I said, *"Bonsoir."* One of them nodded but otherwise ignored me. That's what a Marine would've done, and I took comfort in it.

It was too late for counting guns or sketching maps that day, and I didn't feel like chasing after Connor. I undid my neck-cloth and wiped my face and neck with it and wondered what to do. It'd been wrong in me to speak so provocatively to a man who went around unarmed. But I was pretty sure it wasn't fear that had stayed his tongue.

He'd been sounding me out. Traitors riddled the insurrection, or civil war, or whatever you wished to call it. After Rigaud had slaughtered the people of Petite Goâve last June, the locals began calling it the War of Knives: a cut here, a slash there, and always the threat of a blade in the back. Come right down to it, all Franklin had done was mention the subtleties of alliance that made the war so tarnal difficult to grasp. But—and here's the thing—it weren't our war. It weren't my business to meddle in it, any more than it was Franklin's. But it might be my business to meddle with *him,* if he was poking around where he didn't belong.

I retied my neck-cloth and shook out my sleeves. If I was quick, I might be able to get out of doing anything about it.

I found my way through the pelting rain to the habitation where Dessalines had his *katye jeneral.* I had to do a bunch of talking before I could get in, and even then I didn't get far. The officer who conde-scended to speak with me knew nothing of boats or the comings and goings of ships in the bay. Neither did he admit to knowing how to communicate with ships offshore.

"*Télégraphe?*" I asked, pantomiming the arms of a semaphore.

He pursed his lips, shook his head.

"*Les feux de signalisation? Les bateaux? Les lettres?*"

My suggestions produced a Gallic shrug, the kind that begins at the belt, travels out to the fingertips, and ends with a *moue* of the lips. "I know nothing of the signal fires, the boats, or the letters," he said. "However, some cannoniers of marine were landed up the coast some weeks before. They will remain independent of their ships until some unspecified time. Perhaps until Jacmel has been captured."

"Navy gunners, you say? English or American?"

"English, American—there is a difference? Now go away. We are very busy here."

I left angry and unsatisfied. I didn't believe the gunners had been left on their lone. They'd need food and ammunition, two things that Toussaint had little to spare. Somewhere boats must be carrying sup-plies and orders from the *Croatoan* or some British ship.

And here was that stupid horse again, looming large and damp out of the darkness to bump me with her shoulder.

"Dang it, Joséphine, why d'ye keep following me? *Pourquoi me suis tu partout, hein?*"

She just looked at me sideways. Finally it occurred to me that she probably wanted to be fed and watered and to have her saddle removed. She followed me around the habitation till I found the stables. Catching wind of the other horses, or perhaps the hay, she trotted ahead of me across the stable yard, shoved a roan aside, and stuck her muzzle into a manger.

A groom came out. I gave him a shilling to brush her down, not that I gave a hang what happened to her. But I didn't say it aloud, in case he decided to turn her into soup. "She'd be pretty stringy anyway," I told myself, slinging my recaptured saddlebag across my shoulder. "Probably not even worth the trouble of eating." As I stood there scratching my seat and listening to my stomach rumble, I heard hooves coming my way.

Juge splashed across the stable yard and leaped down from the saddle. *"Mon ami!"* he said, holding out his arms to embrace me in the French style, which I had to submit to or offend him. "You are found at last! I hope you have not forgotten my invitation for this evening."

"After I've eaten I'll be up for anything," I said. I didn't recollect any invitation, but I was idle; if he had girls or drink in mind, I was just the man for it. I'd have preferred to sluice off a couple pounds of dust first, but the rain was doing a pretty good job of that and I didn't guess the doxies around there would be any too picky. But he gave me an appraising look that stopped my musings cold. "Why, what have you in mind?"

"Well," he said, "I was going to go and fetch the cannons of that flying battery I pointed out to you. But after we managed to kill the horses and most of the gunners it came upon me: without the horses the enemy cannot drag his guns away, but neither can we, ha ha!"

"But I am disappointment itself," says I, thinking maybe I'd get my bath after all, and go out for to *cherchez les femmes* on my own account. "I desire to knock a few heads together."

He clapped his hands. *"Très bien!* This is what I like to hear. Come, we eat while I tell you the entertainment I have planned instead."

Supper was pumpkin soup—not very good and little of it. While we ate it Juge outlined the evening's entertainment, as he insisted on calling it. "My dragoons I leave in the care of Grandfather Chatterbox," he said. "Tonight calls for subtlety and silence. For this work I take along some of my comrades from when I first arrive to serve Father Toussaint. Take a pistol if you wish, in case things go wrong, but I caution you not to shoot otherwise. A pistol flash at night, and *bon sang!* You are blind, and the enemy knows exactly where you are."

The rain had let up, and the ravine of the River of Orange Trees cut a dark swash in the moonlight. My blue pantaloons passed muster for night fighting, but my white shirt and vest were right out. Juge made me strip to the waist, and then laughed. "*Bon sang!* Your skin is brighter than your shirt."

"How you exaggerate."

"But even so, you will stand out like the shooting star, even in the shadows." He tugged at the tear in the seat of my pantaloons where my drawers showed. "And it seems the moon has risen. Here, we fix this."

He slathered me with muck from the bottom of the trench until I was as black and smelly as the dozen friends he'd brought with him. They were a ferocious-looking lot, some of them with teeth filed to a point and all of them scarified across their chests and arms. Half of them were naked as Adam—and about as unconscious of it, too. For weapons they carried the ubiquitous cane knives as well as short lengths of rope with a wooden handle athwart each end, which the Spanish call a *garrote*.

"We wrap your sword in your clothes and leave them here along with your fancy hat, *mon ami*," said Juge. He handed me a cane knife. "The small-sword is hesitant where the *manchèt* is decisive. No dainty poking about, no *en garde* and the *touché*. Just a chop or two, and you will find that a man is no more trouble without his hands."

The manchèt was about a foot and a half long and six inches across at the end, narrow at the tang and squared off at the tip like a butcher's cleaver. Although it was the first time I'd held one, I found it to be less awkward than it looked. Naturally it would be easy in the hand, being designed for cutting sugar cane from sunup to sundown, but with its sturdy blade and razor edge it also seemed admirably suited for whacking men up into their component parts. Still and all I'd rather have had a cutlass, with its point for thrusting and its heavy handguard for socking a man in the head.

Touching his lips in a final warning to remain silent, Juge led us slithering over the edge of the ravine and down into its gloomy depths. The air stank of corruption, but whether from corpses or stagnant water I wasn't sure till I crawled across a soft body. Before I'd realized what it was I'd sunk my hand into its belly, releasing such a noxious vapor that I puked.

Juge sputtered into his fist, trying to smother his laughter. "I should have warned you, *mon ami*," he said when he was able to control himself, "this is the graveyard of the mulattoes. But as it is their graveyard and not our own, we do not bother to bury the dead."

I had vomited so violently that strands of the stuff hung out of my nose. I sneezed and spat, but said nothing. I'd been eager for a fight once I'd resigned myself to being up all night, but now I wasn't so sure.

Keeping to the banks of the river—more of a creek, really, running along the bottom of the steep-sided ravine—we crept downstream under the low branches of a thorn thicket for about a mile. I had no more accidents with bodies, after I learned to identify the concentrated stench and the pale phosphorescence of corrupted bones that emanated from them. I learned to avoid getting snagged on the thorns, too, after someone in the dark had kicked me a time or two for making too much noise in getting unstuck.

I was feeling ill-used and beginning to wonder if I was being made the butt of some evil jape when at last we came to a place where the ravine bent to the left. There it narrowed sharply and the brush formed a thorny blanket from one wall to the other. Other than the brushy tunnels through which we crawled, the only open passage was the streambed itself, and it was choked with boulders. Half of Juge's men shinned up into the trees that grew along the waterway and inched their way out along the overhanging branches. The rest of us he took farther downstream, telling off his men in pairs on either side till only he and I remained.

"Here we wait in the ambuscade," he whispered. "We let them go by, and then we follow. Just watch me, and you will know what to do. Until then, *mon ami*, absolute silence or I shall leave you to your fate."

Not caring to guess what that fate might be, I crouched beside him in the brush and tried my best not even to breathe. Insects filled the air with their chirring, and off in the hills the voudou drums sent their eerie rhythms throbbing through the forest. When I grew tired of crouching I lay back on the damp earth, clutching the manchèt across my chest and watching the stars pass over from east to west. About the time the moon began to peep over the rim of the ravine, I heard a clattering of stones downstream to my left and soft curses in French.

I sat up, but Juge put a hand on my shoulder to indicate I should stay where I was. He crept past me in the shadows toward the river. Even though I could feel his boot touching my own, he lay so still that if I hadn't known he lay there in the dappled moonlight I would have took him for a pile of stones or a heap of dirt. Perhaps a fathom beyond him I could see the creek sparkling in the moonlight, and hear it tinkling and gulping as it passed among the jumbled boulders and broken branches that littered its bed.

The clatter to our left grew louder and more frequent, interspersed with hissed warnings to shut the hell up: *"La ferme! Ta bouche!"*

From around the bend crept a grenadier. His white trousers and gaiters shone in the moonlight. Even his long dark coat was faced with white, and as he turned to gesture to someone behind him, the white *X* of his crossed equipment belts made a beautiful target across his back. He turned again and moved slowly up the middle of the stream toward us, stooping low and using the bayonet on the end of his musket to poke around in the underbrush. A file of men began to appear from around the far end of the bend. I counted eighteen of them as I peered through the thorn bushes. At last their officer showed himself, using his bayonet to pink the bottoms of men who stopped too long to look around them.

"*Grouillez-vous!*" he said. "Get a move on!"

"*Doucement, citoyen lieutenant,*" whispered the sergeant at his side. The drums thumped like heartbeats in the hills.

"What do you mean by telling me to be careful?" said the lieutenant. "No one can hear us over that fucking voudou racket. How they screech and wail!" He took off his bicorn, adjusted its plume, wiped his forehead with his sleeve and put his hat back on. "We'll be here all night at this rate. *Pousse-toi,*" he said, telling the man he'd just pricked to move aside. He threaded his way along the file of grenadiers, hopping from boulder to boulder to keep his feet dry. When he got to the head of the line he turned and said, "See? There is nothing to fear. *Allons!*" And pointing his musket to show the direction, he said again, "Come on!" He disappeared to the right around the far side of the bend.

"You heard him, you miserable bastards," said the sergeant. "And so did the niggers, if they're about. On your feet, there." He splashed along the line, kicking the men into motion. "Nothing for it now but to keep your eyes open and your powder dry! Move!" He slapped the men on the back as each passed him in the direction the lieutenant had gone. "Don't worry, my little chicks, mother hen will watch your backs for you. Off you go." When the last had gone he leaned on his musket and shook his head. "Ah me," he muttered, "and what am I to tell their mothers? I know what I shall tell their sweethearts, ha ha!"

He took off his hat and mopped the back of his neck with his kerchief. Then he lowered his hand to swab out his hatband. Juge rose to his feet and took a silent step toward him, raised both arms, and suddenly jerked his fists apart. The sergeant kicked his legs out and tried to turn, but Juge kept him in place with a knee in his back.

I stepped up to see what I could do. The sergeant turned his bulging eyes toward me and held out his hat and musket, as if to ask would I mind holding them awhile. When I took them from him he fluttered his fingers along the cord biting into his throat. Then with increasing urgency he tried to dig his fingers under it, but Juge's grip was firm.

At last the sergeant's hands fell away from his throat and his arms dropped to his sides.

Juge laid him down in the stream and unwrapped the garrote from around his neck. "We take them one by one from behind," he whispered. He took the musket from me. "Your turn is next."

We crept along the bank till we spotted a grenadier crouched down and peering upstream. Juge touched my shoulder and waved his hand before him, as if to say, "After you."

Somewhere there is a line between war and murder, but it isn't drawn in San Domingo. I stepped up behind my man and swept the manchèt down with all my strength. Blood surged from his neck, filling my nostrils with its iron stench, pulsing hot on my hand, glittering in the silvery light. I thought of Mr. MacElroy's hat, hanging on a peg in my cabin. I yanked the blade out of the bone and swung again. The head thumped off downstream.

Juge gripped my shoulder. *"Très bien, mon ami,"* he whispered. *"Allons.* We see what fish the others have caught."

From a curious distance I noticed that my legs trembled. I ordered my lungs to take deep, regular breaths. It's one thing to walk a deck while cannon balls and jagged bits of the ship are flying around: they either hit you or they don't. But this sneaking up on men in the dark was something else entire.

Upstream a musket fired, and another, and then a volley. Horrid cries intermingled with the shots. As we rounded the bend I saw half a dozen grenadiers tangled up in the thorn bushes, jabbing their bayonets at shadows—till they poked at a wrong shadow and a black arm knocked the musket aside and a cane knife snicked through flesh and bone. One by one the grenadiers joined their comrades sprawling in the creek or hanging grotesquely from the brambles.

Farther upstream a mob of eight or nine grenadiers bunched together, trying to reload, trying to bite their cartridges open with mouths that screamed. Juge's wild men rose from the bushes and swung their cane knives. They were pissing on the bodies by the time we reached them.

I leaned against a tree to catch my breath. Beside me, a naked black man faced the grenadier lieutenant in the shadow of a limb that jutted out across the stream. The black man had his hands above his head and sported a ferocious erection. I turned away, not wanting to see what he was about to do to the lieutenant. But then I noticed the tip of the lieutenant's sword-bayonet sticking out of the black man's back, and that the black man was gripping the handles of his garrote, which looped over the branch and around the lieutenant's neck. They hung together in the gross shamelessness of death, with their toes dabbling the surface of the clean water that rushed beneath their feet.

The moon was full overhead now. By its light the Africans stripped the grenadiers of weapons, food, shoes, ammunition. They chopped their former comrade's hands free of his garrote, slung him across the biggest man's shoulders, and melted away into the shadows.

"A good harvest this evening," said Juge. He put his arm through mine. "Now, *mon cher petit ami,* we may walk upright like men again. Should you like a glass of wine? I have a thirst like the sponge."

As we hiked up the River of Orange Trees I heard more grenadiers clattering up the ravine behind us, and out of the corners of my eyes I caught the ghostly traces of men drifting down to meet them.

Eight

Apparently I had passed some sort of test. Juge still laughed when he saw me, but now it seemed more out of pleasure than amusement. I couldn't rely on him for companionship, however. He was often off doing something or other that I wasn't privy to. Our conversations were mostly limited to a hello and a wave as he trotted by on one of his unending errands with his dragoons and Grandfather Chatterbox trailing behind him.

I spent my mornings sketching the black troops, disguising diagrams of the trench works and unit locations in them. I sketched and disguised Pétion's defenses in the same way. I had no intention of going anywhere near speaking distance of the citadel, but I guessed if any of Dessalines' officers found me with diagrams of the mulatto positions, he might wonder what else was in my sketchbook, and I had no doubt that Dessalines would be happy to think up an appropriate punishment for a white man caught spying. Not *spying*, I reminded myself, but I was uncomfortably aware that it might not seem that way. With my watercolors I painted a landscape that included a nice view of the trench works with the citadel in the background. It was the sort of thing that any visitor would wish to immortalize, and as it was a view that the black troops looked at every day I didn't guess anyone would take it amiss.

One gloomy morning I also visited the ruined fort at the far left of the lines, where the houngans conducted their rituals at night. It had been built without benefit of mortar, and the walls had scattered the stones in a disordered jumble. Vines had crept out of the forest and entwined themselves around the stones, and the roots of trees had further buckled the walls. An open-sided thatch-roofed hut stood in a clearing within the walls; it seemed ordinary enough at first glance, but it gave me the shrinking scrotes, as if it had been imbued with some black mystery far beyond my ken. As long as I kept away from the hut, however, it was an infinitely soothing place, with nothing to disturb me but the drowsy humming of insects and the trilling of birds. I stood for a while watching the pigeons I'd disturbed wheeling across the sky, their wings flashing white V's against the gray clouds until they circled around and gathered once more atop the guano-streaked stones.

The old fort had a commanding view of the citadel and the anchorage. A ramshackle wooden pier jutted out from the black-sand beach on the near side of the fortress. A few boats lay alongside the pier, and a sentry stood out at the end of it, but there were no coils of rope or stands of barrels or anything else to indicate it had been used recently. I had a wonderful view down into the fortress, too. I counted the guns and noted their positions, and estimated the number of troops and horses, and wrote it all down in my sketchbook.

I turned to the north, to my right, and scanned the black army's lines, looking for the American and British units the officer at the *katye jeneral* had hinted at. As I swung my glass around to the northeast I was startled to have a close-up image of a hussar officer picking his way on horseback toward me. He wore his short coat hanging from one shoulder, the way hussars do, and looked at me in a way that made me feel I'd been caught doing something filthy. I lowered my glass and saluted him anyway. *"Comment allez-vous, compagnon?"*

He waved my greeting aside as if fanning away a stink. *"Que faites vous la?* What are you doing up here? Get away. You have no business looking around up here."

"I am an American officer, working with the staff of General Dessalines."

He reined up at the name, but he didn't go away. At his gesture a pair of troopers rode up beside him.

"Très bien, mes amis," I shrugged, and they trailed along behind me

until they were satisfied I was returning to headquarters.

It was time I got back there anyway. From midmorning on I belonged to Connor. He kept me busy translating bone-achingly dull documents, which I memorized as best I could, not daring to make copies: notes on troop movements, readiness, morale; the unit number of every battalion in every demi-brigade, and the names of all nine captains, lieutenants, sub-lieutenants, and quartermasters in each battalion; remarks on the bloody stalemates at Jacmel and the Goâves up on the north coast of the peninsula; and guesses as to when, not whether, Toussaint would seize Santo Domingo, the Spanish side of the island, and how soon first Consul Buonoparte would try to reoccupy Saint-Dómingue, the French side.

"Saint-Dómingue," I said to Franklin in the little office we kept at headquarters. "Better make that 'San Domingo,' so whoever reads this in the War Department will know what Mr. Connor means."

"I have already done so, Mr. Graves," said Franklin, scribbling away. "Just translate. Leave the thinking to me."

I wasn't allowed in the meetings that Connor attended, though I could hear the muttering and sometimes shouting beyond the door, and had an occasional glimpse within. A skittish white secretary translated everything from Creole into French—when they spoke Creole, anyway; most of the officers spoke French—and I translated everything into English, and Franklin scratched it all down on his bits of paper and tied them up with his seemingly endless supply of red tapes.

I sighed, reaching for another letter and squinting at the French script. Connor strode through the room.

"Oh, Mr. Connor," I said. "I really ought to get about my work, y'know. I still got my report to prepare for Commodore Gaswell."

He stopped with his hand on the latch of the far door. "I should think you would find everything you need to know in these notes."

"They're a mountain of information, but I need to know for myself what's reliable," I said. As I spoke I realized I'd gotten some ink on my nose. I tried to wipe it off with my sleeve and then remembered my handkerchief. "I need to sketch out a proper map, which I can't do without I see the ground. And there's nothing about logistics here at all. For instance, where's the landing place for these supplies they're supposedly getting from us?"

"Soon, soon," he said, "you will be your own man again. In the meantime there is matter after matter that needs my urgent attention, and no one can help me as well as the inestimable Mr. Graves." He went through the far door and shut it behind him.

"There's always some excuse," I muttered. I scrubbed at my nose, but all I managed was to ruin my handkerchief.

Franklin bent again over his portable desk. Even with a proper desk to work at, he used his portable one. I longed to smack the smirk off his face with it. Actually, I wouldn't have minded stealing his traveling desk and all that was in it, but I didn't guess that would go over too well—not with Connor, and probably not with Gaswell, neither. Certainly not with Dessalines.

The door that Connor had gone through came ajar, and through the crack I saw Grandfather Chatterbox sitting in a corner next to Juge. The old man was playing with a little vial filled with corn kernels. Some of the kernels were black and some were white. He tapped it patiently until the black kernels were on top. Then he nodded to himself, shook the vial up and began tapping at it again. He never said anything, nor even seemed to be listening, and Dessalines and his officers paid him no mind that I could see. After a while he cocked his head at Juge and the two of them went outside. I watched them through the window as they mounted up, Grandfather Chatterbox on Bel-Argent and Juge on a handsome roan.

Juge had discarded his torn-off trousers and old coat in favor of a regulation staff-officer's uniform. The gold-trimmed blue pantaloons, tassled Hessian boots, and double-breasted white vest were regulation, anyway; but he'd found a silver-spangled tailcoat that was gaudy even by the standards of Toussaint's army. Between the uniform and the dragoons that followed him around, I had begun to guess that Juge was more important than I'd first supposed him to be. Now, as I gazed out the window at him, he touched the brim of his hat to me and then thundered off in a cloud of dragoons with Grandfather Chatterbox at his side. He would outride his escort by evening, I knew, and would return to camp with only the old man left to guard him.

I'd gladly have faced Joséphine again for the chance to ride with him. By day at least, the war was uncommon dull. Even the ogre Dessalines was a disappointment. The only time he had spoke to me was once at dinner. *"Passez moi le sel, je vous prie,"* he said. *"Mais oui, mon général,"* I answered. It wasn't exactly the sort of thing I'd be telling my shipmates over dinner for the next twenty years. I could just see it: "The monster Dessalines, you say," I'd drawl, sprawling in my chair as the decanter made its rounds. "Sure, met him at the siege of Jacmel during the War of Knives. He even spoke to me. There he sat, across the table, as near as I am to you. 'Pray pass the salt,' he says, offhand like, just as if he weren't a murdering fiend. And did I blench? Did I quail? I did not, gentlemen. 'But of course, General,' says I, and passed him the salt."

I'd have snatched myself bald out of sheer boredom if Juge hadn't been there to see I was entertained of an evening. He was generous to a fault when it come to fighting. I was particularly curious about his troublesome hamlet down by the Grand Rivière, so we found a couple of muskets one night and went down there. It proved to be pretty much like repelling boarders in a ship-to-ship duel, what with the cannons banging away on both sides, and us jostling for space to poke our bayonets at the mulattoes as they clambered over the chevaux-de-frise. There was even the danger of drowning, what with the mud that got churned up underfoot.

A cheval-de-frise, by the way, is a log pierced through with sharpened stakes. It has advantages over a boarding net for keeping men out, the sharpened stakes being an obvious one. Trouble is, the stakes also make good handholds for climbing, and before too long the mulattoes found a weak place in our line and began to pour through it, shoving and kicking and clawing in the most ferocious no-holds-barred wrassling match I ever seen. I'd been schooled in the genteel art of gouging and biting at Judge Breckenridge's academy when I was a boy, but adding guns and swords gave it a whole new twist.

Major Matou, the commander of the blacks in that part of the line, kept packing in reinforcements until everybody was gummed up so close they couldn't hardly use their cane knives. It didn't bother them none—they went at each other like bulldogs and badgers tied together, trying to snatch each other's throats out with their bare teeth. I figured out pretty quick I didn't like it. I tucked myself into a hole under the breastworks. I got kicked and stepped on plenty, but it was a damn sight better than mixing with that crowd. It relieved my curiosity about infantry fighting, anyway—*I* was satisfied. But it ruined my night's sleep, and in the morning Bertrand gave me Johnny-shitfire about the state of my clothes.

A week dragged by slower than a dog chasing a porcupine in August. I soon got the better part of the commodore's work done and was eager to be gone. How I was to accomplish that, I didn't know; each morning and evening I climbed the hill from which I'd first seen Jacmel, but though I plied my pocket telescope over every wave from the bay to the horizon, I never saw so much as a hint of the *Croatoan*.

Franklin absented himself from the office one glorious day. The cannons had ceased their tarnal roaring, the birds sang innocently among the splintered stumps of the trees, and Dessalines and his crew were off hatching plans for a major assault that evening. I wasn't privy to their plans, nor cared to be. I spent a pleasant morning putting the finishing touches on a watercolor that was prime if I squinted at it right. Just as I had begun to wonder if I would be lucky enough to get dinner that day, Connor stood himself in the doorway and blocked my light.

"Mr. Graves," says he, "the time has come to go see Pétion. We may be gone several days."

"I'm glad to hear it," I said. "I can use the time to finish my maps."

"You mistake me, sir. Between your translations and Franklin's notes, I intend to bring back a report to his Excellency the president that will make my name. I shall give you a mention, of course, but until my work is done I shall need you at my side."

I looked at my watch. "But it's near two o'clock already. Pétion will have seen the men massing in the trenches. I don't guess he'll find it too convenient to open the gates for anybody right about now."

"We have hours yet."

"I promised Juge I'd ride with him."

He slapped himself on the forehead and then pointed out the door. "Go. Pack your bags and meet me back here at headquarters, *if* you please. I have arrangements to make."

"Very well." I shrugged. I'd picked up the gesture from Juge, and I found it to be useful for when I needed to say *something,* but not what was on my mind. "I got a letter to deliver there, anyway."

"Oh? Whom do you know in Jacmel?"

"No one." I blotted my watercolor and rolled it up. "It's from a dead man."

"A dead man?" he called as I tromped across the porch.

"Fellow name of Villon," I said over my shoulder.

"Wait, wait," he called. He followed me as far as the porch and leaned over the rail. "Villon, like the poet?"

I stepped off the road to let a battery of horse artillery go by. The horses were wild-eyed and lathered, and the gunners hung for their lives onto the caissons as they jounced down the road. I shaded my eyes and squinted up at him. "That's right. Why, have you read him?"

"Of course: 'Where are the snows of yesteryear?' as the famous line asks." He laughed self-consciously, the way a man does when tossing out quotations from books he maybe hasn't read. "Have you opened the letter?"

"Of course not. It's to his wife."

"Have you the letter on you?"

"No," I lied. I had no idea what he wanted with the letter, but something in his eye made me think I should keep a close watch on it.

"I see," said Connor. "Ah well, it don't signify, I'm sure." He snapped his fingers. "Oh, I just thought of something—I haven't seen that rascal Franklin since noon."

"So?"

"So before you pack, go find him, please. He likes to watch the action down by the river, at the hamlet they have so much trouble with. Go, go quickly!"

Come to think of it, I hadn't seen Franklin for a while, neither. I broke into a trot.

"A black American gentleman?" said Major Matou. "This is something I would like to see. I didn't know there were any."

"I was told he spends his time down here."

"You were told falsely. I have never seen this man. But tell me, do you plan to join us for the assault this evening? I make it my business to take this annoying village once and for all."

Sweet jumping Jehoshaphat, not that again. "I am engaged to ride with Juge tonight, Major. How it distresses me to think I shall not be with you and your brave fellows this evening." I gave him my best disappointed look. "However, I may not even be able to ride with Juge if I do not find this Franklin first."

"Don't be so downcast, my American friend," he said, patting my shoulder. "I shall miss you, but I'm sure you will find your own share of glory this evening. *Bonne chance, mon ami!*"

"Good luck to you too, sir. Oh," I said as I turned to leave, "by the way, have you seen any American or British units?"

"Not for several days, no. You wish to show Juge how your compatriots fight, *hein?* This is fitting and seemly." He gave me a smart salute, kissed me on both cheeks, and bid me adieu.

I let myself be carried along by the columns moving on the road behind the trenches till I came onto a ridge overlooking the River of Orange Trees. There I found a breeze to blow the dust away, and I climbed up onto a large boulder where I could take advantage of the air and not be stepped on for a while. Nearby a couple of batteries of artillerymen stacked round shot and cartridges in preparation for the evening's labors. I don't mind work, usually, when someone else is doing it, but at that moment the sight oppressed me, and I cast a despairing eye out to sea.

And there I saw a frigate rounding Cape Jacmel from the west, near bows-on to me and close-hauled on the starboard tack. I had no doubt she was a Frenchman that had slipped out of Brest to reinforce Pétion; certainly she would fetch the anchorage if she kept on her present course. But no! She flew her jib sheets, and I snapped my glass to my eye. She surged prettily about—for a Johnny Crappo, anyway—and as she turned toward the open sea I counted her ports and estimated her length. She was a thirty-two-gun frigate of maybe a hundred and forty feet from stem to stern and perhaps thirty-five feet on the beam. Then as she brought the wind onto her larboard beam I saw the Stars and Stripes streaming from her ensign staff, and I took her in all at once. I knew her—I *knew* her!

I jumped to my feet and whooped. "That's the *Croatoan*, boys!" The battery commander looked up at me, and I hollered, *"C'est une frégate américaine!"* He gave me a wave, but he was too busy to look where I was pointing. "Then tend to your work and be damned," says I, "for I won't be here to see it, ha ha!"

An officer of one of the passing brigades, his trouser legs rolled midway up his ankles and his shoes and stockings white with dust, stepped away from his company and strolled toward me. At least I guessed he was an officer—I took in the red-and-yellow striped kerchief knotted under his narrow-brimmed round hat, the long red-lined tails of his blue *surtout*, the gold earrings bright against his black skin, the heavy-bladed hanger swaying against his knee, the gilded epaulets and, most of all, the hands clasped behind the back and the remote indifference.

Definitely an officer. I touched my hat, and he returned the compliment. *"Pardon, citoyen,"* I said. "I'm an American sea officer on detached duty. I am told there is an American unit near here, perhaps some sailors and Marines. Can you tell me where they are?" I wasn't sure how to say "marines," but *soldats marin* seemed close enough.

"If you've lost your unit, you must be very detached indeed," he laughed. He identified himself with the surprising name of Forcené, and said, placing subtle emphasis on the correct term, "The *fusiliers marin* and the seamen have gone down to join the assault. They are with the British light company. *Là.*" He pointed to the plain below.

Far off on the army's left flank, over by the ruined fort that the hussars had chased me away from, fluttered a yellow banner emblazoned with a cross of Saint George. A look through my glass showed me it had a Union Jack in the canton. Around it I could make out some black men in scarlet coats that glowed in the heat haze. Near them was a small group of white men in blue uniforms trimmed with red. They were U.S. Marines, without a doubt, and with them were a few sailors in checked shirts and tarpaulin hats.

"*Merci beaucoup, citoyen Forcené.*" The former slaves of Saint-Dómingue had a facility for choosing noms de guerre, I thought, as I hopped down off my boulder. Matou meant Tomcat, and Forcené meant Madman.

I ran double-quick toward the farmhouse where Franklin and I were billeted, aiming to gather up my papers and hook on out of there.

A pair of black-caped horsemen trotted along the road, heading away from the farmhouse and perhaps a hundred yards beyond it. The one in the lead glanced over his shoulder. He turned away again as soon as he saw me, and I didn't recognize him, but either he was wearing a mask or he was the darkest Negro I ever saw. His face was like a black void in the shadow of his hat. The other one glanced over his shoulder and then reined up. It was the Parson. I swallowed sickly as he drew a pistol from his saddle holster and trotted toward me. I was all set to make a dash for the house when his companion gave out a sharp whistle. The Parson turned like a sullen dog called to heel, and the two of them sped away.

The door of the house stood open. The sentries were gone. I drew my sword and crept in, feeling naked without my pistols. All was still inside. I poked my head into both of the rooms downstairs. All quiet there. I looked into the little lean-to in the back where Bertrand did the cooking and the washing and mending. The crockery stood neatly on the cupboard, and his blankets were folded shipshape on his cot, and the sun shone through the open back door, but the little man was gone. I ran upstairs, expecting to find Franklin with his throat slit or his brains blown out.

Instead, I found the son of a bitch standing in our room, holding my saddlebag upside down and shaking it. My clothes and papers were scattered across the floor, the bedstead had been upended, and the mattress had been torn apart. Wads of straw lay thick around his ankles. He nodded at me.

"Hey now," says I. "What the hell are you doing?"

"Looking for what that man missed," he said.

"What man?"

"The man in the black cape and mask. He has just now left. Surely you saw him."

"I saw two men. One of them was the Parson." I put my sword away and looked at the mess he'd made.

"The Parson?" said Franklin. "If you mean that man we saw in the woods the other day—"

"Stow it. The man that came in here—just what is it you think he missed?"

"I have yet to discover that."

"Then what makes you think he was looking for something?"

"It is self-evident." He spread his hands to indicate the mess.

"You know what I think happened here? I think maybe you're in cahoots. Maybe you tore everything up yourself. Maybe you stole something you knew where it was, and want it to look like it was stole by someone who had to ransack the place to find it."

He gave me one of his rare smiles. "That's so farfetched as to be plausible. But here is the way of it." He tossed my saddlebag onto the ruined mattress. "I was on the back porch drinking coffee when the door banged open and someone charged upstairs. Whoever it was made noise enough to be you, but I have never known you to be in a hurry. So I came upstairs to see what was the matter. From the landing I saw a man in here, throwing things about and muttering."

"Who was he?"

"He wore a mask. A black kerchief." He made a *V* of his first two fingers and pointed at his eyes. "With holes cut in it to see through."

"That sounds like one of . . ."

"One of what?"

"Like that chap that almost ran your writing case through in Port Républicain." I didn't guess Franklin needed to know about the Knights of the White Hand till I knew where he stood. "What was he looking for?"

"That's what I want to know, which is why I was picking through your belongings just now." If he was embarrassed to be caught at it, he didn't show it. "So, will you tell me what it was?"

"Why should I? Assuming I even know." It was that damn letter, is what it was.

"I am an agent in the employ of the War Department."

"Agent! His secretary, you mean. You ain't nothing but a clerk."

"My guise as an humble amanuensis enables me to perform my mission, which is to keep an eye on Connor."

"Why?"

"I'm not at liberty to say."

"Let's see your credentials." I held out my hand.

He laughed. "You expect me to carry proof that I'm a spy?"

"Well, do you have anything that says who you are?"

"Certainly." He reached into his pocket and extracted a slim leather wallet. "I have here a certificate identifying me as George Franklin, twenty-six years of age, and a freeborn black man of the city of Philadelphia." He handed me a letter. "It describes me very well, I dare say, right down to the annoyingly superior attitude."

It was headed *Philadelphia, War Office, 20. Jan'y. 1800,* and signed *yr &c Jas. McHenry.* I had nothing to compare it to, but I figured if it weren't James McHenry's honest-to-God signature, Franklin was foxy enough to make sure it was a passable likeness. I glanced through the short paragraph. "Says here you're haughty and saucy, Franklin. That's pretty good."

"Thank you. I wrote it myself."

"You wrote it yourself?"

"No, but I might have. Don't trust papers. They are easily fabricated. Trust your eyes and your brain." He took the paper back and put it away. "Now. So. The question is twofold: What was our man looking for, and did he find it?"

"I was talking to Connor just a little while ago," I said reluctantly. "I told him I had a letter to deliver to Jacmel. He perked his ears up like a dog at dinnertime when I said it was from a man name of Villon."

"Villon, like the medieval poet?"

"Have you read him?"

"I was not aware he'd been translated into English. Have you read the letter?"

"That's just what Connor said. And the answer is no, I didn't read the letter. It ain't addressed to me."

"You speak of it in the present tense. You still have it, then?"

"Maybe."

"Then perhaps you can let me have just a peep."

"I bet it's in French."

"And of course I don't speak French." He bowed slightly, as if I'd scored a point of some kind. "Now listen very carefully," he said. "I warned you about Connor, did I not?"

"Yes, but I weren't listening."

"Your former foolishness is neither here nor there. But you must listen now: He has aspirations."

"Aspirations?"

"*Plans,* you naïf. Plans, such as transporting Toussaint's slave rebellion to the Southern states."

"Toussaint won't go for that. He's already bit off more'n he can chaw right here."

"Oh, give me strength," he said, glancing up at the ceiling and then seizing my arm in a surprisingly strong grip. "Listen, you pumpkin-headed tatter-ninny. Of course Toussaint won't 'go' for it. What *he* wants is to make a free black republic here in San Domingo. That will be dangerous enough for him without giving the world an excuse to come down on his head was he to let it spread. No. This is not in his interest, and it would mean Connor's life was he to propose it to him."

"It'll mean *your* life if you don't let go of me." I brushed imaginary fingermarks off my sleeve while I tried to wrap my head around what he was saying. "Anyway, I don't catch your meaning."

"Are you an imbecile? Connor intends to present his plan to Pétion. He has gathered every bit of information about Dessalines' army that he can. That information will be invaluable to Pétion when he breaks out of here to join with Rigaud at Petite Goâve."

"But Rigaud needs Jacmel to anchor his right flank. He'll never go for it."

"If Pétion stays here he will be destroyed, and there goes the right flank anyway. Rigaud needs Pétion and his army more than he needs Jacmel."

"So how does a slave uprising someplace else help Rigaud?"

"Even a single regiment set loose in, say, South Carolina could force us to withdraw from the Caribbean. Just the threat of it would seriously hamper our efforts here. We would have to break off our blockade until his transports were found."

"And if we withdraw from San Domingo, he can be resupplied by sea."

"Now you begin to understand," he said. "And if the transports *do* reach our coast—well, our army is scarcely worth the name. Pétion's veterans would sweep them aside in a few weeks. And he won't need to take any cities, either. If he controls the plantations, he controls the South. And don't forget it was the great mobs of freed slaves that tipped the balance here in Toussaint's favor. Imagine if that happened back home. Imagine the raping, looting and burning from Georgia to Delaware! Is that what you want?"

"Don't you want the slaves to be free? And you a black man." I admit I kind of enjoyed seeing him so agitated. It beat his usual blank stare any day of the week. He looked at me all goggle-eyed, like a squeezed toad. "Listen, it'd never work," I said. "Once they let the genie out, how're they going to get it back in the bottle?"

I had him there—but only for a moment. He tapped his fingers on his cheek, and then said, "They'll do it the same way they will do it here. They'll quiet them with promises of land and emancipation—but in the meantime, fellows, there are crops to be picked and goods to be shipped. Food doesn't grow on trees, you know."

"Yes, it does."

His back stiffened and his spectacles flashed. "Do I look like an ignorant field nigger to you?" For a second I thought he was going to smack me, but he smoothed his lapels instead and said, "No one's going to free any slaves, I tell you. Connor intends to run off the planters and replace them with his own men. And when the dust settles, he'll be sitting on top of an empire."

"Franklin, are your papers intact?"

He gaped, the first time I'd ever seen him taken by surprise, and he dove under the ruined mattress. "Yes!" he said, rooting through his carryall. "They're all here. But—"

"But they're in English and no use to Pétion. Connor has the French originals, I bet."

He stood. "No doubt." He thought a moment and said, "No, there is doubt. Let us say it wouldn't surprise me."

"Looks like your job ain't done, then."

I began packing. Crumpled in the corner I found the clean shirt I had brought in case I needed one, and I found my extra pair of socks hanging from the lamp. My compass and my telescope were already in my pockets, along with the letter, and I was wearing my sword. I found my orders, my passport, and my commission, and slipped them next to the letter in my pocket. I stuffed the shirt and socks and my sketchbook into my saddlebag, and slipped my pistols into my belt. There were plenty of other things that lived in my carryall, but they were too heavy to bother with. I needed to move fast. I walked out the door, throwing my saddlebag over my shoulder.

"Where are you going?" said Franklin. "I shall come with you."

"No you won't, mate," I said. "You still got time to find Connor and go with him to the citadel, which I expect is where you need to be. Me, I got a ship to catch."

Nine

As I dodged along the crowded road that would take me around to the left flank, where I'd seen the Stars and Stripes flying, I met Juge riding his handsome roan and leading Joséphine. The late afternoon sunlight sparkled on the silver lace of his flash uniform. *"Bonjour, mon ami!"* said I, looking warily at Joséphine. I misliked the way her lips quivered when she stepped toward me. "I need a horse. I went to the stables to get one, but they said I could have only her. Then they said she was gone and they wouldn't tell me where. I thought surely they had thrown her into the soup pot."

"Bon sang! You are not too late," he said, grinning. "I have been looking for you. I thought you would miss the battle I promised you! Have you ever been in one?"

"Of course I have," I said. "Have you forgotten the troublesome hamlet? But I must ride immediately to Cap Maréchaux. I have seen a ship at sea."

"Indeed, the sea is an excellent place to find a ship," said Juge. "It is where I have always seen them myself. But I do not mean a little skirmish of no consequence. Have you ever fought in a grand assault, with the chosen men leading the way?"

"Well, not a grand assault." Nor did I care to see one, not that night, whether I disappointed Juge or no. "Listen, *mon ami,* I go to Cap Maréchaux. On the way, I must speak with the American contingent. They're over on the left. I must find out if they are in communication with the sea."

"So soon said, so soon done," said Juge. He indicated Joséphine. "See how she pines for you. I have been feeding her with bits of carrot and whatever else I could find. But she always gives me the sad eyes: 'Oh, where is my dear little friend Mr. Graves,' she says."

She *was* nuzzling at me instead of biting me. Truth be told, I'd visited her a few times in the stables and spread shillings with an open hand among the grooms. I still didn't guess she was edible, but you never know what a Frenchman will put in his mouth.

While I strapped on the spurs that Juge handed me, a bugle sounded in the camp, and then another and another. The horses raised their heads.

"This Joséphine, she is a soldier," said Juge. "See how she strains her ears at the sound of the trumpet—she is ready to charge any bastion!"

"Last time I tried that on her, she threw me over her head. Anyway, I go to the left flank." I draped my saddlebag over Joséphine's shoulders and settled myself in the saddle. It was a cavalry model worn smooth with long use, with a long sword hanging from one side and a carbine in a scabbard hanging on the other. At Juge's insistence I shrugged the sword belt over my shoulder, saying, "Yes, yes" when he said that my small-sword was fine for sticking rude gentlemen in the street, but a cavalry saber, long, straight and heavy, was what I wanted for whacking off heads in a real set-to. I unbuckled my own sword and tucked it among the rigging that held Joséphine's gear in place. She quivered at the rising sounds of drum and trumpet.

"Come," said Juge, his eyes bright. "Let us go where the generals are!"

"No, I tell you! I go to the left flank, and then to Cap Maréchaux." I nudged Joséphine in the ribs and we trotted down the track.

"Oh, very well," Juge grumbled, following me. "But Connor, he is going to be very angry."

I spared him a glance. "What makes you say that?"

"*Bon sang!* Was he not annoyed to find you gone when he snapped his fingers?"

"Snapped his fingers?"

"Yes, like that." He demonstrated. "Called you his boy. 'Where's my boy?' he said. 'I need him, the stupid fellow,' just like that."

"How do you know? You speak no English."

"'Ow you know I don'?" he said, recognizably if indistinctly in English. He switched back to French. "I am the great linguist. But insolence knows no language, and it is clear what sort of man this Connor is. I am surprised you can restrain your hand, sometimes, so ill bred is he."

"He has a higher opinion of himself than the evidence might warrant, and he is short-tempered at times, but never insolent."

"When you are there to hear him, yes, but you do not hear what he says when you are away, no?"

"What does he say when I am not around?"

"Too much, just as I have. Franklin, now," he said, "there is a curious fellow."

"Not Franklin."

"But yes!"

"But no!"

"But yes! Have you ever talked to him? So knowledgeable! So intelligent! So cultured and witty! We have the amusing conversations."

"I can imagine," I said. "Between your horrible English and his nonexistent French, you must be quite a pair."

"Ah, but no, my friend! He speaks the most elegant French, almost as well as I speak the English. You might be surprised."

"I *am* surprised." I gave Juge a close look, but he seemed his usual honest self. "He has told me several times that he has no French at all."

"No French?"

"He admits to being able to say, 'I am an American,' but that's all."

"A very curious fellow," said Juge, reining up. "So like a hummingbird. Sticks his nose into everything."

"I bet he does." Joséphine took advantage of the halt to snatch a mouthful of brush. A troop of hussars clattered past us on the road, scattering the columns of infantrymen. "He told me Connor has some wild plan to transport the rebellion to our southern states."

"This is the pure fabrication," said Juge. He urged his horse forward; Joséphine followed, with bits of grass hanging from her lip. "We are true Frenchmen and not in rebellion. Besides, Father Toussaint has all he can manage here."

"No, not with Toussaint's help. With Rigaud's."

"Ah yes? No wonder Connor was in such a hurry to get an escort to the citadel. *Bon sang,* did you not hear the drums and bugles? He wanted to be very sure they knew he was coming, so there would be no shooting by mistake. Never have I seen a man wave a white flag with such energy."

"Was Franklin with him?"

"But of course. He with his little writing desk, following along behind Connor and the ghost."

"The ghost?"

"Yes. That white man we saw at the ravine where we ambushed the chasseurs. He surprised me, that one. I thought someone would have shot him by now."

I looked at the soldiers slogging along the road. They none of them spared me so much as a glance. I felt kind of like a ghost myself. "How does he come and go, then?"

"He must have a passport. Am I a sentry, that I would know this?"

My head thudded in time with the horses' hooves as we cantered along. This part of the line was closest to the mulatto defenses, and was drawing fire from the blockhouse that stood across the road from Fort Beliotte. A grenadier toppled over as we rode past, and a sergeant bawled at the men to close the gap.

"Juge," I said, "was Connor dressed all in black?"

"He wore a black cape, yes. He and the ghost look most unnatural together, as if the devil and his brother are loose in the land."

I thought of Connor's last words to me before he'd sent me off to find Franklin—at a place where he knew Franklin wasn't. "Tell me, Juge, has the poet Villon ever been translated into English?"

He shrugged, which is a pretty good trick when you're booming along on horseback. "Villon is barely translated into French, I think.

He wrote a long time ago, and the language has changed. But all know his famous line: *'Mais ou sont les neiges d'antan?'"*

"Connor knows it too. Only he said it in English: 'But where are the snows of yesteryear?' I think he speaks French as well as I do. And I think he has copies of every note and letter that went through your headquarters these past few weeks."

It was the first time I'd ever seen Juge look worried about anything. He reigned up so sharply that his horse sidestepped and tried to throw him. I near about fell off, myself.

"Ho! Doucement—ho!" he said, easing up on the reins and patting the roan's neck until the animal grew calm. "But is he a spy? *C'est une véritable catastrophe!"*

"If it's true, certainly."

"I should tell my superiors," he said, but he had an unhappy look on his face when he said it.

"It'll mean his neck. I only have Franklin's say-so on this."

He looked puzzled. "Franklin's word? What does Franklin have to do with this?"

"I don't know, entirely." Although I didn't fully trust Franklin, I didn't want to get him shot. "But he's the one who told me these things about Connor."

"There is too much we don't know." He shook his head. "But surely we must do something. What do you intend?"

"I intend to go aboard that frigate in the bay and speak with her captain."

"But this is passing along the responsibility!"

"Isn't that what you were about to do?"

He laughed, a bright and cheery sound in that miserable landscape. "This is so, my friend."

"Naturally the captain will require more evidence," I said. "And I doubt he'll want to risk his own officers when he can just as easily send me. So maybe I'll return, *hein?"* I held out my hand. *"Au revoir, mon ami.* It has been a pleasure to know you."

"Adieu." He took my hand and held it before looking unhappily

toward the center of the line, where a gathering of banners showed that Dessalines and his staff had arrived on the field. I could see the general amid his staff, stripped to the waist like a prehistoric warlord. Grandfather Chatterbox rode beside him on Bel-Argent. The soldiers near them waved their hats and cheered, and the cheering spread in a great deep-throated roar along the line.

"But no," said Juge, and the old mischievous look came back. "I do not leave my friend until we arrive at the end of the line. There is time yet. This intelligence that Connor has gathered—it makes no difference to the assault. Come, let us ride!"

With cannon balls shuddering overhead, we splashed across a filthy stream and rode behind rank after rank of colonial troops. There were regulars in smart *uniforms nationale,* straw-hatted and unshod militia in blue and white stripes, and who-knew-what units in grimy homespun. I saw men of all shades of black and brown, and once a whole regiment of white men, many of them yellow with fever. All were drawn together under the Tricolor. Some stared anxiously toward the forts, others affected unconcern, and still others stood cow-eyed and indifferent. Some troops were drawn up in rigidly straight lines, three or four men deep, depending on the type of regiment. Others sat around, smoking, talking or just staring into themselves. I had heard that soldiers threw their cards and dice away before going into battle, lest they die with instruments of Satan in their possession, but here and there I saw clusters of soldiers gathered around a tree stump or a blanket, gaming away as if it were a long Saturday night and no Sabbath in the morning.

A gully running down from our left forced us out onto the open ground in front of the line. At the bottom of the gully lay the Baynet Road, a smooth white streak leading eastward from Pétion's front gate, through the black army's lines, and off into the hills above the *katye jeneral.* Beyond the gully we found a battery of mortars at work. The fuses traced bright arcs against the rapidly darkening sky as the shells rose impossibly high and then fell with a flash and a distant roar among the forts.

Between the mortars and the wing of hussars that screened the end of the line, I saw the yellow banner with the Union Jack in the canton. A company of redcoated black soldiers stood around it. But oh, glorious day, beyond them waved a lone Stars and Stripes, the sweetest of ensigns.

I pointed it out. "There," I said. "The Americans!"

"Come on!" said Juge.

We touched our spurs to our mounts, galloped along like generals past the lobsters, and reined up before a group of Marines and sailors. Their banner was a small flag with a competent but homemade look to it, as if a sailmaker's mate had stitched it together as a favor for the Marines who carried it. Strictly irregular, that—only ships were authorized to carry the national colors into action—but my heart leaped as it snapped in the breeze.

The sailors were all enlisted men, without even a petty officer in sight. I spotted a Marine sergeant, but I ignored him. A sea officer would be in charge of the detail. The nearest sailor removed his hat to me, and I said, "Where's your officer?"

"Got none, sir, 'ceptin' the Mick, there." He pointed his thumb over his shoulder at the sergeant. "You readin' y'self in, sir? Takin' over, like?"

"No." It was none of his business, but a hint of a sneer crossed his face when I said it. "Are you from the *Croatoan?*"

"Aye, sir."

"I need to get aboard of her. Is there a boat?"

His face settled into a look of studied indifference. "Dunno, sir."

The sergeant stepped toward us. He was a compact man like most ship's soldiers, of little more than the minimum five and a half feet tall, and sported a robust set of ginger side-whiskers. His red vest and blue uniform were dusty but not what you'd call dirty; he himself was clean, shaved and apparently sober; and he had a pleasant cheerfulness in his blue eyes.

"You, sergeant," I said, "who's in charge here?"

He stamped his feet and thrust the butt of his spontoon into the ground. "It's Sergeant Michael Cahoon I am, sir, United States Marine Corps, *sir,* off the *Croatoan* frigate."

"But where's your officer, Sergeant?"

"An it's an officer yar wantin', 'tis himself over there, sir."

Though he still stood at attention, he managed with a twitch of his shoulder to indicate a young Royal officer of the line, who slouched in the saddle as he walked his horse toward us.

"No, man. I mean your *ship's* officer. Where is he?"

"Himself copped it in the shenanigans yesterd'y, sir, an' was took back aboard the frigate. No, I tell a lie—'twas the day before. Mr. Dentz it was as got his yesterd'y, he being one o' the young gentleman and not what you'd say in command, and t'ree o' the boys as well. So with only meself left in charge o' the detail, and no more reason than that to miss out on a grand cavort, yon English kiddie took us under his wing, after a manner o' speakin'." He tilted his head toward the advancing Englishman. "He's a good lad, sir, only don't tell him I said it, if it please yer honor."

"Sergeant Cahoon, I need to report at once to Captain Block. Where's your rendezvous?"

Before Cahoon could answer, the Englishman rode up out of the dusk and touched his hat with a languid glove. "Leftenant Treadwell," he said, "commanding a thoroughly detached company of the Seventh West India."

I returned his salute and looked him over. I guessed he was no more than a few years older than me, but he had an old man's weariness about him. His coat was threadbare and patched, and had faded to pink in the tropical sun. There were remnants of silver lace on it, and its facings had once perhaps been yellow. He must've had money once, to buy a commission.

"I'm Lieutenant Graves, sir, of the U.S. Navy, and this here's Mr. Juge." It occurred to me that I had no idea what rank Juge held; I had no idea how much he could understand, either, but I had no patience for translating right then. "How'd you come to be detached, Mr. Treadwell?"

"Didn't come to be detached, sir—came to reinforce Môle Saint-Nicholas. Had to take the place after the French pulled out, y'know.

Too good a base for controlling the Windward Passage. But Toussaint showed us the door in 'ninety-eight, and whilst we were coverin' the army's rear, the general covered his arse and buggered off, aw haw haw." He didn't smile when he laughed.

"Sweet jumping Jupiter," I said. "You've been here two years?"

"A year and nine months, anyway."

"But what are you doing *here*, Mr. Treadwell?"

"When one is given the choice of bein' flayed alive or joinin' up with Toussaint, sir, one jolly well joins up with Toussaint."

"But sure you could've been picked up by now."

He looked over at his company. They were all black men, even the sergeants, and were keeping an eye on us. "Couldn't leave the lads behind," he said. "Wouldn't look right. Dare say they wouldn't let me, regardless. Only way out of here for me is to take French leave."

"French leave?"

"You know—toodlin' off from a to-do without kissin' milady's hand and thanks for a lovely party." He looked over at the forts and then flashed me a grisly half-smile. "Just struck me as amusin': Your name is Graves, and that's where we're headin', aw haw haw. I say—glad you're here to take charge of these Marines of yours. Damned rotten influence. Got drunk as lords on purloined rum last night. Got me an' m' fellows soused, too."

"But I'm not—" I stopped myself before I could blurt out that I wasn't intending to attack any damn fort. Instead I said, "Is this true, Sergeant Cahoon?"

"Oh, God aye, sir."

I looked away to keep from grinning back at him. "Mr. Treadwell," I said, glancing around at the ground they faced. Night had fallen while we talked, and firelight glowed behind the walls. "Ain't there supposed to be parallels and approaches and breaching batteries and things? Sure you ain't fixin' to charge across this open ground."

He surveyed the field with distaste. It lay hidden in shadow, now that the sun had gone, but I recalled that it sloped sharply down toward the ancient fort overlooking the anchorage, and then dipped again into a gully before climbing up to the foot of the prison. A wall running between the prison and the main fort had come down in places, and I supposed that would be their objective.

"No sappers, no artificers, an' no engineers to tell 'em where t' dig. But with any luck we'll get bogged down in the ravine there. Excellent cover, that." He gave me a twisted smile to show he was joking. "Oh, bit of advice if you'll forgive me. Should leave m' horse behind." He tapped the side of his nose with a finger of his dirty glove. "A white man on horseback makes a simply marvelous target—for both sides." He trotted back to his company, where he dismounted and sent his horse to the rear.

"'Tis off that beast you should be gettin', as himself said, sir," said Cahoon. "We was after needing a officer, as ya know how Jack hates takin' orders from a sojer. Well now, the sun has set and there go the bugles, sir. I'll just get me lads lined up there, and you can look 'em over."

Juge reached over and nudged me. "What is going on? It sounds as if you have acquired these men."

"That's what *they* think. I need—"

"Oh, if you please. It would be very amusing!"

"Amusing! You know I can't spare the time to get sidetracked. Sergeant Cahoon here has merely asked me to inspect his Marines. There's no harm in that, and will probably make them happy. But after that I must find a way to get into that frigate."

Cahoon barked and growled the Marines into order. They stared stolidly in front of themselves, but the sailors eyed me curiously. Some of them even grinned as they stood at what passed for attention among seamen. I suppressed a sigh and dismounted, walking up one short line and down the other, my hands clasped behind my back as I pretended to look them over. The soldiers seemed clean enough—Marines keep themselves in good order without any interference from sea officers, I've always found—and the sailors were sober.

"An excellent turnout, Sergeant Cahoon," I said. "I'll mention it to Captain Block."

Cahoon gave me the foot-stomping salute again. "It's grateful I am to hear it, your honor, and so I am."

Joséphine skittered and snorted as I hoisted myself aboard again, and she laid her ears back across her head, but she made no effort to nip at me. If anything, she seemed eager to get going. The skin across her withers rippled, and she shook herself as if settling her gear in place before a run.

"Right, lads," Cahoon called out. "Present . . . *harrrm!*" In a normal tone he added, "Right, me boyos, pull yer socks op."

The Marines didn't pull their socks up that I could see, but they did bring their muskets to with a snap.

"Fix . . . bay-*nets!*"

There was a great rattling of metal on metal, and some hollering and stamping that seemed to be an expected part of the procedure. The seamen drew their cutlasses and tomahawks.

"Now listen here, Sergeant Cahoon, I need to get to the *Croatoan*. Where is—"

Cahoon gave me a gap-toothed grin, pointing at his ear to indicate a temporary deafness as trumpets blared and drums roared along the line. His own drummer, a boy of maybe ten, was pounding away like a crazed monkey. A shout began far off across the valley and raced around the line and back again.

From the army's center a band of chosen men—the forlorn hopes, the half-companies of men who led assaults in expectation of promotion or forgiveness of crimes should they survive—strode out onto the field, with the single white chevrons on their sleeves seeming to glow in the darkness. Most carried muskets with bayonets fixed. Some carried ladders and grenadoes as well. A subaltern capered in front of them, waving his sword and pointing the way.

Fireballs—burning bales of oil-soaked wool—came whooshing over the walls of Jacmel. "Trebuchets," shouted Juge at my look. He swung his arm in imitation of a medieval catapult. In the light of the fireballs, groups of chosen men pelted head-down across the plain toward the forts. The defenders' small arms and artillery opened up. As men fell, their comrades snatched up their ladders and raced toward the gaps in the wall. Little trails of sparks rose toward the wall and exploded beyond them as the chosen men threw their grenadoes.

"Sergeant Cahoon," I said again, when I thought I could be heard, "tell me at once where—"

Everyone seemed to be shouting now. No one was paying attention to me. Lieutenant Treadwell bellowed something. His sergeants and Cahoon repeated the bellow, and the soldiers and Marines and sailors stepped out with their blades glittering in the light of the fireballs.

Juge drew his saber.

"Juge! We must dismount!"

Joséphine minced around and tossed her head as she fought me for the bit.

Juge cupped his hand behind his ear.

"Juge, we must advance on foot!"

He shook his head, laughing. "Draw your sword, my friend!"

I had to do it, with him watching, but hell if I was going with him. The forlorn hopes had mobbed up around a breach in the wall. A fire burned there. The subaltern I'd seen before scrambled up the rubble into the breach, a black figure against the flames, turning around and raising his hands in encouragement. A dark spray blossomed around his shoulders, and his headless corpse fumbled down the slope.

Juge urged his mount forward. Joséphine tried to follow.

"Avast there!" I sawed at the reins. "Stand and be damned!" I had to dismount—I *must* dismount—but it was all I could do to hang on.

Juge had circled back. "You have trouble with your horse, *mon ami?*"

"Yes, damn it! She won't—"

"Naughty Joséphine!" he cried. "How you shame us!" He smacked her in the flank with the flat of his sword.

Juge whooped. The Marines and sailors yelled. Joséphine shot to the fore, with me swinging my saber in a wild circle and roaring, "Whoa, dammit! Whoa!"

Men streamed through the fire-streaked dark toward the walls of

Jacmel. The pounding of boots and drums drowned out the pounding of my own heart. Joséphine sailed down the hill past the ancient fort and across the little ravine. As we crested the rise I saw the gap in the wall. In front of it a trench had been dug, and it was filled with soldiers raising their muskets. They disappeared behind a wall of smoke. Bullets whispered past my head.

Juge careened alongside me. "Woe, dammeet, woe!" he shouted merrily, as if my words were a battle cry. He spurred his horse, his saber at the point.

We plunged into the enemy's line. Juge rained down death and mayhem with his saber. The soldiers and sailors caught up with us and scattered the mulattoes, and then we were through the wall and clattering down a narrow cobblestoned street.

The prison wall rose up on our left. Beyond a head-high wall on our right glowered the ramparts of Fort Beliotte. The street ahead was filled with fleeing mulattoes. Juge cut them down as they ran. A man he missed fell to his knees before me, his hands raised in supplication. A green strand of intestine ballooned from under his vest as Joséphine planted a fore-hoof in his middle.

A man on my left tried to run me through with a sword. Something blew his face off and he fell.

A bayonet poked at me from the right. I kicked it away and yanked out my saber. I swung down at a head. The blow was pure reflex, training mixed with terror, but the saber split the skull from crown to chin.

And it got stuck. I didn't think to let go of it, and the weight on the end of the blade snatched me right out of the saddle. I hung in air, head down and face up—stars twinkled beyond my boots—and then my momentum ceased and gravity brought me crashing down square on my back. The air left my lungs, my arms and legs flopped uselessly, and I lost the saber. Joséphine and Juge thundered off without me.

I gained my knees, wheezing for breath. Treadwell and Cahoon arrived. "Good evening, sir," said Treadwell, jogging past, and then the Jamaica company and the sailors and Marines knocked me flat again as they jostled by.

Except for the groaning of the wounded and my own sobs as the air returned to my lungs, all in my immediate vicinity was quiet. I gained my feet and looked around. The mulattoes had retreated to an inner line of fortified rubble. It had caught fire in places, and in the firelight I saw men swarming over it like cockroaches on a garbage pile. There was a frantic tumult there, trumpets blaring and drums roaring and banners waving or wavering, suddenly broken up by a horrifying swirl of canister from the defenders' cannons.

As I yanked at my saber, trying to free it from the corpse's ghastly grip, an ebb tide of retreating troops sent me sprawling face-first into something hard. I felt the blow from my skull all along the length of my bones. I tried to get to my knees but only managed to turn over. Even my toenails hurt.

Like shadows from a magic lantern, men moved forward and back, tripping over me, frantically concerned with things I couldn't see. And here was Juge, leaning down from the saddle, tugging at the front of my coat.

"Get up, my friend! We regroup!"

I recognized the individual French words, but their collective meaning escaped me. My head throbbed and my stomach heaved. As soon as Juge had gotten me to my feet I fell to my knees again, puking like a poisoned dog.

Juge spoke to me in French, laughing about a mulatto graveyard and an uneasy stomach.

"I seem to have lost my ability to speak French," I said, surprised that it came out in French.

Joséphine shoved her way through to me. A pair of seamen picked me up and threw me into the saddle.

Our men had formed around us. The nice young English officer, his carefully patched coat singed and torn, pointed his men here, pushed them there, organizing a double rank of muskets across the narrow street. I wished I could remember his name.

Cahoon drew up his remaining Marines in a third rank behind the

British, with the sailors behind all. Through the smoke I saw the dim figures of infantry sweeping down the narrow street toward us.

"Prime and load!" said the Englishman. The Marine drummer boy reinforced the order with a tattoo on his drum.

The redcoats and Marines bit the ends off their cartridges, primed their pans, poured the remaining powder down their barrels, spat the balls in on top, and rammed the charges home.

"Make ready!"

The soldiers and Marines cocked their muskets.

"Pre-e-sent!"

They leveled their muskets. A mob of mulattoes loped out of the smoke, shrieking as they came.

"All ranks together," shouted the Englishman: *"Fire!"*

The mulattoes staggered as the triple rank of muskets spat flame and lead. The mulattoes' front collapsed, and the men behind them wavered.

"Now, me boyos," cried Cahoon: *"Charge!"*

With a furious yell, they flung themselves on the enemy. Juge dashed after them with a shout. Joséphine followed, ignoring the stranglehold I'd thrown around her neck.

The boys were doing pretty good until a troop of cuirassiers slammed out of a flaming side street, their steel breastplates gleaming scarlet in the hellish glow. The soldiers and Marines parried the sabers with their bayonets, but the weight and speed of the heavy cavalry was too much for them. They scattered like ninepins or simply fell under the lashing hooves and sabers, till the sailors slipped low into the fight, hacking with their cutlasses and tomahawks at the horses' hamstrings. Horses screamed and fell, throwing their riders.

The cuirassiers on foot were clumsy in their jackboots and breast-plates. The boys plied their bayonets and tomahawks on the unpro-tected legs and arms and heads.

Lights flashed in my head. I couldn't see who was who. I swayed in the saddle.

Men strained for footholds in the gore as they tore at each other. Blades glittered in the firelight. Blood misted from the sky. I saw a Marine astride a mulatto grenadier, gouging his eyes out with his thumbs. Then a cuirassier was hacking the Marine to pieces. I saw the Marine's upraised arm come off, and then most of his head.

I hauled my carbine out of its scabbard. A .69-caliber ball at thirty yards will penetrate five inches of oak. At two feet, I discovered as I shot the bastard in the back, it goes through a steel breastplate like tinsel paper.

Then things got out of hand as a fresh wave of mulatto infantry joined the fray.

"Oh, blast," said the English lieutenant as he took a bayonet through his thigh. Then he fell and our line broke. Our men and the enemy alike disappeared into the smoke.

I seemed to have fallen out of the saddle somehow. Joséphine stood over me, screaming and kicking at anyone who came near. She knocked a grenadier into the wall, his pigtail slithering in the smear the back of his head left on the stones. She lashed out with her hooves and teeth as the mulattoes streamed past us. Then she collapsed with a shriek that fair tore my heart out.

I scrabbled up the street on my hands and knees. And here came Juge, whacking left and right with his blade as he fought his way toward me.

Then he too was unhorsed. He dragged me over the blood-slick cobblestones. I tried to tell him to run for it, but speech had left me.

I was on my feet again, leaning on him while the world swayed. I took a step, and then another. My head buzzed. All around me men were shooting and shouting and falling down. Some got up again. Some didn't.

I saw a hole in the wall and stumbled through it, leaving the insane din behind. And there, outside the wall, resided a blessed peace. I leaned against the wall and sank down.

Cahoon's face swam into view. With a terse "By yer leave, sir," he bent my head back and swiped at my hairline with his sleeve. He hauled me to my feet, and we staggered a few steps before a shocking pain in my head buckled my knees.

I slumped against a pile of broken stones next to the English lieutenant. The whole world seemed on fire.

Blood dribbled into my mouth and bubbled in my nose. I sneezed and a crimson spray spattered my pantaloons. *I'll catch merry hell from that little fellow—what's his name,* I thought. *You know, the little fellow who does for me and Franklin at the farmhouse.*

"Am I dying?" I asked, but the words bumped into each other. I was annoyed to notice that my ass was damp from sitting in the mud. I didn't want anyone to think I'd shit myself.

Cahoon winked. "'Tis but a wee scratch, sir. A bit o' rag an' ye'll be right as rain." He plucked my kerchief from my sleeve and knotted it around my head.

He'd lost his hat. His hair was cropped down to stubble like an old cornfield, which struck me as comical. I couldn't recall ever having seen a Marine on duty without powdered hair before. I started to say so, but then a long red crease appeared in his scalp. He jerked upright, looking surprised, and then flopped onto his back.

Juge stood up—to my eyes he seemed to keep on standing up and up and farther up for quite some time, limned against the far-off starry night—just in time to get a musket butt across the back of the head. I tried to push him off my legs so I could get the hell away from there, but then a muddy boot swung toward me from a great distance and sparked against my nose.

Mulatto soldiers marched me and Juge down the street. I thought the Englishman must be behind us, but they had me by the elbows and I couldn't turn around to see. My head hung so heavily I could barely lift it. I fell and they dragged me till I made myself walk upright again, and I shrugged their hands away and they let go of my arms.

I saw Joséphine on her belly among the corpses, looking at me and trying to rise. She got her haunches up, but her forelegs were broken and her hind hooves skittered on the cobblestones.

"*S'il vous plaît, citoyen,*" I said to the officer in charge, noting distantly that my French had returned to me. My scabbard was still strapped to her rigging, but my sword was gone. I wiped the snivel from my face. "I implore you. May I have the loan of a pistol?"

He glanced at Joséphine and then motioned the soldiers to let me step aside. "What do you care about a horse?"

I shrugged. "She is my horse."

"We have no ammunition to spare for the stroke of mercy. However—" He drew his dirk and handed it to me.

I cradled Joséphine's head in my arms. Her breath was warm in my ear as she nuzzled my neck. I gave her two quick strokes across the throat, with the dreadful weight of finality behind them. She gazed at me in wonder, and then the light fell from her eyes.

Ten

"We are in a quandary about you fellows," said Négraud, a mulatto lieutenant with a big nose. It wasn't just a honker, it was a colossus. He squatted next to us in the courtyard of Fort Beliotte, exactly filling the only spot of morning sun. The stones where I sat were still clammy from last night's rain. "The ammunition to shoot you we cannot spare," he said, "but to let you starve distresses us. Not to mention the inconvenience of guarding you. It is a big dilemma." He scratched the black bristles on his heavy jaw. "We could bayonet you, I suppose," he said as if to himself, "but that might upset the men."

"Bon sang!" said Juge, lifting his head. "They are the delicate ones, *hein?"*

"As delicate as your fellows," snapped Négraud, and Juge's head sank back onto his knees. The lieutenant turned back to me and said, "Which is to say, not at all. The bayonet, she lacks a certain exuberance. Most of the boys prefer the manchèt for such work."

I glanced at the Englishman and Cahoon, and resented their ignorance of French. I looked Négraud in the eye. "Why not just murder us and be done with it, then?"

He looked away. "Oh, la la, this word *murder* is such a harsh one. It is more in the line of the stroke of mercy. Like your nigger friend here, we do not normally take prisoners except for the torture."

"To extract information?"

"Ho ho! No, I told you—for the torture. It eases the ill feelings."

The cannons were banging away again, like hammers in my head. The sky was dotted with brilliant clouds, so pure and clean it was near enough to make me weep for the glory of it, but the salt breeze stank of corpses. I took my bloody handkerchief away from my face. "Is there no alternative?"

"But of course, my dear friend the American!" said Négraud. "If you are rich or have friends with money, perhaps we can arrange for your welfare. The commandant has condescended to observe this bourgeois custom in such cases as yours. How about it, then—are you rich?"

"It depends on what you have to sell."

"Please, sir," whispered Sergeant Cahoon, "what's yer man sayin' there?" Ghastly pale with a filthy rag wrapped around his head, he shivered despite the heat. I was surprised to see it in a Marine.

"The dog wants a bite of our breakfast." I couldn't talk very well. My nose was flattened all over my face. I wasn't sure which was buzzing more, my head or the flies on the pool of human ooze in the corner of the little courtyard.

"No beastly idioms, please," snapped the Englishman. "Do you be a good chap and speak plainly."

Treadwell was his name. It came to me in a flash. I was pleased to remember it, but he seemed to have left his manners somewhere. A bayonet through the thigh will do that to a fellow, I thought. "He says we better find some money if we want to eat."

"But this is monstrous! Supposed to arrange for our pay till we're exchanged and extend us credit in the meanwhile. And we'll be exchanged soon enough. Tell him that."

Lieutenant Négraud nodded as I translated. "This may be true in your case, young Englishman," he said, "since Britain is at war with France. Although this unpleasantness could have been avoided had you stayed home. But hospitality," he said to me, "it goes out the window when the cupboard is bare. The empty-handed guest is not welcome, my dear friend the American."

"But you've already stolen everything we own," I said. "Our money and swords, my epaulet, my silver watch with so much engraving on it that it can't possibly be valuable to anyone but myself—everything."

He shrugged. "You still have your clothes and boots, not to mention your lives."

I translated for Treadwell.

"I shan't pay a share for the sergeant," said he. "Work is the rightful lot of the enlisted man, anyway. He should be billeted among the ranks, not with officers."

"Lieutenant Négraud," I said, "what's become of the enlisted men who were captured?"

"The private soldiers are all dead," he said flatly.

"Not a gentleman, y'see," Treadwell was saying. "Neither are you and this nigger, in any sense that matters."

"All dead?" I asked while he babbled. "Every one of them?"

Négraud pursed his lips. "Well . . . every one of them we caught, anyway."

"Mr. Treadwell, will you pipe down?" I said. "There ain't any ranks left for him to join."

"Don't be stupid. A score of my niggers surrendered, at the least. And I saw perhaps a dozen Marines and sailors withdrawing at the double-quick. Which is to put it kindly. Anyway, I shan't billet with a sergeant. One doesn't associate with his kind of fellow."

The madder I got the more my head hurt, and the more my head hurt the madder I got. "Well, his kind of fellows is all dead or scattered now," I shot back, "so shut your hawse-hole. And if you're so fucking concerned about rank, you can address me properly. Why, damn your eyes, sir! A navy lieutenant outranks an army lieutenant, as I guess you know."

"Well I do beg pardon most humbly, sir." He fell back on the hot stones, laying his arm across his eyes to hide his tears.

I turned away in disgust. "Say, listen," I said to Négraud. "I'm not really a legitimate prisoner of war anyway, and neither is the sergeant. We should be sent to the jail in Guadeloupe."

"How do you figure this? You were caught bearing arms against us."

"But our countries are not at war."

The lieutenant shrugged. "It is my opinion that in such a case you are criminals who should be executed at once. But this is a question for the big officers, *hein?* And as for your nigger friend, a picturesque ending will be his fate soon enough. The Englishman—him I do not know about."

Juge just sat, holding his head and staring at his feet.

"The point is," I said, "we are here, and if you were going to murder us you would have done so by now. We would not be bickering about our upkeep otherwise."

He tapped his nose and grinned. "You have found me out. The truth of the matter is that the commandant saw your colors last night and sent orders that you were to be captured if possible. He wishes to speak with you as soon as you have been settled comfortably."

"And if we are indeed settled comfortably, I'm sure there will be something in it for you."

"Ah well," he smiled, "all is good in the world. Come, gentlemen, I show you to your suite. The sergeant will stay here."

"No," I said. "As officers, we require a servant. He'll go where I go and eat what I eat."

Négraud shrugged. "If you can pay for his dinner, what do I care? Follow me, please, gentlemen."

Juge and I supported Treadwell between us while Cahoon wandered behind, trailing his fingers along the stones of the wall as if he were afraid of getting lost.

Négraud took us through a gate that led into the lane we'd fought in last night. The cobblestones were sticky with congealing blood. A soldier was using a shovel to scrape up toes and fingers and whatnot.

"Good day, Jean-Paul," said Négraud. "Quite the harvest, *hein?*"

"*Oui, citoyen lieutenant,*" said Jean-Paul.

Négraud indicated the goo the man was dumping into a barrel. "For the dogs and pigs," he said to me.

Joséphine had been taken away. I closed my mind to a vision of her dismembered body hanging up in some kitchen somewhere.

Négraud took us around a corner and pounded on a large iron gate. "Something nice for the gentlemen," he said to the soldier who swung the gate open. "An upstairs suite with a sea view." He held out a hand. "But stay, corporal. I take them up myself."

"Upstairs?" said I, as we passed into the central yard. Mulatto soldiers sat against the walls or slept in the dirt. A man or two looked at us without curiosity.

"Certainly, upstairs," said the lieutenant. "This floor is reserved for our own fellows. Drunkenness and other minor crimes."

I looked up. The inner walls were lined with little barred windows. Here and there a black face peered out. "I do not complain, of course," I said, "but the dungeon is more usual, is it not?"

"You cannot expect to be put in the dungeon!" he laughed. "The dungeon, he is our bomb-proof. No, no, if someone is going to catch iron from that ogre Dessalines, it will be you fellows." He swung back an ironbound door that led to a stone staircase and motioned us through, saying, "Up-up-up, my ducklings!" After we had climbed two flights of stone stairs, he led us down a corridor and opened a door with a great clanking of keys. "I trust this will serve the gentlemen," he said, with an ironic bow.

We settled Treadwell into a pile of greasy-looking straw in the corner. "It will do," I said. "Unless you have something better?"

"I regret we do not."

"Very good, then." I turned to grin at Juge, but he was helping Cahoon lie down next to Treadwell.

"Lieutenant Négraud," said Juge, "fetch a surgeon at once. These men are very bad off."

Négraud gave him an evil look around his massive hooter. "I am sure he is very busy after your little nastiness last night, but I will pass the word."

"And water. Clean water, immediately."

"Surgeon, water. Sure, sure," said Négraud as he left.

The door fell to with a clang, leaving the room in darkness except for a square of light from a small window opposite the door. As I waited for my eyes to adjust, I felt bits of plaster and small wriggling things misting down from the rafters onto my head. Dessalines' guns sounded like corn popping in the distance. I heard a shout in the street followed by a metallic rumbling.

Juge's teeth flashed in the dim light. "A round shot bounding down the street," he said. "May God in his infinite mercy see that it takes off a few legs before it comes to rest. Come, help me make our friends comfortable. And by the way, Matty, please do not call me Juge in front of the *gens du couleur*. They will discover who I am soon enough."

Even the unflappable Juge seemed startled a few hours later when a short sturdy white man with wings of gray hair poking out from under his bicorn strutted into our little cell, carrying a lantern in one hand and an enormous black bag in the other.

"Je suis le Colonel-Docteur Pepin," said the man. He swept off his bicorn in a bow and set his bag on the floor. "No time for the niceties," he continued in English. "Where is the patients? Ah yes, I see them." He jammed a pair of pince-nez onto his beak and removed the bloody handkerchief that Treadwell had used to patch himself. *"La baïonnette,* she is a nasty weapon. But then they all are nasty, *n'est-ce pas?* Yes. Hmm."

Putting his nose over the wound, he sniffed first delicately and then robustly.

"Not yet the putrefaction." He fondled the proudflesh at the edges of the puncture, gazing at Treadwell's face. "Quite warm to the touch. This hurts you, m'sieur?"

"Unbearably." Treadwell's face grew paler and the sweat stood out in beads on his forehead, but he didn't cry out or even make a face.

"Yet m'sieur must bear it," said Pepin, not unkindly. "I recommend rum or cognac, if it can be found, and if you can buy it. But, he is well enough for now. I bind the wound—*là, et là*—in her own blood and hope for the best. Later, perhaps, I amputate. There is no medicine, but between you, me and the lamppost, I think it does no good anyway. Keep the flies away, and I prescribe the *moustiquaire* as well."

THE War of Knives

Next Pepin scrubbed Sergeant Cahoon's scalp with a rag, peering into his face as he did so. "Only a graze to the scalp, which does not account for his condition." He looked into the sergeant's mouth, smelled his breath, counted his pulse. "You have the chills, eh? Dreadful pains in the head, the back, and the limbs?"

"Oh, God aye. 'Tis like the very divil poundin' on his anvil, and so it is."

"The fever is high. The bowels, they are costive?"

"What's costive, Mr. Graves?"

"He means are you seized up."

"Oh aye. 'Tis the great shame to me."

"The urine, she is scanty and albuminous?"

"What's 'yoo-reen,' sir?"

"Piss."

"Oh aye—scanty's the word, sir, and never a truer one spoken. Dunno about albu-whoosis, though."

"Like the egg white," said Pepin.

"Oh aye, 'tis that I can barely squeeze it o't, sir, when it comes a-tall. 'Twasn't always this way."

Pepin bled him, saying, "This should provide great relief." But afterwards he drew me aside, supposedly to examine my nose under the light of the little window, and said in a low voice, "He should have calomel at least, but there is none left. And you must make for him his own pallet, as far away as you can manage. I will speak to that jailer with the big nose about moving him to another cell, but I fear it is already too late."

"Too late for what?"

"Yes, poor fellow," said Pepin, as if he'd answered my question. "I will check on him again in a few days. Should the fever return after a period of recovery, let me know *tout de suite*.

"And you," he said to me in a louder voice, "in my expert opinion, have received a nasty bump on the head and a kick in the face. If you do not die, you will live. Hold still."

And with that he seized my nose and yanked it. A horrible crunching noise filled my skull, and for a moment I was blind with pain, but when I ventured to touch my nose I found that it was near about straight again.

Pepin packed up his things and settled his hat on his head. "Now, my friends, to the business. How is it you propose to pay me? I assume the jackals have stripped your pockets."

"Pay you? I thought . . ."

"You thought what? That a learned man such as I works for free?"

"But I—you're an army surgeon!"

He held up a finger. "I am the physician, not a lowly surgeon."

"My apologies, sir." There was no point in showing contempt, and perhaps harm, though I was hard-pressed to disguise it. I tugged off my left boot and fished around in the little inside pocket. I held out a small handful of gold and silver, which I hoped he would think was all I had. "You might as well have it as anybody else," I said. "Go on. Take it. Don't wait for any more, because there ain't any."

But Pepin selected only a Spanish quarter real, worth two bits American. "*Merci*. Now I am retained as the personal physician to you and your friends. Do not hesitate to call me if I am needed. *'Voir*."

"*Au revoir, monsieur le docteur,*" I said, both ashamed and relieved. "*Merci beaucoup.*"

"*Pas de quoi!* Don't mention it!" Stopping at the door, he glanced out through the Judas window and then said, as if he had just thought of it, "Besides, I may have the favor to ask of you sometime, *hein?*"

"*Moustiquaires,*" snorted Juge when the doctor had left. "Where does he think we will get mosquito nets here, when he cannot even put a clean bandage on Treadwell? Fah."

We made Treadwell and Cahoon as comfortable as we could, which wasn't very, and looked around. Aside from Treadwell's pile of straw—which was now greatly diminished, we having appropriated most of it to make a separate bed for Cahoon—by way of furniture we had a battered table, a pair of plank benches and a few empty crates. A lantern with a stub of candle in it hung from a hook in the ceiling.

"I'm surprised no one's eaten this yet," said Juge, taking down the lantern and putting the lump of tallow in his pocket. "I hide it, in case someone comes looking for it."

Behind a low door that sagged on its hinges I found an indoor seat of ease, which consisted of a rickety platform with a hole in it, laid over a stinking shaft. A sloping plank ceiling protected the user from contributions from above. That much I saw before the stench forced me to close the door again.

I dragged a couple of crates over to the window and stepped up on them. There I had a fine view of the bay and of the *Croatoan* lying hove-to between the headlands. I hoisted myself up by the bars and studied the ground below. Beside an alligator pear tree at the base of the wall, a little creek emptied into the bay. It was more of a bright green streak of scum than a creek, really, and I supposed it to be the outlet from the latrine.

I jumped down and put my hands on my stomach. My guts gurgled and my kidneys ached, but I wasn't ready to face the shit hole again. I felt horribly weary and envied Treadwell and Cahoon their filthy beds.

Juge was gazing down into the latrine. "Look," he said, "this hole leads to other apartments."

"Well, of course it does," I said. "Everybody above and below shits into it too, don't they?"

He took off his coat and rolled up his sleeves. "Watch the door," he said, and heaved on the seat. With a squeal of wood on stone, it lifted right out. He stuck his head into the shaft and peered around. *"Bien,"* he said when he came up for air. "The shaft is wide enough that one could brace oneself with the feet and shoulders and so maneuver up and down. It looks horribly damp and slimy, but cleaner than one might think. If one were to fall, however . . ." He grinned. "Later, someone will have to see what he can see."

Two soldiers in dingy homespun brought our supper, along with a bucket of dubious water and an unsigned note: *Because you so kindly*

supplied us with fresh horsemeat, we return the favor by sharing it with you.
Good appetite!

"From Lieutenant Négraud, I bet," I said, handing the note to Juge and fishing a gobbet of something out of one of the pots. From the shape of it and the hairs, I figured it was a part of a muzzle, perhaps even a nostril. Trying not to think of Joséphine, who couldn't have been the only horse killed last night, I put it in my mouth and chewed it. It tasted exactly the way you might expect a horse's nostril to taste.

"Not bad," I said. "Like stewed shoes, only not as tender. Mr. Treadwell, may I help you to some? The broth will do you good. And you, Juge?"

Juge shook his head. "Father Toussaint says to avoid meat when possible. And when I smell it roasting—feugh! It makes me ill. What is contained in this other pot?" He lifted the lid and sniffed the steam. "Ah, *navets!*"

"What's yer man sayin' there, sir?" said Cahoon.

"He says we have *navets* for dinner."

"What's 'navvies'?"

"I don't care as long as it ain't turnips. Juge, what are *navets?* I do not recall hearing the word before."

"*Les navets sont des navets,*" he said, meaning they were what they were. He shrugged as he chewed a mouthful. "A root vegetable. Some kind of a radish, I think."

But I was already staring into the pot with disgust. "Turnips, by God!" said I.

Eleven

While playing at Continental privateer as a boy, I'd considered that someday a determined enemy might capture me after a desperate action. The hayloft that served as my quarterdeck did double duty as a dungeon, where my dastardly captors threw me with sneers on their cowardly lips (or with polite regrets because of the spirit I'd shown in the face of the usual overwhelming odds, depending), leaving me there to rot on well water and cornbread hooked from the kitchen. As I ate and drank I languished in a drift of sweet-smelling hay, which to my mind was dank straw alive with vermin. And after the bread and water—the daring escape!

But it hadn't occurred to me how dull prison would be. Our primary entertainment was catching rats, which we soon discovered were a commodity of exchange. That first meal of horsemeat and turnips was the only official meal we got, but Lieutenant Négraud (and my diminishing supply of gold and silver) saw to it that we got enough to keep us alive. We suspected the guards of dipping into the pots before bringing them in, and I made the mistake of complaining to Négraud. He expressed shock, outrage, deepest concern, and then invited himself to dinner.

"My friends," he said, "it is the only way I have to satisfy myself that you receive your fair share. Now, I see you have a small store of rats. I have here the playing cards. How about a game of *vingt-et-un* or piquet?"

"I'm for that," said Treadwell. To Négraud he said, "Let's have a round of *vingt-et-un,* then, shall we?" To me he said, "Harder for him to cheat at twenty-one, I expect. If I can amuse him enough, maybe I can keep him from simply confiscating the lot, eh?"

"I guess you'll want me to translate."

"I should think not," he said. "Gaming is the universal language. But do you tip me the nod if I win too many rats once I've figured out how he's marked his cards. Watch and learn, sir, watch and learn."

I yawned. "Not this child." Gaming is one depravity at least that I never had much appetite for. "Lieutenant Négraud, I'd like to stretch my legs."

"Oh, sure, sure," he said, waving me away. "You have the run of the entire floor. Stay off the stairways and probably no one will take it amiss." He cut a king to Treadwell's three.

I asked Juge to keep an eye on things, and took myself for a stroll. There were fewer inmates than the day before, and no new ones. They were all of them black men, and eyed me with suspicion, but race was the smallest thing that separated us. Walking among them was like walking through a feedlot of doomed beeves. Except beeves don't know they're going to die, and their death serves at least some purpose.

I saw a man I recognized, an immensely tall officer of the line. "*Bonjour, monsieur le capitaine,*" says I, all chipper and good cheer. "How are you today?"

"*Sa pa gade-w,*" he replied, which was the only thing he ever said to me. I assumed it was an insult. I thought letting myself be insulted was the least I could do. I considered it a kindness, I guess.

"*'Voir,*" I said, and walked on down the corridor. Later I learned he'd only been asking me to mind my own business.

I stepped against the wall to let a pair of guards pass. They dragged a black man between them. He'd been beaten pretty well, and glared at me through swollen eyelids as they hauled him away. A welcome breeze puffed through the northern windows, and I put my face against the bars to breathe it in. But that also gave me a view down into the courtyard between the prison and Fort Beliotte. A naked black man knelt there. Soldiers forced him face down in the dirt. I jerked my face away from the window so I couldn't see what they did next. I had thought Négraud was exaggerating when he talked about the utility of prisoners, but I knew better now.

I returned to the cell in time to see Négraud gathering up his cards and chuckling over the brace of rats he'd won. Treadwell hung his head in defeat—and slipped me a wink while the lieutenant's back was turned.

General Pétion sat in an elegant carved chair behind a paper-covered desk. Behind him, the brilliant tropical daylight shone in through a pair of south-facing doors that had once been set with glass panes. They led out onto an iron-railed balcony, which would have had a view of the sea if someone hadn't put a prison in the way.

"I am sorry to say I cannot countenance your complaints," he said, showing me into a straight-backed wooden chair. Like many mulatto officers, he had attended one of the military colleges in Paris and spoke handsome French. "We are all hungry here. We are all prisoners here."

"Perhaps then we should all leave, sir," I said. "General Dessalines has promised you safe passage, has he not?"

He waved aside the notion of believing any promises made by Dessalines. "I am no more free to leave than you are, Lieutenant Graves. What would you have me do? I cannot exchange you because our countries are not at war. Dessalines will not take the town by storm, because our position is too strong; and we will not surrender because he will put all in the town to the sword, no matter what he says while we are safe and sound behind our guns and redoubts. So they must starve us out, barring the arrival of more artillery. You will starve alongside us if we do not shoot you or hang you first. I say this not to frighten you, my young friend, nor to insult you. I can see you are not afraid. You are young and have not yet learned that fear is your friend."

He walked over to the double doors of his office, looked into the corridor at the guards, and then closed the doors. He led me out onto the balcony. It looked out over the same courtyard that was visible from the prison. Beyond the courtyard's far wall was the bloody lane.

"I have forty-five hundred troops at my command—as long as I fight for Rigaud," he said, so low I could barely hear him. "My officers are rabid supporters of his cause and would not hesitate to slit my throat were I to hesitate in my conduct of our defense. Dessalines had nine thousand troops when we began: six thousand of the line and perhaps three thousand of militia. Henri Christophe has two demi-brigades. If he is up to strength, that is another six thousand men. Odds of three to one in Dessalines' favor. He needs perhaps twice as many men as he has to storm this place, I think, but he could not feed or arm them even if he had them. So I am not angry about the presence of a few British and Americans. Fear not. I will keep you and your friends alive as long as I can." He patted my shoulder. "So let us not complain anymore about the food, as long as we have some, *hein?*"

"But sir," I said, "all we had yesterday was boiled grass!"

"And many of my troops had not the fuel to boil theirs." He waggled his finger. "Let us not complain, for fear of getting something worse. Now, surely you do not wish to use your time with me to complain about the cuisine."

He had sent for me, of course, but you don't point out that kind of thing to generals. "When I was captured, sir," I said, "the soldiers stole my epaulet and my watch. The epaulet was gilt, not gold. It is of little worth, but a friend gave it to me and it has sentimental value. It is the same with my watch, a silver one with an engraving of an American sailor crushing the English tyrant's crown beneath his foot. It has my initials on it and the date, Christmas 1799. A friend gave me that, too, and I would like it back if it turns up."

He shrugged. "When one's life has been spared, Mr. Graves, one must not complain of being relieved of a few trinkets. It is the way of war. Besides, one cannot eat a watch or an epaulet. No doubt these things have changed hands many times by now. Why bother me with this?"

"Mere trinkets, as you say, sir," says I, throwing my helm over and coming around on the other tack. "What I mean to say, sir, is that when I was captured I was left four things of value."

"In addition to your boots and your life, you mean?"

I gulped. "Yes, of course." I pulled my papers from my coat pocket and held them like a hand of cards. I played the first. "This is my passport signed by Mr. Blair, the assistant United States consul at Port Républicain. You see it has been countersigned by General Dessalines."

"No doubt he signs many such documents before they are filled out, to save himself time and effort." He looked it over. "Ah, but it is written in French and English both. All to the good." He examined the French part of it before turning it over to the English side. "This man," he said, flicking at Blair's signature with a pink nail, "he calls himself assistant consul. But your Dr. Edwards in Le Cap, surely his senior, claims to be no more than a commercial agent charged with looking after American business interests in the island—if smuggling arms and ammunition in exchange for coffee and sugar can be said to be a legitimate business interest. This Blair, France does not recognize him. He is no ambassador or anything like."

"Yes, sir. And between you and me, he is what in English we call a scrub."

"The *scroob?*" he said, trying out the word. "I do not know this term."

"It means a coward and a liar, an ungentlemanly fellow."

"Ah. Him you do not like. We are in accord. And yet you wish me to trust what he says in this paper?"

"That paper, sir, is what gives me permission to travel in this island."

"This paper gives you permission to travel in those parts of the island held by the rebel Toussaint. But Toussaint, he does not hold this part of the island."

"Well, yes, but of course," I stammered, looking for a way out of my blunder. "But I accepted it in good faith, and it was not my intention to come here—into the citadel, I mean. I came entirely against my will, I assure you. My arrival was as much a surprise to me as it was to you, sir."

"And yet you were caught fighting on the field of battle—in that very street below," he said, pointing to the bloody lane.

"I was swept up in it against my wish, sir, as I said. But once I was in it, naturally I defended my life."

"And you think any common soldier would do less? And yet for them . . ." He drew a finger across his throat. Then he crooked the finger at me and I followed him back indoors.

"You make my point exactly, monsieur," I said. "I'm not a soldier, I'm a sailor. I'm no horseman. I was on my way to that ship in the bay when my horse bolted toward your lines. I fell off and spent most of the battle sitting in the mud with a headache."

"The headache? Yes, the din of battle is frightful—all that shouting and bashing of heads. And it was all your horse's fault. And yet, and yet. Ah," he said as I played my next card. "This is your credential as a lieutenant of vessels, is she not?"

It was easy enough for him to guess—*lieutenant* is the same in French, and it was wrote in large capitals among the spidery script.

He handed me back my commission and passport. "Very good," he said. "You are an officer in the United States Navy and your government thinks you have some business here. I did not suspect otherwise."

He held out his hand again. I put my third set of papers in it.

"These are my orders from Commodore Gaswell, sir. He requires me to make my way overland to this place, where I am to report to the squadron that was—that was supposed to be offshore."

"The squadron that was supposed to be blockading this port, you mean. Such a thing is illegal without a declaration of war, my young friend."

"But that's my point exactly, sir: we are not at war. Despite their outrageous treatment at the hands of Citizen Talleyrand, who demands millions of dollars merely to sit with them, our emissaries do their utmost to straighten out this unfortunate misunderstanding."

"At war, act of war—" He shrugged. "It is the tiny difference."

"But it is the great difference, General Pétion!"

"It all depends on one's perspective. The bucket does not contain a great deal of water compared to the ocean, you agree? Yet the bucket contains a great deal of water when one's head is thrust into it. As yours may soon be if you do not say something soon to convince me you are not a spy."

He had shed his bantering friendliness as you might blow out a candle. It was all I could do to keep the shaking in my legs and out of my voice.

"But I cannot be a spy, sir. I came here in uniform with my commission and orders in my pocket, not sneaking around pretending to be something I am not. I am here to find out the facts as they are, not as one might wish them to be. It is right there in my orders, sir."

He chewed his mustache, considering. "What kind of facts do you hope to find?"

"The commodore wishes to know what the situation is here. He cannot trust Dessalines or even Toussaint to tell him honestly. They want to put the best appearance on things, of course."

"For why does he wish to know?"

I gave him my best French shrug. "I can't speak for him, of course, but perhaps the president wants to know which horse to bet on."

He laughed. God, what a happy sound that was. "You have turned the tables around me. This is the American idiom, yes?"

"Yes, sir, ha ha. You have it right exactly."

"Of course his Excellency Mr. Adams wishes to know who is the stronger—not for liberty, equality and fraternity, but for the fat pockets, *hein?* I begin to believe you. But my little friend, you are so young. Tell me how it happens that you of all your commodore's officers are given this important mission."

"Because I am of mixed blood, sir."

He stared at me a moment, a skeptical smile on his lips while the word *sang-mêlée* hung in the air between us. Then he said, "I was unaware a man of color would be welcomed among your officers. In the ranks, yes. But among gentlemen? Surely they would not countenance it."

"If they knew of it, certainly. The commodore knows because he is a friend of my father, and he keeps it to himself because he is my patron."

"He keeps it to himself so he can use you for his own purposes, I think," said the general. "But, *la*—it is so fantastic it may be true. Your father loves you very much to see you have a career! Not many do as much for their natural sons."

Natural son was the polite way of saying bastard. "No, sir, he hates me. But he loved my mother." A dark pain crept into my head.

"Ah. Your mother was his slave, yet he loved her. I know this to happen, even in America."

"Yes, sir, I believe he did—but you mistake me again, if you'll pardon my saying it. She wasn't a slave." Not that I knew of, anyway. I rubbed my temples. The light from the balcony was blinding. "I express myself poorly. I am told she was a Creole woman from Louisiana. I never met her."

"Ah me! You were taken from her as a babe in arms." His voice softened. "Or perhaps she died in the childbed, *hein?*" He clucked his tongue. "Either way, it makes no difference. We men of color see things differently, having one foot in the white world and the other in the black. One day, with God's infinite justice, we shall have our boots on both their necks, *hein?*"

If that's what he thought I thought, I wasn't about to set him straight.

Again he held out his hand. "And now your last paper, if you please."

I gave it over, wishing I had read it first. "This, sir, is a letter from one of your officers, whom we captured near Cap Dame-Marie last month. It was his wish that I see it delivered safely to his wife here in Jacmel."

He glanced at the address. "To Madame Villon Deloges in the Rue Rigole-Haut? But there is . . . ah ha! Very good! You have read this letter, of course?"

A sickening lurch had overtaken me when he read the address aloud. *Rigole haut,* which I had assumed referred to a high ditch or channel, was also a pun. *Rigolo* meant odd, funny, a sham. "Of course I have not, sir," I managed. "A gentleman does not read letters not addressed to him."

"No, no, of course not. A shocking thought." He tucked the letter under his blotter. "This I will see put into the proper hands. Now we may turn our minds to more interesting matters. Tell me what you know about Citizen-General Buonaparte's coup d'état . . ."

I caught Pétion up on news from the outside world as best I could, spending what would have been a pleasant hour if I hadn't been so worried about the contents of that damn letter. As aides came and went with papers to be signed or words to be whispered in the general's ear, we sat at his desk feasting on turnips stewed with their greens and a tiny scrap of salt pork. There was also a dish of what Pétion called *polenta;* I called it cornmeal mush.

"What was it the Englishman said in his dictionary?" said Pétion, doing me the honor of spooning the last of it onto my plate. "That the oat is a grain fed to horses in England and to men in Scotland? So too it is with you Americans and your Indian corn, I think."

The coffee that we drank afterwards was mostly chicory, but I'd grown up drinking chicory and eating cornmeal mush, and was acquiring a taste for turnips. It was home-cooked fare as far as I was concerned, and I would have felt right at home if my guts hadn't been chasing themselves around my spine.

"Regard the *cigarro*," said Pétion, running a cheroot under his nose after we had finished eating. "A Spanish introduction, got from the Indians. The *cigarro* becomes quite the popular method of taking one's tobacco. But of course I forget that you would be familiar with them. It is said the Spanish colonies enjoy a great deal of commerce with the United States, despite the Spanish law."

"The *puertos habilitados* are always eager for business," I said, "especially as prices are better in the illegal ports. And even women and boys smoke cigars during the yellow fever epidemics, to keep the bad air away. It is where I picked up the habit," I added hopefully.

The thin black cigar he gave me was as fragrant as burning rope, of the kind that cause men to sniff the air in envy and women to ask who's burning garbage. With reluctance I quit smoking it halfway down, trimming off the ash with Pétion's knife.

"By your leave, sir, I would like to save the rest for later. We have no tobacco, and I know Lieutenant Treadwell craves something for his pipe."

He nodded behind a puff of smoke and waved a hand over his cedar box. "Pray take your friends each a *cigarro* with my compliments. I would entertain Mr. Treadwell but he is ill, and I would even entertain your staff officer friend if these were still revolutionary times. But as he is a nigger and I am a man of color, the situation demands other sorts of entertainment for him."

There were only five cigars in Pétion's cedar box, but he frowned when I hesitated.

"I am still commandant here," he said. "Do you think I cannot smoke every *cigarro* in the city if I choose?"

"But of course, General. Perhaps fate will allow me to return your kindness someday."

"Hospitality is an honor, not a hardship," he said, watching with muted sadness as I tucked the cigars into my pocket.

Twelve

Juge and I sat with our knees up and our backs to the wall, watching Sergeant Cahoon across the cell as he writhed in his own filth.

"For pity's sake, will someone clean him?" said Treadwell. "I simply cannot abide the stink any longer."

"That's easy for you to say," I snapped. "Your leg excuses you from duty."

"I earn my keep with the cards."

"You lost five rats last night."

"It's a controlled loss. That big-nosed nigger would just take 'em all, if I didn't keep him entertained."

"Well, try to win some firewood tonight or we'll be eating raw rat."

"The Froggies eat raw meat all the time. They call it *tartare*."

"Oh, what a lie."

"What does he say?" said Juge.

"He thinks we should clean Sergeant Cahoon."

"What do you mean by this *we?* I am a major. I outrank you. *You* must clean him."

"Since when are you a major?"

"Since Father Toussaint chose me for his staff."

"You're pretty young to be a major, aren't you?"

He shrugged, "And you are young to be a lieutenant of vessels. But there it is for all to see."

"Yes, my rank was there for all to see," I retorted, "until I lost my epaulet. But you wear a uniform that could mean anything or nothing."

Treadwell propped himself on his elbows and glared at me. "For the love of God, man, stop that bloody Frog babblin' an' tell him to jump to it. You're the rankin' officer."

"You're wrong there, chum. He says he's a major."

"Oh, don't be stupid. Niggers can't be majors."

"Can around here."

"Well, then it's damn convenient for him, isn't it? I mean, never says a word about it till some unpleasant work needs doin', and suddenly he's a bloody major."

"Being in here ain't exactly nuts in May for him neither, y'know."

"Oh, *God*." Treadwell turned his face to the wall.

Cahoon stared at me. I didn't know if he could see me or not. I didn't know if he could see anything. He vomited again, spewing out great splashes of stuff like wet coffee grounds.

I sighed. "Fine. I'll fucking clean him up. No, I tell a lie: I'll see if I can't get Dr. Pepin up here."

I went to the barred gate at the top of the stairs and kicked and hollered until a soldier opened the door at the foot of the stairs and yelled at me to shut the hell up.

"We need more water, clean rags, and Dr. Pepin," I yelled back.

"You won't get 'em," said the soldier. "So shut the fuck up before I come up there and beat you."

I rattled the bars some more. "I will not shut up! I have nothing better to do all day than to kick this door, and if you come up here without the things I ask for I will put a fist in your eye again like I did yesterday."

"I will not come up there," he said. "That man has the black vomit, I know he does. I have never had it, and I don't intend to get it now."

"Everyone in this whole prison will have it if he does not recover soon," I shot back. "And the cleaner we can keep him and the sooner Dr. Pepin gets here, the less danger for you."

From up the stairs rose the smell of the gunpowder and tobacco the guards were burning to purify the air against the bad miasmas that caused the fever.

"Oh, very well," said the guard. "I will fetch him now and beat you later."

Dr. Pepin arrived with five soldiers in tow, three of them carrying buckets of water. The other two carried a tub in which several bed sheets lay soaking in vinegar.

"Do not ask how I get this vinegar," said Pepin. "Suffice it to say you owe me a small fortune, which I trust you will repay me before long. And now for the patient."

"He's burning up," said I. "He turned yellow this morning, and he's been puking black stuff all day. Shits and pisses himself, too."

"Can't help it, sir," Cahoon muttered. It was the first coherent thing he'd said in a while.

"Ah, he is aware of his surroundings," said Pepin. He surveyed the mess around the sergeant. "You see the stale blood that has expelled from the anus? It indicates a hemorrhage in the intestinal mucus membrane. He is stuporous, yes?"

"A stupid man I well may be," said the sergeant, trying to rise, "for who else would go t' sea? But 'tisn't a man who'll say I'm the stupidest."

"*Stuporous,*" I said. "He means you're in a daze."

"Oh aye, daft is it? But 'tis fair enough I suppose." He fell asleep again.

Dr. Pepin knelt beside him. "The pulse, he is rapid yet feeble. The patient exhibits a dry brown tongue accompanied by incontinence. La, la," he clucked. "But perhaps there is hope. *Allons,*" he said, turning to one of the soldiers, "be so good as to throw that water on him."

Cahoon sat up yelling. "What the bloody fuck!"

"Ah ha!" chuckled Pepin. "There is hope indeed! *Encore une fois*—once more with the water!"

Several bucketfuls later, Cahoon was not exactly lively, but he was awake.

"'Tis yer eyes I'll be havin' for poached eggs," he muttered, adding, "I'll be murderin' yis in yer sleep when I find me strength. 'Twill be a thought for to savor, these black nights."

"Clap a stopper on it, Sergeant," I said cheerfully. "At least you're clean now, which is probably as much a relief to you as it is to us."

"And now we wrap him in a sheet soaked in the vinegar," said Pepin. "I find this works well at this stage. Sometimes two or even three patients out of ten survive this treatment."

"Survive the treatment, is it?"

"Ha ha! I misspeak, Sergeant—I mean, survive after receiving this treatment."

I was pretty sure Pepin meant that so many of his patients survived *because* of the treatment, but I didn't care to press him further.

"*C'est bien, garçons,*" said Pepin to the soldiers. "*Merci.*" He gave them each a coin, and they went away laughing.

We'd stripped Cahoon of his clothes already, he being so leaky there didn't seem any point in keeping them on him. As Pepin began swaddling him in the sheet, I said in French:

"Dr. Pepin, what are those little red bumps on his arms that look like mosquito bites?"

"They are called *petechiae*," said he. "You'll notice more of them on his chest. They often appear in concert with bilious remitting fevers, and some regard them as a sign of impending death. In my opinion, however, they are what they appear to be: mosquito bites."

"Is there a connection between them and the fever?"

"No, I think your Dr. Rush has destroyed that notion entirely. You yourself have many such bites, do you not?"

I admitted I did.

"And yet you exhibit no signs of the fever. Oh," he said, switching back to English, "speaking of mosquitoes, you must, how you say, swab up the floor or you will have clouds of them in here." And then, without changing the tone of his voice, he said, "Would you be so kind as to check if any of our friends linger in the passageway?"

I opened the door and looked out. "All clear."

"Good. I think none speaks English anyway, but it is just as well to avoid being heard altogether. Now listen very carefully. You are soon able to pay my fee in full, perhaps. Pétion must break out very soon. There is almost no food left, and he no longer can replenish his ammunition, thanks to your frigate at the mouth of the bay. We have had no more supplies since she arrives. Yet he dithers. Perhaps a nudge from your frigate—a timely bombardment, say—might help him make up his mind, *hein?* Maybe you signal this to the frigate."

"I got no way of doing that. With a set of signal flags, maybe."

"But do you sailors not send signals at night with lamps and rockets and such?"

"Sure, but they're agreed upon beforehand. You know, 'If I light a blue fire, attack the enemy to windward; if I send up a red rocket, come alongside.' That sort of thing." Not that I had any blue fires or red rockets. "There's no established code for signaling with lights."

"A pity. Such a system would be so useful. Now, as you are a sailor, I am certain you know when is the next full moon."

"Yes, sir. The eleventh."

"Exactly. This, I think, is when he intends to go."

"But wouldn't the new moon suit him better? It'll be dark then. Harder for Dessalines to see what he's up to."

"And nearly impossible for Pétion's troops to see where they are going, once they get into the woods. They do not know the terrain. No, he needs the full moon. The exact hour is a mystery to me, but I am willing to bet my life that he will break out on the eleventh. When is the moon at its highest?"

"Midnight, with a full moon. It rises at sunset and sets at dawn. It's just the opposite with the new moon."

"Mariners are walking almanacs." He settled his hat on his head and picked up his bag. "Now, you remember what I have told you, in case you think of a way to signal or if you suddenly find yourself away from this place. Today is Sunday, the second of March. You have nine days, *mon ami.*"

"Eight days," I said to Juge the next morning. "We must think of something by then, if we are to be of any use."

"Very good," he said. "Some opportunity will present itself. Or perhaps it will not. In the meantime, idleness is our enemy. I shall use the time to teach you fellows the Creole."

I looked at Treadwell. He lay on his back counting the spiders in the ceiling, or something. He'd been doing that all morning.

"Hey, Treadwell," I said, "how'd you like to learn to talk Creole?"

He propped himself on an elbow. "No. I shan't learn the nigger gibberish," said he. "It's no language, not a proper one, and not at all necessary anyway. With blacks, you point and the sergeants yell, and everyone muddles along admirably, thank you very much."

"I thought your men were Jamaican," I said. "Don't they speak English?"

"Of course they speak English, after a fashion, but that's hardly the point, is it?"

"It'll take your mind off things."

"Right." He caressed his leg. "And speakin' of takin' things off, if Pepin decides to take off the old pin, I shall be all set to beg my bread in any street in the island, once I've learnt Creole. Great lot of good that'll be. Is *that* your point, Mr. Graves? Eh?"

There were plenty of sailors with only one leg, but I guessed it was different with soldiers. I left him to his sulk. "How about you, Cahoon? Want to learn the French Creole?"

"Oh aye? The Irish and the English are plenty to be livin' together in me head as it is, sir." He tapped his temple. "'Tis six to a bed in here as it is already, thanks all the same, there."

"Suit yourself then." I switched to French. "Looks like you have a class of one, Juge. I won't bother to translate Mr. Treadwell's views on the subject, but he leads me to wonder: Toussaint himself speaks only Creole because his French is wanting, *n'est-ce pas?*"

"Father Toussaint speaks as he wishes."

"But it is said he has little French and hates to use it. Is this because he does not wish to be thought of as one who puts on airs?"

"Palé frasé pa di lespri pou sa," said Juge in Creole, and looked at me expectantly.

"Er . . . Speaking French isn't, um . . . proof of intelligence? Or wit, perhaps?"

"Bon sang! You have it exactly so. You have learned your first lesson. See how easy it will be?"

"But—and I mean no insult to General Toussaint and all—but isn't it a sort of prideful ignorance that prevents him from speaking proper French?"

He gave a look that killed the smile on my lips. "I should not put it that way, even in jest," said he. "Let us say instead that he takes joy in his own language, and if one wishes to consult with him, one must speak as he does. But he speaks French well enough, I assure you, and reads English. And Latin, too. You should hear him say the Mass! He is a great one for the church and all the saints." He crossed himself. "How he despises the maroons in the mountains who pound away on their drums, shrieking for demons to possess them as they dance and drink the night away. Of *course* the voudou brings on a trance, with the amount of rum they consume. But anyway, anything Father Toussaint misses in French, Delatte and his other white secretaries are sure to tell him."

"But of course," I said, wondering what Connor and Franklin were up to.

"Silence, classe!" said Juge, clapping his hands in exactly the way my tutor used to do when I was cutting up instead of paying attention. "Today we begin with the syntax. Once one commands this and a basic vocabulary—a great deal of which is taken directly from the French— one is well on the way to learning this simple but useful language. First, one must know that in Creole, one does not conjugate the verb. One could not if one wanted to, for the simple reason that it is not done. Why this is I do not know, so do not bother to ask. Second, one indicates the tense by placing a sort of marker before the verb."

"A marker? What's that?"

"*Asé palé,*" he said, holding a finger to his lips. "Stop talking and I shall tell you. Ready? We begin: If no marker appears, it means the phrase is cast in the simple past—or perhaps in the present. Context will tell you which. But when markers appear, they will take the forms *ap, a, pral,* or *te.* For example: *Map palé,* I am talking. *Ma palé,* I will talk. *Mpral palé,* I am going to talk. *M'te palé,* I have talked. Do you follow?"

"Yes, yes. But shouldn't I write this down?"

"No, the Creole is not a written language. Do not be foolish. *Encore,* we continue:

"The indefinite article, *yon,* precedes the noun, and the definite article, *nan,* comes after: *yon gason,* a boy; *gason nan,* the boy. One makes the plural by omitting the article: *gason,* boys. And of course the definite article changes when one speaks of something feminine: *fi a,* the girl. And *la* for things that have no gender: *elev la,* the student."

"Oh, a thousand thanks," I said.

"Ha ha! No, say *mesi anpil,*" he replied. "You will soon acquire an adequate vocabulary. In the meantime, a few stock phrases and aphorisms will get you through most situations."

"Yes, I have a collection of those already."

"No doubt the ones that sailors acquire in every port. No, I mean you must learn some local ones in order to understand the people. For instance, *Yo trené kadav la na la ri.* That is, *They dragged the corpse through the street.* This is an example of the lack of a passive voice. One never says *the corpse was dragged,* but always *they dragged the corpse.*"

"Who dragged the corpse?"

"Why, the people who drag corpses through the street, of course."

"This is a common saying?"

"Oh yes, one hears it quite often these days."

Dr. Pepin came by again in the afternoon to stroke his beard and look at Treadwell's leg. Négraud came with him because he had heard about Pepin's quaint notion of bathing Cahoon.

"Can't you just wipe him off?" he asked. "Surely this constant bathing injures the health."

"Such nonsense. You yourself could benefit from a bath," said Pepin, "you with your constant chewing of garlic."

"But chewing garlic keeps away disease," said the lieutenant.

"Yes, because it drives other people away. Speaking of which, go away while I examine my patients."

"Treadwell's leg has closed up," I said. "It's a little swollen, maybe, but it looks well enough to me."

"It looks well enough to the unlearned eye, yes," said Pepin. "But tell me, does he toss and turn at night with the delirium?"

"He talks in his sleep, sure."

"Ah me, ah me," said Pepin. "The leg is red and swollen, and hot to the touch. I should have come sooner. Why did you not alert me when I tended to the sergeant?"

"You're the doctor," I said, cross because I felt guilty. "I thought you'd see to it."

"The wound has healed on the surface only. Inside, she festers. I should have put in a thread to allow the pus an avenue of escape. M'sieur Treadwell, I am afraid I shall have to open you with my little knife."

The Englishman put up a good front, but Juge and I had to hold him down. I didn't look to see what Pepin was doing, but judging from the way Treadwell gasped and bucked, it wasn't pleasant. At last Pepin pronounced himself satisfied, and Treadwell fell asleep from exhaustion.

"I have been remiss," said Pepin. "I am sorry for the shortness of my tone earlier. But I think this operation will help. Perhaps one day by the grace of God he will walk again. And now for my other patient. Sergeant Cahoon, 'ow are you today?"

"Weak as a babbie, your honor, but I sat on the seat of ease this forenoon watch. 'Twas the world's great satisfaction to me."

"The seat of ease?" said Pepin.

"He means he used the head," I said. When Pepin still looked puzzled, I added: "The latrine, sir. The necessary. Juge and I held him steady while he walked himself over there. It was a great satisfaction for us, too, not to have to sluice him off anymore."

"Oh, God aye," said Cahoon. "'Tis the delight to me. A man's not a man that cannot be trusted with his own bowels. Who knew what pleasure could be had in the mastery of—oh Jezzus!" He clutched at his belly. "Mr. Graves, sir, 'tis touchin' cloth I am!"

Pepin had Cahoon's trousers down before I had marched him halfway to the latrine.

"And now," said Pepin, while Cahoon was busy and Juge and Treadwell had turned away to give him some privacy, "here is something I must prevail upon you to take." He slipped a piece of paper into my hand. "It is written in such a way that even the unlettered may grasp its meaning, so hide it quickly and do not look at it again until you may deliver it to General Dessalines or some other such person of authority."

And with that he plucked his pince-nez from his nose, stuffed his bicorn onto his head, picked up his bag, bid us adieu, and marched out the door.

Seamen are a prudish lot by and large, despite the stories that people tell. Etiquette demands that they avert their eyes when another man strips, for instance. I believe it comes from being so crowded together below decks. Juge, Treadwell, Sergeant Cahoon, and I were so crowded together in our little cell that before long we had few secrets from each other anymore, at least not of the kind that showed.

One morning after breakfast time, to distract myself from the fact that we'd had no breakfast, I said, "Juge, when I first met you, you wore no shirt beneath your coat."

"Yes, I find it gives me a savage look that frightens the men of color."

"Like a red Indian in full war regalia. But if you will indulge my vulgar curiosity, what I wish to know is this: How is it you have your name branded on your chest, and how did you get such a name?"

"Ah," he grinned. His shirt was open, which is what had reminded me of it, and he ran his fingers across the raised letters J-U-G-E. "It is an interesting story. I will tell it to you. Juge is not the name given me at birth, of course—it is my name of war. But as the man who christened me did not consult my mother in the matter, any more than he consulted her in the fathering of me, I did not feel obliged to keep the name when I became a man.

"But how I came to be called 'Judge' is simplicity itself. Our Lord Jesus gave me the name," he said, crossing himself, "and it came about in the following way.

"For the *J* and the *E* I claim no credit. They were my former master's initials—and mine, too, for Javier-Étienne. That was how I was called as a boy: Javier because I was born in January, and Étienne for the saint."

"Why Saint Stephen?"

"I don't know. It is innocent of meaning." He traced the *J* and the *E* with a fingertip. "His lady insisted that all their slaves be branded so, one letter on each breast. She even caused to be branded the ones like me whom she knew to be her husband's children. Yes," he said, anticipating me, "I am a *griffe*. My mother was black and my father was half white, an *affranchi*—this is an insulting term, as it supposes that freedom is granted by men and not given by God. He was too proud of his land and slaves to know it. But as in appearance I am like the true *nègre*, I trust you will not hold it against me."

"So you're a mulatto, then?"

"Mulatto! Do not call me this."

"Why? What's wrong with it?"

"What is wrong with it? It means mule, this is what is wrong with it." He wagged his hands on either side of his head to indicate ears. "Anyway, you would have liked his lady, I think. She was a great beauty and a charming hostess, much admired and sought after. She was very kind to me as I got older, if you understand me." Tenderness mingled with contempt on his face. "She even persuaded her husband to send me to the College de la Marche in Paris to be educated."

"The College de la Marche?" says I. "You must be older than you look."

"Yes, and so? I have twenty-four years, but this is not the point. The point . . ." He leaned his head back and stared at nothing.

"Fine, that's the *J* and the *E*. But what about the *U* and the *G* in between?"

"I arrive at that shortly." The smile had gone. "My older brother Joseph-Eugène was my lady's pastry chef. On the evening that I returned from France, he was so excited to see me that he burned the shells for the pear tarts. They were her favorite. She flew into a wrath that she could not contain. And so she had Joseph-Eugène thrown into the still-glowing oven. You understand now why I say I cannot abide the smell of roasting meat."

"But what did you do?"

"What *could* I do? I was a slave. Slaves died all the time, in worse ways than did my brother. And it was a remote habitation. They knew about the revolution, of course, and Dutty Boukman's uprising."

"Who's Boukman?"

"Who is Boukman? He was the houngan whose ceremony in the Alligator Wood set fire to the spirit. The French cut off his head, and now he is a loa. This was in 1791. Surely you know of it."

"No, I confess not."

He shook his head, as if in sorrow at my ignorance. "Stories reached us, of course, even way off in the mountains as we were, but it was like a distant cry. We did not heed it. I brought further news when I returned from Paris. I landed in Le Cap and saw terrible things as I made my way home, but no one believed me. I did not wish to believe it myself. I wished to hide away, but once a man is infected with revolution, he cannot be cured. And then one day, all was in turmoil. The fields were burning, and out of the flames came black men with knives in their hands, naked like savages and seeking revenge. My master and lady begged me to place them and their children under my protection. I was the overseer by then, having my letters and of course being my lady's favorite. I swore on the Holy Bible that I would let no harm come to them at the hands of the mob. This promise I kept to the letter. I took their money into safekeeping and put their children on a boat to

THE WAR OF KNIVES

France. Whether they arrived safely I never discovered."

"And your master and lady?"

"I assumed control of the entire plantation, such of it as was left. My lady I put to work as my chef of cuisine, she who had never dirtied her fingers in her life. And then one evening she burned the tarts."

"Juge, tell me you didn't—"

"But I did, my friend, I did. Then I stoked the coals with the same fireplace poker that I had used to dash out her husband's brains, and with the red-hot tip I burned the *U* and the *G* into my chest. As I say, it was at the command of Jesus Christ." Again he crossed himself. "The money I gave to the other slaves and told them to do as they wished. Then I took my master's boots and sword, and rode off in search of Father Toussaint. And *bon sang!* How my lady's screams rang in my head as I rode."

Thirteen

One morning a pair of grenadiers came and slapped a pair of darbies on my wrists. I asked where we were going. "Colonel Cravache," said the uglier one. I asked who that was. "You'll find out," he said. He jerked a thumb over his shoulder. "March."

They took me down the stairs and through the yard. Lieutenant Négraud shook his head and looked away as we tramped out the gate. The grenadiers shoved me along the street to Fort Beliotte. The usual hullabaloo was going on down by the walls—cannons barking, muskets popping, men bellowing or screaming, depending. It was a normal day. It was a beautiful day, too, as usual—or it was overhead, anyway, and probably up in the hills and out on the bay. I didn't much like how the day in the citadel was shaping up. It was hot in the fort, hot even for San Domingo, but a cold draft ran up my coattails as we turned down a narrow stairway to the basement. There we passed through a low doorway, above which a guttering torch shone on the words "Adjutant's Office" painted in brown paint. The office, if it can be called that, was a dim, stinking room furnished with a rough table, some stout chairs and a leather-padded sawhorse streaked with dried blood. The table, chairs, and sawhorse were equipped with straps and ringbolts. A collection of manacles and whips dangled from the stone walls.

A narrow-headed colonel with skin the color of a cockroach stood by the sawhorse and watched the grenadiers strap me to a chair. They did it without being told. It was all in a day's work to them. When they were done the colonel bent over me to test the straps. His breath stank of rancid cheese. His mustache looked like a nest of spiders had crawled under his nose and died. "Go," he said to the soldiers. Then he walked around the room, studying me from various angles as if there was something interesting about me.

"I am called Cravache, the whip." He folded his arms and leaned against the sawhorse. "Who sent you here?"

"Commodore Gaswell, the commander of my squadron."

"For why?"

"To assess the military situation here and to write a report about it. I have already discussed this with General Pétion."

"You are a sailor. Why did you not come by sea under a flag of truce?"

"I did not come under a flag of truce because we are not at war. I came by land because it was faster. God's truth, Colonel," I said. "I never intended to come to Jacmel. I was on my way to Cap Maréchaux when my horse bolted in the excitement."

"It is convenient to blame this on a horse."

"Nonetheless, Colonel, it is true."

"Liar. No one storms a city by accident."

I shrugged. "I just got caught up in it."

"We are all just caught up in it. That is the nature of war. Where did you learn your French?"

"Baltimore."

"Who taught you?"

"A refugee from Le Cap."

"Why did you hire him?"

"I didn't. My brother hired him."

"You split hairs. For why was he hired?"

"My father wanted me to learn French."

"For why?"

"My mother spoke French."

"Why did she not teach you?"

"She died when I was born."

"She was French?"

"Yes."

"From where?"

"The Louisiana country."

"So she was not truly French. She was Creole."

"So I am told."

"You do not know whether your mother was French or Creole?"

"I told you, I never knew her."

He slapped me across the face, once, twice and again till my eyes stung. He smiled. "That is to remind you to keep a civil tongue in your head. Now, why this refugee?"

"He was cheap."

I got slapped again for that.

"This man whom you call *cheap*, he was a former planter?"

"I think so."

Cravache pressed his lips together and blew air between them. "He *thinks* so." He looked up at the ceiling. "You see why we fight? A gentleman reduced to teaching beautiful French to snotty boys. '*Un, deux, trois.* I have a yellow pencil. Is this a yellow pencil? Yes, it is a yellow pencil.' Bah. Now tell me what is so important about this." He tapped me on the nose with Villon's letter.

"I don't know, sir. I haven't read it."

He slapped me three times again. I tasted blood. "Not *sir*," he said. "You must call me *citizen*. I do not care for your bourgeois niceties. Now, we commence again. Why are you here?"

He was good at his job, was Colonel Cravache. His earlier questioning was patty-cake compared to the games we played when he finally presented me with my set of watercolor sketches.

Somebody tugged at my arm. "Where's Juge?" said I. My face seemed to be glued to the floor with blood.

"Extraordinary," drawled Treadwell. "Could've sworn he was here. No? My mistake." He put his arm across his eyes and pretended to sleep.

"Himself was took by a couple o' sojers," said Cahoon as I peeled my face off the floor and he helped me sit up. "Are ya a-tall well, sir?

Yer a sight for the ages, there, and so ya are." He sopped my face with a filthy rag. It made me see lightning, but he did it so tender I near about wept.

"A couple of soldiers took him where? When?"

"Didn't say, sir, not that I'd be understandin' if they did. 'Twasn't but half an hour ago, when they brought ya in an' dropped ya on the floor there. Brave grenadiers they was," he said darkly, "them with their great hams for fists an' their bullyin' ways."

I couldn't remember anything between the watercolors and waking up there on the floor, although from the rawness of my throat I guessed I must've done some screaming. I hoped to Christ they hadn't taken Juge away because of something I'd said. But that was my worry, not the sergeant's. I asked him how he did.

"'Tis the world's great wonder how the body heals, sir. I even took meself to the head while you were gone."

"I'm obliged to hear it."

"The board's wobbly, sir. A man might fall to his doom and death, and such a one as no one bears thinkin' about."

Talking to him was like talking to a three-year-old who was proud he hadn't shit himself all day. I ignored his prattle while I tried to think of a way to make myself scarce. I'd gotten off lightly with Cravache, I was sure of it. I hated to think of what was happening to Juge while Cahoon nattered on about the state of his bowels and Treadwell sulked in his bed. And well they might, too—no one was savoring the thought of murdering *them* slowly.

Every inch of me ached, and I believed Cravache had broken my nose again. But I was damned if I was going to let Dr. Pepin set it for me, not after the last time. I straightened it myself—and it was a damn good thing I sat down before I did it, too.

I looked at Cahoon blithering and Treadwell pouting, and decided I'd had enough of them both. Stranding Cahoon in the middle of a sentence, I took myself for a walk along the corridor, stopping on the far side of the prison to look out the window of an empty cell toward the courtyard under Pétion's balcony. A group of soldiers had staked out a chubby white man face down on the ground and were painting crimson stripes across his naked back and buttocks with switches cut from the lemon tree in the corner. I turned my face away. My heart felt colder than a Labrador clam as I continued down the corridor.

I tried the stairwell door out of habit, and to my surprise it opened. There was no point in going down, where the first turnkey I met would just send me back to my cell if he didn't knock me down first. I went up.

The door at the top of the stairs had come off its hinges. It was propped up against the wall, and was fuzzy with grime and cobwebs, as if no one had thought about it in years. Several sets of footprints led away from it along the dusty floor. Only a few footprints came back out. Daylight glimmered beyond the turning of the corridor. I felt a puff of cool breeze on my face. I could still hear the man screaming in the courtyard below, but the sound was muffled by walls and distance, and I didn't want to think about him anymore. I trod lightly along the corridor as if in a church, ignoring the empty cells on the right and the narrow windows on the left, and looked around the corner.

Shafts of sunlight streamed through holes where the wall faced the far left of Toussaint's lines. I stuck my head and shoulders out the biggest hole and looked down into the trench that we had blundered through on the night we were captured. Soldiers hunkered in it, obviously bored despite the occasional musket balls kicking up the dirt. It occurred to me that if I had a rope I might shinny down—right spang among the soldiers, who might not take it too friendly. But I didn't have a rope anyway.

I continued along toward the seaward side. The cornerstones at the turning had been smashed in and the ceiling had come down. I climbed up the broken stones to the roof.

The prison had been built to keep people in, not out, and there were neither battlements nor guards on its pitched roof. It would have been a dangerous as well as an uncomfortably hot place to be posted, anyway—the heat radiating off the slates would roast a man in about an hour, I guessed, if the sun didn't boil his brains first.

A slate skittered out from under my foot as I crawled to the peak. I held my breath at the noise it made as it shattered on the stones four stories below.

A soldier on the parapet of Fort Beliotte looked in my direction. I waved, and he waved back.

I was surprised to see that the sun hadn't yet reached the zenith— the interview with Cravache seemed like something that had happened to someone else and long ago. On my left I could see the *Croatoan* working her way to windward on her usual patrol route across the mouth of the bay. To my right I had an excellent view of Pétion's forts and redoubts and Toussaint's lines beyond them. I inventoried Pétion's guns out of professional curiosity. He had mostly four- and eight-pounder fieldpieces with maybe half a dozen twelves in the main fort, all of them facing toward Toussaint's trenches. Not one gun that I could see covered the seaward approach.

A sergeant joined the soldier on the parapet. I waved at him, too, but he didn't wave back.

As the *Croatoan* came about to make her leeward leg to the southwest, a string of bunting broke out on her far side. Her shivering main topsail masked the flags until she braced her yards round, but as she settled on her new course I could see them just as plain.

Make your number, they read.

And there, due south and close-hauled on the larboard tack as she made her easting to clear Cap Jacmel, was a fourteen-gun schooner with an old-fashioned raised quarterdeck. I'd have recognized her at once even without the familiar three-flag number fluttering at her forepeak. It was about all I could do not to blubber at the sight of the *Rattle-Snake.*

I glanced at the sun again. Nearly eight bells in the forenoon watch, when Peter Wickett and John Rogers, the sailing master, would shoot the sun with their sextants and Peter would declare it to be noon, when today would officially commence by sea reckoning. And after the declaration had been duly entered in the duty log along with various remarks about the bearing and distance of landmarks to pinpoint the schooner's position at precisely one point on the globe and no other, the sun would continue in its course across the sky, the half-hour glass in the binnacle would be turned, the watch would change, and the schooner's carefully plotted position would be left forever behind her as an unmarked spot on the unmarkable sea.

But the people, now—there probably weren't three hands in fifty who'd give two shits to know where the schooner was or where she was going until she got there. Of infinitely more importance to them would be that dinner was on its way. And afterwards Bosun Klemso would pipe *All hands to splice the mainbrace* while Corporal Haversham's Marines stood watch over the serving out of the grog and all was right in the world.

I had a chest full of clean clothes over there, and all the whiskey and tobacco and fresh air a man could want, and friends, and a berth that, while it tended to be dampish in any kind of a sea, had sheets and blankets that Ambrose aired out whenever the weather permitted. Pinched and crowded though she was, *Rattle-Snake* was a regular floating palace compared to the prison of Jacmel. As suddenly as my joy had come—it was joy, I decided—it upped anchor and slipped away, leaving me floundering in a whirlpool of self-pity.

A musket ball whined past my head. It wasn't near enough to have actually been aimed at me, but the next one might be. The sergeant handed a smoking musket to the soldier, who handed him a fresh one.

I scooted down the roof to the hole, scampered down the pile of rubble, and continued along the corridor on the seaward side. I reckoned I should be grateful to the sergeant, for the brief excitement had cheered me considerable, enough anyway that I noticed that the air and light let in by the broken wall made the cells there almost pleasant. I poked my head into the unlocked ones and peeped through the Judas windows into the locked ones. There was nobody in any of the cells I looked into, just some gooey paint pots and scraps of old furniture and such. Since the mulattoes seemed to be in the habit of doing in most of their guests, I figured they used that floor for storage. I looked for a rope, but found nothing sturdier than some bits of spunyarn and other small stuff.

I came to the last cell before the stairwell and glanced through the Judas window. I glanced in only because it was the last cell, and my seaman's sense of tidiness demanded that I look in every one of them. But a remarkable sight met my eyes: A four-poster bed had been set up in there. Through the mosquito netting that draped it I saw a white man reclining on a pile of pillows, his face hidden behind a writing desk propped on his knees. He was dressed only in his shirt with his legs spread wide, giving Charlie and the boys some air.

Across a chair beside the bed lay a black suit of clothes, and on the wall above it hung a black cloak, a broad-brimmed black hat, and a gentleman's small-sword with a steel hilt.

The Parson, I thought, pulling my face away from the window in alarm. But then I drew close again and peeked in from another angle to get a better look at something I'd seen out of the corner of my eye.

At a basin beneath the window stood Franklin, washing out a pair of socks.

They'd done for Juge better than they had for me. His head looked like a rotten pumpkin. He grinned when I knelt beside him. It was a fearsome grin, with raw gaps where some of his teeth had been yanked out, but he laughed at the look on my face. *"Bon sang!"* he spat. "Someday I will feed that bastard his balls! You will see."

"We must get out of here, *mon ami*. They will kill you."

"Oh no, I think not. They will let me rest a few days, then again with the beating and the tooth-pulling. I have many teeth. They will not let me spoil the fun by dying."

"I go tonight."

The smile faded. "How?"

"The cannonade has left a large hole in the wall upstairs. No guards will be able to see me over there after dark, and there is no one on the seaward side. I will find a way down. When I have found it, I will come back and show you the way."

He shook his head. The movement tore a groan out of him that I felt in my bones. "No, I cannot move. I have really stepped in the shit this time." He giggled. "And so should you, to share my misery! You should climb down the latrine instead of the wall."

"I think the footing will be better outdoors. I shall make like the fly, crawling on a wall."

He put his hand on mine. His grip was weak, and the skin was dry and cold. "Take care you do not fall, Matty. The noise will attract the guards."

"Bon sang!" I laughed, wondering who we were trying to cheer up, him or me. "What do I care if I make a noise? The fall will probably kill me."

"What do I care if you fall?" He took his hand away. "I only worry that the guards will be angry with me and the sergeant."

After washing his face as best I could, I bandaged his head with his shirt and went down the corridor to kick on the gate.

"Stop that!" called Négraud. "It is the heat of the day. We try to sleep down here."

"We need Dr. Pepin right away!"

"This is too bad!" He said something to one of the turnkeys, and then they both laughed. "Today he has a more pressing engagement!"

"He will be very angry with you, Lieutenant Négraud!"

"No, not he. He's gone to wait upon the adjutant. Do you think you're more important than the adjutant?"

"When will he be back?"

"Oh, he'll be around. And around and around, sometimes up, sometimes down."

Again he laughed. I guessed if Pepin had business with Colonel Cravache, the joke probably wasn't very funny.

"Will you tell him when you see him?"

"Yes, yes."

"You promise this?"

"Yes, I promise. Now, Monsieur Graves, will you shut up like the good fellow?"

"Yes, of course, Lieutenant Négraud. A thousand thanks."

I went back to the cell and climbed up the stack of crates to look out the window. The *Rattle-Snake* had come up into the wind and backed her fore-topsail. "Juge," I said, "Dr. Pepin is busy with that cunt Cravache right now, but he will be along later. Négraud has promised this."

"It is of no matter," said he, but so quietly that it scared me.

I jumped down from the crates and found his coat, folding it up and slipping it under his head for a pillow. "Is it better so?"

He muttered something I couldn't catch, and reached for my hand. "I die, or I live," he said. "This is up to God, not to you or me. I am content."

I folded his hands across his breast and climbed up onto the crates again, scrubbing my face with my filthy coat sleeve. Juge would laugh if he knew I would weep for him, and dog me if I'd let Treadwell see me with slobber on my face.

The *Croatoan* and the *Rattle-Snake* were hove-to. I recognized Peter Wickett—no other officer in the squadron was that tall and skinny— in the stern sheets of *Rattle-Snake*'s gig, going over to have a confab aboard the frigate and probably stay for dinner.

I stepped down again and knelt beside my friend. He had fallen asleep, but at least he wasn't dead. I checked.

"Don't go anywhere, now," I said to Treadwell, just to see if I could hurt his feelings. "Sergeant Cahoon, come with me."

We returned with our arms laden with the paint pots I'd seen up-stairs, along with some string, a few sticks, and a paintbrush that with a little work I figured could be brought into service.

"Fetch over one of them sheets we wrapped you in," I told the sergeant. "Fold her in half and we'll lash one of these here sticks athwart each end."

"What *now?*" said Treadwell.

"I calculate on letting someone know we're here, Lieutenant."

"Toussaint knows we're here. Fat lot he cares."

"I ain't talking about Toussaint. He's got his own troubles."

Despite himself, the Englishman raised up on an elbow to watch as I smeared paint on our improvised banner. "And what's that supposed to be?"

I'd painted a large outline of an *S* with a small *Y* at one end and a series of decreasing circles at the other. I began filling in the *S* with little *X*'s. "A rattler, Mr. Treadwell. What's it look like?"

"Looks exactly like shit, is what it looks like."

Well, I had asked him what he thought, hadn't I? But I didn't give a damn what he thought, and I answered mild: "It's the right color, sure enough. And them bits around the edges, that really is shit. Now: Sergeant, I ain't tall enough to reach out the window from the crates. You must hoist me up while I lash this to the bars."

"I say, might let it dry first. You'll smear it."

"No time, Treadwell. Somebody might come afore then."

Despite having been a near goner the day before, Cahoon was as steady as an oak stump when I knelt on his shoulders. He straightened up as easy as if I was a kid on his back.

I lashed a double strand of line around one end of the top stick, ran the line through the bars and lashed it to the other end of the stick.

"It'll flap around in the breeze and get all mussed," said Treadwell. "Then where's your pretty painting, eh?"

"Dog me if it ain't so, Treadwell—you're right. Gimme your shoes."

His smirk faded. "My shoes?"

"You heard me. Give me your shoes, unless you got a better idea."

"I shan't give 'em to you."

I jumped down from Cahoon's shoulders. "Sergeant, take his shoes."

"Aye aye, sir. You heard himself, Mr. Treadwell. I'm after havin' them brogans, and no arguin' if ya please."

"But—but Mr. Graves, they're my *shoes!*"

"You won't be needing 'em," I said brutally. "Thank you, Sergeant. Lash 'em on good and tight."

"'Tis the great pity, sir, as I'm no sailor that can tie the pretty knots."

I did it myself and got back on his shoulders, paying the banner shoes-first out the window, handsomely so as not to smear the paint. When I was sure it would lie straight and not flap around, I got down again and wiped my hands on my front.

"Very good, Sergeant. Drop the paint and the leftover stuff down the head and no one's the wiser."

"Yes," drawled Treadwell, "surely no one will notice the paint all over your weskit."

I looked down at my vest. "Well, I am pretty splattered up," I said, "but it blends right in with the dried blood."

"And what now?"

"And what now, Lieutenant, is when my shipmates in the *Rattle-Snake* see that banner, they'll know I'm here."

"Is it your ship is out there, sir?" said Cahoon.

"Hell yes, and so's yours. Don't you ever look out the scuttle?"

"The old *Croatoan*, sir?" He ran to the window and hoisted himself up. "Oh aye, so it is herself, sir! Did you never see such a fine sight?"

"Right, then," said Treadwell. "Someone might see your banner, and he might mention it to some officer, who might deign to look at it, and then what? 'Well, bugger me with a corncob iffen it ain't ol' Mr. Graves up there!' How the bloody hell will they know it's you?"

"How they'll know it's me, Mr. Treadwell, is before I left the *Rattle-Snake* the captain said if I was ever in trouble I was to signal him somehow. I guess he'll know it's me the minute he sees it."

"Then what? Will they fetch a boat? Do think, Mr. Graves? Eh?"

"What the fuck's gotten into you?"

He threw his sheet aside and sat up, but that's as far as he got. He clutched his leg and panted. "You're getting ready to pull out and leave me here. I was abandoned once before, you know. Don't think I don't know the signs. Two years it took me to get this far." He thrust a pair of fingers at me. "Two years! All for nothing! Nothing but to die in a rotten jail."

I looked at Cahoon, who pretended he didn't see me looking at him. I looked at Treadwell's leg. "What am I supposed to do? I can't carry you."

"The sergeant can."

"No, he can't. And he can't come with me, neither. He's woozy yet. He'll fall."

"God!" Tears welled in his eyes. "Just give me a fortnight. Ten days, even. My leg will be better by then, I swear it."

I didn't know which I hated more, his tears or my terror. "We ain't got ten days."

"A few days, then."

"I'll think on it."

The sound of marching boots came down the corridor.

"Oh, for God's sake, shut up," said Treadwell. "Just . . . Please, just shut up." He drew the sheet over his face and blew his nose on it.

Négraud thrust open the door. He jerked his thumb over his shoulder at the pair of grenadiers behind him and said, "My little friend the American, these fellows have come for you. Be a good fellow and hop along, *hein?*"

Thirteen

Ugly and Uglier weren't the same lads who'd taken me to see Colonel Cravache, but they could've been their twins. They took me around Fort Beliotte to a side entrance, rather than through the courtyard under Pétion's window. I was glad to go the long way around, for beyond the courtyard wall I could hear unearthly howls and roars of laughter. We strode smartly up the broad stairs and into Pétion's office. One of the grenadiers slapped my hat off my head, and we came to attention.

"You men are dismissed," said Pétion, looking up from the mass of papers on his desk. He took the cigar out of his mouth. "Stand easy, Mr. Graves. I trust I find you well."

"Just a broken nose and some bruises, sir."

"Good." He indicated that I should sit in the same hard wooden chair as before.

"I'll mend soon enough, sir, but it isn't me I'm worried about. My friends need Dr. Pepin right away. I implore you. One has a broken head, and the other's leg does poorly. You may remember he was stabbed with a bayonet."

He tut-tutted—not too convincingly, I thought. "I am afraid the doctor is unavailable," he said. "Perhaps one of his assistants can help you later. Now, as to the matter at hand: The presence of you and your friends, as you call them, is most inconvenient and embarrassing. Will you have a *cigarro?*" He snapped open the lid of his cedar box.

"Yes, a thousand thanks." I selected one of the larger, but not the largest, of the half-smoked stubs and lit it at the lamp.

"Most inconvenient and embarrassing, you and this Englishman."

"Yes, sir. He is in a bad way. His leg—"

"Yes, yes. If I kill you or him, Lieutenant Graves, the other will bear the tale to the world. And if I kill you both, your governments may perhaps ask unanswerable questions, once this unfortunate quasi-war is over. Someone will talk. It is always this way." He puffed at his cigar. "Lieutenant Treadwell should have been exchanged, but I am told he is too ill to travel."

Here was the answer to one problem, at least. "Pretty soon he'll be too dead to travel, General, because he despairs. Exchanging him would save his life."

"Hmm? Yes, I shall look into the matter. But you will let me finish, if you please. You, Mr. Graves, have no business here at all. You should have been sent away long ago, and would have been except Colonel Cravache saw enemies in every doorway. I despised him for it, I admit. And I like you. And one hates a bureaucrat, is it not so? It is entirely natural to harbor such feelings, I think. Come, you must have a glass of Cognac to go with your *cigarro*."

It was good brandy, real French stuff. Down in the courtyard the screams stopped as if they'd been cut off with a knife. The locusts began chirring again in the cracks in the walls, the brandy did its magic, and just like that it was a peaceful afternoon.

"Your friend Juge," Pétion continued, "would have been disposed of immediately, except I suspect even yet that he may prove useful. He really ought not to have carved his name on his chest like some wild nigger right out of the African forest. I might not have known him, otherwise." He leaned back, blowing smoke.

The brandy and tobacco made me lightheaded, as if I had drifted out of myself.

"But forgive me," said Pétion, "you spoke of needing a surgeon. Come, I have a little surprise for you. You will find it elucidating, I think. Elucidation is a good thing, is it not?" He ushered me toward the balcony, catching my arm as I wobbled. "After you my dear sir, I beg."

Out on the balcony I swigged down the rest of my brandy, took a nonchalant puff on my cigar, and looked down. I choked on the smoke.

I was prepared for a pile of naked men pinned together with bayonets. I was prepared for the abattoir that follows a session with the cane knives. But I wasn't prepared for Pétion's little surprise.

"You should not have shown me that letter, Mr. Graves. It left too many questions in my mind. And when a question presents itself to me, I cannot rest until I have answered it. Now look!"

I peered again at the naked remains of Dr. Pepin. His arms and legs had been broken into lengths convenient for wrapping him around the rim of a wagon wheel. The sun had swollen his tongue and blackened his lips into an obscene leer, and his ruined eyes stared unseeingly into the sky. He had been flogged first, fore and aft, and a mass of flies crawled over the gory stripes on his body.

"*C'est horrible,*" I whispered, ashamed that my first thought was gratitude.

"Better he than you, *hein?*" said Pétion, reading my thoughts exactly.

I braced my shoulders and put a sneer on my face. "*Tant pis! Que le diable l'emporte!*"

"Yes, to hell with him," agreed Pétion. "We caught him trying to pass through our lines."

"Perhaps, sir, he was just trying to get some medicine. You know when any two armies face each other for any length of time, there is considerable trade for necessaries."

"Alas, no. He merely said he was sick of war and wanted to go home. The unfortunate presence of certain documents sewn into the lining of his coat made this excuse impossible to entertain." He leaned on the rail, looking down at Pepin. "But so much the better, *hein?* Now you are free from the worry of when you will be caught. Now you have only to worry about what I shall do with you."

"Do with me, sir? What do you mean?"

"I mean spies are usually hanged, is it not so? The honor of the firing squad is not for them."

"I'm no spy, sir. I told you how I came to be here."

"Ah, but I have received another story from two men who know you. Their accounts arrived independently, though nearly simultaneously. They corroborate each other. They both tell me your real reason for being here. And with the letter you brought, I can have no doubt that what your friends say is true."

"Who are they and what do they say?"

"Later, perhaps, I will present you with the evidence. I am under no obligation to do so, you understand. Under French law a man is guilty until proven otherwise, and your guilt is proved to my satisfaction. Although, I shall add, it is proved to my sorrow as well."

"But—but I have no idea what's in that letter!"

"What counts is that you brought it here. But let that not worry you at present. You will live a while longer. Come along, now."

With Ugly and Uglier clearing the way, Pétion and I marched through the front gate and along the edge of the city's main street, passing between Fort Beliotte and the blockhouse and on toward the forward defenses. Here, on the high ground above the battle plain, lay hidden redoubts packed with men and guns.

I could see how misconceived it had been to try to take the fortress by storm without sapping toward it first. The blockhouse standing before Fort Beliotte and the other blockhouse on the left, across the ravine through which the River of Orange Trees flowed, provided the crossfire that had punched holes in the waves of Negro infantry advancing across the open ground. Pétion's men had lain in wait here in these trenches and redoubts, out of sight and out of the line of fire, until Dessalines' brigades had marched within pistol shot. Then the mulattoes had stopped the black soldiers with a fury of grape and musket balls. The bodies lay out there yet, reduced to bones by the vultures that lurched and hissed among them.

But it was equally clear that Toussaint, with his greater numbers, would slaughter the mulatto army if he could catch it in the open—which Captain Block could bring about if he chose. I tucked that thought away as Pétion stopped before a pit sunk behind an earthen breastwork.

"Here is what I have brought you to see," he said.

I had been mistaken to think he had no artillery but light fieldpieces. A pair of huge mortars squatted in the pit.

"Ah, I see the delight in your eyes," said Pétion, although my expression hadn't changed that I was aware of. "As a military man, you will find this procedure of great interest. Know you anything of mortars?"

"A little, sir." I eyed a group of black men, naked but for their chains, who huddled together to one side of the battery. Beyond them a group in remnants of uniforms clanked with hammer and chisel at something I couldn't see.

"Captain!" cried Pétion, as a scabby white man in a filthy white uniform approached. *"Le capitaine Fontenot, n'est-ce pas?"*

"Oui, mon général, it is I, loyal Fontenot, busy as always!"

Fontenot's clothes were sun-bleached homespun rather than the white Bourbon uniform, but the sight among the blue coats and red vests of the revolution was jarring. I guessed that, like Treadwell, he had been marooned years ago and had found it necessary to change masters. He grinned like a monkey on a leash as he swept off his faded bicorn and said, "How may I serve your Excellency?"

"Explain for my guest, please, what you do here."

"Well, m'sieur . . ." Fontenot licked his lips, not meeting my eye.

"Forgive me," said Pétion. "Where are my manners? Captain Fontenot, this is Monsieur Graves, an American lieutenant of vessels. I have no doubt he shares your interest in gunnery. Now go on, loyal Fontenot! Explain everything there is to know about these infernal machines of yours."

"Ah yes! Well. These mortars are probably the only bronze pieces in the entire island, Monsieur Graves. By themselves—aside from their mounts, you will understand—they weigh an astonishing four thousand one hundred and thirty-five kilograms apiece."

"Astonishing indeed," I murmured, calculating in my head. That was eighty-one hundredweight and a bit over, nearly twice the weight of one of our long twenty-fours.

Fontenot hooked his thumbs in his lapels. "They are in caliber three hundred and thirty-two millimeters and a fraction."

"A fraction? Why the odd size?"

"Because it is thirteen English inches, to be exact." He grinned. "We stole them from his Britannic Majesty, you understand."

"That must make finding shot for them difficult."

"Not shot, shells." He held up a finger, like a schoolmaster. "But we stole those, too, so we're content. Each projectile weighs eighty-seven and half kilograms. That's a hundred and ninety-three pounds, by the English system."

"Yes, yes," broke in Pétion. "We are conversant with mathematics. And they require how much powder?"

"As much as thirty-two pounds," said Fontenot, abandoning the French system of measurement, "which, at a fixed elevation of forty-five degrees, gives us a maximum range of forty-two hundred yards."

"Two miles and a third," I said.

"And a little over, yes, but that is academic for now. At this range we use much less powder."

"I am glad to hear it," said Pétion. "You will understand, Monsieur Graves, why we have been reluctant to fire these fellows before. But an amusing use for them has been brought to my attention. Proceed if you please, loyal Fontenot."

"*C'est bien, mon général.*"

Fontenot's crew poured powder into the mortars' gaping maws, first from kilogram bags, then from smaller bags, and then a few ladles from a keg. Fontenot added a final pinch to each.

"Just for luck, really," he said, patting off his hands. "Otherwise it is like a kiss without a mustache, as the girls say: something is missing without it."

Then two crews, of four burly men apiece, each picked up a shell where it had been laid on a sort of iron stretcher with a cradle in the middle and rolled the shells into the mortars. The shells had a band around their centerlines that rested on a shelf inside the barrel.

"Now, sir, as a naval officer," said Fontenot, "you are accustomed to round shot, and chain shot, and grape shot and all sorts of shot, but not to shells. Too dangerous except in ships especially equipped to handle them, no?"

"Bomb vessels, we call them," I said. "Or just bombs for short."

"Bombs! Yes, I like that. Bombs, in case the gunners mishandle their shells and the whole ship blows up, hee hee! But of all your various types of projectiles, I will bet you have never seen this new type we have developed."

A squad of gore-spattered grenadiers confirmed my notions of Fontenot's new type of projectile when they dragged a pair of the naked black men, kicking and screaming, down into the mortar pit and chained them across the muzzles.

Fontenot selected a pair of fuses—powder-filled wooden cones with the times marked on the sides—trimmed them to length with a small folding saw that he took from his pocket, and tapped them into the touchholes with a little hammer. He gave no litany of commands, but merely stepped out of the way, stuck his fingers in his ears, and nodded to the men with the linstocks. They touched the glowing match ends to the fuses. As the fuses sparked and fumed, one of the prisoners shrieked prayers and the other expelled the contents of his bladder and bowels. Then the guns roared, a fine red mist tinted the smoke, and the grenadiers tossed the smoking remnants of the murdered men onto a pile, where the prisoners with the hammers and chisels pounded the twisted irons off the mangled hands and feet.

Only Fontenot had watched the fall of the shells. "Short and to the left," he said.

Pétion had kept his eyes on me. "Your beloved Father Toussaint, Monsieur Graves, from whom we got the idea, no longer uses this method of execution. He has begun instead to take boatloads of prisoners out to sea. He has them tied in pairs, with weights attached to their feet. They are skewered on bayonets and then thrown overboard, like so much hay on the end of a pitchfork. What do you think of that, hmm? Are you still glad you came to meddle in our little war?"

I leaned over the breastwork of the mortar pit so I wouldn't puke on my boots. *"Bay kou blié, poté mak sojé,"* I gasped, reciting one of Juge's aphorisms: *He who strikes the blow forgets, he who bears the mark remembers.*

"Pepin is dead and I have been accused of spying," I said to Juge when the grenadiers had returned me to the cell. His head was still ugly, but he was alert. I filled him in on what I had seen.

"Who has accused you?"

"I don't know," I said. "But Pétion told me it was 'two friends,' and Franklin and the Parson are in a room upstairs. They obviously know each other, although Franklin pretended not to recognize him when first we saw him. I think you were wrong about Franklin. I think he's mixed up in some sort of a plot and has used me as his stalking-horse."

"You have spoken with him?"

"I have not. He's with the Parson, as I told you, and the Parson has his sword to his hand."

"They let him keep his sword?"

"Odd, isn't it?"

"But what if you are mistaken? Surely you will not murder them."

"I can't do anything about them at the moment." *Murder* was coming it a bit high, I thought, but that's just what I'd have done if I'd been armed. "Juge," I said, "they have furniture—a bed! And cushions, and mosquito nets! Very strange if they are prisoners, isn't it?"

"Perhaps he has given his parole . . ." He closed his eyes and drifted off.

"Must you always talk to the nigger first?" said Treadwell. "As a white man I find it rather insulting, I must say."

"He's the ranking officer."

"So he says."

I cared even less what Treadwell had to say than I had earlier in the afternoon, but courtesy demanded I speak to him. "Now look'ee here," I said. "Pepin's been broken on the wheel. He got caught trying to get his warning out to Toussaint. That means it's up to us to finish the job, see?"

"A great lot of use I'll be, as you said so eloquently. You can jolly well count me out of any capers, thanks all the same." He had tossed his sheet off again, and the sweat glimmered on him in streams.

"I've just come from seeing Pétion. He says you should've been exchanged already. You'll be out of here soon enough."

"Oh, right. And with Pepin dead, what will happen to me?"

"Hang it, man, I don't know. I can't take you over the wall with me." I'd been willing to carry Juge, I remembered, but dog me if I'd risk my neck for Treadwell.

"Sergeant Cahoon can do it. He's strong as an ox and almost as smart."

"Here, sir, none o' that, if ya please!"

"Hush, Sergeant. You'll have to stay here and nurse Mr. Treadwell as best you can till I come back."

"Ya will be comin' back is it, sir?" said Cahoon.

"Of course, Sergeant. You don't think I'd abandon you, do you?"

"Oh aye, never in life, sir."

But damn me for a dog, I calculated on doing just that. If I made it down the wall and out to the *Rattle-Snake,* bugger me with a belaying pin if I'd set foot in that prison again. A broken nose was soon forgotten, but I had no intention of getting myself strapped across one of Fontenot's mortars.

I lay on my belly and peered over the edge of the roof. The last of the daylight cast shadows along the wall, throwing the bumps and crannies in the sandstone blocks into high relief. The holes on the side facing Toussaint's artillery were tempting, but it was already dark on that side, making it impossible to plan a route, and besides there was that damn trench guarding the gate to the lane.

But there was nary a soul on the narrow strip of rocky beach. When the sunlight had winked out, I tucked my socks into my boots and dropped them over the edge. They hit the ground with a soft thump.

As I waited to see if the small noise would attract any unwanted company, I watched the *Croatoan* and the *Rattle-Snake*. The sun still cast its rays out beyond the point, picking out their sails and sides in a ruddy glow. The *Rattle-Snake* had taken up station just beyond the mouth of the bay, where with her nimbleness and shallow draft she could snatch up any small fry trying to slip into the anchorage; the *Croatoan* stood on the horizon, ready to engage any French force of strength that might make an appearance.

A skiff rode to a painter down at the far end of the jetty. I could see it bobbing on the lesser dark of the water and hear it as the wavelets thumped it against the pilings.

Below me in the corridor a light wavered and wobbled, casting moving shadows on the stones. I heard footsteps and a mutter of conversation.

"I tell you, I heard someone moving about down here earlier today," Franklin's voice said.

"There is no reason to suppose we are Pétion's only honored guests," said another voice. It was a raspy but full-chested whisper that carried easily down the passageway. The hair stood up on my neck, and I knew it was the Parson who spoke. I backed away from the hole and stretched out flat.

"I see no reason for levity," said Franklin. As the light drew closer he said, "Here is the opening I mentioned. The upper wall is entirely caved in. If you are not yet ready to walk out the front gate, perhaps you will be good enough to lower me down the wall by means of a rope contrived of bed sheets knotted together."

"What, and let you out of my sight? Not a chance, Mr. Franklin."

"Are we not allied in a common cause?"

"Merely an alliance of convenience, Mr. Franklin, fated to expire as soon as we have left this place."

The light played across the stones. "It is hardly my fault that Connor abandoned us."

"He's got nothing to do with it. I'll deal with him separate."

I hugged the roof, breathing slowly and easily so as not to be heard. They were so close beneath me that I could've bounced a sword off their heads, if I'd had a sword.

"Do you hold the light for me," said Franklin. The shadows moved, and then his head and shoulders appeared as he clambered up onto the broken wall and looked over the edge. "The light is insufficient to reveal any handholds, and we dare not shine the lantern about. I see soldiers moving around down there."

"Come back down, then," rasped the Parson. "We shall see what the Lord has in store for us in the morning."

If Franklin had leaned out any further I'd have been able to topple him off to his certain death. But Juge's word *murder* had stuck in my craw. I had no doubt that Franklin was one of the traitors Pétion had mentioned, but I had no proof. And if you're going to claim the side of righteousness, you have to play by the rules. Besides which, if I did for Franklin I'd then have to face an unpleasant interview with the Parson and his sword.

The light retreated back the way it had come. There came a squeal of hinges as a door closed, and the corridor went dark.

I swung around and felt with my bare feet for the first of the toe-holds I'd fixed in my mind. I began inching down the wall. The legs were the hardest, for when I reached down with one the bent knee of the other threatened to shove me off into space, and my legs were un-accountably trembly.

I'd made it as far as the story below when the shouting began.

Fourteen

I ran my bare foot down the wall and felt for another toehold. The shouting didn't have a thing to do with me. I could've ignored it. I was a mite preoccupied to want any truck with people who shout—the wall couldn't hold a candle to a topgallant mast in a January gale, but it was all-fired steep and crumbly.

The breeze began to kick up, and a sheet of rain splashed across the wall and slicked it up pretty good as I clambered down. Before long I couldn't see where I was going next, except maybe straight down in a hurry. I hunched at the bottom of the long fissure that ran down from the top of the wall, cussing under my breath at a freshet that poured down the back of my collar. I looked out at *Rattle-Snake*'s and *Croatoan*'s stern lanterns sparkling through the rain, and then down at the stones below. And as I crouched there I thought that the law of gravity is all very good when you've got both feet on the ground—it brings comfort to a man in an uncertain world, to have a scrap of dead-certain reality to hug to his breast and know that it applies to all men equal—but I thought that a suspension of it would be only fair at certain junctures in one's life. While I was thinking this, I noticed that the shouting was coming from a window a few yards to my left.

My rattlesnake banner hung from the bars, with Treadwell's shoes dangling below. I clearly heard Treadwell bleating, "Oh mind what you're about, you horrid bumpkin!" and Cahoon swearing aloft and alow in Irish. I guessed he was swearing, I mean—it's hard to tell with an Ulsterman. But then the sergeant hollered, "Mr. Graves! For Dear's sake, gi'e us a hand!"

I had just about figured that wall couldn't be climbed any farther, not by me in the shape I was in, and I confess I was that weak and maybe scared that my legs might mutiny. But even more than that, somebody was bound to miss me sooner than was convenient if I didn't shut those two fools' mouths for them. I swarmed up that wall a heap faster than I'd come down it.

When I crested the top I saw Franklin down the corridor to my left, holding a lantern aloft and peering out from his door. Then the Parson pushed him through the doorway and followed him out, his black cloak over his shoulders and naked steel in his hand. I didn't wait around to say hello. I slid down the loose stones and lit out for our cell.

The guards never bothered to leave a lantern on our floor. I scampered along with one hand trailing on the wall to keep my bearings and the other out in front of me in case of obstacles, but I didn't think to slow down when I got to the cell. Cahoon was wailing like a banshee and Treadwell was doing his damnedest to outshout him, though John Bull ain't got a patch on Paddy when it comes to lamentation, you hear *me*. All a-quiver to help or hinder, depending on who was getting the worst of it, I ran full tilt through the dark and took a flying tumble over someone lying on the floor.

"*Bon sang!* You have trodden on me," said Juge.

I had just time enough to wonder at the mildness of his tone before I clonked my noggin against the far wall. I staggered back a step or two and sprawled on something soft.

"*Merde!* Am I now the chaise longue, that you should sit upon me?"

"What the tarnal hell is going on here?"

"Oh, Mr. Graves, yer puir man in his despondency has gone and threwn himself dine the bog-hole!"

"Down the bog-hole?"

"I shall have no more of your gum, you fen-watered turnip," came Treadwell's voice. "Surely even a blockhead such as you can understand why I took my breeches down."

"Someone strike a light, for chrissake." I rubbed my head.

"An' how was I to know ya had yer britches dine, with the light as dark as the divil's arse? Himself is after doin' him a hurt, Mr. Graves. Yer man's wits have wandered these several days."

"That's a lie," said Treadwell, somewhat calmer. "I meant merely to pay my respects to Tom Turdman. And when I sat down, the seat gave way and I tumbled in. Embarrassin', really."

"Tumbled in?" said I, laughing.

"Yes, damme, tumbled in. Quite stuck now, I'm afraid."

"Oh aye—stuck are ya? 'Tis after gettin' ya o't I'll be, Mr. Treadwell, or me name's not Michael Cahoon. Which it is, and all."

"No! Keep your distance, you whey-brained moose—"

There was a snap of wood breaking, a grunt, and then a slithering sort of wail.

"By Jezzus, he's goin' dine!"

There was a click and a spark of steel on flint, and Juge held up a lighted stub of a candle. By its flicker I saw Treadwell's hands clutching Cahoon by his side-whiskers, and his stocking feet sticking out on either side. The sergeant was reaching down into the hole, presumably trying to get a better grip, when he slipped in a puddle of muck and went headfirst down the hole after Treadwell. I grabbed him, but he slobbered through my hands.

"Sweet mother of glub—" said Cahoon as he disappeared.

"Help," added Treadwell in a muffled and unhopeful sort of way. I heard a pair of diminishing wails, a *sploop,* and then nothing more.

I stood away from the latrine, shaking filth from my hands.

"Bon sang!" said Juge. "What shall we do?"

"Get them out again, I guess." I leaned over the hole. "Ahoy below! Ahoy there! Can you hear me?"

I heard a low moan, and the sound of someone puking.

"Oh, God, not on *me,*" said Treadwell, faint and far away.

"Well, they're alive at least," I said.

Juge spluttered through his fingers as he tried not to laugh. He held out his other hand and I hauled him to his feet.

"Ahoy below," I called again, and then a beam of light swept through the room. I spun around.

"Stand where you are!" rasped the Parson.

Franklin stood in the doorway, holding up his lantern. The Parson's deathsome face loomed over his shoulder.

"*Mon dieu,*" breathed Juge, making the sign of the cross.

"*Bonsoir,* Monsieur Juge," said Franklin, stepping into the room. "I thought I had heard your voice these several days." His French was stiff but serviceable. The Parson stepped around him with his sword at the ready.

"*Bonsoir, mon ami,*" said Juge. He took a small step toward Franklin. It was a subtle move, as if he'd merely shifted his weight, but it put him between Franklin and the door. "Monsieur Graves has already informed us of your presence."

"Oh, is that you, Mr. Graves?" said Franklin, switching to English as pretty as you please and shining the light on me. "You look as if you have had a chamber-pot emptied on your head. 'Ye shall know them by their raiment,' it is said."

"Nay," said the Parson. The tip of his sword quivered. "Matthew seven-sixteen: 'Ye shall know them by their *fruit.*' The next verse is 'A corrupt tree bringeth forth evil fruit,' and eviler fruit I never seen."

"It ain't fruit," I said. "It's shit. Anyway, I calculate to serve you out, Franklin." I eyed the Parson's blade. "In about a minute. I'm busy at the moment."

"Serve me out? Whatever do you mean?"

"I mean you're in league with the Knights of the White Hand. You told Pétion I'm a spy, and I aim to bring you down for it."

"I—? In league with whom?"

"You heard me. Now be quiet, I'm trying to listen." I bent over the hole again.

"I shall not be quiet," said Franklin—then, "No, sir, put up your sword!"

The Parson shoved past him and came at me. I was all set to hop down the bog-hole after Cahoon and Treadwell, but Juge punched him in the side of the neck. The Parson dropped like a wet sack, and Juge snatched up his sword.

"And now, my friend," said Juge, placing the point at Franklin's throat, "perhaps you will be so good as to explain your association with this man."

"I have not heard of these Knights of the White Hand, Mr. Graves," said Franklin. "I would swear it on a Bible, had you one handy, although I am not a great reader of that work." His eyes were bland behind his glasses. "Besides, you would not believe me in any case."

"Damn right I wouldn't. I heard you two talking, and I'm getting pretty sick of your lies."

"Ah. Well, I can tell you this, then." He pointed at the Parson, still stretched out on the floor. "Mr. MacGuffin there is dedicated to thwarting a conspiracy on the part of some of Rigaud's followers. It is their idea to foment slave rebellion to the southern states. If he is a Knight of the White hand, I have no official knowledge of it."

"Then why did he go for me when I mentioned the White Hands?"

"Perhaps he believes you to be part of the conspiracy."

"Me? My orders are to find out who's involved in it. That's what I'm doing here."

I didn't know a man could look disgusted and superior with his back against a wall and a sword at his throat, but Franklin managed it. "You got yourself jailed to discover a conspiracy? Your methods want work."

"Shit and perdition! I keep telling people I didn't come here a-purpose."

"Regardless, this is far beyond the Navy's jurisdiction." He looked down at MacGuffin and nudged him with his foot. "And what about that letter from Villon?"

"What *about* that damn letter? Everybody keeps asking me did I read it, and I never did. All's I did was, I swore to Villon before he hanged that I'd deliver it to his wife here in Jacmel."

"There is no Madame Villon."

"So I gathered." I said it pretty bitter, too; I didn't think my dislike of Franklin was entirely justified, but I still hoped Juge would stick him in the throat. "But anyway, I never read it."

"It's immaterial whether you've read it. What matters is that *I* should read it."

"What makes you so special?"

"I follow the conversation with difficulty," said Juge. "May I trouble you to speak French?"

"Au certainment." I filled him in on what Franklin had said.

"We are presently at an impasse," added Franklin. He kicked the Parson again, a little harder than before. "Monsieur MacGuffin and I have made an uneasy sort of pact to find and destroy elements of a conspiracy to foment a slave rebellion in the southern states. Monsieur MacGuffin is of the opinion that Monsieur Graves has been sent to Jacmel as part of that conspiracy, but what part he plays, if any, I have yet to ascertain. However, he has delivered a certain document into Pétion's hands. I believe this document to contain a ciphered list of co-conspirators."

Juge kept the blade at Franklin's throat, but his eyes wavered. "Matty, surely you would not allow this to happen? Rigaud, he could use this list to buy the support of your President Adams—or at least to withdraw his support of us. *Bon sang!* I thought you were in sympathy with our struggle."

"Of course I am. Franklin doesn't know what's in that letter any more than I do."

"You deny giving it to Pétion?" said Franklin.

"If it's in cipher, how do you know he's read it?"

"That's not what I—" Franklin cocked his head. "Do I hear voices?"

"Halloo, Mr. Graves! Are ya hearin' me there?"

Franklin stared at the latrine. "Has someone gone down . . . ?" Unable to finish his sentence, he merely pointed.

"Some friends of ours have had the mishap," said Juge.

"But how did they—"

"Quiet," I said.

"—come to fall in?"

"Shut up!" I leaned over the stinking hole. "Ahoy, Sergeant Cahoon! Are you hurt?"

"No, sir. As filthy as a Belfast hoor, but we landed soft for all that. Mr. Treadwell's in a bad way here, though, with his puir leg and all."

"Can you climb back up?"

"That I cannot, sir. The hole widens o't at the bottom an' there's naught to grab hold of."

"Can you see a way out?"

"Oh aye. There's a low bit of tunnel with a wee gate at the end."

"Can you open the gate?"

"Dunno, sir. It's all I can do to keep Mr. Treadwell's head above—above water, sir."

"Stand away from below, Cahoon. I'm coming down."

"Aye aye, sir. I'm away." I heard a receding series of splashes.

I held out my hand. "Juge," I said, "give me that sword, if you please. It's the closest thing we have to a crowbar."

"You go after them, *hein?*" He watched Franklin a second longer and then handed me the sword. "Happy landings, *mon ami.*"

Franklin wiped a smear of blood off his throat. "We have much to discuss, Mr. Graves," he said, "but I think the curiosity of our hosts has been piqued at last. I hear several pairs of boots coming up the stairs." Without so much as a grunt of effort or a glimmer of expression, he grasped MacGuffin's wrists with one hand, grasped him behind the knees with the other, and hoisted him onto his shoulder. He scooped up the lantern and stood up. "You will have to serve me out another time. Meanwhile I shall return to my cell."

The first ten feet or so was just like climbing down a chimney, albeit a belly-lurchingly filthy one. Then suddenly there was nothing under my feet but air and I went down the shaft like a rock. After a brief eternity I landed with a muffled plop.

It was worse than I could possibly have imagined. The air was saturated with a stench so foul that I felt I would rather suffocate than breathe it. But breathe it I did, in a shallow gulp that my lungs

immediately expelled, followed by what little there was in my stomach. I was on all fours, and the filth splattered back into my face as I
puked. Not that it mattered much. I seemed to be drenched with the
stuff through and through.

I gained my feet and stood with my hands on my knees, gasping
and dry-heaving. I still had MacGuffin's sword in my hand. I used
it like a blind man uses a stick, groping my way toward a place that
seemed less dark than the rest of the pit.

"Halloo! Mr. Graves, what was it that ya dropped? A great rope,
I'm hopin'."

"Hush," I said. "The turnkeys are out and they'll hear you."

"By Jezzus, ya did not coom dine yerself?"

"No, I sent your granny." I felt around till I found his arm in the
dark. "Now where's that gate you were talking about?"

"'Tis only a wee bit from here. I left puir Mr. Treadwell propped
up nearby it. 'Tis loose, but I cannot get a grip, it bein' so muckish
underfoot."

We sloshed along under the low roof of the tunnel till it rose a bit
as we came to the end, and I could see the rain and the bay through
the gate. Treadwell sobbed in great gasps with his face against the
bars.

"Ease him away handsomely, Sergeant," I said, and Cahoon took
the lieutenant under the arms and gently pulled him a few feet back
up the tunnel.

"Just set yerself there, me darlin'," he said, "for what hurry is on
ya until the wee door is open at all?"

"I'm well enough for now," said Treadwell. "But for God's sake,
hop to it, man."

"We aim to," said I. "The guards'll figure out where we went in
about a minute, if Juge can't hold 'em off."

"Is himself not comin' then?" said Cahoon.

"No, he ain't. Said he'd rather take his chances where he was. Then
he blew out his candle, and I guess that's the last I'll see of him."

"'Tis the great pity o' the world," said Cahoon. "He's a fine man. Sure, an' he's as brave as—"

"Here, you Hibernian hobbinol, do you get that gate open! The air in here is thick enough without your boggish nattering. Any more of it and I shall surely perish."

"Feeling better, are we, Mr. Treadwell? Bear a hand, Sergeant."

The bars of the gate were fuzzy with rust, but for all that they had a core of solid iron and wouldn't budge. Even when Cahoon braced himself behind me and I pushed with both feet, all we did was slide back up the tunnel.

"That's no good, sir," said he. "But how are the hinges now, I'm wonderin'?"

I banged on the frame of the gate with the hilt of the sword. It moved. "The pins are set in sandstone. If it's as rotten as the rest of the stones . . ." Using the sword as a crowbar, and with Cahoon pulling me from behind, I felt the frame begin to give way.

"Handsomely! Handsomely now," I said. "If the blade breaks, we're sunk."

There was a squeal as one of the pins slid out from its stone shaft. "D'ye hear that, by Jezzus? Only one more t' go—"

"'Vast heaving," I whispered. "Listen!"

From upstairs came the sounds of a to-do in French. A gruff voice was demanding to know where we'd gone, and Juge was saying that he'd been asleep till just that minute, and anyway it wasn't his job to keep track of prisoners. *Bon sang!* Maybe if they'd lock the doors now and then, as they were supposed to, perhaps prisoners wouldn't wander off as they pleased and tumble down the stairs in the dark and break their heads or worse. It was a shameful way to run a prison, he thought, and they'd better go look around the corridors and perhaps upstairs if they meant to find us before Lieutenant Négraud did. And they'd better keep their voices down while they did it, too, or they'd be found out before they were done. I heard a few slaps and a groan, and then a bang as the cell door slammed shut.

"He just bought us some time," I said. "You still got your boots—see if you can't kick out the other pin."

We switched places. Cahoon braced himself against my back and gave a mighty kick.

"Ooh, 'tis me foot that's broke," he said.

The heave had sent me under. I had to swab out my ears before I could understand him.

"You broke your foot?"

"Bless ya no, sir, just in a manner o' speakin'."

"See is the gate loose," I said.

"Aye aye, sir. Oh God aye, sir! It's comin'—" He shoved it open with his shoulder and tumbled out into the open air. He was so greased up that he slid right down the slope into the bay.

"Come along, Treadwell." I turned him around and slid him along on his stern.

"Was that a splash I heard?" he said.

"Yes. I hope the sergeant can swim."

"First time he's ever been glad for a bathe, I should imagine. I say, hope you remembered the soap and flannel."

Rain never felt so good. I reveled in it as I oozed down toward the bay. The sea was as warm as bathwater, though a bit fouled from the muck the sergeant had already sloshed off himself. He sat up to his waist with his feet splayed out in front of him, using one of his boots to pour water over his head.

"Oh, 'tis grand," he said. "Is it a bucketful you'd care for there, Mr. Treadwell?"

"Yes, I should like that."

Leaving Cahoon to sluice Treadwell off, I placed the gate back over the mouth of the tunnel and then crept down to the end of the wall to see where my boots had landed when I'd tossed them off the roof. Campfires glowed around the corner and I could hear men moving about and talking in low tones. Rain hissed in the flames. No excitement, no hue and cry, which meant no one there was expecting us.

I looked over at the pier where the boat was tied up. There was no sentry in sight, but if there was one, and him a proper soldier, he'd have found himself someplace to shelter from the rain.

I found my boots and scooted back to the others. "How's the leg, Treadwell?"

"Took a bit of a pounding, sir. Shouldn't think I could walk on it, but I'll hop if I must."

The water lay calm along the shore. "You won't have to. We'll take you in tow." I wrassled my socks over my wet feet. "Cahoon, there's a boat tied to the end of the pier over there. Let's float Mr. Treadwell on his back and keep our heads low. And remember, sound carries well over water, so no talking unless absolutely necessary."

"Aye aye, sir."

"Can you swim, Treadwell?"

"Like a fish."

"Good man. But just lie quiet and let us do the work."

"Right, sir."

"Let's shove off, Sergeant."

I didn't think it was the right sort of terrain for caimans, but I was pretty sure the carcasses floating down the river made the bay an attractive place to be a shark. No point in mentioning that—if somebody got bit, we'd know it soon enough. We half-waded, half-swam toward the pier, with Treadwell calmly keeping his nose above water as he bobbed along on his back. The hair rose up on the scruff of my neck every time a fish nipped at the filth on my legs—or it would have risen, anyway, if it hadn't been so thoroughly pasted down with muck.

The rain drummed on the pier above our heads. I hoisted myself up to eye-level to have a peek. There were several soldiers between me and the campfires, but they were all hunched down with their cloaks over their heads against the rain.

I worked my way around to the end of the pier, where the boat lay gently knocking against the piles. Some lubber had tied the painter with no thought to getting it undone again. Pure soldier's work, that was—a sailor would've thrown a clove hitch over the bollard and had done with it. I had to heave myself onto the pier to get at the knot.

Of course it was soaked, and I tore off several nails before the obvious occurred to me. I slipped MacGuffin's sword out from my belt and cut the line.

A tarpaulin in the boat moved, and somebody stuck his head out. "Is it you, Paul-Charles?"

"It is not." I stepped into the boat and slashed his throat for him.

It was an excellent blade. It cut so deep that he made no more sound than the sighing of the wind as his life gushed out of him.

I found the oars under the tarpaulin and fitted them into the row-locks. When I'd eased the boat down to where I had left Treadwell and Cahoon, I said, "No noise, you two. Just grab ahold of the stern for now, and keep your yaps shut."

A little way out into the bay I boated the oars and helped Cahoon get the Englishman aboard. I thought the spirit had left him, until he said, "Do you not tread on my leg, Mr. Graves. It's all I can do not to scream."

Cahoon shot out of the water so suddenly I thought he would upset us. "Forgi'e us, Mr. Graves," he croaked, "but 'tis himself the leviathan below. I saw his shadow about me feet, and himself rubbin' against me."

Its dorsal fin broke water as he spoke. It was a leviathan in truth. I watched it as it rolled alongside, working its maw. I stuck it in the eye with my sword, and it shot away in a flurry of foam.

"You're a braver man than I am, Sergeant." I took up the oars and began pulling for the lights out on the bay. "I don't guess I could've held back, was I in the water with that."

I shouldn't have said it—he being an enlisted man, and a soldier to boot—but it was worth it to see the grin on his face.

"An' troth be told," said he, his eyes as big as eggs, "had I known the beast to be so huge as that, I'd a shrieked like a babbie."

Fifteen

"Sorry about the deck, sir."

"No harm done, Mr. Graves." Command had made Peter Wickett complacent about dirty decks. That was my department now, not his. "Holystones and water will make it pure as a maiden in white flannel. Your clothes, however, were a lost cause."

He'd made us shuck our duds in the boat. Even in the rain, the Rattle-Snakes had smelled us coming, just about. After reluctantly allowing us aboard they had subjected Cahoon and me to jets from the pump and made us scrub down with hard yellow soap and rough towels, while the bosun's crew had snaked Treadwell aboard on a carrying board. Surgeon Quilty packed him off to the sick berth, clucking all the way.

Now that I was decked out in a soft white shirt and nankeen trousers and carrying a pound of fried salt pork (quite against Quilty's orders), a mess of greens, and a couple of pints of hot sweet Navy coffee in my belly, liberally laced with rye whiskey from my father's own distillery, I felt as good as I could ever remember. I drew on the cigar Peter had given me and kicked off my slippers under the table.

"I guess Captain Block will be glad to have his sergeant of Marines back," I said. "How is he, anyway?"

Peter cocked an eye. "Block? To serve with, you mean? He is as lax with me as he is with his midshipmen. No order there: the midshipmen's berth is a veritable monkey's den, if monkeys can be said to live in dens. But that he is amiable and not afraid of a fight, I doubt not. I have heard him called the 'fighting Quaker' when he is out of earshot. He has taken several prizes, so his people like him. And I almost persuaded him to let me send a party ashore when I saw your signal."

"So you saw it, then! Much good it did, though, and Mr. Treadwell's shoes still dangling at the end of it."

He smiled, but there was little joy in it. The skin was stretched taut over the sharp bones of his face. "It did me good to see it, Matty. When Mr. Connor came back aboard, he told us you had been captured. I feared the worst."

I almost bit through my cigar. "Connor's aboard?"

"Nay, not he. He has ensconced himself in the *Croatoan*. Much more suitable for a gentleman, I believe he said. More room. More servants."

"But he's not ashore."

"I just told you he is not. We plucked him off Cap Maréchaux a week ago."

"He's a bad 'un, Peter. He aims to raise a slave rebellion back home."

He had been lounging with his feet on his desk, but he sat up at that. "Have you proof of this?"

"No, sir, I ain't. All I know is what Franklin told me. And him I can't figure out. He's all the time lying, and then he turns around and points out his own lies." I rubbed my head. My thoughts were all muddled up. "Connor or Franklin is a traitor, only I can't tell which yet." I told him what Franklin had said and how Connor had gone through my things at the farmhouse.

"But you only have Franklin's word that it was Connor," Peter said. "Assuming anyone else was there at all."

I thought back. "Now you mention it, Franklin didn't say it was Connor. He let me think it, but all's he said was the man's face was covered. And you'd think he'd recognize him anyway, mask or no mask. Assuming someone else was there at all, as you say. I never saw anyone going through my things but him."

"But why should he choose that afternoon to do it? Surely he could have chosen a time when he could be reasonably sure he wouldn't be caught."

"Maybe something forced his hand—like that Connor was getting set to go to the citadel, and maybe he wouldn't have another chance. Maybe it just hadn't occurred to him before, I dunno. But here's the strange thing: Franklin and MacGuffin had the run of the place at Jacmel. They had furniture, and MacGuffin even had his sword."

"MacGuffin?"

"A weird white man, dresses all in black. I figure him for a Knight of the White Hand, only he don't entirely act like it. Him and Franklin have some sort of partnership, apparently—an alliance of convenience, MacGuffin called it. Strictly jury-rigged, but it seemed to be holding up for the moment."

"Perhaps Pétion allowed this MacGuffin to keep his sword. It happens from time to time."

"For what, gentlemanly acknowledgement of a gallant action? He ain't a soldier nor a sea officer. And Toussaint and Pétion wouldn't neither one of 'em acknowledge gallantry if it kicked 'em in the ass. They got too much at stake. No, MacGuffin and Franklin got something going with *someone*. My guess is, it's Pétion."

"Pétion has no idea when he'll be able to leave Jacmel, so he can't be much help to them," said Peter. "Perhaps they've merely combined forces until they can escape. If this MacGuffin is one of these Knights of the White Hand, why else should he abide Franklin? I have nothing against Negroes, yet I cannot stand him."

I tried to remember their conversation at the hole in the wall. "Connor stranded them there. Whether he meant to shuck 'em or just hoofed it in a hurry, I don't know. But MacGuffin was pretty put out about it." I thought some more. "I hate to think well of Franklin, but Juge thinks he's sound."

"Who?"

"A black officer I was mates with. He was captured with me. He's in good with Toussaint and is a prime fellow. He covered our retreat. And Pétion *does* have an idea when he'll be leaving Jacmel. He aims to break out on the eleventh. If Captain Block was to give the citadel a good pasting from the sea . . ."

He ran his hands across his face.

"You look a mite peaked, Peter, if you don't mind me saying so."

"Peaked? I am weary as I have never been. It is that young MacElroy. His death rests heavy on me."

"Who?"

He blinked. "Young Mr. MacElroy, who got his head shot off."

"I'd forgotten about him." I had a sudden vision of wiping his brains off my face with my sleeve. I didn't want to remember him. "Softness ain't a good quality in a fighting man, Peter."

Some of the old coldness came back to him. "Neither is indifference to death, Mr. Graves. For shame, to forget a dead shipmate so quickly."

"If you'd seen what I seen in the past two weeks, Captain Wickett, you wouldn't care about one frightened little boy. I have seen so much slaughter and viciousness that I don't care if I never fight again." The bitterness of my tone surprised me.

"That does not sound like you, Matty. I have never known you not to care about a shipmate, nor to shy from a fight."

"Never say I'm shy, Peter," I said in a low voice. If there was an implied threat in my tone, I didn't care. "There was a man in the boat we took. I slit his throat without a thought. I must've tossed him overboard after, because he wasn't in the boat when we got here, but I don't remember it at all. No, I ain't shy of a fight, Peter. It's what I'm good at, and I'll keep on doing it as long as I'm able."

The silence hung heavy between us. He reached for the sherry on the sideboard. "We could both of us use a dram." His hands shook as he poured.

The sherry was weak stuff. I wanted more whiskey. I wanted to get drunk. I thought of Billy with a hole in his chest and decided I'd better not get drunk. I pushed the glass away, but not so far away that I couldn't get at it again. "What is it about MacElroy that bothers you so much, anyway?" says I. "You seen boys and middies killed before. A cannon ball don't care who it hits."

"I have yet to write his parents."

"You know the drill." I drank off the rest of my wine. It was perhaps a mistake on top of the greasy food and the whiskey, but after a moment I felt the warmth spreading through my veins and guessed it would stay down. "'A gallant young man who fell defending free goods and sailors' rights. Promising officer, behaved in exemplary fashion, didn't flinch when Johnny Crappo peppered us with grape shot.' That kind of thing."

"I find your flippancy offensive, sir," he said.

"So do I, sir. My apologies."

"Very well, then."

"Honest, Peter, I'm sorry. I liked MacElroy. What's happened to me that I could talk about him so?"

"This isn't about you. And what you said is true, and it's what I shall do. Consider yourself forgiven, if it makes you feel any better."

"I'm also sorry to say I lost your epaulet."

He dismissed it with a wave. "A gift not given freely is not a gift. It was no longer mine, and an epaulet can be replaced, in any case. It is only cloth and metal."

"And my watch."

"What?" He laughed at that. It wasn't much of a laugh, but it took some of the grayness out of his face. "Lost your watch again? Villon was hanged for stealing that watch. You really must be more careful."

"It's too dang gaudy to stay hidden for long. It'll turn up, I guess."

We discussed the merits of different watchmakers for a while, and where the best shops were in Port Républicain and Le Cap for getting new uniforms and epaulets, before turning our heads to business.

"Now," said Peter, "Although I could not persuade Captain Block to send a party ashore to look for you, I have almost got him to do something about Toussaint's dearth of artillery. I think a good smashing from an unexpected quarter, was it coordinated with an assault by Toussaint's forces, might be enough to drive Pétion out from cover."

"I'm right there with you. And, like I said before, I have good reason to believe that Pétion intends to attempt a breakout late in the evening of the eleventh." I told him about Dr. Pepin and showed him his cryptic note. It was plenty waterlogged but still readable.

"Ah, the eleventh," said Peter. "The full moon."

"Near as I know, he figures on shoving off when it's at its fullest and highest. He don't want his men blundering around in the woods, bonking their heads on tree trunks. He aims to get as many of 'em as he can to Petite Goâve and join up with the rest of Rigaud's army."

"Then Toussaint will have the same problem as here, without the chance of our guns to help him out."

"Depends on how many survive the breakout, sir, if I may. The blacks know every road and trail thereabouts by now, and I bet it'll be more of a turkey shoot than a running fight. But as for our end of it, Pétion has no guns facing the bay." I reached for a pencil. "Here, I'll draw you a map. Bear in mind I got no idea of the ground under the bay, except that everyone I asked said it was deep right up to the shore. Which I can say that it ain't, at least right hard by the prison. But that's not where you want to hit, anyway. And it's dead calm under the cliffs, so we'll want our sweeps handy—if I may offer the advice," I added hurriedly as the birthmark on his forehead darkened. "And Block may have to kedge off before the night is through."

"I am far ahead of you, Matty. I sent Mr. Rogers out in the longboat to sound the anchorage, it being a perfect night to do it unobserved. I expect him back shortly."

"Then will you excuse me to go check on Mr. Treadwell in the meanwhile? He's a sort of shipmate, I guess, and he's in a bad way."

But I didn't go down to the sick berth. Treadwell would be either tearfully contrite or obstinately ungrateful, and I couldn't have stood either. I sat in my bunk with Billy's old longhair cat, Greybar, on my lap instead, staring at the deck and thinking about something Peter had said. Connor had told him that I'd been captured. But since he'd gone to see Pétion right before the assault, I didn't see how he could've known that. Unless Pétion had told him—in which case, why hadn't he vouched for me and taken us with him when he made his rendezvous?

After a while I got tired of staring at the deck. So I took out MacGuffin's steel-hilted sword and looked at it instead. Now that I had it under a lamp I could see exactly what I thought I would see. It bore the same death's-head pommel and bizarre Latin engravings as the one we had taken from Connor's would-be assassin in Port Républicain. I didn't know who MacGuffin was, but I knew *what* he was.

"A little island in a sea of uncertainty," I said to Greybar. He sniffed at the sword and touched it with his paw, but when he tried to lick the blade I put it away.

"Mr. Connor, thee says?" said Block, the fighting Quaker, shaking my hand the next morning in the great cabin of the *Croatoan*. He was a handsome if plumpish cove, about forty, with grizzled hair that was thin aloft and tied at the nape with the usual black bow. Unlike most Quakers he was clean-shaven, and he addressed us by title instead of "friend." He introduced me to Williamson, his first lieutenant, who looked up from the bottle of Madeira he was opening and said, "Good on you for escaping, Mr. Graves." Block waved Peter and me into chairs and continued, "No, Connor went ashore again. Invaluable man for keeping in touch with the Negroes. Toussaint dotes on him, to hear him tell it. Hey, pipe down out there!"

This last was directed through the door leading onto the maindeck, where a crowd of mids jousted on piggyback with mops for lances and buckets for helmets. They just laughed until the bosun chased them into the rigging, where they scampered around like monkeys and jibbered among themselves.

"With your permission, sir," I said, near about dragging the words out of my mouth, "I ought to go ashore again. Dessalines had a spy in the citadel who slipped me a note. They found him out, and I feel sort of obliged to see it delivered." Matty Graves, messenger boy, that was me. I showed him Pepin's note. "It tells when Pétion intends to break out."

"Assuming he does, and assuming it happens when thee says it will." He looked at the note upside-down and right side up, and turned it over, and looked at the front of it again. "Why'd he draw it? Why didn't he just write it?"

"Dessalines can't read."

He shook his head. "An illiterate with thousands of souls in his hands. Yet thus it was with kings of old." He gave me back the note. "But I think thee will have to explain it to him, even so, if Captain Wickett can spare thee."

"I've grown accustomed to his absence, sir," said Peter. "Also, it might be well to land a pair of your twelve-pounders on the west side of the river to provide enfilading fire, if I may say so." He went to Block's chart table and spread out the map I had sketched. Block and Williamson looked over his shoulder while I tried to peep between their elbows. "On this hill here, sir. It has a gentle slope, but I have measured its height—trigonometry is a wonderful thing, is it not?— and I am persuaded a heavy battery there will make things hot for the mulattoes at little danger to the guns or their crews. Toussaint usually keeps a regiment of hussars at the foot of it as a screen for his forces on that side of the river, which itself provides a hindrance that even cavalry would be loath to essay under fire. If the hussars fight as well as I have heard, we should fear no sorties from the citadel."

"Draw up plans for moving the guns and select the crews, Bill, if thee will," said Block to Williamson, who excused himself and departed. Block rubbed his hands together. "Oh, what a caper this will be. No chance of a prize, but I took plenty of powder out of our last one, and it's burning a hole in my pocket." He grinned. "So to speak. Thee shall have thy twelve-pounders, Captain Wickett, and Mr. Williamson will see to their landing. And thee, Mr. Graves, being already ashore as thee will be, may send up a pair of lights when the breakout commences. Now then, was there anything else?"

"Yes, sir. I believe your third lieutenant is a friend of mine. Mr. Towson."

"Towson!" He shook his head. "He'll never rise any higher without he don't knuckle down and learn his navigation, but he's a regular terror as a gunnery officer. I think Captain Wickett and I can spare thee a few minutes for an old shipmate." He glanced at the watch bill tacked to the bulkhead. "Thee'll find him in his cabin. See does he have his nose in a book, hey?"

Dick Towson did have his nose in a book, strictly speaking, but he couldn't be said to be studying of it. What he was doing was lolling in his cot with his legs dangling over the sides, keeping tempo with one fist in the air as he sang verses of "Ben Dover was a bully mate, and the captain's favorite, he." He sang it kind of muffled on account of the unblemished copy of *The Practical Navigator* that lay across his face.

"Here, you," I growled, snatching the book away. "Ye'd give your Auntie Griselda the quivering fantods was she to hear you singing such things."

He bolted upright. "Oh! Ha ha, you gave me a start! I'll say you did. I thought you was Mr. Williamson here to lambaste me for a buffoon again." He put his bare feet on the deck and yawned. "I'm to carry the *Navigator* with me wherever I go till I have learned it stem to stern. Then I'm to carry a sextant night and day till I get the hang of that as well."

He didn't look near as glum as he might have. I said, "Leading you a dog's life, is he?"

"Nay." He reached out for the *Navigator* and then tossed it onto the foot of his cot. "I'm a lieutenant! It's still all nuts and oranges to me. But say, you ain't dead! Now I can write that letter to Arabella I've been putting off."

Arabella was Dick's younger sister, blond like Dick but a sight prettier—which is saying something, as Dick was about as fair as they come. Arabella always turned my knees to jelly and tied my tongue in knots when I saw her, and she knew it, too. And truth be told I was sweet on Dick's young stepmother as well, but that was a truth I dasn't tell to anybody.

"Sure," I said. "I'll write her myself. I ain't wrote her in, lessee now . . ."

"You haven't written her once this entire cruise." He pointed at a stack of letters on his desk. "As she reminds me at least once a week.

That's no way to court a girl, you know. They're funny that way."

"So are fathers," I said glumly. "I ain't wrote *him* since he stopped my allowance."

He lay back on an elbow. "Stopped your allowance? Why ever for? You're still four years away from your majority."

"He thinks an acting-lieutenant draws a lieutenant's salary. But there's something else I need to ask him, and I'm dogged if I know how to go about it." I took a deep breath—and let it out again without speaking. Dick's father owned half a hundred slaves to winnow his wheat and run his hogs and dredge his oysters and hew his timber at the family's White Oak Plantation on Maryland's Eastern Shore. And here was Jubal, Dick's personal slave, to serve us cider and cakes. The glasses looked like thimbles in his fists. But he set them out delicate as kittens next to the cakes, and said, "They be anything else, Mars Dickie?"

"No, go away. Oh, wait—my boots've been griping. See if you can limber them up."

"Yes, suh, I get on it directly. Good to see you again, Mars Matty." He bowed his shiny head on his bull-neck and went away with the boots.

I was glad to see him go, too. He'd be tucking Mars Dickie into bed in about a minute, just about. I didn't guess either one of them meant anything by it, it being natural to them, but Jubal's meekness and Dick's expectation of it like to made me puke. Dick was the last person I could talk with about my mother. Not if I was perhaps one day to marry into his family. He looked at me around his cake, and I had to say something.

"Listen, Dick, I was just wondering. How does a man tell his children are his own?"

He handed me a glass of cider. "Well, you know what the philosopher said: Women love their children more than their husbands do, because women are more certain they're their own. Why, have you got a wench someplace saying you got a brat on her?"

"No, I—"

"Because if you do, just slap her on the rump and buy her a bauble. And if she's a colored girl, just slap her on the rump and let her count herself lucky, I say. Drink up, now."

I dropped the cider down my throat and decided I'd better not have any more. I wanted it too much.

"And speaking of girls," said Dick, "I'll tell you this. If you don't write Arabella pretty soon, she's going to go off with one of them beaux of hers. They buzz around her like bees on a honey pot."

"Now, that's something I don't care to think about, thank you very much."

"Then that's a pretty good sign maybe you ought to *start*," he said, and I was thinking about it, too, till he whomped my head with his pillow. "Ha ha! You should've seen the look on your face. Listen, I don't know what you're on about, but *I* know a thing or two about women. Like for instance the more you go on moping about her like a moony calf, the faster she's going to find someone to compare you with. Not in *her* eyes, but your own. A woman always holds trumps, but it don't do to tip your hand."

"Dang if you ain't right as always, Dick. Well, listen." He was my best friend. I'd thought I missed him, and here I couldn't get away fast enough to suit me. "I better get back before Peter Wickett gets his color up."

"Tell Captain Block I had my book open."

"I'll tell him your were up to your eyeballs in it, mate. And thanks, Dick. You've taken a load off my mind."

That was a lie. I felt worse.

General Jean-Jacques Dessalines himself presided over our little game of tell-me-true, with a colonel and four majors in reserve. Despite not caring for my story at all he made me repeat it over and over while two secretaries, one white and one black, wrote it out anew each time, translating Dessalines' questions from Creole to French, and my responses back again. I'd decided it would be best for now to keep mum about my growing command of Creole.

Dessalines looked at me like I was something he'd just found under his boot. "Are you certain you understood what the doctor said?"

"*Oui, monsieur le général.*"

He held up Pepin's hieroglyphic note. "Explain."

I didn't guess there was any point in repeating Pepin's assessment that even the unlettered could grasp the note's meaning. "*Oui, monsieur le général,*" I said again. "This circle with the numeral eleven in it indicates that Pétion is to attempt a breakout on the evening of the eleventh of this month—"

He held up a massive hand. "Stop there. Why the eleventh?"

"Because, General, that's the evening of the full moon."

"No, no," said the colonel. He was a tall and handsome man, but he had a look in his eye like he might come unhinged someday. "The general means to say, why did Pepin not use the revolutionary calendar? The eleventh of March is the twentieth of Ventose. Why did he use the old method?"

"I can't say, Colonel, because I don't know. All I know is that he wrote it."

"Assuming our servant Pepin wrote it. And assuming he didn't mean the eleventh of Ventose, which would be . . ."

"March second," said Dessalines. "Which is already past. Colonel, did Pétion break out on the second?"

"He did not, General Dessalines."

"There, you see? Oh, it's refreshing to see a white man admit he knows nothing. I'm enjoying this. Continue."

They were a pack of lunatics, I thought, but it's best to play along when the lunatics have taken over the asylum. "The plan is for Pétion to attempt to break out on the eleventh, sir, when the moon is full." I pointed at the note. "The circle that's crossed out, the one with the numeral twelve in it, means he wants us to think that he will wait until the twelfth, but he will not. The drawing of the bayonet with the hand blocking it indicates that he will commence the breakout with a feint along the Baynet Road. However, where the real breakout will be attempted I don't know."

"*Très bien.*" Dessalines bared his fangs in a massive yawn, all yellow ivory and blood-red throat, and handed Pepin's note to the black secretary. I wondered if anyone would ever see it again.

My jumping into the sewer, however, was of great interest to the panel. Some of the majors doubted that such a thing as a sewer existed, until one who had visited Roman ruins in France assured them that it was so, though he hadn't heard of such a system at Jacmel. At any rate the thought of Juge persuading a *grand blanc* to jump into ten thousand gallons of shit struck them silly.

"You bear no evidence of this on your person," said Dessalines. "Why is your uniform clean?"

"I bathed when I went aboard the *Rattle-Snake,* sir. And my old clothes are probably floating around in the bay somewhere."

"You dared to return to your ship before delivering this news?" He frowned. He was a great one for frowning—he did it with his whole body. You could see the frown rising from his thighs to his shoulders to the huge muscles of his neck, gathering fury as it went, and then twisting in his face like a badger in a bear trap. "This information is of much more importance than your personal comfort. Father Toussaint will not be pleased."

"I'm grateful to hear the news I bring is important, sir," I said, giving him a bow. "And I am distressed to think I have evoked Father Toussaint's displeasure. But I did not presume to present myself while covered in shit."

"And yet, gentlemen," put in the colonel, "a white man will always have a certain offensive air about him, *n'est-ce pas?*"

The panel dissolved into laughter—but Dessalines did not. He pulled out a pistol and banged on the table with it. We all shut up. He roared, "How did the American lieutenant of vessels say Pétion's defenses are laid out? Liar! How many men would he say remain to Pétion? Four thousand? Liar! What food have they? Lucky to get rats? Eating grass like the cow? Liar! How is morale? Liar! Why didn't they keep him in irons? Liar!" He pointed his pistol at me, and I waited in dread to see if he would cock it. "Until Father Toussaint has had time to review the minutes of this hearing, the lieutenant is not to leave camp without my express permission." He reversed the pistol in his hand and tapped it like a gavel on the table. He did it so dainty that I almost laughed. "I release you into the custody of your compatriot Monsieur Connor. You will find him in the anteroom. Don't shame yourself by keeping your betters waiting. And have another bath!" he shot at me as I bowed and scraped my way to the door. "You still stink! Now then, what is next on the agenda, citizens? Well, I can tell you with just one glance at this document that we could save twice as much powder if we dispose of prisoners in ways other than by shooting them . . ."

Connor led me outside. All concern and jolly good cheer, he was, and complimented me on my escape.

"I don't guess I had a choice," I said. "Just like my being here now. If Dessalines don't like it, why not just send me away instead of threatening me? And what's he mean, I'm released into your custody? I'm an officer engaged in the lawful business of the United States."

Connor had gotten himself a black suit. He looked both rich and severe in it, like a parson who fleeces his flock and then charges them for a shave. "If one is to travel in the higher strata, Mr. Graves, one must learn to cultivate friends. One does that by making oneself appear to be what one is wanted to be. And in such a place as this, I find, friends are by far the most valuable of commodities." He slipped his arm through mine and steered me along the road. "Speaking of friends, did you see my secretary at all?"

"That ornery Negro with the gold specs? I been wondering where he got off to." I misliked his touch, but couldn't remove my arm without insult. "Didn't he go to see Pétion with you?"

He looked at me sideways. "He disappeared about the same time you did. I had it from reliable sources that he meant to do you a mischief, and I am relieved he was thwarted in his purpose."

Franklin, hurt me? That was an odd notion. I'd thought his chief danger to me was that he might provoke me into murdering *him*. "I never made any bones about disliking the man, Mr. Connor, but why should he want to do me harm?"

"Why does any of us harm his fellow man? Through a misguided sense of rightness, I suppose. God, king or country, it's all the same. Ah, here we are," he said as we arrived at a group of tents. "I heard the general give you an order as you left."

"You astonish me. I said before I ain't under his authority." The only order I remembered was the one forbidding me to leave camp.

"I, however, hear and obey. Besides, I daresay you'll enjoy this." He steered me under a huge canvas awning stretched across a network of poles and ropes. In its shade a platoon of washerwomen engaged their particular enemy, soiled clothing, over an array of wooden tubs.

"My dears," Connor announced in his rich fruity voice, "my young friend is in dire need of your services. He is here at the direct order of General Dessalines. Although he is clean in word and deed, I fear he has an absolutely filthy mind—can you translate that, Mr. Graves?"

Now this was something like! Every one of the washerwomen was young and pretty. *"J'ai grand besoin d'un bain,"* I said as some of them smiled and some of them giggled. "Does anyone speak French? I am in great need of a bath, please, and my uniform needs a brushing. I fear then that I shall have to run around naked . . ." The smiles and giggles changed to merry laughter. Apparently some of them did indeed speak more than Creole.

"I'm rambling, Mr. Connor," I said in English. "But apparently I've made an inroad. How much does one pay?"

"It depends on what one wants. But no fear, she will tell you if you do not give her enough. I will collect you when you have finished. There is a soiree this evening, and you must be decked out proper. Till then," he said, and left.

"Dezabiye-w, tanpri," said a chocolaty girl in a crimson Madras turban. "Take off your clothes, please." I reached for my buttons, but before I half knew what they were about, she and another likely wench had stripped me stark staring naked—except for my leather pocket of coins,

which I shook cheerfully. The girl in the red turban shushed my mild protests with fingers to my lips while the other held up my linen on the end of a stick. They both shrieked. "I surrender, ladies," says I.

"Leave him to me," said the girl in the red turban. "He has nice legs."

An older woman of maybe twenty poked them with her laundry pole: "Get to work, you gabbling hens!"

The girl in the red turban grasped me above the elbow and marched me over to a canvas partition. On the other side of it were more tubs, filled not with clothes but with men. Most of them were black, but there were a few whites and *gens de couleur* among them. Some of them were smoking cigars or pipes, some had bottles and glasses next to their tubs, and none paid any but the most casual attention as the girl propelled me toward another screened-off area.

She snatched up a bucket of steaming water that sat waiting and poured it into the tub. "Here we are," she said in passable French, her smile brilliant with strong white teeth and a tongue as pink as baby roses. "Into the water we go, that's the good little gentleman. Though there seems to be more *grand blanc* than *petit blanc* about you," she said, eyeing the place in question. "No, no—how can I wash you if you cover yourself that way? Hands on the side of the tub, please, that's my dear. How you act! You'd think you've never been washed by a black woman before, and you a rich American gentleman."

"But I never have," I said. "When I wash, I wash myself. And I'm not rich."

"*When* you wash is right." She soaped me up. "Never have I seen such a dirty people as you Americans. You'd think bathing was unhealthy, the way you avoid it."

"Well, of *course* bathing's unhealthy," I grumbled, "if you do it too often. It removes the essential oils and lets disease in through the pores. Any civilized person knows that."

"Civilized people, indeed. Your doctors and the French and English ones too, always stuffing sick people into dirty breathless holes. No wonder you die from fever so much. Anyone would get sick, packed together in their stink like salt cod in a New England schooner." She shuddered, her breasts quivering most interestingly beneath her checked cotton kerchief. She squeezed her sponge out on my head. "Now, take your hair. Greasy and full of nits!"

"But I washed and combed it yesterday," I said.

"You *think* you washed and combed it," she retorted. "You know nothing about washing and combing, obviously. You will see when I am done with you. You will be as pretty as Juge."

I blinked at her in surprise, and she said: "Sure I recognize you— you are his friend, and he is my friend, so now we are all friends. So you just stop your squirming. While you soak I'm going to comb out your hair, and you just sit still for it or I'll get one of those old hags to scrub you down with a hog's-bristle brush. That won't be nearly so nice, which this would be if you'd just stop wiggling and let me clean you up."

It *was* nice, which that particularly private part of me manifested on its own accord. It rose proudly up through the now sludgy water to greet her.

"I don't think we've been properly introduced," I said.

She laughed. "Well, I believe we have been now." She gave me a stroke that like to curl my toes. "They call me Marie-Celeste."

"Matty Graves. I am enchanted."

"And enchanting," she murmured, lifting off her dress and joining me in the tub.

Sixteen

Refreshed inside and out from Marie-Celeste's ministrations, in spotless white vest and breeches and a freshly brushed uniform coat with a black crepe band below the left elbow, for we still had three months of mourning left for General Washington, I sallied forth from the baths feeling quite the lad. While I'd waited for my smallclothes to dry, the barber had shorn my curls and brushed them forward in the new style after squealing with indignant horror at their length. I had cleaned my teeth with the brush kept handy for the bathhouse patrons, and my buttons and buckles shone so bright they might've been mistook for gold. All I lacked was an epaulet.

"Not bad, young fellow," said Connor, staring at my hair. "But don't you think perhaps a touch of powder—?"

"No." Connor had seen a hairdresser too, obviously, who had powdered his ringlets to a snowy whiteness. "I can't countenance wearing flour in my hair when the troops are starving."

He shrugged. "You are sadly out of uniform, however," he said. "Perhaps this will help." He held out an epaulet. It was old and sprung in the wires and with the brass showing through the gilt in places, but it was regulation U.S. Navy.

"Hold on, this is mine," I said. "Where'd you get it?"

"Yours? What an extraordinary coincidence." He flashed an embarrassed smile that might have been genuine. "There is a trade of curios back and forth between the lines. Naturally I recognized it at once as American. I snapped it up for a trifle, and now I present it to you. Of course I had no idea it was yours."

I bet he didn't, either. It was a slip. "Much obliged, I'm sure," I said as he pinned it on my shoulder.

He gave me an appraising look, the way an artist squints at a portrait to see if maybe he's slapped on too much paint. His eyes traveled up and down and then came to rest on my midsection. "That is an interesting sword you are wearing," he said.

I had worn MacGuffin's sword, having lost my own. It was perhaps a dangerous thing to carry in that camp, lest someone should recognize it—but it was my hope that someone would. I studied Connor's face. "Look familiar?"

"I did not say that. May I ask where you acquired such a thing?"

"There's a trade in curios inside Jacmel as well as out. Say, ain't it time we shoved off?"

With our hats tucked under our arms so's we wouldn't mess up our hair, we strolled over to Toussaint's headquarters. An old black man in a crimson velvet suit took our hats and gloves and accepted with barely a glance the *carte de visite* that Connor gave him. I doubted he could have seen past his nose anyway, he held it so high. He sniffed because I had no card, but he nodded when I told him my name.

We followed him through the house to the back garden, where brass-helmeted dragoons clicked their boot heels and the major domo or whoever the old man was pounded on the step with his silver-mounted ebony stick and announced us to no one in particular. His duty done, he bowed to his knees and went back indoors to sneer at the next batch of visitors.

Beyond the dragoons, in a large sort of arbor where a small band honked and tootled its way through what I guessed were the latest dances, the mostly black officers and their mostly black ladies mostly ignored us. An occasional white or mulatto face spared us a glance and sometimes a smirk before turning elegantly away. I was about to ask Connor how long I'd have to stay before I could make a polite exit when the colonel from Dessalines' board of inquiry approached us with an expectant half-smile.

"*Bonsoir, m'sieurs,*" he said, resplendent in his well-cut uniform and a wig as sleek and white as ermine. He was a handsome version of Dessalines, with the same wooly side-whiskers and closely trimmed mustache, but with much less of the general's lurking fury. "*M'sieur Graves de la Marine des États-Unis, n'est-ce pas?* I trust I find you recovered from your recent tribulation."

"*Mais oui, monsieur. Merci beaucoup,*" said I, straightening up from making my leg. I wondered which tribulation he meant: my imprisonment or my time in front of Dessalines. "It was as nothing. But I beg the colonel will forgive me, as he has me at a disadvantage. We were never introduced."

"It is I who must beg forgiveness. Allow me to name myself: I am *chef de brigade* Henri Christophe, of the first and second demi-brigades and commander of the forces in and around Le Cap. I beg you will forgive the impertinent questions regarding the information you so kindly delivered from"—he hesitated just a fraction, glancing at Connor— "our friend inside Jacmel."

"I have heard a great deal of the colonel and am most honored to make his acquaintance," I said, bowing again. "May I name Monsieur Connor?"

"This Connor and I have the acquaintance."

They eyed each other like a couple of tomcats squaring off.

A white lady fluttered her fan at us, and then turned it just so and minced at Connor.

"Ah, Mr. Connor," said Christophe, giving the lady the barest of bows, "it would seem Madame Bréde desires your attentions."

His words needed no translation. Connor met the lady's eyes and smiled, murmuring apologies to us as he withdrew.

"She has the pox, alas," said Christophe, watching them go together. "I hope they become very well acquainted." He took me by the elbow and threaded me through the crowd till we came to the punch bowl. "You will pardon my unseemly curiosity, sir, but what is it you have heard of me?"

"Of your victories in the field, naturally. And the executions at Le

Cap, and also the affair of the Englishman Rainsford, of course. The newspapers were filled with it."

"But yes, *Capitaine* Rainsford." He ladled me out a glass of *sanguinaire*, a spiced wine punch with chunks of paw-paw and oranges in it. "About a year ago he presented himself as an American, and then had quite a bit of difficulty explaining himself when we found out he was no such thing. Not that he was in any real danger, of course—if he'd been French I'd have shot him out of hand, but the English enjoy certain protections here, despite their attempts to bring back the *ancien régime*. He disappointed me. I had liked him . . . One tells you and your former masters apart with difficulty, if you will forgive my saying so."

"Not at all, sir. People are the same all over, I find. We, for instance, have difficulty telling the French and the *gens de couleur* apart, much less all the other color gradations. *Nègre, sacatra, griffe, marabou, mulâtre, quarteron* and *sang-mêlée*—I can't remember them all. We can't tell the difference, and I am ignorant as to what all the fuss is about. Such an eye it must take to detect such minute differences!"

"Oh, foo," said Christophe, sipping his punch. "I have heard of your quadroons and octaroons, and it is said that your people are as conscious of race as we are, if not more so. We have white men and mulattoes fighting alongside us, and the same can be said for André Rigaud, though he is a keening dog if ever there was one. And as far as telling the difference between the blacks and the mulattoes and the French, of course it is difficult, for we are all as French as the first Consul himself."

"So you are, sir. Please forgive my stupidity," I said.

"It is of no moment."

"You are very kind, sir. But Captain Rainsford, now—I read an excerpt of his report in the papers. At least he was forthright in his admiration of your tactics. Is it true what he says, sir, that your infantrymen shoot and load so rapidly and conceal themselves so well that they are nearly immune to cavalry attack?"

"Yes, yes—how gracious you are to mention it. I have them run, and throw themselves down, and switch from their bellies to their backs, from van to rear, all while maintaining an impressive rate of fire. It's astonishingly effective in the dense forests. My hussars are my particular pride, of course, gorgeous on parade, but between you, me, and the woodpile I confess that except along the coasts and a few of the valleys, even light cavalry is useless except as mounted infantry. Too damn many trees."

"We have watched a squadron of hussars across the river by the hill near the water. Are they yours, colonel?"

"Indeed so. You noticed them, *hein?*"

"How could I not? But I ask for a particular reason. Captain Block wishes to mount a pair of twelve-pounders on the hill there to help dislodge Pétion. He is particularly concerned that a force remain before him to discourage any sorties from the fortress."

"Yes, I know. General Dessalines has promised this, is it not so?"

"Indeed, sir. But Captain Block instructed me to take particular care to speak with the cavalry's commander as further assurance that they will be there when the time comes."

A faint displeasure crossed his face. He finished his punch and tossed the glass onto the table.

"It is not that Captain Block lacks faith in the general or the chef de brigade," I added, "but only that things can change very quickly in battle, and he does not care to lose his guns and powder, and particularly not his gunners."

He dabbed at his mustache with his handkerchief. "It will be as he wishes. On this I give my word."

"The colonel's word is sufficient, sir. I thank you on the captain's behalf. I beg you will pardon me for speaking of such matters at a social occasion."

"It is the ladies, I think, who have made such rules." He smiled again, holding out his arm, and we walked some more. "But now you must tell me what you know of Lieutenant Juge. How fares he?"

"*Lieutenant* Juge! Except that he gallantly covered our escape, sir, I can't tell you much, I'm afraid. For instance, I wasn't certain of his rank until just this moment."

"He did not tell it to you?"

"Er . . . he did, but not at first."

"Yes, he is cautious that way. He does not reveal himself until he is sure to whom he speaks."

I laughed. "He played a joke on me. He told me he was a major."

"Ha ha! That is Juge. No doubt he did it to avoid some unpleasant task, *hein?*"

"Exactly so." I laughed again, imagining the look on Treadwell's face was I to tell him about it.

"You ought to feel flattered that he condescended to joke with you. As it happens he is a particular favorite of Father Toussaint, who in fact is eager to discuss a certain matter with you."

"Indeed, sir? But is the governor-general around at all?"

I had half imagined that the great man would be seated on a throne of human skulls, perhaps, or at least surrounded by a buzzing cloud of courtiers and toadies. It would need a glorious presence to outshine the splendid ladies and gentlemen posturing on the dance floor out beyond the trees, or sipping punch and conversing in loose groups, but I could see no one who fit the bill.

"No, not *here,* sir," said Christophe, amused. "This is just the great circle. Everyone who is anyone may come here. But the small circle is exclusive. Follow me, will you not?"

Beyond a grand latticework archway, which was woven with blossoms and guarded by a matched pair of brutes dressed as grenadiers, milled a group of ladies and gentlemen even more resplendent than their less-favored counterparts outside the archway. It was difficult to tell the colors of some of the uniforms, so covered were they in gold and silver lace. The men's gorgeous epaulets tugged at their shoulders, and the ladies' breasts thrust and jiggled at the fronts of their diaphanous gowns. The gowns must have been copied from the latest dolls from Paris, I guessed, for I'd never seen their like before. And such a daring profusion of décolletage and slender bare arms!

Mess sergeants in fancy dress came to light the lamps. No formal supper was in sight, but as more soldiers began to set dishes on the tables, there was a general rush in their direction. Heedless of order or sex, and without waiting for forks or even plates in some cases, the inner circle sat themselves and began gulping down food as fast as they could.

"Our timing is excellent," said Christophe. "Come."

I caught sight of a little black man in the shadow of a calaba tree, gumming something out of a gourd bowl and gazing at the glittering soldiers and gauzy ladies. A bowl of uncut fruit and a loaf of bread sat on a cloth by his side. Someone had dressed him up in a gaudy uniform complete with a broad sky-blue sash over his right shoulder. There were stars on the sash and a forest of gold lace on his collar and cuffs, but no epaulets, no sign of rank.

"One moment, please, Colonel Christophe," said I. "I've just seen someone to whom I should say hello. We rode together for a short time."

"You 'rode together'?" said Christophe with an amused look. "So you know him already?"

"Sure, he's Grandfather Chatterbox. An odd duck, but he seems to know people, and Juge dotes on him. *Bonswa, Gran-pè Bavard,*" I said, sidestepping a startled grenadier and bowing deeply. *"Kouman ou ye?"*

"M' byen wi," he answered. "I'm fine. I am expecting you. No, leave him be," he said to the grenadier, who had placed a paw on my shoulder. The old man put a hand across his mouth as if hiding a smile.

"I am very sorry to say I left Juge in Pétion's care," I said, "but he insisted on covering my retreat."

The hand dropped, and he wasn't smiling. "Ah Pétion, he was a friend of mine." He made a rude noise after he spoke. He had no teeth in his upper jaw and his lips hung loose, rendering his mouth admirably suited to the purpose. Then his sad old face lit up in a smile. "So! You didn't waste the time you spent with my protégé. You speak Creole even worse than you speak French!"

I took that as a joke, as my French was a damn sight more elegant than my English. "Monsieur is too kind," I said.

"But Juge, he thrived when you saw him last?"

"Li pa pli mal," I said, meaning that Juge was well. As the idiom liter-ally meant that Juge was no worse, I added, *"Tout bagay byen,"* but the old man nodded to indicate that he'd understood the first time. "Pétion seemed most careful to preserve his life," I continued. "Perhaps he in-tends to use him to bargain with Father Toussaint. Me he considered useless, or perhaps damaging to hold, considering my government's at-titude toward Rigaud. No doubt he is relieved I am gone."

The old man set down his calabash of soup. "No, you're not useless. If he is relieved at your absence, it is because it has placed you in front of me to speak in his favor."

"Oh no, sir, hardly in his favor."

"Then to present him as less than despicable." He took up his vial of black and white corn kernels and shook it, examining the effect. "So, what do you think of Pétion's chances?"

I glanced at Christophe, who smiled behind his hand but offered no help.

"Well," I said, "I think his chances are not good. The only thing that could save him is if Toussaint were to lift the siege."

The intensity of the old man's reaction startled me. *"Sa ki lans coeur gnannc, se couteau seul ki comain,"* he snarled, meaning that what was in his heart could only be cut out with a knife. "No, the city must fall. Everyone in it must die. It will be so." He shook his corn kernels some more while he calmed down.

The splendiferous ladies and gentlemen who had finished with their dinner stared at us anxiously. Christophe looked up into the darkening sky, as if he had spotted something up there of great interest.

Me, I was scared. No—not scared, I realized, but awed. The old man had a power of dignity that bordered on the supernatural, as when he'd shut me up with a gesture on the road from Léogâne. *"M' regrèt sa, gran-pè,"* I said. "I don't know what I said wrong, but I'm sorry for it. If I could help Juge, I would."

"You would? Why is that?"

"Because I like him."

"Because you like him. Is that reason enough? He's black and you're white."

"My mother was Creole."

He shrugged. "This means nothing."

"He is my friend."

He lifted his chin in a gesture that was part challenge, part warning. "Where are you from?"

"My home port is Baltimore, but I'm from—"

"Baltimore is in the Maryland, is it not?"

"Yes, but—"

"This Maryland is what you call a southern state, is it not?"

"In a sense, yes, but—"

"Do you own slaves?"

"Pa sifè non."

He gave the crowd a droll look. "Of course he says, 'Of course not.'" The ladies and gentlemen tittered. He looked back at me. "But you avail yourself of their labor, all the same. Who unloads your ships? Who harvests your wheat and tobacco? Who scrubs your kettles and serves your meat and hauls away the night soil? You don't want the niggers around you, yet who else would do the things you won't do for yourself?"

"Well, I—"

The ladies and gentlemen had drawn closer, clearly enjoying my discomfort. Some laughed outright. Christophe tugged on my arm, but I shook him off.

The old man waited, his tongue snaking along his parted lips. His head was too big for his body, I thought, and the teeth that lined his underslung lower jaw were brown and snaggled. I looked into the depths of his fathomless eyes and a pain shot through my heart.

"Nan dan-ou! At least we don't shoot them out of cannons," I said hotly. "No, and we don't tie them up and fork them into the sea with bayonets, either! And Dessalines—he should be standing trial, not presiding over them!" I remembered Juge's devotions, and guessed the old

man might be Catholic, too. "Is this what Jesus said? 'Do unto others as they do unto thee'?"

Christophe pulled on my arm in earnest, hissing, "*Mon dieu*, Graves, keep these thoughts to yourself," but the old man held up his hand and Christophe's mouth snapped shut.

"It is impossible to reign without terror," said Grandfather Chatterbox. "Look at France. She is the very soul of civilization, yet how many thousands of thousands has she killed? The guillotine, the firing squad, the garrote—what difference does it make in the end? None at all to the man most concerned, I'm certain. You should read my newspapers for the full story: *Le Cap François* and the *Gazette officielle*. Or my pamphlets, of course."

"*Your* pamphlets!" I fell to one knee as I suddenly realized the grossness of my error. "Oh, good lord. Do you mean to tell me, sir, that you are Toussaint L'Ouverture himself?"

It was Grand-père Bavard's turn to be surprised. "Of course! You knew that, surely?"

"I did not, sir. I thought you were just a harmless old—that is to say, I thought these people were humoring you."

Echoed after a second by the courtiers, Toussaint laughed, loudly and suddenly and shortly. He made a curt gesture, palm upward. "On your feet. Bootlicking is a time-honored art, Monsieur Graves! Don't acquire it. Sometimes I wish I could preside over my court the same way I do over my armies, with a pistol in my hand. But you, boy, are under my protection."

He shook his vial of corn again, frowned at it, and then shook it some more. Finally he held it up, and the people around us applauded. The black kernels had risen to the top and the white kernels had sunk to the bottom.

"This is how it will be here, too," he said, "make no mistake about that, Monsieur Graves. But in the meantime, there is a great deal of work to be done." His eyes softened. "So. As for you, it is sufficient to know that a friend is in great peril of his life. A friend, I may add, who admires and trusts you. I send a man with you to fetch him out. Also, as I believe you mentioned to Christophe and Dessalines, one of your own agents is captive there—George Franklin, the black man with whom we traveled from Léogâne, yes? You must get him out lest Pétion realizes who he is and cuts his throat."

"Oh, no, sir. Franklin is not an agent of my government."

Toussaint winked. "Just as you say."

"I crave the governor-general's indulgence in this last matter, sir, but I'm afraid I can't return to the citadel." Dog me if I'd go back into that hellhole! "I must be here to coordinate the bombardment. This is very important, as the governor-general says."

"The bombardment is important, but your presence here is not. Captain Block is free to fire as soon as he is in position. I think we will know it when he has begun." His eyes had hardened again. "No one else can do what I ask of you." He gave me a kindly look that didn't fool me for a second. I could feel his spirit pulling on mine, the way a quagmire sucks on your boots. "I do not order this," he said. "I *ask* it. Put it that way to Captain Block and you will see what he says."

Seventeen

"I still say it's a stupid idea, Mr. Connor."

Dick and I had spent all afternoon hauling the pair of twelve-pounders ashore and siting them on the hill west of the river. Well, we'd seen to it, I mean, the men having done the actual donkey work; but now Dick was having a whee of a time pasting the redoubts with round shot while I slogged around in the crick mud down at the mouth of the Grand Rivière. I poured water out of my boots. The rain was coming down by the hogshead and I didn't see how I could get any wetter, but I hate having water sloshing around in my boots. "I know how *I* got hornswaggled into being here, but ain't no reason for you to come along."

"Dessalines has placed you in my custody."

"I done told you before he don't have the authority to do that." I had a hole in my sock and my big toe was sticking out.

"He has the authority in this camp to shoot you on sight if he feels like it."

"We ain't *in* his camp. We're on an island in the middle of a fucking river."

"Come along now, we don't have all night."

I peered out toward the bay. "They ain't anywhere in sight yet. But you mark me, we're going to have a power of iron around our heads in about a minute."

He looked at his watch. "It's barely nine o'clock. We have an hour yet."

"Shit and perdition! Are you in a hurry or ain't you?"

"Let's see if we have any dry powder left, and get on with our business."

He said it so mild I wanted to kick him, but I checked my pistols anyway. "They're both of 'em soaked."

"No time to reload," he said, more cheerful than I cared for. "Besides, it's too damp for that anyway."

"Damp!" says I. "Damp ain't in it." I shoved my pistols back into my belt. "I don't see how that old Toussaint thinks I'm going to rescue Juge, anyway. Once Pétion busts out, he can just walk out all by his lone."

"Pétion will see he is killed before the troops move."

"Well, what am *I* doing here, then?"

"It's a classic manipulation." He snapped his fingers at me to put my boots back on. "Dessalines threatens to see that an accident befalls you if you fail, and Christophe and Toussaint offer you friendship if you succeed. You are caught between fear and greed, the two motivators for all human behavior."

I stomped around till my wet feet had settled in my boots. My socks were all wadded up around the toes. "I don't think wanting to live makes me exactly what you'd call *greedy*," I said. "Naturally I want to live." And see to it that someone get what's coming to them, I thought, but I shut my mouth and checked the contents of my bag. The bread and cheese were soaked, but the bottle of wine was intact.

Voyou, the man that Toussaint had sent along with us, was a middle-aged *rouge*, a mix of African and Indian, with filed teeth and straight black hair that looked like half a cocoanut stuck upside down on top of his head. He wore a coil of rope over his naked shoulder and, in the belt he'd buckled on over his breechclout, a U.S. Navy tomahawk that I'd given him as a present. He waded up out of the dark and waved the crowbar in his hand, singsonging in Creole.

"He says the coast is clear, Mr. Connor."

"Then let us go."

Dick's twelve-pounders flashed and roared as he traded shots with the flying battery the mulattoes had brought up across the river. He'd beaten it down to one gun by sundown, but that gun had survived for hours by moving after each shot. It was firing slowly now, even accounting for the time it would take to limber up and resituate, as if most of its gunners had been killed. Flying batteries were meant to hit and run. They were murder on massed infantry but suicidal against emplaced artillery.

One of the twelve-pounders began concentrating its fire on a redoubt on the bluff above us.

Connor snuck another look at his watch. "Right on time," he said. "That will keep their heads down while we cross the stream."

The water was no more than knee-deep over the sandbar that ran from the triangular island at the mouth of the river to the bluff the redoubt stood on, but storm runoff boiling down from the mountains had set up a fierce current. It would've been better for us to wait for the flood tide to stem the river's flow, but that would've meant sneaking into the citadel while the *Croatoan* and the *Rattle-Snake* were doing their best to knock it down. My boots filled up with water again, but I had sense enough to keep my mouth shut about it.

Another load of ball and canister rumbled overhead and slammed into the redoubt. Yells came from inside the little wooden fort, but I doubted much damage had been done yet. As soon as the twelve-pounder's shot had struck home, the musketeers inside popped up their heads and began shooting. Their defiance was impressive, but I doubted they'd hit anything—Pétion's full moon, so necessary for his plan, lay hidden behind the clouds.

We reached the far side of the river and made our way upstream along the little bit of beach at the foot of the southernmost stronghold. Fort Beliotte was a beacon to the north, its wooden roof burning steadily despite the downpour. We came to a stretch where water willows crowded the bank, and we stepped into the river again. Alongshore the current was sluggish and greasy, but to our left it rushed and foamed and was rich with the stench of death. Firelight danced on the stream and sparkled in the falling rain.

We left the stream and half-crawled, half-swam across a fetid series of trenches filled with liquid mud. Equipment lay scattered around as if it had been abandoned in a hurry. No one challenged us, but I did meet one man, who lay so still that I didn't notice him till I'd oozed into his arms. He was buried in the slime with just his head and hands sticking out. Even though he was about as dead as a man can be and still stink, his left eye moved—maggots, writhing in the socket. I rolled away, swallowing puke, and at last we came to a low breastwork.

"*Vil mi,*" whispered Voyou. His Creole pronunciation was worse than mine. I didn't know what language he was used to speaking; some Indian tongue, maybe, though I thought the Spaniards had wiped them all out centuries ago. I imagine it was his pointed teeth that made him sound like he had a mouthful of porcupine quills.

"He says it's the town wall," I told Connor.

"Oh, how wonderful to have a guide," said Connor. "I could not have figured that out for myself."

There was a good deal of shouting and screaming coming from beyond the wall, interspersed with the rattle of musketry and a distant clinking of steel on steel. I peeked through the spikes of a broken cheval-de-frise.

Figures in silhouette flitted through the streets, fleeing, chasing, while others marched in orderly groups. Beyond them rose Fort Beliotte, its lower walls as bright as brass in the glow of burning houses, its upper reaches flaring and smoking in the rain. A group of white officers dashed past, pursued by a mob of mulatto fusiliers.

"They're off their nuts," I said. "They're killing their commanders."

"Good," said Connor. "Then they won't notice us."

Wrapped in our cloaks and with our hats pulled low, we slipped into the confusion unremarked and worked our way along back streets toward the prison. Through the rafters and broken walls of the houses along the way I saw a group on the next street over that stood out because of its regularity: a long string of men dangling from jury-rigged gallows. Looters were at work stripping the corpses. A squad of soldiers charged the looters, who returned like flies as soon as the soldiers had passed on.

We stopped in the rubble of an abandoned house hard up against the south wall to catch our breath and reconnoiter. A bit of its roof remained, and we bunched together out of the drizzle.

"Did you see the upper part of the prison this afternoon?" I said. "Looked like it caved in."

"Yes. It may be bad for poor Franklin," said Connor. "You say you saw him up there?"

"Top floor on the seaward side, on this side of the building. That part seemed intact."

I hoped Franklin was still safe and sound in his cell so I could pound a straight answer out of him. The sooner MacGuffin was in hell the better, as far as I was concerned, but I hoped he was alive, too, so I could acquaint him with the wrong end of his sword. But Juge, now . . . I cringed with shame as I recalled the way I'd caviled in front of Toussaint. Juge would be laughing and eager, was he in my place. I hoped someone had moved him before the wall collapsed.

My teeth were rattling like a couple of skeletons fucking on a tin roof. To mask it I said, "My pistols ain't getting any drier. I better draw the charges and reload while we're out of the rain."

"I'll not waste time on that," said Connor. "My powder is dry, and we both have swords. Now, where is the place where your remarkable sewer empties from the prison?"

We climbed the wall and sat astride it. "Over there, by that alligator-pear tree," I said. "No, the short one with the fat leaves."

Voyou pointed. *"Ahuacatl,"* he said.

"Ki sa?"

"Ahuacatl," he repeated. Then, *"Aguacate."* He cupped his crotch.

"Good God, Mr. Graves, what's he saying?"

"Dunno, but I'm pretty sure it ain't Creole." I thought about it and then laughed. *"Aguacate's* Spanish for alligator pear. I bet the other thing he said is the Injun word it come from. I calculate it means *balls,* ha ha!"

"You are entirely too frivolous ever to amount to anything, Mr. Graves."

"As you say, Mr. Connor." His displeasure had put me in a good mood. "Let's shove off."

Someone had hammered the gate back in place, but Voyou managed to pry it open about six or eight inches with his crowbar. A foul reek issued from the tunnel. I felt my gorge rising. "I can't go back in there," I said.

"Nonsense. You're the smaller man. Come along, there's little time to waste."

"I'll puke. I can't do it."

"It was the plan agreed upon. Now get along."

It was the plan, all right. And it was my plan, too, which didn't make me feel any better about it. However, I took off my coat and weapons and bag and handed them to Connor, who promptly set them on the wet ground. Telling myself that I could always strangle him later, I squeezed through the gap and slid on my knees into the dribbling filth.

"Oh, fuh! *Fuh!*" I gagged. *"Lordy,* but it don't *half* stink in here!"

"Shh!" hissed Connor. "I am quite aware of the smell. Tell this nigger to put his back into it or he will never get inside."

"I don't think he'll find that much of an enticement, Mr. Connor."

Voyou was willing and strong, however, although his efforts were diminished somewhat by his tendency to giggle, and between us we managed to pry the grating open enough for him to slip inside. He literally slipped inside, grasping the front of my shirt when his legs went out from under him. We performed an obscene waltz on our knees for an awful moment before we could be certain not to fall on our faces. There was an oily sploosh as Voyou dropped the crowbar.

"What was that?" hissed Connor.

The moon broke through the clouds, and beyond him I caught a pale glimmer of sails as the *Croatoan* drifted in across the bay with the *Rattle-Snake* in her wake.

"Voyou lost the crow."

"Well, pick it up then."

"I'm not grubbing around down there for it."

"Damn you for a recalcitrant ninny! Do as I say, blast you!"

"You're in luck, Mr. Connor. Voyou has picked it up." I passed it through the bars without wiping it off first.

Connor took it without thinking, the way you do when someone hands you something. "Oh God," he said, dropping it like a dead thing. He wiped his hand on the wall. "Get a move on." He passed me my things, using my coat as a glove to return the crowbar. "Remember, I wait half an hour, no more."

"What, ain't you coming?"

"Duty takes me so far and no farther."

I slipped my coat on, reslung my sword and bag, and stuck my pistols in my belt. I hadn't bothered to bring a lantern; carrying a flame into those vapors would be as crazy as striking a light in a powder magazine. We knee-walked in darkness through the slimy tunnel until at last we could stand upright again. A faint light glowed in the passage above our heads.

Voyou boosted me up into the bottom of the shaft, but then a new problem presented itself. Though the upward passage had been as filthy when I had slid down it on my way out, it was much wetter now, as if the rain had found a passage into the shaft. When I braced my back against one side and my feet on the other and tried inching my way upward, the streaming ooze on the walls and the sludge on my boots sent me slobbing downward onto Voyou's head. Giggling, he caught my feet and shoved me as high up as he could reach. By standing on his hands I was able to gain a rough place that allowed me to hoist myself up and hold my perch.

About a fathom and a half above me I saw candlelight glimmering through a crack in the door to the guardroom on the first floor. Voyou below me was a blacker shadow in the reeking gloom. I whispered to him to toss up his coil of rope.

With the rope draped around my neck and my hands behind me, I put my back and feet to the wall and inched upward until I reached an

outcrop. With its help I was able to haul myself onto the bench strad-
dling the shaft, where I sat for a while, listening for any hint of sound
above the plashing of water and the thrumming of the pulse in my
ears. I heard nothing.

I measured out two fathoms of rope. Taking a bight around myself
and bracing my feet, I tossed the end down to Voyou, who swarmed up
the line and squeezed onto the bench beside me. He hauled up the rope
and re-coiled it. Then he drew his tomahawk, I drew my sword along
with one of my useless pistols for style, and slowly, slowly, I pushed
the door open a crack. No movement in the guardroom. I pushed the
door open a little farther, waited some more. Still no movement, still
no sound. I saw a pair of legs sprawled on the floor by the far door. I
waited. The legs didn't move.

Then at my nod we burst yelling into the room.

A candle burned in a dented old dark-lantern on the table. The air
was heavy with the smell of rum and blood. Except for ourselves the
only person in the room was Lieutenant Négraud, and he was dead.

He'd been stabbed in the belly and had a disappointed look on his
face. The blood that he lay in was fresh. I touched his throat, and it
was still warm.

His ring of keys was missing from his belt. I pawed through his
pockets.

"My watch!" said I, holding it up.

Voyou's eyes glinted. He held out his hand. *"Ala bel!* How pretty!"
He waggled his fingers.

I closed my fist over the watch. *"Vouzan! Nan dan-ou,"* I said, telling
him where he could put his fingers. "This watch is very expensive. You
can't afford it."

"Ah wi? Poukisa ou di sa?" he said. "Oh yes? Why do you say that?"

"Because it killed two men already. If you try to take it, it will kill a
third." I stood up and took a step back.

He looked at the sword in my hand and shrugged. *"Byen.* I take
what is left."

"Mete-w alez. Be my guest."

He got the best of the bargain. Négraud's cartouche was filled with gold coins. The Indian chuckled as he slung the cartridge belt over his shoulder.

"*Eske-w kontan?*" says I.

"*Wi, anpil!*" Yes, he was amply content.

I glanced at my watch before stuffing it into my pocket—half past nine, if Négraud had kept it wound and correct. Half an hour until the bombardment commenced. I stepped to the door and peeked out.

The corridor was empty, thank God. A tarnal pair of dead idiots we'd be if someone had heard us a-whooping like Shawnees as we flang ourselves out of the latrine. I sheathed my sword and checked my cartouche for dry cartridges. A couple of them seemed serviceable. I dried the pans of my pistols on Négraud's shirttail, wormed the damp charges out of the barrels and reloaded.

"*Suiv mwen,*" I said, snatching up the lantern. "Follow me, and stop laughing." I led the way to the stairwell, hoping we didn't meet any guards coming from the other direction. Even more than that, I hoped we didn't run into whoever had done for Négraud.

Captain Block had given Toussaint as much powder as he could spare, and Dessalines' guns had smashed blocks of the outer wall inward, letting in the wind and rain and strewing the corridor floor with stony rubbish. Whether it was stupidity or merely bad marksmanship that had caused his gunners to pound the prison, I could only guess, but they'd done a good job of it and at least they'd stopped by the time we got there. Black holes gaped in the floor, and I thanked a beneficent universe for having placed the lantern in the guardroom.

I barely recognized our old third-floor cell in the rubble. The iron-bound wooden door had sagged outward, splintered at the top but still attached by its massive lower hinge. I flashed the light around the cell, holding the lantern and a pistol out at arm's length. The man who lay slumped against the far wall was the right size and shape, but his face was all wrong.

"Juge? *Parlez fort,*" I said. "Speak up!"

"Ah, Matty, *mon ami*," came the familiar voice, "you still speak French like a Spanish cow."

"Juge, my friend, is it you?"

"Of course it is I," he mumbled. "Who else would dare answer to my name?"

I examined him in the light of the lantern. "You have paid Cravache one too many visits, I think."

He smiled at me with broken teeth and scabby lips, his gums black with congealed blood. "Our hosts, they did not wish me to leave." Around his wrist was a shackle, and attached to the shackle was a heavy chain that was pinned to the wall.

"I just found Négraud downstairs," I said. "He was murdered."

"No! Perhaps he was caught stealing rats, *hein?*"

"Have you seen or heard anything?"

"There was a banging on the walls, but once that stopped, all was silence until someone crept by a few minutes ago. I heard him go upstairs."

"Did you see who it was?"

"*Bon sang!* It was so dark, I would not have recognized my own sweetheart unless she farted." He worked his lips. "You wouldn't have any wine, would you, and a scrap of bread?"

"Of course I have." I handed him my bag and suppressed a pang of guilt. "Am I the simpleton, that I would not think of it?"

He stuffed a wad of damp bread and cheese into his mouth and swallowed it without chewing. He choked a bit, but waved me away when I tried to whack him on the back. He snapped the neck of the bottle off against the wall and poured wine into his mouth.

"Ah, this is much better." He ate more bread and cheese and slugged down some more wine before setting them aside. "Enough. Now the important thing is to remove this chain from my wrist. Someone is trying to knock down the whole city, I think."

"Pétion's breaking out tonight, and the city's gone mad. Father Toussaint sent me here to get you out. But I also need to find Franklin and MacGuffin. Do you know where they are?"

"Pfff! How would I know this? They did not invite me upstairs for cakes and lemonade this evening. But get me loose and l help you find them."

It was no good trying to get him free of the shackle, but the pin in the wall seemed promising. Voyou braced himself with a foot on the wall and yanked with his crowbar, yanked again, and the pin came free. Juge reached out his hand, and I hauled him to his feet. He yawned and stretched, the chain clanking. He gathered it up for want of anything better to do with it.

I climbed up the crates and looked out the window. The *Croatoan* and the *Rattle-Snake* lay below me and to the right. They had anchored fore and aft to secure themselves in position for the bombardment. They had boats out, rigging the springs, the heavy lines attached to the anchor cables and run around the capstans, that would allow them to traverse their guns across a wide arc as they chose their targets.

I hopped down. "I am going upstairs to see that justice is done," I said. "You can wait here if you want. You may not want to help me do what I need to do."

Juge was leaning against Voyou. "You intend to murder Franklin?"

"No. I intend to arrest him."

"But you will not mind if he resists, I think. I shall accompany you."

"No, you're too weak. You stay here and rest till I come back."

He drew himself away from Voyou. "I am a remarkable fellow. Too weak? Fah. It is my fervor to see justice done."

A light flickered in the cell at the end of the corridor. I shuttered the dark-lantern and handed it to Voyou. "Be silent as death, now," I said. With sword and pistol in my hands I crept down the passageway till I came to the lighted room. I peeked inside.

Franklin sat on the floor, with a smoldering dip in a clay bowl beside him casting an uncertain light. He sat in a puddle of blood, and in his lap he cradled MacGuffin's head and shoulders. The death's-head hilt of our missing dagger of the White Hand protruded from the Parson's lower spine.

"George Franklin," I said, pointing my pistol at his face, "or whatever your name is, in the name of the United States I arrest you for treason. Murder, too, it looks like." I sidestepped into the room away from the doorway as Juge and Voyou entered behind me. *"Venez donc,"* I said, switching to French to be sure that Juge understood. "Get up. My friends here will bear witness that everything is clean and above board."

"Vous êtes un parfait idiot," said Franklin. He stayed where he was and kept his hands in sight. "You're a perfect idiot. Connor stabbed this man, not I."

"Connor's waiting downstairs, so who's the idiot?"

"You're mistaken. He left not a moment ago. No doubt you met him in the passageway and let him escape."

He said it with such conviction that I gave him a second look. "How'd he get up here, then? We had to come in the back way up the shit-hole."

"He knows people, and they know him. I imagine he simply said hello and walked in the front door."

"So where's he now, then, if you know so much?"

Juge rattled his chain. "Maybe he heard us coming and lay in some dark corner until we passed. Or maybe he hides in one of the cells. Remember I heard someone going up the stairs."

"I didn't see him."

"That proves nothing," said Franklin. "Perhaps he was there, perhaps he was not."

"And maybe you're lying, and maybe you're not." I wanted an end to it. I gave Juge my pistol. "Please go see if Connor's hiding around here. Are you strong enough for that?"

"Mais oui, I am the Hercules. You do nothing rash while I am gone?"

"I won't kill him unless he forces me to it."

"I'll not move a finger," said Franklin.

"Bien. I leave Voyou here to keep you company."

"As for your charge of murder," said Franklin, switching back to English as Juge left, "MacGuffin still lives."

"Then lay him down and stand aside."

"No," rasped the Parson, so faint I had to lean close to hear him. "The blade is in my vitals. It will kill me if I move."

"Fear not," said Franklin. "I shan't drop you." He cradled MacGuffin's head and shoulders tenderly but distantly, as you would a sick kid that wasn't your own.

I sheathed my sword and squatted beside them. "It's over, MacGuffin. I know what you are. I can't promise you clemency. In fact, I'm pretty sure you'll hang if you live."

His lips were drawn back in pain—or perhaps wickedness, I couldn't tell. *"Deus vult,"* he said.

"Amen, brother. God wills it, yessir." If that's what it took to get him to talk, I didn't see any harm in mouthing the words. "But you have time yet to redeem your soul. Tell me what you know."

"Iure divino." He rolled his eyes toward me, a chuckle rattling deep in his chest as he muttered the word that Quilty's fever victim had said just before he died: *"Dixi—"* He jerked away from Franklin and thrust himself onto the dagger. "Oh, sweet Jesus!" The blade sythed through his innards and cut his screams short.

"Shit and perdition, Franklin, why didn't you stop him?" I put my hand to MacGuffin's throat.

"It's pointless to throttle him now," said Franklin. He leaned away from the body but stayed where he was on the floor.

"I ain't trying to strangle him. I'm seeing is he still alive."

"Is he?"

"No he ain't, no thanks to you."

"You had the same opportunity as I to stop him." He tapped two fingers against his chin, considering. "Fortunately, Mr. MacGuffin and I had a little chat before you arrived. He told me where Connor plans to rendezvous with the ships that will take him and his men to a certain place."

"What d'ye mean, 'a certain place'?"

"I will divulge that to the senior officer on this station."

"You should tell me in case something happens to you."

"That is exactly why I won't tell you. I want you to take very good care of me. In the meanwhile we must arrest Connor, which we may yet do if we act quickly. I suspect he is going through Pétion's files in Fort Beliotte as we speak, looking for certain documents that might prove dangerous to him. He also absconded with all my notes when he abandoned me here."

"Who cares about your notes? Pétion's about to move," I snapped. "He's already got all the intelligence he's going to get about Toussaint's army. He's already committed."

"I mean my notes on *Connor*, you fool. He's as white as you are. There are also documents that could prove damaging to a certain highly placed American official, whose name I can't divulge as yet."

I eyed him up and down, wondering if he was trying a new piece of bait. Either way, he knew it was too tempting for me not to snap at it. "You wouldn't be talking about a certain assistant U.S. consul, would you?"

He gave me a fishy stare from behind his spectacles. "As I said—"

Juge ran back into the cell. "*Bon sang!* What is the screaming?"

"Mr. MacGuffin has spared us the trouble and expense of a trial." I filled him in on what Franklin had said. "I take it you didn't find Connor."

"No. Let us fetch this villain at once."

I yanked the dagger out of MacGuffin's spine. With Voyou and Juge on my heels, I marched out of the room without looking back. A clever man, Franklin—I'd lost interest in him.

As we dashed through a confused crowd of soldiers toward Fort Beliotte, a pair of rockets rose from the bay and burst overhead, lighting up the clouds with a sullen crimson glow.

"*Gare à vous!*" says I. "Look out!" And then a roaring filled the air, followed an instant later by the boom of the frigate's twelve-pounders and the crack of the schooner's sixes out in the bay. The wind of a passing ball spun me around and threw me on my face. I looked up to see my companions scattered around me—Juge sprawling on his back, moving his arms and legs like an upended turtle; Voyou on his belly, peeking through his fingers; and Franklin fumbling around on his hands and knees, as if looking for his stolen writing desk.

"Come *on*," I said. We might have two minutes before the next salvo, and the air would be filled with a steady rain of iron once the faster gun crews began to outpace the others.

Officers were herding the mulatto army into the central square and sorting them into their proper units. Another salvo sailed in, kicking up stone chips and knocking men around.

"Stand steady! Close up," cried the officers.

"Let us move or let us lie on the ground," called a soldier.

"Non, garçons!" cried Pétion from astride a gray charger. "Am I not more exposed than you, as is fitting and proper? We must not move until we move as one. If you trust in me and do your duty as Frenchmen, we will soon be drinking rum with our comrades in Petite Goâve. This I promise you! In the meantime, we must give Dessalines time to swallow the bait. Hear the fighting to the east? Already he falls into our trap!"

The soldiers gave him a cheer, too preoccupied to bother with the four of us.

We shoved our way along the edge of the crowd till we came to the gates of Fort Beliotte. But for the torches sputtering in their sconces in the arched entry hall, all was quiet. In the guardroom three grenadiers had been stabbed to death. There was no one else around, neither in the hall nor on the wide stairs as we ran up into smoky darkness.

Connor arose from behind Pétion's desk as we burst in. On the desk stood a lighted candle, and beside the candle lay his pocket pistol—on full cock, but out of easy reach. It was hellish hot in the room. Smoke beyond the balcony glowed in the firelight, and from upstairs came the moaning of flames.

"Oh, good," said Connor, as if he had sent me on a minor errand and then forgotten about it, "you have found Juge." Ignoring the pistols in our hands, he went back to rummaging through the drawer he'd pried open. "Your work here is done, Mr. Graves. You may go now." He started to put a paper in his inside pocket, but then he looked again at my pistol and thought better of reaching a hand into his coat. He placed the paper on the desk and gestured at Juge. "Toussaint will wish to see his protégé as soon as possible. Oughtn't you to be going?"

"It's a little crazy outside right now. I think I'll wait a bit." I sidled around till I could see everyone in the room. Franklin followed me, uncomfortably close.

"Do put up your pistol, Mr. Graves," said Connor. "It is one thing to be shot a-purpose, but it should gall me severely to be holed through carelessness."

"Mr. Connor, I aim to bring you aboard the *Croatoan*."

"I appreciate the escort," said he, riffling through a sheaf of papers and then tossing them aside, "but I am expected elsewhere. Ah." He pulled a familiar-looking paper out of the drawer. Villon's letter. Holding his coat open by the lapel, and moving ever so slowly, he tucked it into his breast pocket.

"I'm sure Dessalines will be eager to have a chat with you," I said, "if ye'd rather go see him instead."

"No, no, that will not be necessary." He closed the drawer with his thigh and leaned on the desk, looking at the shuttered lantern that Voyou carried.

I snapped my fingers, the way he'd snapped his at me. "Step away from the desk. And I want that letter."

"I believe your powder is wet, Mr. Graves," said Connor.

I was watching his hands, but he made no move to pick up his pistol. He blew out the candle instead. And then in the sudden darkness, Franklin grabbed me in a bear hug and threw me against the wall.

Out of the corner of my eye I saw the door of the lantern snap open, fixing Connor in the glare of its bull's-eye lens. Then Connor's pistol blazed, and Voyou dropped the lantern with a grunt. Juge's pistol flashed in the pan—a misfire. The lantern clanked across the floor, the light flicking on and off as the shutter opened and closed.

In the points of light that punctuated the darkness I caught a glimpse of Juge shaking out his length of chain, and of Franklin, who but never carried a weapon, lurching after me with a knife in his hand. Cuss me for a slackjawed ninny—I'd taken the dagger out of MacGuffin's back but forgotten to search his body. Then the lantern went out and Franklin was on me like a duck on a June bug.

"You son of a bitch! You traitor," I squeaked. I tried to kick away from him, but he was stronger than I'd took him for. The point of the dagger scraped along my ribs. I grabbed his wrist, but he grabbed my pistol with his other hand. I pulled the trigger and hoped to Christ I'd shot him for his trouble. He let go suddenly, at any rate, and I lurched face first into the corner of the desk. That lit up the inside of my head like jubilee, but of the room I couldn't see a damn thing. I stood up, holding out my sword the way a blind man does with a cane.

A shadow on my right ducked under my guard. I backhanded the son of a bitch with my elbow and then punched his head with the steel handguard of my sword. I heard the crunch of teeth or bone—*oh, happy day!* thinks I, pretty proud of myself—and as I went to follow through with my blade, there was a flash and a bang in my skull.

A pistol must've gone off right behind my left ear. A roaring silence filled my head. *Oh, lordy,* I thought as my legs gave way, *I'm struck deef as well as blind.* I stretched out on the floor. It was cool and smooth— quite comfortable, actually, in the tropic heat. I gazed thoughtfully up at the flames licking through suddenly bright seams in the ceiling as someone tripped over me and stumbled off toward the doorway. *Ain't deef after all,* I thought, pleased with the notion. I heard a whoosh and a clank and a yelp, and then I decided to sleep for a while.

We trudged beside a road that ran straight as a rifle bullet toward— I looked up at the stars in the clear night sky—toward the east. The Baynet Road, I decided, though I couldn't remember how I knew that name. The road was silvery in the moonlight. All around us women struggled along with their children in tow. Squadrons of cavalry trotted past us on the road, filling the air with the tang of horse lather. My companions and I walked without speaking. The snorting of the horses and the jingling of the harness seemed horribly loud in the unnatural quiet. I wanted very much to tell someone that the rain had stopped, and that the stars and moon were out, but everybody seemed so anxious to get wherever we were going that I thought maybe they didn't care about rain and stars and moonlight. The clouds had gone and the moon hung in the sky like a bloody eye. It was the smoke that made it look that way. The air was filled with smoke. I walked with my hand on a litter on which a groaning man lay, clutching his belly and coughing up smoke.

The musketry behind us increased, answered by cannons. Two pieces, I judged, nine-pounders or maybe twelves—heavy field artillery. Somebody back there was getting it, sure as shooting.

"Sure as shooting—ha ha!" I said to the litter-bearer next to me. He shushed me, and whispered something in what sounded like French. I could've sworn I'd spoken in the same language. No, that couldn't be right. The joke didn't make sense in French.

From off to our right came a pounding of hooves, closing fast. The cavalry that had been screening us wheeled to meet them.

The men carrying the litter stopped. The black man who was leading us said something that wasn't in English or French, but which I understood well enough that I wasn't surprised when they hurried their burden behind an outcropping of rock.

The sounds of a terrible fight came from our right.

I was proud that I spoke French. I conjugated various verbs as I continued walking, uncurious about the fight or where my companions had gone, but the black man came back and grabbed my arm.

"*Bonsoir,* Juge," I said, surprised that I hadn't recognized him before. "*Parlez-vous français?*"

"Idiot! Shut up and come with me!"

"That's no way to talk to an old shipmate."

He pulled me down behind the rocks. I heard thunder. I popped my head up again. A line of shrieking hussars fell on the women and children. Juge yanked me down again. I threw him off and stood up, watching in horror.

"*Aba blan avek milat! Tuyé moun-yo!*" The hussars tore the women and children to pieces with saber and hoof. "Down with the whites and mulattoes! Kill them!" They slaughtered those who raised their hands or fell to their knees—children, women covering their babies with their bodies—and darted like dogs after those who ran.

I sat down on my own accord. "I also speak Creole, apparently," I said, and Juge clamped his hand over my mouth and sat on me. I continued watching from around the edge of the rocks.

The hussars' bugler sounded the recall and their colonel stood in his stirrups, waving his sword overhead. He pointed toward the burning town in the distance.

A company of cuirassiers lumbered up the road toward the hussars, haloed by the inferno behind them. At their head rode Pétion on his gray war-horse. The hussars faced about and charged. Wild yells—a hollow thump of horse colliding with horse—the clang of steel on steel and the soft snickety-snick of long blades slicing through muscle and bone. The cuirassiers reeled, recovered—and then broke as a mass of infantry smashed into their flank. Pétion fled with the black hussars in chase.

The colonel let them go and turned to direct the infantry: "The Second Demi-brigade, form up on me!" His horse carried him near our hidey-hole.

"That's Christophe," I said, but Juge had already leaped up onto the rocks, waving his arms over his head. "Chef de Brigade Christophe!" he called. "It is I, Juge! Over here, Citizen-Colonel Christophe! Do not shoot!"

The mounted cadre that had stayed with the colonel closed in on our hiding place, their horses prancing and their sabers drawn, and infantrymen rushed at us with their bayonets gleaming in the moon-light, but Christophe ran his horse alongside us and plied the flat of his sword among his men until they backed off.

"Well met, Lieutenant Juge!" he said at last. "I trust I find you in good health on this delightful evening—and M'sieur Graves, as well! Father Toussaint will be happy. Sergeant-major, a guard of honor for these fellows. You will excuse me, Juge, but I have urgent work this night." He sloped his saber on his shoulder and trotted off into the sil-very moonlight, with the Second Demi-brigade baying the battle song of the grenadiers as they loped after him:

> *Grenadiers, à l'asso!*
> *Se ki mouri zaffaire à yo.*
> *Ki a pwon papa,*
> *Ki a pwon maman.*
> *Grenadiers, à l'asso!*
> *Se ki mouri zaffaire à yo!*

> *Grenadiers, to the assault!*
> *Those who die, that's their affair.*
> *They have no papa,*
> *They have no mama.*
> *Grenadiers, to the assault!*
> *Those who die, that's their affair!*

Eighteen

"An empty bucket is soonest mended," said Surgeon Quilty as he finished bandaging my head. "It's a lucky thing Mr. Connor didn't hit you someplace vital, ha ha!"

I had a vicious headache, and even the muted light of the *Rattle-Snake*'s sick berth was like an auger in my eyes. I closed them, but that was worse. I seemed to spin in darkness, and my stomach started knocking at my tonsils. I opened my eyes as little as I could. "What did he hit me with?"

He looked at me closely and then nodded as if to himself. "A small knife that he carried in his waistband, apparently. Seems he tried to trepan you with it, but your skull is so hard that the blade snapped off."

"What's 'trepan'?"

"It means to drill a hole in the skull. We do it to relieve pressure on the brain, mostly."

I touched the bandage. "It feels like he stuck it in my head."

He moved my hand away. "None of that, or I'll lash your hands to the cot again." He dropped his mock scowl in favor of his usual cheerful look, saying, "Indeed he did stick it in your head, young sir. You might even say he stuck it in your ear, ha ha!"

"Please, Mr. Quilty."

"Yes. I beg pardon. Well, young sir, the point of the knife struck the left temporal bone, partially severing the ear, passed along the *os parietale*—that is to say the temple—and lodged beneath the *os zygomaticum*, which forms part of the orbit. You would call it the cheekbone. There the blade snapped off, leaving the tip of it stuck in your head, as you say. However, I removed it without incident—the blade, not your head—and sewed your ear back where nature intended it to be."

"He cut my ear off?"

"Near enough as makes no difference, ha ha!" He was entirely too cheerful for my taste. "However, please God it is healing nicely, and the masticular muscles escaped damage for the most part. I was more concerned with your eye, but though the edge of the blade lay alongside the orb, it neither punctured nor even scratched it. At any rate, the danger has passed." Despite the confidence in his voice, he touched the wood of my cot when he said it.

"I don't recollect a dang thing."

"This is entirely usual." He pulled the sheet up to my chin and tucked me in. "When there is an injury to the head, often the patient remembers nothing of the blow, and sometimes nothing of what happened during the several minutes or even hours beforehand. And sometimes he lies comatose for days, weeks or indeed sometimes for the rest of his life, such as it is."

"No, I remember now," I said. "Someone shot me. I remember the flash and the bang."

"It would be natural to interpret the blow that way, but it is not a true memory. A blow of such violence would rattle what little brain you have around in your skull, which would account for your perception of a 'flash and a bang,' as you put it."

"I see." I remembered going into Pétion's office and seeing Connor there, but I was a little fuzzy about what had happened next. "Is Franklin aboard?"

"Not aboard the *Rattle-Snake,* no. Mr. Towson brought you and your entourage off while he was fetching the guns from shore, but my colleague in the *Croatoan* would not let Franklin move once he saw his condition. You, however, insisted on coming here. You made such a row that they were glad to indulge you. Even after you had returned to the bosom of your shipmates, it took quite some doing to convince you that you had indeed arrived home."

"Oh dear."

"Oh dear is right. You blackened Mr. Horne's eye for him. It took great forbearance on his part not to return the favor, I dare say, but instead he sat on you till you had calmed down. Speaking of calm, you must remain so for several weeks more. A dim room and a vegetable diet for you, and this time I mean to hold you to it."

He made me count the fingers he held up and moved a finger back and forth while I followed it with my eyes.

"Let's see," he said. "A history of head injury—you nearly got your brains dashed out in the Bight of Léogâne, I remember."

"Yes. A gun blew up next to me. Knocked me clean out of my wits for a while." That was only last January, but it seemed like something from another lifetime.

"And you have a number of lumps on your head, and your nose has been broken recently. Do you recall bumping your head at any other time?"

"I don't remember, Mr. Quilty. Maybe. I seem to remember falling off a horse at some point."

He nodded. "A loss of consciousness accompanied by a loss of certain memories but not others. Any seizures?"

"Don't think so."

"Numbness in the extremities?" He put the back of his hand against my cheek.

I turned my face away. I didn't want to be touched. "No."

"Nausea and vomiting."

"Only when I stick my hands into rotten corpses."

"I'll take that as a no, but earlier you were a veritable fountain at both ends. Weakness and lethargy, I dare say?"

"You could call it that." Quilty was a kindly cuss, but he was getting on my nerves. "Say, what's this all about, anyway?"

"And personality changes," he said, as if ticking off the last box on a mental checklist. He said it as if it were a fact, not a question. I asked him what he meant by it—and pretty sharp, I guess—but he just put his things away, told me to get some sleep, and left.

➤ ➤ ➤

As soon as he had gone I pushed the sheet off me, the better to take advantage of a cool breeze coming down the forward hatchway. From the schooner's smooth swoops and the way we were heeled over to larboard, I calculated we were sailing large under a brisk topsail breeze on the starboard tack. Which was odd if we were bound for the Leeward Islands, as I supposed we must be.

"Saint Kitts, probably," I muttered, picking at a long scratch in my side. It didn't hurt much, but it itched like Old Harry. I snugged myself down for a nap. "Cousin Billy, that old soak, has overshot his mark, and now we're having to run up from south of Nevis." Commodore Truxtun was based in Basseterre in Saint Kitts, of course, and naturally we would rejoin him now that we had delivered our convoy and Mr. P. Hoyden Blair to Port Républicain . . .

Lightning bolts of pain fired in my head as I sat up. We hadn't been attached to Truxtun's Leeward Islands squadron since a month or more. Billy was dead, Peter was captain . . . I swung my feet to the deck, meaning to run up to the quarterdeck to ask whither we were bound, but a wave of nausea washed over me and I had to hug the cot till it passed.

"I shouldn't, old man," drawled an English voice. "The sick-room attendants are right terrors in this ship. Mind, they'll strap you down again if you ain't careful."

"The *Rattle-Snake*'s a schooner, not a ship, you lubber. And they're loblolly boys, not sick-room attendants." But the voice was familiar, and I turned my head to see Treadwell propped up on one elbow in the opposite cot. "Why, you old cuss! You're looking tolerable."

"Likewise, I'm sure." He looked at me carefully. "You recognize me?"

"Course I do. Why shouldn't I?"

"Oh, no reason, sir. No reason at all." Emotions played across his face: caution gave way to bashfulness, which suddenly gave way to a great sunny grin. He patted a heavily bandaged leg. "Hang it, I'm delightfully well, Mr. Graves, I must say. Tip-top. It's a wonder what a week's rest'll do, along with knowin' one's leg is still in its proper place an' not feedin' the sharks, ha ha! Pepin and his talk of the knife—the old quacksalver was dead wrong, ha ha!"

"Well, dead at any rate," I said, before closing my mind to the memory of the French doctor on Cravache's wheel. I couldn't remember if that had been before or after we'd hauled Treadwell out of the prison. It must've been before, but everything was all jumbled up in my head. "I'm glad you kept your leg, sir."

"Thank'ee ever so, Mr. Graves. Apologize for bein' such a mewlin' prat before. Don't know what came over me."

"Forget it. *I* have. But say—what d'ye mean, 'a week's rest'? I brung you aboard just the day before yesterday. You're out of your reckoning."

"I meant it in a general sense, sir. It's been ten days, actually. But we have been *underway,* as you sea dogs put it, for a week now."

"Ten days! How you talk. I just come aboard this morning."

He shook his head. "Ten days, sir. Every day brings me closer to the day I'll walk again, and so I count each one."

"Ten days," I said again. "Where have I been these ten days?"

"Out of your head, that's where. And not quiet about it, either."

"Lordy. That must be what Quilty meant when he threatened to lash me down 'again.' The people must think I'm gone for a lunatic."

"I'll say. But you seem to have come back to yourself. I'm glad of it, too. Bit disconcerting, bunking with a madman, y'know. There were a few nights I wished for a pistol under my pillow, ha ha!"

I lay back, thinking it over. Except for the blinding headache, I felt fit enough. If we'd been at sea for a week, then obviously I'd had a week to recover. That was long enough for any old salt to be lying about idle, I guessed, but I thought maybe I'd have a nap anyway. I yawned. "Where are we bound?"

"Dunno. Something about chasing a pink . . . erm, monosyllable, and a friggin' arm-flute."

"A pink mono . . . ? Oh! The *Rose-red Cunt* and a frigate armed *en flute,* you mean?"

He giggled. "Well, yes, that's what they said."

I kicked the sheet the rest of the way off and hauled myself upright. "Ahoy! Ahoy, you loblolly boys," I roared, despite the agony it raised in my head. When one of Quilty's assistants stuck a wary head through the door, I said, "You there. My respects to the captain, and I'll come on deck now."

He shook his head, prim as a maiden aunt in fresh-boiled flannel. "Oh no, sir, not without the surgeon gives the word."

"My respects to the *captain*, damn your eyes, and tell him I'm fit for duty."

"Being fit for duty is Mr. Quilty's department, sir," he said, the little priss. "Without he gives the word—"

"Enough." Getting angry just made the room spin around. I waited till it had stopped, and said: "My respects to the captain, and where the hell are my clothes?"

"Them words exactly, sir?" He plucked nervously at a button on his shirt.

"Yes, them words exactly, consarn it." I pointed in the general direction of the quarterdeck. "I'm perfectly in command of my wits, and I just gave you an order. Go."

It took some persuading, pleading even, but at last Quilty allowed me to be strapped to a chair and carried up on deck. To my annoyance he insisted that I be wrapped in a blanket against the breeze, but he also insisted that a piece of sail be set up for an awning to shade my eyes, for which I was grateful. I kept my eyes shut during most of the operation, but after the hands had lashed my chair to a ringbolt between a pair of guns on the leeward side where I'd be out of the way, and most of all after they had stopped *jostling* me, I managed a few squints to get my bearings. It was a piercingly bright afternoon, with a few clouds scudding down the wind high overhead and a rainbow shining in the spray on the starboard bow. My lids were heavy and I settled in for a doze.

"I trust you have found your wits again."

I opened my eyes to see Peter Wickett standing before me with his hands clasped behind his back. The stubble was black along his jaw and the skin was taut across his cheekbones, as if he hadn't slept in several days—which he probably hadn't, with a chase in sight.

"Yes, sir," I said. It wasn't true that I'd found my wits, but the truth was too complicated to explain. "What's our course and position?"

"We are headed nor'west by west, seventy-seven degrees and thirty minutes west of London this noon. Unless we carry something away, we may cross the tropic sometime in the evening watch." The leading edge of the fore-topsail snapped in the breeze. Peter said nothing, but he shot a bitter look at Mr. Rogers at the conn.

"Watch your luff there!" said Rogers.

"Watch your luff, sir, aye aye," said the quartermaster, and the tiller-man repeated the order even though he'd already corrected the error. Rogers needed no rebuke, implied or spoken—but it was a sign of the strain Peter was under that he would notice the sailing master's business at all, and Rogers let it roll off his back.

I pictured the latitude and longitude on the chart in my mind. "That puts us in the Bahama Channel, sir, about ten leagues south of Andros."

"I have noticed this, yes," said Peter. A faint pleasure shone in his cold gray eyes.

"Are we going home, then?"

He gave me a sardonic look. "Depends on our friends." He looked across the starboard bow. "You cannot see from here, but we are in chase of *L'Heureuse Rencontre*—"

"The *Rose-red Cunt!*"

"—And a frigate called the *Faucon*. She is armed *en flute*." He scratched the puckered scar on his cheek. "Do you recall either of them?"

He'd gotten the scar from a musket ball during a fight with picaroons in January. An image came to me of him holding a bloody tooth in his hand and then throwing it overboard. I recalled it clearer than things that'd happened more recently. "Of course, sir. We fought *L'Heureuse Rencontre* off Port Républicain." I recollected *being* in that fight very well, although most of my memories seemed to be centered on Mr. MacElroy's hat. "But I disremember any ship called the *Faucon*."

"I did not know it myself till your Mr. Franklin told us."

"*En flute* means her guns've been taken out of her. She's got nothing but holes in her sides, like a flute. A transport, most like." That rang a bell somewhere.

He gave me a curious look, as if my answer weren't all he'd expected. "Most of the guns, anyway," he said, with the air of a schoolmaster dropping hints. "They still have their quarterdeck and fo'c's'le guns. Ten long eights, I should think. That gives us a slight advantage in weight of metal, if we can take her while Captain Block engages the corvette. They will be loath to allow it. But more importantly they have several hundreds of troops aboard, which will make it unhealthy to grapple with them. I hope to do this in the Straits of Florida."

Little bits were falling back into place. "Is the *Croatoan* with us, sir?"

"Did I not just say so? Last night she was close enough to use her bow chasers. The corvette yawed as if to give her a broadside, but he soon changed his mind when he saw Block was having none of it."

"Block can sail twelve knots to our ten. Why don't he go in and knock 'em around some?"

"I have not presumed to ask."

I chewed that over for a while. With his twenty-four 12-pounders and eight 9-pounders, Block could stand off and shoot 'em both to pieces if he wanted. But as Peter said, it weren't our business to second-guess a post-captain.

"Where did you find 'em, sir?"

"Three days ago off Miragoâne, just as your Mr. Franklin said. They had the heels of us, at least at first."

"Where are they bound, sir?"

"I do not know. Franklin lapsed into coma before he could say."

I could make no connection between Miragoâne and Franklin, but my blood stirred at the sound of his name. I recollected he had a couple of friends who were wrong 'uns. There was a gaunt white man who had a face like Death, or maybe he was just dead, and a dashing mulatto who was as white as I was, whatever that might mean. And the port town of Miragoâne lay some sixteen miles west of Rigaud's stronghold at Petite Goâve. A man on horseback could make it in no time, assuming he lived to make the ride . . .

"How are things at Jacmel, sir?"

"Apparently Pétion made it out, but Toussaint destroyed his army in the forest. I am told you witnessed it."

I had an image of a woman's head rolling across a moonlit road. There had been cavalry—I remembered the smell of the horses and the creak of the harness. And there had been a man on a litter, clutching his belly. None of it made much sense. Or maybe I didn't want it to. And there had been a black knight with white hands, speaking in Latin with a knife in his back.

Peter studied me while I thought. "Mr. Quilty is of the mind that you should be below. Are you fit? Truth, now."

"I 'low I'm glad of this chair, sir."

"I mean in your faculties, Mr. Graves. Are you addled?"

"Oh no, sir, my thinking is entirely clear. It's just that I seem to have forgotten a few things. They're right on the edge of my mind, though, upon my oath."

"Then perhaps we can clear a few things up for you. Here," he said to Freddy Billings, a mop-headed ship's boy who had been hovering behind him and looking at me shyly, "run down to the wardroom and tell our guest that Mr. Graves is on his feet again." He gave me a quick half-smile. "So to speak. It seems you have stirred up a hornet's nest, Matty."

"I calculate I bung-holed it completely, if that's what you mean."

He pursed his lips. "Not at all. Your best thinking seems ever to get you in over your head, but you have a talent for surrounding yourself with competents to fish you out again. Speaking of whom—*bonjour, monsieur le commandant.*"

"*Bonjour, monsieur le capitaine.* How fares our invalid?"

"As well as may be expected, Major."

"*Bonjour,* Juge." I laughed as I remembered something from that horrible night. "Say, do you speak French at all?"

He gave me a puzzled look. "Obviously, as that is what we speak at this very moment." He spoke it with a slur, too. Then he showed his broken teeth in a smile. "And the Creole, too, apparently." He had a patchwork of plasters stuck to his head, white as spinster's lace against his black skin. "He is ever the impertinent one," he said to Peter. "No doubt you chastise him often."

"Not so often as would be good for him, sir," said Peter. "Your pardon, gentlemen." He walked back over the slanting deck to the windward rail, where he stood with his chin thrust out and his fingers twitching behind his back, running his eyes aloft as he watched jealously for any flaw in the intricate balance of sails and spars and rigging that might warn him that something was about to carry away. He'd have been there these past three days, knowing him, wringing every last fathom he could out of the old schooner by sailing her on the edge of disaster and no closer.

I supposed the transport and the corvette were old and hadn't had their bottoms scraped in a while, or they'd have sailed the *Rattle-Snake* under the horizon by now. Block would be playing it sly in the *Croatoan*, keeping the enemy in sight but spilling his wind from time to time to allow us to keep up. It wasn't the dashingest way to snare a pair of weasels, but maybe it was the smartest way.

When I was sure Peter was deep in his thoughts I said, "My God, Juge, you didn't tell him you're a major, did you?"

Holding himself with stiff dignity—belied by the hasty way he grabbed at a backstay as the schooner corkscrewed over a roller—he said: "How do you know Father Toussaint did not promote me for my gallantry?"

"Did he?"

He gave me a lazy grin and said, "*Bon sang,* how you raved! You are not so tough, *hein?* I, however, am the remarkable fellow."

"The remarkably *green* fellow," I retorted, eyeing the color of his cheeks and the little beads of sweat on those parts of his face that weren't covered in plasters. "How's the stomach? Does it lie easily within you, or does it rise up and down with the sea?"

He lost hold of a little groan as the *Rattle-Snake* took an inconsequential lurch to leeward, but he steadied himself on the backstay again and recomposed the grin on his face. "I have the *sea legs* now," he said, the English phrase sounding odd on his lips. "In time I become the veritable Sinbad." Sea legs or not, he perched himself on the gun carriage beside me and gave me a close look. "But why so downcast, *mon ami?*"

"Seeing you has brought it all back to me. Connor, Franklin, MacGuffin and the Knights of the White Hand—I completely buggered it, didn't I? Franklin was right about Connor, and I let him get away."

Juge nodded. "Yes, it is so—Connor eludes us for the moment, but we know where to find him when we need him."

"Where, then?"

He pointed forward. "Why, in one of those ships, of course!"

I wished I could stand up and take a look for myself. I could see the *Croatoan*'s topmasts about half a mile ahead, though, as we crested a roller. The sea was chopping up, and she was getting her studding sails in. Rogers looked up at our own topmast studding sails and raised an inquiring eyebrow at Peter, but Peter ignored him.

"Connor made me his pigeon," I said. "And there he goes with all the evidence. He's probably burned most of it by now."

"No, he has burned nothing but his fingers, ha ha!"

I grabbed his wrist. "You got his papers?"

"*Mais oui!*"

"How, if he got away?"

He ducked his head, mumbling, "After I smote poor Voyou with my chain—"

"I *thought* I heard you hit someone."

"An unfortunate accident. It was dark, you will remember. Anyway," he said, sitting up straight again, "I grabbed Connor by his collar. I *collared* him, as I think you Americans say, no?"

"You nabbed him, yes. Then what? You arrested him?"

"Indeed so. I said to him, 'I detain you, monsieur, in the name of France.' At least this is what I started to say. Before I could finish, he slipped out of his coat and ran away like the deer, leaving us with all the papers in his pockets. Were it not that my friends are so much weaker than I—you with the bump on the *caboche*, Voyou with a chain wrapped around his head, and Franklin with a bullet in his middle and his teeth knocked out, I should have had him."

"I recall hitting someone, and I remember you carrying a man on a litter. So that was Franklin?"

"Yes, of course. And Voyou was the man at the other end of the litter. A very tough fellow, that one. Never once did he complain of the headache."

I started to scratch my head, but thought better of it in case Quilty was lurking where he could see me. "So, Connor shot Franklin, did he?"

Juge held up a finger. "Connor shot Voyou—through the lantern and not the body, I am glad to say, though I hardly think this was his intention. And before that, my pistol misfired." He waggled the finger at me. "Only one loaded pistol then remained in the room, *mon ami.*"

"Franklin attacked me, Juge. He tried to kill me." I thought about it. "Well, he tried to take my pistol, anyway."

"Hardly the same thing, *mon ami.*"

"He had a dagger in his hand."

He shrugged. "So he had a dagger in his hand. Did he stab you until you are dead? He did not. You mustn't take offense. I think, *mon ami,* he tried to prevent your killing Mr. Connor. He wants very badly to take him back to Washington, no? Although for my part, I think the sooner the cockroach is stepped on the better."

"Well, now, Franklin and I have our differences, but it's a bit much to call him a cockroach."

"Ha ha! I speak of Connor. But I tell you true, my interest is to see that he does not associate Father Toussaint's name with a lie. To prevent this, I would have him die." He touched my arm. "Assuming he still lives, of course. He may have died trying to leave Jacmel. All was chaos that night, and perhaps the buzzards have eaten his eyes these several days ago. But because these ships try to elude us, I think it is impossible he is not aboard one of them."

"Of course they want to elude us. They're full of soldiers bound for places they aren't supposed to be!"

"Yes, but without Connor, they would not go in the first place, *hein?* It is self-evident."

"I should talk to him."

"*Bon sang!* Have I not said that many people wish to talk to this Connor?"

"No, I mean Franklin."

He shook his head angrily. "There is no chance of speaking to him, assuming he still lives. Your captain refused me in the most astonishing terms when I asked it of him. I said to him he could just put this nimble little boat next to the big clumsy one and I could jump from one to the other. Simplicity itself, no? But he said it was dangerous. As if I, Juge, care about danger."

Doing such a thing would risk staving in the schooner against the frigate's stout timbers. I had such a perfect picture of the look of horror that must've crossed Peter's face at the suggestion that I had to laugh.

"*Bon sang*, but you sailors are merry fellows," said Juge, looking cross. "Always the laughter whenever I open my mouth."

We crossed the Tropic of Cancer shortly after the first bell in the evening watch, on as pleasant an evening as ever there was. The stars and half-moon lighted our way, and green phosphorescence creamed along our bows and folded over itself in our wake, but Quilty cut my pleasure short.

"You must go below to take a light supper of portable soup," he said. He took my pulse and examined my tongue, though I couldn't imagine what he hoped to find there. "And after you've eaten, sir, you will confine yourself to your cabin, where you will stay except to take the air for an hour or two in the forenoon watch. Weather and your head permitting, of course."

Portable soup, which is a sort of thin, reconstituted glue with bits of decayed vegetables floating in it, was reserved for the infirm and the addled. And because why? Because no one with the strength or the wits to resist would eat it. I ate it with a bit of ship's biscuit with hardly any weevils in it yet. The *Rattle-Snake* had only been at sea for three and a half months, and the bread was no harder than a brick and probably as nutritious.

Juge had risen from his bunk to join me, taking only a biscuit and some tea. He watched me tap my biscuit on the table before I ate it. He mimicked my motions as if he'd been tapping his bread all his life, but curiosity got the better of him and he asked me why I did it. He blanched when I showed him what had crawled out among the crumbs, but he soaked his biscuit in his tea and made himself work a mouthful down before setting the rest of it aside.

"It counts as meat," he said. "I really mustn't eat it. And I of course have already eaten, anyway. I merely keep you company."

"There are two kinds of sailors, Juge. Them that's been seasick and them that's going to be seasick. It's nothing to be ashamed of."

"I tell you I have not the hunger."

I let it go. If he could take a beating and slit a throat without a thought, it was his right to blanch at a few weevils in his bread. I sat there, gnawing at my biscuit, trying to get a purchase on it with my teeth the same way I was trying to get a purchase on a puzzle in my mind. "Juge," I said, "when you took those papers from Connor, did you give them all to Franklin?"

He fished some weevils out of his tea. "And why would I not?"

"But did you?"

"All the important ones. All I kept was a letter of no consequence."

My hand jerked and my spoon flew across the table. "A letter! Addressed to a Madame Villon Deloges, perhaps?"

"I think so." He wiped soup off his sleeve and handed me back my spoon. Then he took the letter out of his coat pocket and looked at the back. "Yes, the Madame Villon Deloges in the Rue Rigole-Haut. A funny name—"

"Give me that!"

"You need not snatch it. Is it so very important?"

"Franklin and Connor thought so. And Franklin thinks Madame Villon Deloges doesn't exist." I spread the letter open on the table.

"And so did Pétion, although he seemed mighty glad to have this."

"So, why?"

"I don't know. Can't you see I'm reading?"

It began:

> *"Mais où sont les neiges d'antan. O, where are the snows of yesteryear?" How often I reflect with remorse on the years that pass between us . . .*

It rambled along in that vein for a while. It was pretty flowery stuff, I thought, even from a doomed man. "French script is squiggly enough as it is," I said, "but the writing is funny in places. I can hardly make it out, sometimes."

"I noticed this too," said Juge. He had come around the table to read it over my shoulder. "He mentions you."

"Where?"

"Down at the bottom. There." He pointed at the last paragraph.

> *I entrust this note to a monsieur Graves, a noble but naïve young acolyte in the navy of the United States. He assures me I will not hang. If you read these words, my dear, you will know he was mistaken.*

I had been mistaken, all right. I'd even laughed at him while he clutched at my coat and begged me to help him escape. I thrust the memory back into the dark corner where I kept it and read the last of the letter. There were a couple of words crossed out, and then it finished with:

> *The Steersman comes for me, as he does for all. When he comes for you, give to him this answer and cross the sea of woe.*

"What is this *timonier*?" said Juge, pointing at the word.

"Steersman. Haven't you ever heard of a steersman?"

"*Bon sang!* Am I the Columbus that I should know this? And what steersman?"

I shrugged. "Charon, I suppose. He ferries the dead over the River

Acheron, according to the Greeks. And Acheron means River of Woe."

"Then for why does he not just say 'Charon'? And why does he say *sea* of woe when it's a river?"

I poked my elbow into his ribs. "It's poetry, man. You can't just come right out and say what you mean, you know, otherwise the words just kind of lie there."

"I prefer to say what I mean and leave it at that. And for why does he use the masculine when he says 'my dear'?"

I shrugged. "Maybe he was a sodomite. What I want to know is what 'this answer' is." I peered again at the misshapen letters. "That son of a bitch!" I shook the letter at Juge. "*This* is the answer!"

I dashed into my cabin and lit the lamp.

I went through each line with a pencil, underlining the oddly shaped letters. I found "Isla de Galvez," which I didn't know where it was, and the name Tejaz, which I guessed belonged to a Spaniard or a Portugee. In the back of my mind I was aware of a cry of dismay that floated down from above. It seemed to come from a distance, as across water.

"What is that?" said Juge. He went to the door and peered toward the hatchway.

"Nothing aboard of us." If Peter didn't want me, he could sail his own damn schooner. I worked my pencil across the lines of script. Here was a misshapen *B,* and an *L* in the next word, and then an *A.* "We'd have heard a great crack and plenty of shouting if we'd lost a spar or a sail. Someone will let us know if it's important."

But his fidgeting was making my head hurt again, and then the *Rattle-Snake*'s motion changed suddenly, as if we'd brought the wind forward of the beam. I heard the sound of the main topsail yard being braced around. "Maybe we'd better have a look," I said, but he was out of the wardroom before the words had finished leaving my mouth. I stuffed the letter into my pocket and ran up the ladder after him.

Bosun Klemso was shooing gawkers away from the rail. "Get on about yer business there!" he bellowed. "Them as ain't on watch, get below!"

His directives didn't apply to us, of course, so we stepped up to the quarterdeck and glanced around. Despite my words to Juge my first thought was to look aloft. I was still half-blind from having had my head under the lamp, but all seemed shipshape up there, with no topmen bustling around in the rigging and trying to wrassle down a cracked spar or busted sail. My next thought was to look toward the chases, but we were nearly abreast of the *Croatoan* and it was she that caught my eye.

She had flown up into the wind, and her profile was all wrong. As we surged up to windward of her I could see her main royal and topgallant masts hanging down on her leeward side, and I could hear her topmen shouting and the desperate thumping of an axe. The rest of her sails flapped and thundered as if they meant to tear themselves apart.

"Back the fore-tops'l," said Peter, and raised his speaking trumpet. "Ahoy the *Croatoan!* Do you require assistance, sir?"

"Nay!" came Block's shout. "Light thee along after the enemy! Cripple 'em if thee can. I reckon I'll be along shortly."

That was a hell of an order, I thought. He was sending us to do what he'd been scared to do himself. It was also unneeded. All we had to do was keep them in sight till we reached the American coast. Once they dropped anchor we could annoy them enough to keep them from landing their troops till help arrived.

"Very good, sir," said Peter. "I shall attempt to lure them to windward. Perhaps I can run one of them onto a cay between Andros and Grand Bahama."

"I don't give a hoot how thee does it! Go! Lose not a moment!"

"Aye aye, sir." Peter returned his speaking trumpet to the beckets, we braced our fore-topsail around, and the frigate disappeared in our wake.

"What is it?" said Juge.

"We're going to take a pounding," said I. "We've been ordered to play hounds and hares with the enemy."

"Hounds and hares? What is this?"

"It means we're off to catch a Tartar by the tail."

"A Tartar has a tail?"

"Dammit, I can't think of the French for it. It means we're going shark-fishing, with us as bait."

"Ah, I comprehend at last—we are to fight them!"

"Not if we can fucking help it."

"You astonish me. For why have we chased them these several days if not to fight them?"

"We were supposed to fight them with the frigate."

"But this is marvelous! The glory will be ours alone, ha ha!"

"Have you always been a lunatic? You don't know what we're getting into."

"Feh." The look of disgust he gave me exactly mirrored how I felt about myself. "Why don't you run along to bed now, as Monsieur Quilty orders. As for me, I shall find a way to make myself useful."

Already I could see the *L'Heureuse Rencontre* corvette silhouetted against the starry sky ahead. Her captain would have noticed instantly any change in *Croatoan's* position—once he was sure she was safely out of the way, he'd let us catch up or even turn on us. She and the transport, the not entirely toothless *Faucon* frigate, stood a much better chance of arriving unnoticed if they could shake us now.

"Mr. Rogers," said Peter. "Pray come a point to starboard."

"A point to windward, sir, aye aye. To the braces there, some of you men."

As we settled on our new course, trying to edge around upwind of the chases, Peter said, "Clear for action, please."

"All hands!" cried Rogers. "Clear for action!"

That was *my* line, I thought, but no one had even acknowledged my presence. I stepped up to Peter and saluted. "Present and ready for duty, sir."

"Get off my quarterdeck, sir!" he said. Then he added in a gentler tone, "I may need you later, Matty, but for now I think it best was you to stay out of the way. Mr. Quilty advises me that you are very ill."

Men scurried around striking everything below that wasn't needed on deck—which included me. Quilty appeared out of the bustle and grasped me by the arm, intending to march me off to bed like a little boy being sent to his room.

"I will not go down into the cable tier, Mr. Quilty."

"Then you'll come into the sick berth with me."

"No—you'll be needing every inch of deck space soon enough."

"Shush!" He gripped my arm tighter. "You know better than to talk like that. Very well—go to your cabin and stay there."

I sulked on my cot in the dark—all lights having being extinguished except the battle lanterns on the deck—and listened to the happenings in the various parts of the schooner. I could hear the Marine drummer boy beating "To Quarters," and the rumble as the guns were cast loose and run out. I even imagined I could hear the squeaking as the quarter-gunners screwed the flintlocks into the six-pounders. I definitely heard Master Gunner Schmidt mutter in his beard, "*Ja,* ve goink to catch hell this time, by golly by gumbo" as he made his way down into the depths of the magazine.

He said it quietly to himself, not knowing anyone could overhear him. I, on the other hand, had expressed my doubts quite clearly—to anyone who spoke French, anyway, but I marveled that I had spoken about it at all. It wasn't exactly pusillanimity, that odd word for cowardice, but such talk was expressly forbidden under penalty of death "or such other punishment as the court shall adjudge." Yet it made me wonder about myself, and if I wondered about myself then surely someone else would, too—Juge, for instance, and perhaps even Peter.

Then Peter called for silence fore and aft, and all I could hear for a long time was the rush of water past our hull. I opened my scuttle and looked at my watch in the dim light. Nearly nine o'clock—about an hour since Block had lost his topgallant mast. Surely he was under-way again by now, unless the falling spars had done the *Croatoan* some further mischief. In that case it might be hours and hours before he came wallowing up under jury rig, if he came at all.

Two bells struck. I got a pair of pistols out of my chest and loaded them in the dark. I felt around and hooked them alongside the death's-head sword and dagger on the belt that hung at the head of my cot. I lay down again, trying to find a soft spot for my head. The bandages itched. I wanted to tear them off and feel a hat on my head again. I got MacElroy's hat down off its peg and lay with it on my chest.

A distant boom rolled across the water from ahead and a bit to leeward. My cabin was on the leeward side, the aftermost wardroom cabin on the larboard side, but I couldn't see anything out the scuttle. The angle was wrong, and the scuttle was too small to stick my head through. I peered at my watch again. Nine fifteen. Peter called for the sail trimmers, and we came up another point, close-hauled now and thrashing to windward. My hanging cot bucked around like a bee-bit mule. Two more guns, closer this time, and then the thump and rumble of an answering gun overhead. The noise hurt like hell, and I wrapped my pillow around my skull. Then I thought I wouldn't want to be found with my head down and my ass in the air, and forced my-self to stretch out on my bunk. That way if anyone came in they might think I was asleep. "Nerves of steel, mate," they'd say. "So uncon-cerned he was, he slept right through the fracas, ha ha!"

We yawed to leeward and rolled off our starboard broadside. We continued the turn, wearing right around in a circle, and fired off the seven guns on the larboard side as well. I copped another squint through my scuttle.

L'Heureuse Rencontre, her hull lit from below by the glowing foam in her teeth, was perhaps half a mile away—say eight hundred yards, which was well within range of her guns. Then a happy thought struck me. The French wouldn't risk a formal declaration of war by letting their ships be used to land troops on American soil. That meant the men in the *Faucon* would be renegados, just like Connor. Probably sol-diers manned her guns; sailors were harder to come by than soldiers,

and they'd be busy sailing the ship anyway. Not that French artillerymen weren't any good—they were just about the best in the world—
but they weren't used to firing from a moving platform, and most of
'em were probably puking their guts out with *mal de mer.* But the corvette was another matter altogether.

She presented her beam. Then her side lit up all at once, which
cheered me considerable. Her firing in salvo meant her captain didn't
trust his gunners to hit anything on their own.

"Ya!" I said, thumbing my nose. "Ye lubbers couldn't hit a bull in
the ass with a—"

Then my cabin exploded.

Something heavy lay across me. As I gave the something a shove, I
realized it was my cot—what was left of it, anyway. The rest of it had
been knocked to flinders. I kicked it off and sat up. Above my head was
a jagged hole. It was right below where I'd been lying. Oak splinters
from the impact had torn away the partition between my cabin and
the wardroom, as if a giant shotgun had been fired off in there. It gave
me an excellent view right across the breadth of the schooner to where
the ball had smashed in the opposite partition and exited through a
matching hole on the other side. I could see moonlight shining on the
water over there.

I yanked my boots on, slipped my sword belt over my shoulder, and
stepped into the wardroom, where I stumbled over a pile of planks that
once had been our table.

We completed our turn and settled again on the starboard tack.
Water slopped in through the hole in my cabin.

"Ahoy the carpenter!" I found the companion and hauled myself
onto the main deck. "Pass the word there—we've been holed on the
waterline!"

Chips, the carpenter, bustled up with a maul in his hands. His two
mates had their arms full of wooden shot plugs. "Where away?" said
he.

"My cabin. There's another hole on the starboard side, in the master's cabin, but it's above water yet."

"Well, get out the way then, sir," he said. "By your leave," he added, as he and his mates shoved past me.

I ran up to the quarterdeck and found Peter. "Beg pardon, sir—"

"Why are you not in the sick berth, Mr. Graves?"

"Mr. Quilty allowed me to go to my cabin—"

"Then why are you not in your cabin?"

"Ain't got no cabin to be in, sir. We been holed twixt wind and water on the larboard side, and another hole higher up to starboard."

"Are we taking on water?"

"Some, sir, so long as we stay on this tack. Chips is already dealing with it."

"Very well. Mr. Rogers, I have the conn. Send some men to the pumps."

Rogers touched his hat. "Aye aye, sir, and I'll have a look below as well. Mr. Horne," he said to the burly bosun's mate, "get some men on the pumps until you're relieved."

We tacked, the schooner bringing the eye of the wind across her bow as prettily as ever. With the wind on the larboard beam, she heeled over enough to raise the hole out of the water. Peter and I peered over the side at it. Already Chips had stuffed the hole with my nice wool blankets and was pounding a plug into place.

Peter looked up as *L'Heureuse Rencontre* fired again. The balls shot the depths with weird green streaks as they plunged around us. "Not even in what charitably could be called a pattern," said he. "It was luck not skill that guided that ball. But I should like to have a greater distance between us."

He should have chosen his words more carefully. The corvette turned away, cracking on sail as she ran north after the *Faucon*, while we had to keep to eastward until Chips had finished his repairs. The thumping of his maul below decks echoed the thumping in my own head. Then I was lying on the deck looking up at Peter looking down at me.

Nineteen

A great roaring awoke me. "Great guns!" says I, trying to sit up. Something prevented it. I looked down along my body. I had a sheet over me, and three leather straps had been buckled athwart the sheet. Lashed down like a loony, by God! Some son of a bitch had put me back in the sick berth.

A thumping ran along our side—iron balls hitting the poor *Rattle-Snake*. The schooner shuddered as she fired off her broadside. Amid the booming of the six-pounders I caught the high barking of the murdering-pieces along the quarterdeck rail. The enemy must be close if we were using the swivels.

I turned my head. Treadwell was rolling around in the opposite cot. "Great guns, ha ha!" says I. "Did you catch that, Treadwell? I said *great guns.*"

He was trying to get his bandaged leg out from under the bed-clothes. It was lashed to a long splint that extended past his foot and which had gotten tangled in the ropes the cot hung from. "Yes, yes," he said—pretty testy, I thought. "What's happening?"

"How the hell should I know?" I squirmed under the leather straps. I spotted my pistols and sword hanging by the door. My britches and coat hung there, too. "Sounds like we've caught that corvette and the transport, or maybe t'other way around. Let me out of here and I'll go find out."

"No fear," said he, shaking his head. "You're mad!"

"Mad? I ain't mad. I'm *mad!*" No, the word is *angry*, I thought.

"You're a lunatic. How you've shouted this night and day."

"Don't be in such a pucker, Treadwell. What d'ye mean, night and day? Have we been fighting this whole time, and you just lying there?"

Fear and indignation mixed in his face. "What? No, it was quiet all day until now."

I made about as much progress under the straps as a fly in molasses. "Say, I don't aim to be caught abed if we get boarded. Come on now, be a good fellow and unstrap me."

"Shan't do it." He got his leg free at last and hobbled toward the door.

"Hey! Come back here, sir, and be damned!"

Just then a Marine and a loblolly boy shoved in, lugging a jack whose foot was a dripping mess of splintered bone and hanging flesh. Their momentum carried Treadwell right the way back to his cot.

"Set him down handsomely now," said Quilty, following up the rear. He leaned over the writhing man and clamped his thumb on the inside of the knee. "The tourniquet, quickly. You sir," he said to Treadwell. "I'm glad you're up. We'll need your cot." He looped the strap of the tourniquet around the man's lower thigh and gave several twists to the screw. "You," he said to the Marine, "help Mr. Treadwell to the wardroom."

"And me, too," says I, trying to make it an order and not a plea.

"No, he stays," said Quilty, and turned back to his patient. "Blankets, now—no, double them—and lay his head on a pillow." The loblolly boy made the wounded jack as comfortable as he could in preparation of the coming horror.

After Treadwell had gone I stared up at the deckbeams, listening to Quilty and the loblolly boy laying out knives and saws. The sailor had fainted, for which I was grateful. The last thing I wanted was for someone to scream. I might scream right along with him.

But I couldn't *not* look. Quilty had wrapped some tape around the man's calf, about a hand's breadth below the kneecap. While the loblolly boy held the leg straight, Quilty with a wicked curved knife sliced through the outer half and then the inner half of the calf, just above the tape.

More cannon fire shook us, followed by a long tumbling sound. We've had something shot away, I thought. The deck canted as we came about, and then our larboard guns fired—double-shotted with canister on top, from the sound of it. Must be desperate, to overload the guns like that and fire 'em off all at once. Bad for the guns, bad for the timbers. Anguished shrieking followed the bellowing of the guns. I twisted under the straps. The guns fired and fired again, as fast as they could be loaded, and between the blasts came the steady popping of the swivels.

The loblolly boy hauled on a leather strap to draw the flesh of the upper calf farther up the bones. Quilty set to with the bone saw—*zip zip zip*, and off came the lower leg. He tossed it into a bucket on the deck.

Something struck us with a tremendous bang amidships, and the schooner canted over to starboard. Rammed, by Jupiter! I heard a rush of feet overhead, and Peter crying, "Boarders away!" The deck timbers above me shook—a crowd of men stamping back and forth, with the clank of steel and the snap of muskets adding to the din.

"Shit and perdition, Mr. Quilty, they're aboard of us! Let me up!"

"Tenaculum," said he, as if I hadn't spoke, and the loblolly boy handed him a sort of awl with a curved tip, which Quilty used to fish around in the stump. The end of the man's leg looked just like an uncured ham, I thought, wishing I hadn't thought that. Quilty winkled something out with the tenaculum and then used a curved needle to throw sutures around it. He repeated the process on the other side of the protruding bones, tying off the veins or arteries or whatever they were.

A grinding noise reverberated through the schooner's timbers, and we settled upright again. "They've beat 'em off!" says I. "Hurrah for the Rattle-Snakes!"

"Sh-sh," said Quilty.

A boy led a blinded man in and ran topside again. The Rattle-Snakes were yelling fit to raise Old Scratch, but among their shouting I heard a greater shouting. French shouts, coming closer as if floating down the wind.

Of course they're floating, you ninny, I said to myself, for we're far away at sea. *There's a lofty ship to windward and she's sailing fast and free, sailing down along the coast of the High Barbaree!*

"Stop that singing!" said Quilty.

"Who, me?" says I, surprised at the notion.

"Yes you, Mr. Graves. Hush now, that's a lad." He placed lint over the ends of the bones and added some small pieces of linen around the skin where it had been cut. He sprinkled flour on some more lint and packed that in, slipped some tow over the end, laid linen bandages lengthwise across and over the end of the stump, and wrapped it round and round with more linen. He finished it off by slipping a seaman's woolen stocking cap over all. He and the loblolly boy lifted the unconscious sailor into Treadwell's cot.

Another thump amidships, and the screeking of timber on timber as we canted over again—to larboard this time. The blinded man fell down behind the table.

"Sail high, sail low, and so sailed we-e-e—"

"Get him out of here," said Quilty. He sat the blinded man on the table and began to wash out his eyes. "Take him to the wardroom. It's been set to rights now, and Mr. Treadwell will keep an eye on him. They're mates, I believe."

"I know the way, thank'ee," I said as soon as the loblolly boy had unstrapped me. As Quilty peeled back the blinded man's eyelids, the fellow threw a punch and the loblolly boy jumped on him. I hooked my sword and dagger and pistols on my way out, humming *"No quarter did we give them—we sank them in the sea, cruising down along the coast of the High Barbaree!"*

More men were coming down the ladder, some on their lone, some being carried. And here was a curious thing underfoot: a trail of blood, leading aft. I followed it in the gloom and came across Quarter-gunner Samuels, hunching along the wrong way with a wooden splinter sticking out of his side.

I turned him about. "Over yonder." I pointed back the way he had come. "Straight through the bulkhead right for'ard. Can't miss it. Here, I'll bear a hand."

"I thanks you kindly, Mr. Graves," he said. We got as far as the forward companionway. There he knelt down, feeling for the bottom step.

"Light along, Samuels," I said. "Just a little further."

"No, sir, I reckon I'll just set here a spell." He lay on the steps and closed his eyes.

I touched his throat, feeling for the life in him, but I felt nothing. More wounded were coming down the ladder, and I dragged him aside. A horrid shriek came from the sick berth. I would not be going back in there for anything you cared to name, no sir. Clad in nothing but my shirt, I slung my weapons over my shoulder and ran up to the fo'c's'le.

The foremast had been shot away about six feet off the deck. It was still attached by a tangle of rigging and lay all ahoo across the forward guns on the starboard side. I could see dead men under it. Horne stood astride it, flinging chips every which way as he labored with a broadax to cut the mast away. His stocking cap had come off, and his long crazy matted braids flew around like Medusa's snakes as he swung the blade and yanked it free, swung the blade and yanked it free.

The *Faucon*'s jib boom had stabbed into the main shrouds on the larboard side, the end of it jutting abaft our mainmast above the mainsail gaff. Our guns on that side were so heated by prolonged firing that they leaped from the deck as they bellowed point-blank into the frigate's bow. Mulatto soldiers crowded along her bowsprit, trying to reach our deck, but the murdering-pieces on the quarterdeck and our Marine sharpshooters were making it hot for them. They wavered as they tried to negotiate the narrower spar of the jib boom, and then began a-falling into the sea as more men crushed in behind.

This was a strange thing. I went to the side to look. The two hulls working together in the swell were grinding some of the fellows up.

Others were trying to swim through a pack of sharks that thrashed about in the pink foam. They weren't doing so well. The men weren't, I mean. The sharks were making out like Billy-o.

Dead men lay everywhere underfoot. I looked at them as I made my way aft. Most of them were mulatto soldiers, but every now and then I saw a man I recognized. Along the way I ran into Doc, our one-eyed cook, hopping along with a big iron skillet in one hand and his peg leg in the other.

"Hello, sah, Mr. Graves," said he. "I done lost my laig!"

"Really?" says I. "Where did you see it last?"

A ferocious scowl crossed his face. "Now, if I knew dat, would I aks yo' about it?"

"No, I guess not. But, tell me—do you recollect when you last had it to hand?"

"Why, sho! Some ob dem uppity colored men tried to hide in my galley when it got too hot for 'em on deck. Talkin' French at me—some fellas just don't know dey place, I expect. 'Sacker blue to yo' too,' says I, an' I busts 'em on de haid wit' my skillet in one hand and my laig in da uvver."

He transferred his scowl to the peg leg in his fist. The fat end had some gobs of gore on it and a few tufts of black hair. "Why, lookit dat! My stump was itchin' me sumpthin' fierce, an' I unshipped 'er so's I could have a scratch. I done forgot. Here, hold dis." He handed me the skillet, which was decorated in the same way as his peg leg, and strapped his leg back on.

"Dat's mo' *like*," he said, stomping it more comfortably into place. "Now yo' just gimme back dat skillet an' I gon' find me some mo' haids need bustin', I tell you *what*."

He rolled off toward the fo'c's'le, yelling out to Horne to guess what just happen', hee hee, while I continued toward the quarterdeck.

The aftermost starboard guns were playing merry hell with the *Rose-red Cunt*. Her mizzen and main had come down, and she could only lie before the wind as she tottered off to leeward with her stern toward us. Her rudder had been shot away, and her stern gaped like a witch's maw. A crowd of musketmen stood at her taffrail, trying to shoot our gunners, but our six-pounders kept a-roaring and the crowd kept a-dwindling.

I spotted Juge on the quarterdeck. As I ran up the steps, a runty sailor with a white scar across his nose gave me a frantic look and said, "If ya please, sir—"

"One moment," I said. "Name's Brodie, ain't it?"

"Aye sir. The cap'n—"

"In a minute, Brodie." *Brodie, that's right,* I thought. *David Brodie, quartermaster. One of the Irishmen.* "Can't you see I'm trying to talk to the major?"

"Bonjour, mon ami," said Juge. "You decide to join us at the last, *hein?"* He raised his musket and shot a man off the bowsprit. A sailor took the musket from him and handed him another.

"That bastard Quilty strapped me down, else I would have come sooner," said I. "Have you seen Captain Wickett?"

"If ya *please,* sir," said Brodie, at the word *capitaine.* "But 'tis himself the captain I'm speakin' of, who has been felled by a murderous blow, sir!"

I looked around. "You don't say. Where is he?"

"Taken below just this minute, sir," said Brodie. "Still breathin'. Just stunned there, I'm supposin', but ya never seen such a look on a man's face."

Well, what the hell did he expect me to do about it? "Say, Brodie," says I. "Ain't you supposed to be at the helm?"

With a guilty look he said, "Well, aye sir, and so I am."

"Then hop to it. Look, the wind is bringing the frigate around broadside of us. Mind your helm, man! We don't want her laying alongside!"

"Aye aye, sir!"

Having solved Brodie's problem for him—nothing like duty to bring a man to his senses—I turned to take a look along the deck. There was Mr. Rogers down in the waist, calling for fend-offs as the *Faucon* wallowed sideways toward us. Her jib boom bowed as it strained against our mainmast. I thought someone ought to tell those poor chaps they'd better get off the bowsprit—it was going to get a good shaking in about a minute.

She still had a bite in her. One of the eight-pounders on her fo'c's'le, with its muzzle depressed to its limit, was slowly but steadily beating in our deck—and the starboard timbers too, I guessed, with the shot passing right through us. We'd be treading water soon if we let her keep that up. Someone should do something about it.

I looked around—at Brodie manning the tiller, at Juge firing his muskets with a sailor loading for him, at the gun crews busy with the swivels, at the powder monkeys running back and forth with their wooden cartridge boxes, at the Marines potting away at the enemy's quarterdeck—and it seemed to me that I already knew what was missing. Something important.

"Shit and perdition," I said, as I recalled what it was. *"Juge, où est le capitaine Wickett?"*

"Captain Wickett, he is downstairs." He squeezed off another shot. "Did you not hear the commotion? That—" He pointed. "That whatever-it-is fell on him."

The topmast cap lay on the deck. One corner of it was smeared with blood, and the deckbeams beneath it were cracked. I looked up, blinking as if waking from a dream. The main-topmast was gone—no, there it was, floating alongside. The only canvas we had left was the fore-and-aft mainsail, and Peter had brailed it up before commencing the action. Topsails only, when possible, in a brawl; too much chance of a burning wad setting the canvas afire, elsewise.

"Well, then . . ." A shock of bitter shame hit me as I looked at Peter's blood on the topmast cap. *Nothing like duty to bring a man to his senses,* I thought. I was the first lieutenant. With the captain below, that left me in charge. "You men," I shouted to the starboard swivel-gun crews, who'd been popping away at the corvette drifting down to leeward. "Leave her go. Out gaff mains'l, lads! Let go the brails! Man the clew outhaul!"

They gaped at me, the ninnies.

"You heard me!" I stepped to the pinrail and cast off the lines for them. The crack of the sail flapping in the breeze brought them back to their senses.

"Haul taut!" I was in fine voice; brass trumpets weren't in it. "Haul out! That's well your mains'l!"

I found Peter's dented speaking trumpet and stepped to the break of the quarterdeck. There was Rogers down in the waist, still busy with the fend-offs. Setting the mainsail would take some of the pressure off him. "Mr. Rogers! Mr. Rogers there!"

He threw a look over his shoulder and then turned to stare at me.

"Captain Wickett has fallen," I said. But that sounded too final. Peter would brace me up for talking like that. "He is only injured, I believe. I am in command until he returns to the deck. Now cut that goddamn jib boom away before it yanks our mainmast out!"

"But she'll lie alongside us, Mr. Graves!"

"So she will. Grapple onto her when she does, and haul us right up alongside her. Give her a broadside then, double-shotted and damn the timbers. Get your quoins out and fire up through her deck. Then away all boarders—I'm taking every man jack across with me."

"Aye aye, sir."

"Where's Mr. Klemso?"

"Dead, sir."

I looked forward. Horne had finished chopping through the foremast. It rolled along the gunwale and fell into the sea with a splash, and the schooner's bow lifted as if rising from the dead. The sudden motion cracked the *Faucon*'s jib boom lengthwise, shaking men off into the sea, and then snapped it clean off at the base. Our rigging was still snarled with hers, but so much the better—we could use it to pivot.

"Mr. Horne! Come here."

"What happens?" said Juge.

"We're going to take the *Faucon*. Everyone is going across. Are you with me?"

"*Bon sang!* Of course I am." He chuckled. "I had thought—but never mind what I thought."

Horne brought his ax with him. Good and good, thinks I. "Mr. Horne," I said, "gather up the ferociousest, crotch-kickin'est, eye-gougin'est fighters we got. Keep with me and Major Juge here. I aim to take that frigate."

"Aye aye, sir."

"Go." I raised my speaking trumpet again. "Starboard battery, cease firing! Cease firing, I say. Cutlasses and tomahawks, boys, every one of you. We're going hunting for Johnny Crappo."

"But sir—" one of them began.

"But sir, but sir," I sneered. "But sir, what? 'But sir, you're an addle-pated looby, standing there in nothing but your shirt'?" That got 'em grinning. "So ye think I'm a cackling loon, is it? Well, listen here, my bully boys. Them troops in that transport can't afford to let us live, and they won't leave us go till they've killed us all. Look at 'em there!" I looked too. They lined the *Faucon*'s rail, firing away like Old Harry with their muskets. "Now look at me! I'm mad, sure enough—fightin' mad. Them's *sojers* over there—they don't know squat about a sea fight. I aim to learn 'em what happens when ye catch a rattler by the tail!"

That got 'em laughing.

"Besides which, they're bound to shoot me first!"

That got 'em cheering.

"Now get over to the larboard bulwarks and keep your heads down till you get the word. Mr. Rogers, what're you about? 'Vast heaving with the fend-offs!"

"Sir!"

The mainsail had brought us up into the wind, where we hung straight as a weather vane. The *Faucon* swung around like a closing gate. The boobies over there hadn't had sense enough to stow their hammocks as bulwarks nor even to raise their boarding nets. Speaking of which—

"Drop the la'board boarding nets!"

"Aye aye, sir!"

"Now, Brodie!" Our stern swung toward the frigate's side. "That's *well* your helm!" I raised the speaking trumpet. "Mr. Rogers, grapple on—" A ball clanged off the trumpet, and I turned to see Connor on the *Faucon*'s quarterdeck with a smoking pistol in his hand. "—Like lightning, now!"

The grapnels swung through the air and hooked in the frigate's rigging and along her rail. Willing hands tailed onto the lines and hauled us up alongside her. We rode too low for her guns to reach us. In the weird silence I heard the bubbling of water between the hulls, and then a hollow *thunk* as we struck.

"Lash on all a taunt-o! Now fire them guns!"

Seven double-shotted guns roared out. Seven spouts of splinters erupted beyond the *Faucon*'s high sides.

Glory, she's bigger'n houses, I thought, looking up at her. The mulatto musketeers had ducked away from the rail. "You men with muskets," I called. "Shoot any man who shows his head. Again, Mr. Rogers!"

The gun crews reloaded with a will and ran their guns out again, right up against the *Faucon*'s timbers and angled to tear holes through to the sky. Again the guns roared, and again the fountains of splinters shot up from her deck.

"Now, my jolly lads! Boarders away!"

Shirttails flapping and tallywhacker swinging, I leaped to the gunwale and launched myself into the void.

I landed in the *Faucon*'s mainchains with a surging mob behind me. I turned to urge them on, but some enthusiastic soul grabbed my legs and hoisted me ass-over-ears across the rail. The mulatto who caught me seemed as surprised as I was. I gave him a knee in the nutmegs and hauled out my sword. The Rattle-Snakes crowded in behind me, so close I couldn't get my hand up to use my blade. I cleared some room by firing a pistol into a man who blocked my way.

Then here was Horne with his ax, felling a man with each blow. He had the biggest jacks in the crew with him. "Follow me!" says I, letting them go first. "Make for her quarterdeck."

With tomahawks, cutlasses, handspikes—whatever they'd thought to grab—they laid 'em low on either hand along the gangway. To my right, down in the waist, I saw Mr. Rogers and his party snapping at the heels of a confused mass of soldiers trying to get down the forward hatchway.

Horne moved aft with his boys, scattering the enemy before him.

I grabbed Juge's arm and pointed: "We take the quarterdeck!"

"*Mais oui!*" He pushed past me with his sword up and a horrible grin on his face. We played a ferocious game of tag with the mulattoes around the mizzenmast, Horne and his boys sweeping the deck as they went. Then the soldiers were leaping over the quarterdeck rail down into the waist and heading for the safety of the hold.

"Mr. Horne! After 'em!"

"Aye aye, sir!"

I looked around our sudden oasis of quiet. Juge and I were the only living men on the quarterdeck.

"To the captain's cabin," said I. "Let us see if Connor yet lives."

We trotted down a short flight of steps into the waist and found a pair of doors leading aft. A fallen spar and a mass of canvas blocked the one on the right. Juge yanked open the one on the left. It opened into a dark corridor. A familiar figure stood at the end of it.

"Why, Mr. Connor," I said, and fired my second pistol.

He snapped a ball past my ear before ducking out of sight around the corner. I heard a door slam.

I snatched Juge by the arm as he started to dash after him. "Easy," I said. "He may not be the only one back here. We must check each door as we go."

"Have you another pistol? I am embarrassed to say I have not brought one."

"No. I fired them both."

He shook his head. "*Bon sang!* This makes it a little harder." Then he limbered up his sword arm. "It cannot be helped. Let us go!"

The powder smoke smarted my eyes. I felt my way along till I came to a jalousie door on the right. It would lead to a cabin or cabins lying between the two corridors leading aft from the waist. Or maybe the captain's bread room, I didn't know. I kicked it in, revealing a small cabin—the master's or perhaps the first lieutenant's, from the look of it. Empty. I jabbed my sword around under the cot just to be sure and then got down on all fours to have a peek. Nothing.

We stepped back into the corridor. Another corridor ran athwart the end of it. Dog me if I was going to let Juge go first. I pushed him back with my left arm and stepped around the corner—and found nothing but silence.

Two doors were set into the after bulkhead. They would lead to the captain's quarters, one to his sleeping place and the other to the great cabin itself. I busted in the nearest door.

"Nothing, *mon ami!*" I said as I came back out. "Check the other corridor. There'll be another cabin around the corner, there."

"But what about this door here?"

"This door is mine."

"*Bon sang!*" he said. "Do you send me away just as we close on our quarry?"

I grinned. "But of course."

"Oh, but my good friend, this is not fair!"

"Is it fair that we should go two on one against him?"

"Fine," he said. "And when he has you by the throat, I will come in to save your ham, *hein?*"

"Bacon, ha ha! You can save my *bacon* if he gets the best of me. But he won't. Go now."

"No," he said. "I stand here and watch you die. Then I kill him."

"Oh, well thank you very much. I'm pleased you have such confidence in me."

I kicked in the door.

Connor stood right aft behind the captain's desk, over which a silver and glass lamp hung from a chain. At his back a pair of open glass doors led out to the stern gallery, letting sunlight and a pleasant breeze fill the cabin. The door of a gun cabinet to his left hung from its hinges, and he held a heavy sea pistol in his left hand. He leveled it at my chest.

"Please come closer," he said. "I should love so to shoot you."

On the desk between us lay a powder flask, a short brass ramrod, and a shot bag.

I raised my sword. "If you'd finished loading that pistol, you'd've shot me already. Show me your blade, sir."

"Tish tish, Mr. Graves. Surely you do not intend to murder an agent of the federal government."

"You ain't nary such a thing. You're a traitor. You intend to raise a slave insurrection back home."

"No, no, no, that's just Franklin's wild imagination at work. Good God, man, have you no eyes?" He pointed at his face. "I'm a free man of color. A nigger's no use to me if he's running around loose."

"You deny it?"

"Of course I deny it. I'm an adventurer, not a traitor." He got a calculating look in his eye. "I have an empire nearly in my hands. You're a man of color—"

"Who told you that?"

"Pétion. You told him yourself. It'll come out at trial, make no mistake about that. You'll be ruined. On the other hand, now, was you to side with me . . ."

"I want no part of a slave rebellion. You seen what happened here."

He rolled his eyes and sighed. "I told you, that's not the plan. Listen to me and I'll tell you true. My object is Tejas."

"What's a tay hoss?"

"*Tejas.*" He gave plenty of throat to the Spanish *J*. "It's a province of New Spain on the Gulf Coast. We'll build a fort, invite Creole settlers from Lousiana, import a few thousand slaves. It's wide open, man! Some dirty soldiers in some crumbling forts is all that stands in our way." He raised his head at the sound of the ruckus forward. "Well, it *was* all that stood in the way. With a little boat and a blind eye, however . . ."

"You're in league with the Knights of the White Hand. I saw you with MacGuffin outside the farmhouse."

"He was a *former* knight. Every man has his price, and his was low."

He showed his dimples and said, "You should have seen the look on his face when I let Franklin stab him in the back with his own dagger."

"Him! You liar. I read Villon's letter."

"A love letter from a doomed man to his beloved wife. My only interest in it was to see it delivered into the poor widow's hands."

"It's a list of conspirators."

"Don't be foolish. Why would anyone set down the names in writing?"

"Maybe you only knew one or two names each, and it was a way to keep track of everyone. Or you could sell it to the White Hands. I'm sure they'd like a list like that."

"Even if this is true, there's no connection to me."

"It mentions a steersman. A steersman conns a ship. You know, a *conner*, Mr. Connor? That letter was meant to be read by someone who also spoke English."

"An odd coincidence, nothing more."

"And I don't believe you're a mulatto, neither. Hell, you're lighter than I am."

"There is that, yes. Ah, but—" He held up a finger. "If I'm with the White Hands, why would I shoot one of them down in the streets of Port Républicain?"

"You meant to shoot Franklin in the back of the head. A terrible accident. Things like that happen in a close fight, only he stumbled into you and messed up your aim. You shot your own man. That's why you stomped his face in after he was dead. You figured Franklin might recognize him."

He put his hand on his hip and laughed, sharp as old cheese. "No, you're wrong about that. It was sheer petulance on my part. I swear I'm not in league with the White Hand."

"It don't signify either way. You caused a power of trouble, and I aim to see you pay for it."

"*Continuez a le faire parler*—keep him talking," said Juge, lounging in the doorway with his arms folded. "Perhaps he will get a sore throat and die of the pneumonia."

"I'll deal with you in a minute, nigger," said Connor. His eyes darted back to mine. "Franklin was nothing but a trained monkey. He learned how to write down what was told to him, but he had no thoughts of his own."

"That's where you're wrong," I said. "Without him, we'd have never caught you."

A flicker of uncertainty crossed his face. "He lives?"

"He's in the *Croatoan*. She'll be up with us before too long. In fact, I ought to just shut you up in here until she arrives. I'd like to see you pissing yourself at the end of a rope."

"I'll not hang like a common thief."

"Then put steel in your hand, or I'll stick you like a pig."

"You disappoint me, Mr. Graves." He nodded at Juge in the doorway. "Two against one?"

"He won't interfere. *Vous pouvez faire confiance à son honnêté.*"

"*Est-ce vrai, nègre?*" said Connor, staring down his nose at Juge. "Is it so, nigger? Can I have confidence in your honesty?"

"*Bon sang*, but of course you can. See? I put my sword away."

A smile played across Connor's lips. "Yes, and you could draw it again, too."

There was still a great to-do going on in the rest of the ship. I could hear cries of anger and anguish in English and in French. Pistols a-plenty were popping someplace below decks, and the timbers of the frigate vibrated in sympathy as men stomped and struggled in the dark.

"Juge," I said, not taking my eyes off Connor. "It sounds like they could use some help down on the gun deck. It'll be the next one below this one."

"This is an affair of honor between gentlemen," said Connor. "Surely even a nigger can understand that."

"Juge," I said before he could speak. "I need to absolve myself. Let me fight this battle."

"*C'est bien, mon ami.* I do this for you."

"And shut the door on your way out, nigger," said Connor.

Juge mimicked Connor's smile. "I will not be so selfish, Monsieur Connor, as to pray that God lets you live long enough to see me again." The door shut softly behind him as he left.

"I thought he'd never leave, didn't you?" said Connor, flexing his sword arm. "But hold—shouldn't you like to put some breeches on? I've never killed a naked man before."

"A shirt's comfortable enough to fight in. I like it. It's airy."

"I shall endeavor to ventilate you further, regardless. Well then. Let's have at it." He dropped the pistol and drew his sword, jiggling it in his hand till he was satisfied with his grip. Then he put his left fist on his hip and brought up his sword, feeling with the tip of it for mine across the desk. Our blades touched. He tried a simple feint and thrust. I tapped his blade away. He riposted like lightning, whirling his blade around in a tight circle, catching mine and forcing it down.

I snatched my blade out from under his and ducked out of reach. He sidled around the desk. I scooted around the opposite way.

"Won't you come out and fight, Mr. Graves?"

"You've got the reach on me. I like the desk just where it is."

"But you've left the way open for me." He jerked his thumb at the door behind him. "What's to stop me from leaving?"

"A noose. If you stay, you'll at least get a chance to kill me first."

"I take your point. In a manner of speaking." He reassumed his stance, left hand balled on his hip and his blade feeling for mine. "*En garde*, as they say."

We circled around the desk again, our blades skittering and brushing against each other, till we were back where we'd started. Beyond him I saw the *Croatoan* standing toward us from the south.

"Your glass is running out, Connor."

"Yes. And since you will not come out—" He lunged.

I parried across my body. He withdrew and lunged again, his blade piercing my shirt and the hot steel sliding across my naked skin as I rolled across the desk and kicked at his head. He grabbed my leg and I clutched his sword arm beneath my left elbow. And there we hung, locked in a terrified embrace, neither of us willing to withdraw from inside the other's guard. He scrabbled at his waistband for the knife that wasn't there. I chopped at his head, my sword clanging again and again on that damn hanging lamp till he grabbed my wrist and twisted it away from my body. It felt like he was turning my arm inside out.

I felt his breath on my face. He'd had onions for dinner. "Drop your sword!" he hissed.

"I won't!"

"I'll break your arm in about a minute." He twisted harder.

I felt the muscle in my shoulder start to give. My fingers began to open. He jiggled my hand, trying to shake my sword loose. With the sweet inspiration that often accompanies a confrontation with imminent death, I let go of his sword arm and smacked the lamp backhanded across his face. The glass windows shattered.

He jerked back, still twisting my wrist in a fearsome grip—*but let 'im*, thinks I, snatching the death's-head dagger from my belt with my left hand and giving him a wild thrust. I caught him between the bone and muscle of his sword arm, right above the elbow on the inside. It was pure luck, but a thing of beauty all the same, and I gazed upon its splendor with great joy. Him, he just stared. I yanked down through the tendon, and his blade clattered to the deck. Then, with the tip of my sword at his throat, I backed him out onto the gallery till the rail stopped him.

"*Touché*," he said, forcing a smile. "This is just getting interesting. Perhaps you'll bind my handkerchee around my arm and allow me to continue left-handed?"

"No. You must hang."

"I shan't."

"What's to prevent it?"

He answered by lunging forward onto my blade. He looked at me wide-eyed over it, neither of us moving. Then he ever so carefully grasped it with his left hand and eased it out of his throat. He tried to speak, but his windpipe was pierced and all that came out was a strangled squeak.

"Shit and perdition, Mr. Connor." I reached out to catch him, but he turned on his heel and threw himself over the rail. He looked up at me from under the surface, a stream of ruby bubbles shining at his throat, and then the sharks were on him.

Twenty

The sunlight seemed to pierce my skull when I stepped out onto the *Faucon*'s spar deck. The noises of battle below had stopped, but there was a great to-do along the starboard rail.

The *Rattle-Snake* rode lower than I remembered. I went over to the rail and stood looking down at her. Her maindeck was awash. The sea boiled on the far side, where the sharks were having themselves a time with the bodies and bits of wreckage floating there. Rattle-Snakes and a few dazed-looking mulattoes paddled around in the boats, hauling men aboard like so much mackerel. Mr. Quilty waded across the deck with a wounded man clutched under each arm and Treadwell bringing up the rear, dragging his splinted leg behind him. Men leaned over the frigate's rail, helping their shipmates aboard or tossing out ropes to them as the schooner settled in the sea. And here came Ambrose, the wardroom steward, a-galloping through the wash with my coat in one hand and a shark skittering across the deck at his heels.

On the *Rattle-Snake*'s quarterdeck, Peter scooped up Gypsy and flung her across. She hit the *Faucon*'s deck running and lit out for the after hatch. He had Greybar by the scruff in his other hand, and he threw him across, too. Greybar sailed spraddle-legged toward me—and if you want my advice, when someone throws you a wet cat, don't catch it. He wrapped his forepaws around my hand, sank his teeth into my thumb, and tried his best to disembowel my wrist with his hind claws before tearing off after Gypsy.

Peter climbed over the *Faucon*'s rail as the *Rattle-Snake* sank with a groan behind him. He had a bloody gash in his forehead where his birthmark had been, and his scabbard hung empty at his side.

"Congratulations on your victory, Peter." I held out my hand.

He ignored it. "Victory? It is a disaster."

"You've captured a frigate and beaten a sixteen-gun corvette into submission." The *L'Heureuse Rencontre* still wallowed down to leeward, and showed no signs that she was trying to make any repairs. The *Croatoan* would be alongside her in a few minutes. "Two to one, Peter, and both of 'em larger. You'll be promoted, sure." And so would I be, I thought; it was considered a compliment to the captain to promote the first officer after such a fight. My commission was as good as signed.

He looked at the *Rattle-Snake*'s mainmast, still riding above the waves but slowly sinking. "You have sank my command."

"You were outnumbered and outgunned, Peter. You'll be a hero!"

"I'll be a goat," he said. "Both of 'em privateers. One only gets promoted for beating national ships."

"You're ungrateful, is what you are."

His face flushed, and his lips drew back in a gimace. "And you are unbreeched, sir! Where are your clothes?"

"On their way to Davy Jones." I looked down at myself. Connor had managed to slice my shirttails away entire, and I was starkers from the waist down.

Rogers stepped up from the waist and saluted. "Got 'em all nailed down in the hold, sir. About a hundred soldiers, most of 'em still with their equipment. They'll be trouble once they remember they got us outnumbered."

"Put a pair of guns at the quarterdeck rail and train them on the hatches," said Peter. "Do you the same on the fo'c's'le. Corporal Haversham is below?"

"Yes, sir. Him and most of the Marines came through the fight. They're making things hot for the coloreds at the moment."

"Good. Let them keep it up," said Peter. "Secure the magazine. I want all the powder and shot there is. Make that your primary concern.

I would not put it past these fellows to blow us all up, if they can. Go now." Then he turned back to me. "I don't believe I gave you permission to return to duty, Mr. Graves. Leave me."

"But you're shorthanded, Peter—"

"Do not presume to use my first name, Mr. Graves. Go find some dark corner to lurk in, and bother me no further."

I found Juge down on the gun deck, sprawled on his back with a half-circle of dead soldiers scattered around him. He still clutched his sword in his bloody hand. He opened his eyes when I knelt beside him and touched his cheek. "Connor," he said. "You have killed him?"

"Would I suffer him to live, after the way he spoke to you?"

"The shooting has stopped," he said. "Have we prevailed, *mon ami?*"

"*Mais oui.*" I put my arm around him and sat him up. "Come, I carry you to the surgeon."

But he wouldn't rise. "They are destroyed, *hein?* And this we did without the infamous Captain Block and his frigate."

"The *Croatoan* comes up from the south. *Allez-y, mon ami.* You can see her from the deck."

"No, I cannot." He let go of his sword and tried to raise his right hand. I took it in my own and touched his fingers to his brow, his breast and his shoulders in turn. "*Bon sang!*" he said, closing his eyes. "The glory is ours alone."

I sat for a while with his body in my arms. I didn't see what was so damn glorious about it.

Twenty-One

Commodore Cyrus Gaswell squared the pages of my report on his big mahogany table and set it on top of one of his neat stacks of papers. He wore the exact same clothes as he'd worn the last time I'd seen him, or near enough as made no difference—baggy trousers of white nankeen and a seaman's blue checked shirt, open at the neck and sweated through under the arms. He rubbed one bare foot over the other under the table and contemplated me.

Franklin's report, neatly done up in red tape, lay next to mine. It wasn't his entire report, of course; that was for the eyes of the president, and out of my reach—and out of Gaswell's too, for that matter. The writing of my own report had been an interesting exercise in confession and horn-tooting. I'd had the devil of a time deciding what to put in it and what to leave out. Franklin had been no help at all, but then I hadn't expected him to be. He had a pucker in his linen about having missed Connor's aim entire.

"Don't think I sent ye on a fool's mission," said Gaswell. "Pétion's been dislodged and his army routed. Swallowed up whole, just about. I don't guess one man in a hundred has been able to join up with Rigaud. It's a hell of a victory for Toussaint."

"Victory ain't in it, sir. It was a slaughter."

"Yes, well, that ain't your doing. It may feel like it is, but ye musn't give yourself so much credit. Ye followed orders and ought to be content. And ye showed a hell of an initiative in taking the *Faucon*. Paul Jones would've been proud. I'm recommending ye for a permanent commission, and I dare say you'll get it. I'd put Wickett in for promotion too, if I could."

"You mean you can't, sir?"

He tugged at his ear. "I doubt the Congress will promote him to master commandant for losing a fourteen-gun schooner to a ten-gun transport."

"But the *Faucon* was full of soldiers, and he clobbered *L'Heureuse Rencontre*. She was twice our weight in metal."

He ran his pale blue eyes over me. It was like being looked at by God and your favorite uncle both at once. "The *L'Heureuse Rencontre* never surrendered till Block come alongside. Plus she weren't even a privateer, much less a national ship. Nothing but pirates, legally speaking, and ye'll have to take the gun money and be glad of it. She'll be returned to her owners, providing they can be found and will admit to ownership. And if Captain Block had been more vigorous, the *Rattle-Snake* might be floating today. Not that I question Block's conduct, mind ye, but pressing for Wickett's promotion will give Congress the opportunity to ask some questions that ain't none of their business."

"But, sir! That ain't fair to Peter."

"Captain Wickett weren't on deck when you took the *Faucon*. I'm sensible that it weren't of his own volition, but he's entirely recovered already, from what I hear. Recovered well enough to rerig her and the corvette and take 'em up to Charleston, anyway. You may not credit it, but that don't look so good for him." He held up his hand as I opened my mouth. "I don't expect anyone ever told ye life was fair. And considering how your old man brought you up, I don't see how ye could expect it."

"You must tell me about my father sometime, sir." I looked out the stern windows at the *Croatoan* rolling along in line abaft. She hadn't a mark on her, and Block had long since run up new topmasts. I studied the hills of Tortuga beyond her. I didn't care what Columbus thought— that island didn't look like a turtle any more than I did.

"I don't think you grasp the delicacy of the situation, Mr. Graves. Personal considerations don't enter into it, you hear *me*. It don't matter a lick what you or me or Wickett wants. We're in serious negotiations with the French, and I ain't about to let a minor action that no one will ever hear about bugger it up."

If no one ever heard about it, it would be because no one told them about it. I looked at my report on top of the neat stack of papers on Gaswell's desk, and at Franklin's report all done up tidy in red tape. They were both bound to get lost somewhere along the line, I'd bet on it.

"Someone'll hear about it," I said. "You can't keep the Rattle-Snakes from talking."

He wagged his head, more amused than angry. "I hope that ain't a threat, Mr. Graves."

"No, sir. Just an observation."

He took off his spectacles and rubbed them with his shirttail. "Sure, they'll talk. The whole Navy will know about it, and admire ye for your stoic attention to duty. It'll pay off handsome, eventually, don't ye worry about that. The Navy takes care of its own." He stuck his specs back on his nose. "More important to you, *I* take care of my own. Don't you never forget that."

"No, sir. I won't. But I was thinking."

He grunted. "An admirable thing, in moderation."

I looked at his uniform hanging beside his chair, at the beautifully brushed blue broadcloth and the shining gold lace and epaulets. If I had a uniform like that, I'd wear it every day, no matter how hot and steamy the weather. Ambrose had saved my second-best coat and my epaulet, and had made me a decent pair of slop trousers, but the rest of my uniform was a motley assortment that I'd begged and borrowed from the *Columbia*'s other lieutenants. Everything was oversized, third-best, unwanted, threadbare. "I was wondering about my mother."

He shifted in his chair. "Ye'd be better off asking your pap about her."

"I don't believe he'd say, sir. I'll ask him one of these days, if I ever go home again. But I was wondering. You seemed to remember her mighty well, considering you'd only seen her once, in a picture in a locket at Yorktown. Kind of odd how she stuck in your mind's eye for nineteen years."

He leaned back with his hands behind his head. "Forget about position, boy. Lay alongside and fire away. What's on your mind?"

"I think you still have that locket, sir. I'd like to see it."

"Ye never knowed her. Ye can't have any sentimental reasons for wanting it."

I looked him in the eye. "Sentiment don't enter into it, sir. If I'm a man of color, I want to know."

He pulled at his chin. "Some things are best left hid."

"I'll take that chance, sir. I have a right to know."

"Do ye now? I don't recall that particular one being spelled out." He thought about it awhile. His eyes were as blue and empty as the sky. Then he reached into the side pocket of his uniform coat and held out a closed hand. "You're sure now?"

"I am."

He opened his hand, and in it was a tarnished pewter locket on a broken chain. "Go home, Mr. Graves," he said as I took it from him. "I can manage without ye for a bit."

It was a tiny heart-shaped bit of nothing, dented along one side and grimy with age. I pressed the catch and the lid sprang open. My mother smiled out at me, delicate and pretty, hardly more than a girl. I searched her face for my lips, my nose, my eyes, my chin—all there, all there. And like my own, her eyes were dark and her hair was black and curly. But her curls fell long and loose around pale shoulders, and her cheeks were pink as roses.

I shut my fist around the locket. I knew why my father hated me.

Author's Historical Note

This is a work of historical fiction, with the emphasis on that word *fiction*. The major events in the book and the people who brought them about are real enough, but I have condensed some people and eliminated others entirely. Jean-Jacques Dessalines besieged Alexandre Pétion at Jacmel, and the fall of that town on the evening of March 10–11, 1800, effectively marked the end of the War of Knives. Henri Christophe was there with his two demi-brigades, but from most accounts he wasn't nearly as charming as I've depicted him. Toussaint L'Ouverture seems to have been everywhere at once, sometimes as himself, sometimes as Grandfather Chatterbox, and sometimes as strategic imposters. An American frigate helped force the issue by bombarding the fortress, but that ship was the *General Greene*, 28, commanded by Captain Christopher Perry. Perry's son Oliver Hazard was along for the ride, as a fourteen-year-old midshipman in the *General Greene*, but as he accomplished nothing of note during the siege I assigned his dramatic duties to Dick Towson.

Toussaint wrote on March 16 to Edward Stevens, the U.S. Consul General at Santo Domingo, to express with "most intense joy" his gratitude for "the signal and important services which [Captain Perry] has rendered me," but he doesn't specify the nature of the help. Perhaps of most moment to him was that Perry had chased away a privateer brig that had been annoying the small flotilla that Toussaint had assembled to blockade the town. He doesn't mention *L'Heureuse Rencontre* by name, but there's no doubt Toussaint's ships scattered when she hove over the horizon, otherwise Matty would have seen them in the bay.

I painted Pétion and André Rigaud with particularly broad strokes. They were inveterate intriguers, but so far as I know neither was ever involved in a plot to transport the slave rebellion to the United States or to invade Mexico. Certainly Americans feared the first possibility, and that the second was considered more than once is evidenced by the ease with which Aaron Burr, James Wilkinson, and others were discovered in their later conspiracy to carve an empire out of what were then northern Mexico and the southwestern United States—if, indeed, that was their aim. At any rate, if Mr. Connor had consulted a lawyer before he set out, he might have realized he wasn't on such shaky legal ground as he thought. The only charge that stuck against Burr was a misdemeanor, and the case was thrown out on a technicality.

A number of people helped me during the writing of this book. I am particularly indebted to Jackie Swift for her insight and humor, to Rick Crawford for his help with Sergeant Cahoon's boggish brogue, and to Walter Mladina for the swell photograph and his help with French idioms. The inevitable mistakes are my own and not theirs.

B.C.
Los Angeles, Calif.

Glossary

aback, a sail is said to be aback when the wind presses it against the mast, driving the vessel sternward.

abaft, to the rear of a vessel.

abeam, toward or from the side of a vessel.

aft, after, toward, in, or from the stern.

alee, away from the wind.

alligator pear, avocado.

amidships, toward or in the center of a vessel.

astern, toward the rear of a vessel.

athwart, across.

avast, 'vast, given as a command to stop what one is doing.

belay, to make secure, as with a LINE to a BELAYING PIN. Also given as a command to disregard a previous command.

belaying pin, a usually wooden dowel of about 18 inches long, fitted through a rail along the inboard side of a bulwark or at the base of a mast, and used to secure the RUNNING RIGGING.

bend, to attach securely but temporarily, as a sail to a SPAR.

binnacle, a cabinet that houses a ship's compass.

bit, an eighth of a REAL.

black vomit, YELLOW FEVER.

boarding net, a rope latticework meant to keep enemies from coming over the rail.

boarding pike, a spear used by sailors.

boom, a SPAR to which the foot of a FORE-AND-AFT sail is attached. Also a pole used to push a hazard away.

bosun, or boatswain, the senior WARRANT OFFICER charged with the care of a ship's boats and rigging, and often with disciplining the enlisted men.

bosun's mate, a PETTY OFFICER who assists the BOSUN and flogs the men as required.

bow, or bows, the forward part of a vessel.

bowse, to lift or drag using ropes and pulleys.

bowsprit, a heavy SPAR to which the foremast STAYS and HEADSAIL gear are attached.

brace, a line attached to the end of a YARD and used to trim it fore or aft.

brail, a line used to haul the foot of a sail up or in.

broadside, a vessel's artillery considered as a whole, or the GUNS along one side.

cable, a heavy ROPE to which an anchor might be attached or that might be used to MOOR a vessel. In the U.S. and British navies its length was calculated at 100 FATHOMS, which was conveniently close to a tenth of a nautical mile.

cable tier, the place in a vessel where a CABLE is stowed.

can, a tankard.

cane knife, a machete.

canister, a projectile made of small shot in a metal case.

Cap Français, the principal city and former capital of SAINT-DÓMINGUE: Cap-Haïtien (or Kapayisyen), Haiti.

capstan, a vertical winch, useful for moving heavy objects such as anchors.

captain, the top commissioned rank in the U.S. Navy, equivalent to an Army or Marine major, lieutenant-colonel, or colonel, depending on his seniority; by convention, the commander of any vessel. Also the senior man at a given station, as captain of the foretop.

carbine, a short musket meant for cavalry use.

cat, a heavy timber projecting from the bow and that keeps an anchor from damaging the side of the vessel.

cat-o'-nine-tails, a whip of nine strands, each about 18 inches long and affixed to a hempen or wooden handle.

chains, the gear that secures the base of the SHROUDS.

chain shot, a ROUND SHOT cut in half and reconnected by a chain.

channel, from *chain-wale*, an outboard platform on either side of each mast that serves as a base for the SHROUDS.

chasseurs à cheval, soldiers armed as light infantry but mounted on horses. In some services they were armed as HUSSARS but were considered inferior to them.

cheer'ly, quickly, with a will.

chef-de-brigade, a French rank equivalent to a colonel or brigadier general.

cheval-de-frise, a piece of timber with sharpened stakes put through it, laid horizontally in front of a breastwork or trench to discourage unwanted visitors.

Chips, nickname for a ship's carpenter.

clew, either of the lower corners of a SQUARE SAIL or the aftermost one of a FORE-AND-AFT sail.

coatee, a jacket with a high waist and short tails.

commandant, the rank of major in the French army.

commissioned officer, in the U.S. Navy, an officer nominated and confirmed by the Senate. The category included captains, masters commandant, and lieutenants, who could be promoted, and surgeons, surgeon's mates, and (later) pursers, who could not.

commodore, the temporary commander of a naval squadron.

companion, companionway, a stairwell aboard ship.

conn, to steer or direct the steering of a vessel.

cook, the WARRANT OFFICER who supervised the cooking of the enlisted men's food. Officers had their own cooks.

corvette, a SHIP-rigged MAN-OF-WAR with a single row of GUNS, FLUSH-DECKED and smaller than a FRIGATE.

coxswain, a man in charge of a boat and its crew; he usually steers as well.

Creole, a French or Spanish colonial born in the Americas, sometimes but not always of mixed race; also a patois of various European and African languages, specifically the French Creole that evolved into the language now spoken in Haiti.

cuirassiers, heavy cavalry equipped with a steel helmet and breast-plate and mounted on large, powerful horses.

cutlass, a short heavy-bladed sword used by sailors.

cutter, a fast-sailing single-masted vessel, used to carry dispatches or for reconnaissance. Also a broad ship's boat that could be rowed or sailed.

Damballah, in voudou, father of the loa, represented by a snake.

dirk, a long dagger carried by midshipmen as a badge of rank.

Doc, nickname for a Navy cook.

dogwatch, either of a pair of two-hour watches, from 4 to 6 pm and 6 to 8 pm

dragoons, light cavalry that could fight on horse or on foot. They carried sabers and carbines, and often wore a distinctive leather or brass helmet.

fathom, a unit of measure equal to six feet. To fathom something is to understand it.

flush-decked, lacking a raised quarterdeck.

fo'c's'le, loosely, the forward part of the weather deck. From *forecastle*, a fighting platform once carried on a warship's bow.

fore, toward or associated with the front of a vessel.

fore-and-aft, trending along a vessel's centerline. *Fore-and-aft hat*: a bicorn worn with the points to the front and rear.

frigate, a fast ship of war usually armed with 28 to 50 guns that were carried, in theory, on a single deck, and which was meant to cruise alone as a scout or marauder.

fusiliers, lightly armed infantry, often used as skirmishers.

gaff, a spar to which the head of a fore-and-aft sail is attached.

garrote, a piece of rope or wire used for strangling.

gen du couleur, lit. "person of color," a mulatto.

gig, a small ship's boat often reserved for the captain's use.

grand blanc, a white French colonist of the upper class.

grape shot, an artillery projectile made of small shot in a bag or wired around a dowel.

great gun, a piece of artillery firing shot of at least three pounds.

grenadiers, elite infantry, originally composed of a regiment's largest men and used to lead assaults. By 1800, steadiness and experience were considered of greater importance than size.

griffe, a person who is of one-quarter European descent.

grog, watered-down booze.

Guadeloupe, a French island in the Lesser Antilles.

gun, a cannon; GREAT GUN.

gunner, the senior WARRANT OFFICER charged with the maintenance of a ship's artillery and small arms. Loosely, someone who operates a GUN.

gunroom, the cabin where the junior WARRANT OFFICERS ate.

gunwale, the topmost part of a vessel's side, so called because guns were once mounted there. Pronounced "gun'l."

gwo bla, CREOLE for GRAND BLANC.

handsomely, gently.

handspike, a length of wood used to move a GUN laterally or turn the CAPSTAN.

hanger, a sword of medium length and weight designed to hang comfortably at the side of a man on foot; it was the weapon of choice among naval officers.

haul, to haul one's wind: to sail to WINDWARD, particularly to avoid an enemy to LEEWARD.

hawse, the place between a vessel's BOW and where its anchor CABLE enters the water. To cross someone's hawse: to provoke unwisely.

hawse-hole, a hole in the bow through which the mooring CABLE passes.

head, the foremost part of a vessel, and by extension a toilet, because sailors relieved themselves from the head. Also the upper edge of a sail.

headsail, a sail set between the BOWSPRIT and the forward mast.

heave-to, to hold a ship in place by setting one or more of its sails ABACK; past tense is *hove-to*.

Hispaniola, the large island lying between Cuba and Puerto Rico and containing the colonies of SAINT-DÓMINGUE and SANTO DOMINGO.

hogshead, a large barrel for holding liquids, usually about 63 gallons by U.S. measure.

holystone, a block of sandstone used to clean a deck by scraping it.

houngan, a VOUDOU high priest, also called a *papa*.

hussars, elite light cavalry, known for élan and fancy uniforms.

jack, *Jack Tar*: a naval sailor. *Every man jack*: everyone present. *Foremast jack*: an enlisted man.

jib, any of the outer FORE-AND-AFT HEADSAILS.

jib boom, a moveable SPAR extending from the BOWSPRIT.

Johnny Crappo, U.S. Navy slang for a Frenchman. From *Jean Crapaud* ("John Toad").

jolly boat, a small rowboat with a wide stern, carried aboard a sailing vessel and used for light work.

katye jeneral, a military headquarters (CREOLE).

knot, an analogous measurement of a ship's speed, calculated by letting out a LINE knotted at certain intervals (usually 47 feet three inches) for a certain amount of time (usually 28 seconds).

ladder, a stairway aboard ship.

langridge, loose pieces of metal or glass used as ammunition.

larboard, to the left of a vessel's centerline; loosely, to the left.

launch, LONGBOAT.

lead, a lead weight attached to a LINE used for measuring depth; also the entire apparatus. Often it had a concave tip that could be loaded with wax or clay for determining the composition of the sea floor.

Le Cap, CAP FRANÇAIS.

leeward, downwind.

leg, to make a leg: to bow deeply with the forward leg extended.

Legba, in VOUDOU, the intermediary between humans and the LOA.

lieutenant, a COMMISSIONED OFFICER ranking below a CAPTAIN and above a WARRANT OFFICER.

lieutenant-de-vesseau, a French grade of SEA LIEUTENANT.

line, a ROPE that is attached to something.

loa, a VOUDOU spirit, similar to a saint or angel.

loblolly boy, an assistant to a naval surgeon.

lobster, a jeering word for a REDCOAT.

log-line, a knotted ROPE (the "line") attached to a wedge-shaped piece of wood (the "log"), used to determine a vessel's speed in KNOTS.

longboat, a large ship's-boat, usually with a removable mast and sails.

loo'ard, LEEWARD.

lubber, an ignorant or clumsy person.

magazine, a room where gunpowder was stowed and where cartridges were made.

mainmast, the chief mast when there's more than one.

mainsail, the principal means of propulsion in a sailing vessel.

man-of-war, an armed vessel belonging to a government navy.

marine, an amphibious soldier. U.S. Marines stood sentry at sea, but did no actual shipboard work.

marline spike, a long blunt iron needle used for splicing cordage.

master, the commander of a merchantman; see also SAILING MASTER.

master commandant, a sometime rank in the U.S. Navy between LIEUTENANT and CAPTAIN.

master's mate, a senior MIDSHIPMAN or PETTY OFFICER, often but not necessarily an assistant to the SAILING MASTER.

mechanic, an artisan or machinist.

merchantman, a private trading vessel.

mess, a cabin where food was eaten, or a group that customarily ate together. The officers' messes often contributed a set amount toward making large purchases, as for livestock or liquor.

messenger, an endless ROPE passing around a CAPSTAN and to which a heavier one, such as an anchor CABLE, might be attached.

midshipman, a (usually young) WARRANT OFFICER training to be a COMMISSIONED OFFICER.

mizzenmast, the one behind the MAINMAST.

monkey, a mug made of wood or tarred leather.

moor, to fix a vessel in place by means of a ROPE or ropes.

mulatto, loosely, a person of mixed race; specifically, half European and half African.

murdering-piece, SWIVEL GUN.

nankeen, a lightweight cotton fabric.

octaroon, a person who is of one-eighth African descent.

paw-paw, papaya.

petit blanc, a white French colonist of the middle or lower class.

petty officer, a noncommissioned officer usually specializing in a particular task, as a BOSUN'S MATE or QUARTERMASTER.

picaroon, a West Indian privateer of questionable legality.

piece of eight, the Spanish silver dollar, or peso, which circulated widely in the Americas and was worth eight REALES. It was commonly chopped into eight BITS, each in theory worth twelve and a half cents American (hence "two bits," a quarter dollar), although coins worth one-half to four reales were also minted.

pinnace, a boat of moderate size that could be sailed or rowed.

Port Républicain, Port-au-Prince (or Pòtoprens), Haiti, during the French Revolution.

Porto Rico, the U.S. name for Puerto Rico.

post-captain, an officer holding the rank of CAPTAIN and entitled to command a SHIP of more than 20 GUNS.

privateer, a private armed vessel authorized in time of war to seize the ships and goods of the enemy.

quadroon, a person who is of one-quarter African descent.

quarter, clemency, as in not killing a defeated opponent. *Cry for quarters*: beg for mercy. Also, either of the after quadrants of a vessel.

quarters, the place where a man sleeps or fights, depending.

quarterdeck, the after part of the WEATHER DECK, from which the CAPTAIN and his officers CONN the ship.

quartermaster, a PETTY OFFICER who helps to CONN a vessel.

quarter-gunner, a PETTY OFFICER who assists the GUNNER; in theory one was allowed for every four GUNS.

rate, status assigned to a man according to his skills.

ratlines, horizontal ropes strung between the SHROUDS and used as footholds for going aloft; pronounced "ratlins."

razee, a large SHIP made smaller by removing its upper deck.

real, an eighth of a Spanish silver dollar. See PIECE OF EIGHT.

redcoat, a British soldier or marine.

reef, to reduce a sail's area by rolling up the lower part of it.

rope, a LINE that isn't attached to anything.

round hat, i.e., without the brim turned up as in a tricorne, which it began to replace around this time; it often looked like a low-crowned top hat.

round jacket, a short coat without tails.

round shot, a solid ball of iron.

royal, a mast, YARD, or sail above the TOPGALLANT.

running rigging, ROPES used to control the sails and SPARS.

saber, a long and heavy cavalry sword, sometimes but not always curved.

sailing master, the WARRANT OFFICER charged with a vessel's navigation, equal in rank but subordinate to a LIEUTENANT.

sailmaker, the WARRANT OFFICER charged with the care of the ship's canvas.

Sails, nickname for a ship's SAILMAKER.

Saint-Dómingue, the French colony in the island of HISPANIOLA. Now the Republic of Haiti.

Saint Kitts, a British island in the Lesser Antilles, where there was a large naval base.

San Domingo, the U.S. name for SAINT-DÓMINGUE.

sang-mélee, lit. "mixed blood"; the lightest of the racial designations under French law.

Santo Domingo, the Spanish colony in HISPANIOLA. Now the Dominican Republic.

schooner, a FORE-AND-AFT-rigged vessel with a narrow hull and usually two masts, common to North America and the Caribbean.

scuttle, a porthole.

sea lieutenant, "sea" to distinguish him from an Army or Marine lieutenant, whom he outranked.

servant, a seaman who cooked and served an officer's meals, cleaned his cabin, and tended to his clothes. It was also a euphemism for "slave." Marines might serve as mess attendants on formal occasions.

sheet, a LINE attached to a CLEW and used to haul a sail taut.

ship, a SQUARE-RIGGED vessel with three masts; loosely, any vessel large enough to carry a boat.

shroud, a piece of STANDING RIGGING in lateral support of a mast.

sloop, a single-masted sailing vessel.

small-sword, a light, straight-bladed sword carried by gentlemen as a sign of social status and for sticking into rude fellows.

sojer, a derogatory word for a soldier, specifically a Marine; *to sojer*, to perform a repetitive and often pointless task, as for punishment.

spar, a stout wooden pole such as a mast or a YARD.

splice the mainbrace, to have a TOT of GROG.

square-rigged, fitted primarily with SQUARE SAILS.

square sail, actually trapezoidal, but set "square" to a vessel's centerline.

standing rigging, lines used to support masts and SPARS.

starboard, to the right of a vessel's centerline; loosely, to the right.

stay, a FORE-AND-AFT piece of STANDING RIGGING in support of a mast.

staysail, a FORE-AND-AFT sail set to a STAY.

stem, the upright timber at a vessel's BOW.

stern, the rear of a vessel.

stiletto, a narrow-bladed dagger often worn concealed in a sleeve or waistband.

studding sail, a sail set outboard of a SQUARE SAIL in light weather.

stuns'l, STUDDING SAIL.

subaltern, a junior army officer.

surgeon, a ship's chief medical officer. Surgeons of the day were not usually physicians, who held a much higher social rank.

surtout, a long, usually close-fitting coat.

swivel gun, a small GUN mounted on a bulwark and used to discourage boarders.

tack, to come about with the wind across the BOW. Also, the lower corner of a sail's leading edge. *On a (*STARBOARD *or* LARBOARD*) tack*: sailing with the wind on that side.

taffrail, the rail at a vessel's stern.

throw weight, the amount of metal that a gun could fire, or the amount that a vessel could fire from all of its guns in one go.

topgallant, the mast, sail, or YARD above the TOPMAST.

topmast, the second-highest mast.

topsail, a square sail mounted on the second-highest mast.

tot, a small serving of booze.

vomito negro, YELLOW FEVER.

voudou, the ancestral West African religion as practiced in SAINT-DÓMINGUE.

wardroom, the cabin where the senior officers ate.

warrant officer, in the U.S. Navy, an officer confirmed by the president and the secretary of the Navy, and usually specializing in a skilled task such as navigation or gunnery. Senior warrant officers included the SAILING MASTER, SURGEON, BOSUN, and GUNNER. Inferior warrant officers included the COOK and SAILMAKER.

watch, a stint on duty, usually four hours. See DOGWATCH.

watch below, the men off duty.

watch on deck, the men on duty.

wear, to come about with the wind across the stern.

weather deck, a deck exposed to the elements.

windward, in the direction of the wind.

Windward Passage, the channel between HISPANIOLA and Cuba.

yard, a SPAR used to spread the head of a sail.

yarn, a long and often intentionally preposterous story.

yellow fever, an acute infectious viral disease that occurs in the warm regions of Africa and the Americas and is spread by mosquitoes, so-called because of the jaundice that sometimes accompanies it.

yellow jack, YELLOW FEVER.

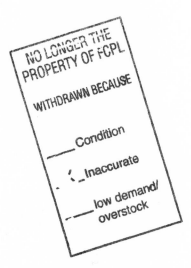